KATE MULDOON FOR THE DEAD

LIZ MATHEWS

outskirts press

Kate Muldoon: For the Dead

v3.0

Outskirts Press, Inc.
http://www.outskirtspress.com

ISBN: 978-1-4787-7582-9

PRINTED IN THE UNITED STATES OF AMERICA

Dedicated with love to my "homegirls."
Always inspiring!

Prologue

Marcy Simpson

The call came late Thursday afternoon; her cell phone buzzed angrily on her desk.

Marcy Simpson was at work—as usual. For as long as she could remember, her life had been consumed by work,always struggling to earn enough to make ends meet. Staring at the stack of tapes waiting to be transcribed, she briefly contemplated the pitiful state of her life.

If I'm not working in the ER, I'm sitting at this desk transcribing doctor dictation, she thought as she clicked off the recorder and reached for her cell phone. The bills were piling up again, and she'd just decided to work through the night—she needed the overtime. She could sleep on her days off.

The caller ID screen announced Zeke Peters, her ex-husband's best friend, would be on the other end if she pressed "talk." The mere fact that Zeke was calling made her stomach churn. It had to be bad news. She considered not answering.

When was the last time I heard from you, Zeke? Marcy wondered. *Maybe a year ago,* she thought, finally hitting the "talk" button.

Zeke delivered the news in a cold, matter-of-fact manner. Marcy heard, "Joe's dead," and then she didn't hear anything else; her thoughts had taken over.

Eventually, she started hearing bits and pieces of what Zeke was saying, ". . . a heart attack, late last night . . . the EMTs couldn't revive him . . . thought you should know . . ."

Marcy discovered she was holding her breath.

He's been dead all day, and I didn't know it? How is that possible? Marcy continued to struggle to process the news. She still hadn't spoken a word.

After a while, she realized Zeke was no longer talking, and the line had been silent for some time. Unsure how her voice would sound, she tried it.

"Thanks for calling, Zeke. My thoughts and prayers are with you all," she whispered and quietly hung up. An odd feeling settled over her; there was suddenly a dead spot in her world. She looked down at the phone in her hand and wondered if Zeke's call had actually happened or if her exhausted mind was playing tricks on her.

Using her smart phone, she clicked onto the Internet, pulled up the *Miami Herald*'s Web page, and located the obituary section.

Nothing about Joe, she thought wearily after a quick search. *A call from Zeke is so implausible; maybe it didn't happened.* She clicked back to the *Herald*'s home page and numbly stared at the ticker streaming across the top of the page. *Certainly Joe's death would be as notable as the local Little League scores they're reporting,* she thought, watching the words roll by.

Then she saw it: *"Prominent cardiologist, Dr. Joseph Dugan, pronounced dead at University of Miami Hospital at 11:10 last night."*

Marcy felt a heaviness in the middle of her chest as if some force was swirling in on her and settling there. She sat back in her chair and concentrated on breathing, trying to process the news.

After several minutes, she turned off her machines, tidied her workstation for the next shift, collected her jacket, handbag, and phone, and went looking for her boss at Jackson Memorial Hospital's transcription center.

"Sue, I'm headed home. I don't feel well."

Sue eyed her suspiciously. "Fine. Just log out and turn in your time card," Sue sighed, turning away.

Marcy swiftly headed for the door.

On her way home, Marcy realized she still felt numb. Joe's death seemed unreal. Examining her emotions, Marcy wondered why she had not shed a tear, and then realized she didn't feel she had the *right* to tears.

This isn't my tragedy, she concluded.

Her tragedy happened years ago—16 years ago. Long enough for Joe to marry his mistress, sire three boys, achieve career success, and build a fabulously huge home. He'd been so successful the new cardiac wing at UM hospital was named after him, and he frequently jetted around the world to speak at international conferences on cardiac surgery—quite a life for a 46-year-old.

Marcy and Joe had met and married in medical school, but Marcy had dropped out after two years so she could support them working as an ER nurse and medical transcriptionist. They'd never had kids, although they wanted them, but they'd agreed to wait until Joe was out of medical school. Then it was going to be Marcy's turn to return to medical school; she'd figured she could handle being pregnant during med school. But, things didn't work out that way. She didn't get to go to medical school or have kids—instead, she got divorced.

She'd never remarried. She thought it was because she was too embittered for anyone to stick around long enough, and, in truth, she wasn't all that interested in finding a new life partner. Joe had been her true love, her soul mate, "the one who completed her." Five years into their seemingly idyllic marriage, Marcy learned Joe was completing someone else—apparently on a regular enough basis to get *her* pregnant.

Joe never denied the affair. He simply said he hadn't wanted to hurt her, and, because he was so grateful to her for supporting him through medical school, he'd been unable to figure out how to end it. Marcy wanted to fight to put their marriage back together, but when Joe said he no longer loved her, her heart shut down, and it never opened up again.

Once she made it to her condo, she called a couple of girlfriends. Had they heard? No, but they all asked how she felt. Numb was her truthful answer, and still no tears. When a couple of her friends encouraged her to break down and "have a good cry," Marcy quickly, but politely, ended the calls.

It's not my tragedy. I don't have a right to cry, she kept thinking.

She poured herself a large glass of red wine and sat at the petite table on her tiny balcony to eat her dinner and think about her strange new situation.

This isn't my tragedy, she thought again.

None of the normal emotional reactions to death seemed appropriate. She'd always hated people who turned everything back to themselves, who made it all about them, saw the world only through their own existence. She refused to do that now.

This isn't my tragedy, she kept repeating over and over to herself like a mantra. But, it was *her* pain, she felt *her* loss, and there was a hole in *her* universe. Then it dawned on her . . . she'd never known another ex-wife whose former husband had died.

Another problem to solve on my own, Marcy thought. She considered the subject for a while, and finally concluded, *I guess the ex-wife cries alone.*

Joe's services were three days later. There was an announcement in the paper—no one called her this time.

Marcy arranged to work the 8:00 p.m. to 4:00 a.m. shift at Jackson Memorial so she could have time off to attend the service. It was the last of her four-days-on work rotation as an ER nurse practitioner at Jackson Memorial. She knew she would have plenty of time during her four days off to recover from the sleepless night ahead.

The church was packed. Marcy came late and sat in the corner of the choir loft at the back of the church, trying to be as anonymous as she could. She truly hoped no one would see or recognize her, and she vowed to slip out the side door before the end of the service when the family would be escorted down the aisle. She kept reminding herself it wasn't her tragedy. But, she had recognized it was her loss too, and she was allowing herself to grieve quietly.

Sitting in the front pew, Joan looked much older than Marcy would have thought possible. She'd been 18 when she married Joe. Now, she looked closer to 44 than 34, but then, tragedy does that to you—Marcy knew that from personal experience.

Joe's two younger, towheaded boys squirmed in the pew next to Joan, largely ignored by their mother. Joe's mom tried to quiet them without much success. The middle son's profile reminded Marcy so much of Joe her heart ached. The young man with the dark brown hair in the front pew, between Joe's mom and Zeke Peters, must be Joe's oldest son she decided.

He'd be 16 now, she thought as she watched Joe's family.

The eulogies were eloquent and touching, with just the right amount of tragic humor these sorts of events call for. At one point during his turn in the pulpit, Zeke's eyes wandered up to the choir loft and landed on Marcy. He paused momentarily, as if trying to sort out who he was seeing. Marcy's heart stopped; she felt like an intruder. Then Zeke looked away and began speaking again.

As the recessional music began, Marcy swiftly descended the stairs and hurried out the side door. She was sure she'd been quick enough, and no one could have seen her hasty retreat. She hurried to her car parked around the corner.

Four days later, Marcy's cell phone buzzed again in the middle of the afternoon, this time interrupting her attention to the stack of patient files in front of her, waiting for a final discharge and documentation. It was Zeke again, and again, his voice sounded strange—steely and cold, almost monotone.

"Was that you I saw at the funeral service?" he asked accusingly.

She thought for a moment of lying, but what did it matter? The funeral hadn't been private; hundreds of people had attended.

"Yes," she replied quietly.

"I wondered what you were doing there," Zeke said.

Marcy decided it was a rhetorical question, or at least one that didn't deserve an answer, so she remained silent.

When she did not respond, Zeke went on, "Well, you should know you'll be getting a call from Joe's estate lawyer later today, and we *all* expect you to do the *right* thing, Marcy."

Whatever is he talking about? Does he feel I've somehow violated Joe's family's privacy by attending the funeral and some legal penalty is appropriate?

"Zeke, no one but you saw me at the funeral, and it was not closed to the public. I can't see how my attendance would require a call from a lawyer, for heaven's sake."

"You know that's not what I'm talking about," Zeke huffed back at her.

"No, honestly, I don't. Frankly, I haven't a clue what you're talking about, and I'm at work. So, I'll simply say good-bye," Marcy said as she calmly clicked off.

She reviewed the conversation and decided she'd sounded reasonable and not the least bit concerned, but in her head and heart, she was panicking. She tried to imagine what in the world a lawyer could possibly have to say about who attended a funeral open to the public or any other reason he'd need to talk to her.

I've never been one of those "fatal attraction" ex-wives. I don't know the Dugans' new phone number or the address of Joe's spectacular new house that was featured in the paper last year. I really don't know anything about the Dugans' lives, except for the occasional photo or article in the paper, and most of that I haven't even bothered to read. I never could figure out why Joe was so involved in all those society events. That certainly wasn't the Joe I married 21 years ago. Of course, the same could be said about so much of Joe's life over the last 16 years.

Marcy went back to her patient charts, hoping she didn't look too distracted.

When her cell phone rang again two hours later, Marcy was finishing her last rounds, taking time with each patient still in the ER to make sure the transition to the new shift went smoothly. She felt jumpy and was ready to bolt for her condo as soon as she could. She needed to process the day's events over a glass of red wine. Glancing at her phone, she wondered who in the world might be calling this time. When she didn't recognize the number on the caller ID display, she seriously considered not answering.

"Yes? she asked tentatively after she pressed the "talk" button.

"Miss Simpson?"

"Yes. Who is this?"

"I'm Ronald Gray, the attorney representing Joe Dugan's estate," he began.

I know who you are, she thought, her anxiety and fear immediately rising. She remembered him well from the divorce.

Marcy simply replied, "Yes?"

"I'm calling to discuss a matter of some seriousness. Is this a good time?"

"Mr. Gray, I cannot imagine it would ever be a good time to speak with you," she surprised herself by saying. "What do you want?"

"Miss Simpson," (*she was pretty sure he was saying "Miss" not "Ms."*) "we're settling Joe's affairs and an irregularity appears to exist."

Marcy had nothing to say to this, so she said nothing. She was relieved he wasn't berating her for attending her ex-husband's funeral, because she didn't know how she could possibly fight this lawyer and his high-priced, high-society law firm. She continued to say nothing.

"Ms. Simpson, are you still there?"

"Yes."

"I said there's an irregularity in Dr. Dugan's estate that I need to discuss with you."

"I can't imagine why, and I'm at work."

"Of course you are, and where is that?"

"How is that your business?" Marcy asked, again, surprising herself with her bluntness.

It was Gray's turn to be silent.

Finally, he admitted, "I suppose it isn't. In any event, I need to speak to you. I'd like you to come by my office tomorrow."

"I'm supposed to take time away from work to stop by your office tomorrow? I don't think I'll be doing that," the new, bold Marcy replied.

"Well, what time *would be convenient* for you?"

Marcy liked this much better. Somehow, the power in the conversation had shifted, and it was now definitely in her corner. She didn't want to lose the momentum, but she also didn't want to continue this private call in the ER, so she said, "How about I come to your office around 6:30 tomorrow evening. *That* would be convenient for me."

"All right," Gray said after a short pause. "We'll be here."

"*We*? Who's *we*?" Marcy quizzed.

"Well, mostly me, but there may be one or two others."

Six-thirty the following day, Marcy sat in the waiting room of Gray and Ferguson, PA, taking in its finely appointed modernistic furnishings. It was a much different office interior than the last time she was here, but then, most everything in the world had changed drastically in the last 16 years.

Gray's secretary finally walked into the waiting area and escorted her into a large room with a conference table that looked like a huge, floating slab of marble. The table had to be 25 feet long if it was an inch. The sheer visual weight of it was impressive and meant to intimidate.

But Marcy had promised herself she would not to be intimidated the way she had been the last time she'd entered these offices. She resolved now to at least *appear* calm and in control, even if her knees felt like they were going to buckle. She quickly sat at the head of the table and rested her hands in her lap to hide the trembling from Gray and the other three men in the room. Two of the men Marcy had never seen before; the third was Zeke. She felt decidedly outnumbered.

Initially, the men were solicitous. They asked how she was doing, Zeke told her she looked great and he could tell she was still going to the gym—she couldn't say the same for him. They offered her coffee, tea, and cold drinks. She accepted only a glass of water.

The conference room got very quiet, and Marcy looked from one man to the other, waiting for someone to speak up. She was dying of curiosity, but she refused to be the first to talk. And so, they sat in silence for several long minutes.

Eventually, the Dugan family lawyer, Ronald Gray, couldn't take the silence any longer, and he seized the stage.

"I'm sure you have an idea why we asked you here, Miss Simpson."

"Actually, no. I have no idea whatsoever. So, why don't you tell me?"

Gray looked skeptical and said, "Let me first introduce these two gentlemen, Mr. Meardon and Mr. Argyle. They're attorneys with the Upton Insurance Company. And you already know Zeke Peters, of course."

Marcy continued to look at the men, shifting her gaze from one to the other, still in the dark as to why she was there. One of the insurance men finally said something. She thought it was Mr. Meardon who had spoken, although he and Argyle looked nearly identical.

"You see, Ms. Simpson, you have been named the beneficiary of an insurance policy Dr. Dugan purchased about 19 years ago, and that he kept current with yearly premium payments." He slid a copy of the insurance policy toward her.

Marcy said nothing. She stared off into space as her mind spun backward, recalling a time, years ago, when Joe told her over dinner that he'd purchased a life insurance policy and made her the beneficiary. It felt like a lifetime ago . . . maybe two.

At the time, she hadn't wanted to think about such things and had told Joe as much. Their "master plan" had been set for years. Marcy was going to work as an ER nurse and a medical transcriptionist until Joe finished medical school and his residency, then they were going to switch. Joe was going to support her while she returned to medical school. The divorce broke their deal and destroyed their master plan, along with a good many other things, including Marcy's heart.

The insurance policy, Joe had told her, would ensure she'd get to attend medical school even if he wasn't there to support her. She recalled telling Joe he couldn't die—it wasn't in the master plan. They'd both laughed at this, and never again spoken about the insurance policy.

Mr. Meardon, or was it Argyle, was talking again. ". . . you see, you are, of course, no longer his wife . . ."

No, duh, she thought.

"Excuse me," Marcy interrupted, "could you repeat what you just said, because I am not certain I heard you." Actually, Marcy was certain she had *not* heard him. She hadn't heard anything but her memory for several minutes.

"I said, Ms. Simpson, Dr. Dugan purchased an insurance policy 19 years ago and the beneficiary is, and I quote, 'Marcia Anne Simpson Dugan, my wife.'"

She continued to stare at him blankly.

"Ms. Simpson, under one interpretation of this language you are the beneficiary of this $4 million policy."

"What?!?" The question was out of her mouth before she could think. She picked up the insurance policy they had slid in front of her and saw "$4,000,000" listed as the insurance benefit on the policy summary page.

They all sat quietly and let the moment sink in. This time, it was Zeke who broke the silence.

"Of course, it wasn't really meant for you. I mean, you aren't his wife, and the money was meant for his *wife* . . . and family, of course," Zeke said, gratuitously providing his opinion.

Meardon and Argyle glared at Zeke, and Argyle said, "That is not how the policy reads, sir. And, the policy was taken out long before Dr. Dugan met his current wife or had a family. In any event, he continued to pay on this *same* policy *every* year. He could have easily let it lapse or convert it, or, even more easily, changed the beneficiary at any point. He was the owner of the policy. It was his to do with as he pleased."

Marcy could not believe what she just heard. One of the insurance attorneys was actually speaking up for her and making an argument that Joe had kept a $4 million insurance policy current all these years naming her as the beneficiary *on purpose*. That argument was hard even for Marcy to believe.

She'd only talked to Joe a handful of times after the divorce, and she hadn't seen him in over 10 years. In the early months after the divorce, she returned a number of his letters unread and refused to answer his calls, even though she missed him desperately and was tempted to reach out to him. That is, until the announcement of the birth of his first son just five months after their wedding day. The insult to her injured heart was devastating. Marcy was barely able to function for a month after hearing about the baby.

"The insurance company, Ms. Simpson, has an obligation to pay the proceeds of the policy to the rightful beneficiary, and we are under a contractual obligation to do so in a timely manner. As of now, we intend to make that payment to you."

This time, Marcy was nearly certain it was Meardon who was taking her side.

Zeke could contain himself no longer.

"That's why you have to tell them you don't want it, Marcy. It's not yours. You have to relinquish any claim to it so it can be paid to Joan and the boys. That is what Joe really wanted."

Meardon and Argyle again glared at Zeke.

Marcy sat as if in a stupor looking down at the table in front of her for several minutes.

Finally, she said, "And what if I chose not to?"

"What?!? You *can't* be serious. It's not yours to keep!" Zeke practically screamed.

"Mr. Peters, you are neither a lawyer, nor a judge. You are here only because Mr. Gray, for whatever reason, thought you might lend some assistance in helping us understand Dr. Dugan's intent. You were not invited here to badger and berate Ms. Simpson."

Marcy stared dumbstruck at Meardon, her new champion.

"If there is a legal contest to our payment of the insurance proceeds," Meardon said, glaring pointedly at Zeke again, "and it sounds like there will be, we will have the money held by the court while the claims are sorted out. We've already prepared the paperwork for an interpleader and declaratory judgment action, that's what this type of legal matter is called. It will be filed tomorrow," Meardon concluded, scowling at Zeke again. "If necessary."

"That would mean, Miss Simpson, you wouldn't receive *any* money until a court determines who is the proper beneficiary," Gray chimed in. "Now, if you would like to take a small fee for waiving any weak claim you could have made due to this unfortunate scrivener's error," Gray continued, now glowering at Meardon and Argyle, "an error which most certainly does *not* reflect Dr. Dugan's intent, Mrs. Dugan has agreed to be reasonable and give you $10,000." Gray paused and pulled a document out from the stack of papers in front of him before he continued. "We have taken the liberty of drawing up the waiver for your signature."

Gray shoved the document and a pen in front of Marcy.

A smile started to form on Marcy's mouth, just a small one at first, but it got larger and larger. Mr. Gray interpreted the smile to mean she would agree to his plan, take the $10,000 and walk away from $3,990,000. He tapped the signature line on the last page of the paperwork now sitting in front of Marcy.

Marcy picked up the pen and held it in her fingers for a few minutes as she pretended to read the document. She thought about her maxed out credit cards, her 18-year-old car that needed four new tires, and the washing machine that crapped out six days ago resulting in an ever-growing mountain of dirty laundry in her condo. She thought about not having to do medical transcription for a while, or maybe even taking a small vacation.

She put the pen down and looked directly at Gray. "No, Mr. Gray. I will not sign this document, or any other that you prepare. I do *not* intend to cooperate with your plan this time. It appears these nice gentlemen are ready to give me a check for $4 million, and, Mr. Gray, I intend to accept that check."

"YOU CAN'T take that money, Marcy! It is *not* yours! It's Joan's and the boys'," Zeke screamed, his face scarlet as he leaped up and rushed toward Marcy in such haste he knocked over his chair.

To her own amazement, Marcy stood to meet him. Not blinking, not stepping back, not cringing, she stood toe-to-toe meeting Zeke's fury. When she spoke, her words were slow and her voice firm, and just loud enough for all of them to hear.

"The money is mine, Zeke. It's mine, and so was he."

Zeke stopped in his tracks, wild-eyed and fists clenched.

Marcy turned toward Meardon and Argyle who, by this point, were also on their feet and moving toward her as if to protect her.

"Do you have my address and telephone number?" she asked the two men.

They nodded.

"Good. Call me in the morning and tell me when you intend to pay me, and what I need to do to collect. Oh, and by the way, I expect you will defend me against any legal tricks Gray and his buddy Zeke may think up."

Argyle and Meardon were smiling as they watched her pick up the copy of the insurance policy and the waiver Gray had prepared and leave the conference room.

The following morning, Marcy called Sue in the medical transcriptions department to let her know she would not be in and might not be in the following day either given how she felt. What she didn't tell Sue was the way she felt was wonderful . . . released and light, and as if the world might have possibilities again.

How long has it been since I felt this way? she wondered.

Oddly, she'd slept well the night before, sleeping in past 6:00 a.m. for the first time in what seemed like decades. As she was brewing a pot of coffee at 8:30 her phone rang.

I wonder what new adventure this call will bring. Lately, each one is more bizarre than the last, she mused.

"Ms. Simpson?" The male voice sounded like one of the insurance lawyers.

"Yes?" Marcy was immediately concerned her newfound hero might have reconsidered his role as her defender.

"This is Mr. Meardon. We met yesterday at Gray and Ferguson. I'm with Upton Insurance Company. I'd like to talk to you about getting an attorney to represent you. Mrs. Dugan's attorney has officially let us know the estate will be fighting release of the insurance proceeds to you. You are going to need representation in what will no doubt be a long and difficult legal battle."

"Don't you have an obligation to represent me?" Marcy asked knowing, yet again, she couldn't match the big bucks Joan could mount to fight her.

"Ms. Simpson, we're just the stakeholders. We can't represent you directly, it would be a conflict of interests," Meardon said, confirming Marcy's fears.

"I can't afford legal representation. I work as an ER nurse practitioner, and I have a part-time job as a medical transcriptionist. I still have school loans, and I'm struggling to keep my head above water as it is. I don't have money for high-priced lawyers. Look, I read the insurance policy last night. You have an obligation to provide me legal representation. I'm pretty sure I read that. Let me get the policy. I'll be able to tell you exactly what it says." Marcy's voice was shaky; her fears were mounting.

"I know what the policy says, Ms. Simpson. The company *is* obligated to *obtain* legal representation for you, but the lawyers at the company can't *provide* that representation. The company will pay your attorney's fees and we have a list of attorneys with whom we work on a regular basis who we can recommend," Meardon explained.

Marcy was silent for several moments as she collected her thoughts.

"I already know who I want to represent me," she said, surprising herself. "I want Kate Muldoon."

Now, it was Meardon's turn to fall silent. After a brief hesitation, Meardon said, "Ms. Simpson, Ms. Muldoon is an excellent attorney, no doubt about it. But, she typically handles criminal defense or civil matters for large corporations. This isn't really in her area of practice." *Plus, she's got to be incredibly expensive,* Meardon added to himself.

"I know and trust Kate, and I want her and only her," Marcy insisted.

"May I inquire how you know Ms. Muldoon?" Meardon probed.

"I dated her brother for five years. He's a cop in Ocala now, but he used to be a detective with the Miami-Dade department before he moved. Besides, why should it matter how I know her?" Marcy said, feeling more sure of herself now.

"It's possible Ms. Muldoon may be too busy to take on this matter. She is highly sought after, and this may not be the sort of case she's inclined to accept."

Meardon was trying to dance around the fact that Kate Muldoon was going to cost at least three times more than any of the attorneys on his approved panel.

"Here's the deal, Mr. Meardon." Marcy felt more confident now just thinking about having Kate on her side, "I've been in a legal battle only one other time, and that was when Joe divorced me. It was so painful I simply gave up," she said, and then paused to collect herself. She refused to start crying now.

"I didn't have legal counsel then because I couldn't afford it, and I didn't make out so well, in fact, I've since learned I got royally screwed. This time, I'm going to be represented by someone who's looking out for *me*; someone who will make sure I don't get taken advantage of again. Is there some limitation on who I can hire, or who your company will pay for? I didn't see any limitation in the policy."

"Actually, there isn't a limitation, Ms. Simpson. The way this policy is written, we are obligated to pay for the legal representative of your choice," Meardon reflected for a moment. "Frankly, Ms. Simpson, just between us, given the opposition I suspect you will be facing, you are going to need strong legal representation." Meardon confided, "You need to know this legal battle will likely be very unpleasant, and you may end up getting none of the insurance proceeds. Or, as often happens in these types of battles, you may enter into a compromise of some sort. I'm sure the $10,000 the Dugans' attorney offered at our meeting yesterday is not the last offer they'll make. They will very likely offer you far more than that before the matter is concluded. You may want to consider that option."

"Thanks, Mr. Meardon. I appreciate your thoughts. I'll be sure to discuss those ideas with Kate. But, to be honest, I don't really feel like negotiating with Joan Dugan. If I walk away with *nothing*, I won't be any worse off than I am right now." She thought for a moment, and then added, "Joan Ferguson blew up my world 16 years ago. I've got nothing to lose. Thanks for calling. I'll take it from here."

Marcy hung up the phone and contemplated her next move as she looked up Kate Muldoon's office number.

Chapter 1

Sophia Touche, Kate Muldoon's legal assistant, buzzed through. "Kate, Marcy Simpson's on line one for you. Can you take the call?" she inquired.

"You bet! I'd love to talk to Marcy. I haven't heard from her in years. Put her through," Kate replied with enthusiasm.

"Marcy! What a great surprise! How the hell are you?" Kate asked when the call beeped through.

"It's great to hear your voice too, Kate. It's been forever. I just hope you're still happy to hear from me after I tell you why I'm calling."

"Uh-oh. What's up? I can't imagine you're sitting in jail somewhere, but even if you are, I'm still happy to hear from you. We haven't talked since right after Sean blew out of Miami for horse country," Kate replied, recalling her brother's hasty decision to move to Ocala three years ago.

"Yeah, well, I've only heard from him twice in three years, and he needed something both times," Marcy sighed and gave a small laugh.

"Sounds like Sean. Sorry, kiddo, he takes after his old man. Dad was never much for commitment and responsibility." The subject of the men in her family had never been one of Kate's favorites. "So, what can I do for you? I hope it isn't anything serious."

"Actually, it *is* serious. I'm not sitting in jail, and it's not a criminal matter, but it is legal, and it's serious," Marcy responded, and took a long breath before launching into an explanation of her rather unusual situation.

"Kate, I know I never told you much about my ex-husband and our divorce. Well, Joe, my ex, died a week ago. You might have read about it," Marcy said. "He was kind of a big deal at UM medical school—a pretty well-known cardiologist."

"Joe Dugan was your Joe, your ex-husband Joe? You're kidding. You never told us that." Kate was surprised Marcy had left out that rather interesting detail the few times she'd mentioned her prior marriage. "I saw the obit and article in the paper. Sounds like he will be missed."

Kate wasn't really sure how one consoles an ex-wife who's been divorced for over 15 years. She couldn't imagine Marcy making any sort of claim on his estate—she just wasn't that kind of person.

"He *will* be missed by many people. But, Kate, the reason I'm calling is Joe's estate attorney called me shortly after Joe died and told me there was 'an irregularity in the estate,' and he said he needed to talk to me about it. He called it something like a 'scrivener's error,' I think. You see, there's this insurance policy, Kate; a policy Joe took out while we were still married. He made me the beneficiary and, well, he never changed that, and oddly he kept paying on the policy each year and . . . oh, Kate . . ." Marcy suddenly felt the tears coming, and she struggled for control.

"Kate, the policy is for $4 million . . . *four million dollars* . . . and they want me to waive any claim I might have to the money. Joe's attorney and Joe's best friend Zeke, they say the money wasn't really meant for me because I'm not his wife . . ."

Marcy had lost the battle against her tears. She was sobbing now, finally able to cry for her loss, the loss of a man who, at one point in his life, had loved and wanted to protect her. And because that man was now gone, she would never know if he thought of her every year when he paid the insurance premium, or ever missed her, or if the money *really* was intended for her.

"Holy shit, kiddo! I'm so glad you called. What an interesting situation. You truly *do* need legal representation. Do you have a copy of the policy? Who have you talked to, and when?" Kate was instantly in lawyer mode.

"Yes, I have a copy of the policy. The guys from the insurance company gave it to me. Upton is the name of the company, and the insurance attorneys were Meardon and Argyle—you know, like the socks.

They were going to pay the money out to me, but Joe's estate attorney has challenged the payout," Marcy said between sobs.

"Now the insurance company has asked the court to sort out the claims. The estate attorney offered me $10,000 to waive my claim. He had a very formal-looking document that he wanted me to sign . . ."

"You didn't sign it, did you?" Kate interrupted.

"No, Kate, but I have a copy of it. They *thought* I was going to sign. The estate attorney, Ronald Gray, and Joe's friend, Zeke, kind of ganged up on me and told me how the money wasn't mine because it was just a 'mistake,'" Marcy said as she wept openly.

"Kate, I got so badly beaten by those lawyers the last time . . . when I got divorced . . . I gave up, it was too hard . . . and I couldn't afford an attorney . . . Oh, Kate, what am I going to do?"

"I'll tell you what you are going to do, so, listen to me carefully. You are going to come to my office tomorrow—are you working tomorrow? If you are, I can meet you before or after work. Just tell me when you can be here. I'm calling Gray and the two insurance attorneys immediately and letting them know you have retained me and they can no longer ethically talk to you directly. They also can't have anyone else do so on their behalf—like Joe's friend, what was his name? Zack?"

"No, it's Zeke, Zeke Peters. He got really angry with me when I told him the money was mine and I wasn't waiving the claim. I thought he was going to hit me." Marcy was crying so hard now Kate could barely understand her.

"It's going to be OK, Marcy, this is going to be OK. You need to relax and let me handle this for you."

I'll take this case for free if I have to. What the hell good is it being a lawyer if you can't stand up for someone who's been knocked down as many times as Marcy? Kate asked herself.

"Kate, I know I can't afford you. I'm not one of your usual celebrity clients I read about in the paper all the time. But, the insurance company is supposed to provide me a defense. Meardon even said so—he also said that I needed a really good attorney, and you're the best lawyer I know. You aren't one of the attorneys they usually work with, but the policy says I get to pick the attorney. Kate, he also told me the Dugan family would probably offer me more to waive my claim than the $10,000 they wanted to pay me when we met yesterday. . . and he said I might end up getting nothing."

Marcy was struggling to pull herself together.

"I told him I didn't care if I didn't get anything. I wasn't interested in making a deal with the Dugans. I don't have anything now, and I won't be any worse off, no matter what happens."

Way to go, Marcy, Kate thought, w*ay to hold your own.*

"Marcy, when can you be here tomorrow? You've handled this enough on your own. I'm happy to represent you. We need to talk strategy, so come prepared to tell me everything you know about this policy. I'll have my associate join us." Kate found herself already intrigued by her newest case.

"I'm off at 4:00 tomorrow, I finally got the day shift; I'm working a 4-days-on, 4-off schedule. Is 5:30 too late?" Marcy asked between sniffs.

"Nope, that will be just fine. If you can send me a PDF of the insurance policy and the waiver they asked you to sign, I can get started right away. I want to call the insurance company and Gray today, and I'd rather review the policy and waiver before I do," Kate explained.

"I have a copier here at my condo, it's a cheap one, but it can send a PDF and it usually works. I'll send the papers to you as soon as we hang up. I'll be there tomorrow at 5:30 . . . and, Kate, I can't thank you enough. I feel so much better already."

Marcy sniffed once more and blew her nose.

"It will be great to work with you, Marcy. I can't predict how this will turn out, but I'll do my very best for you."

"I know you will, Kate. Thank you."

Kate gave Marcy her e-mail address and they said good-bye.

After hanging up, Kate sat back and tried to remember the last time she'd handled a contested interpleader and declaratory judgment action. She decided it was about ten years.

They aren't inherently difficult cases, and the presentation of the evidence is certainly the same as the dozens of trials I've handled over the intervening years.

Kate would have taken this case even if the insurance company hadn't been on the hook for her fees. At one point, she was as close to Marcy as she was to either of her sisters. Kate would have been happy to lose her brother Sean and keep Marcy when they split up. Unfortunately, Marcy felt awkward remaining part of Kate's life; she didn't want to intrude.

Kate buzzed her associate's office.

"What do you need, Boss Lady? I haven't quite finished the Primary Paints response brief. I'll need a couple more hours, but you'll be happy to know it's in good shape. I'll have it to you before we head out of here this evening," Ed volunteered when he picked up the phone.

"Great. But that's not why I'm calling. Would you mind coming to my office? I have a new matter I want to brief you on, and I want you to be on the calls when I talk to the opposing counsel and insurance company. I'd come to your office, but I lose my mind every time I walk in there. I just can't think in all that clutter."

Kate really did find Ed's office disturbing. Whenever she saw it she had serious misgivings about assigning him so much work. On the other hand, he always seems to be able to find things in the chaos and his work was outstanding, so she tried not to think about the mess.

"Sure, I'll be right there," he replied, hanging up.

Kate buzzed Sophia and asked her to run a conflicts check on the Dugan family and Upton Insurance as she looked up the phone numbers for Ronald Gray and the insurance company.

When Ed walked into her office, her e-mail dinged, letting her know Marcy's PDF had arrived—she'd lost no time sending Kate the policy and waiver.

After Kate related the details of her call with Marcy, she and Ed reviewed the two documents. Although the quality of the PDF was poor, Kate could make out the relevant information.

The insurance policy listed Marcy, specifically "Marcy Anne Simpson Dugan, my wife," as the sole beneficiary on an annually renewable, 30-year term insurance policy on Joe Dugan's life. The face amount was $4 million; the annual premium was just under $4,000.

The waiver, on the other hand, was a totally one-sided attempt to trick Marcy out of a potentially lucrative claim. To be valid, the waiver had to be signed on the date it was presented, allowing no time for Marcy to review or seek assistance of counsel before signing. If Marcy had signed the waiver Gray prepared, she would have received exactly one quarter of one percent of the potential insurance payout. But, that wasn't all. The document also stated Marcy would waive all present and *future* claims against the Dugan estate and released any claims she had against any member of the Dugan family, as well as its attorneys, agents, and representatives. Privacy, confidentiality, indemnity, and attorneys' fees clauses, all running in favor of the Dugans *only*, were also included in the boilerplate language of the waiver. In addition, the waiver contained a penalty clause Gray had tried to disguise as a liquidated damages provision. That clause would have required Marcy to repay the full $10,000 in the event she ever challenged the validity of the waiver, or if the Dugans *believed* she'd even *attempted* to violate the privacy or confidentiality clauses. Kate truly despised Ronald Gray when she finished reading the overreaching waiver.

After briefly discussing the two documents with Ed, Kate's first phone call was to the Upton Insurance Company where she was directed to Ralph Meardon.

"Good afternoon Ms. Muldoon. I've been expecting your call. Ms. Simpson told me she would be retaining you," Meardon began. "I will send over our standard fee arrangement agreement, but you'll have to let me know your billing rate. I'm sure your rate is well beyond what we usually agree to. However, this is a relatively old and specialized policy and requires the company to pay for the attorney of Ms. Simpson's choice. I would have never guessed she knew you or an attorney as . . . exclusive as you."

"You mean as *expensive*; you can speak frankly with me, Mr. Meardon," Kate replied. "I appreciate your position, and I will be working with my associate, Ed Evert, who is here with me on this call. That will help keep the cost down a bit. I'm grateful for the assistance you've given my client up to this point. It sounds like Gray and his sidekick, Zeke Peters, may have tried to intimidate Marcy when you all met. It's good to know there was a least one ethical attorney in the room with her."

"It *was* a rather unusual situation, that's for sure. We never thought Mr. Peters would be unable to control himself. At one point, I thought we were going to have to physically restrain him. He charged at Ms. Simpson when she told him she wouldn't waive her rights to the insurance proceeds. My colleague and I were afraid he might physically hurt her. Just between us, I'll tell you I'm glad Ms. Simpson didn't succumb to the pressure Gray and Peters put on her to sign the waiver."

"Well, she won't have to worry about dealing with Gray again, and I may seek a restraining order against Peters just so it's clear he's not entitled to continue to badger her."

Kate paused only briefly to make herself a note to consider the possibility of filing a claim for assault against Peters.

"I'm hoping to fast-track this matter, but that will require your assistance," Kate continued. "As Ms. Simpson's legal representative, I'm making a formal request for documents and information she's entitled to as the named beneficiary. Dugan's attorney may or may not get around to requesting these documents—he may not *want* to know what they reveal. But, the documents and information I want are relevant. Hopefully, we'll be able to find admissible evidence to explain Dr. Dugan's reason for keeping the policy in place all these years without amending it, as he was certainly entitled to do.

"In addition to the full policy, and any riders or addenda, I would like your records regarding the original application for the policy, every document you have relating to payment of the premiums, and the name and contact information for the agent who sold the policy, as well as any other agent who had contact with Dr. Dugan. I'm assuming the policy was kept current and never lapsed, is that correct?" Kate asked as she finished her list of requests.

"Yes, it is, and your request is appropriate. If you can send me a letter stating you're representing Ms. Simpson and list the documents you want we'll get them to you immediately," Meardon said, obviously ready to cooperate. "I'll get our records department working on compiling them today. It shouldn't take more than a day or two. Can I call you when we have them ready?"

"That would be wonderful. I'll send a courier for them once you call. Could you make two copies and send one to Ron Gray? I don't want him crying foul somewhere down the line. Thanks so much for your help."

"My pleasure, Ms. Muldoon. I'm looking forward to working with you."

"Please call me Kate. I'll get the letter of representation and the list of documents we're requesting to you shortly."

As she hung up and called the next number, Kate directed Ed to prepare the letter, and fax, e-mail, and mail it to Meardon as soon as possible.

"Gray and Ferguson, how may I help you?" the British-sounding receptionist asked politely.

"Ronald Gray, please. Tell him Kate Muldoon is calling."

Within a couple of minutes, Gray answered his phone. "Ms. Muldoon, to what do I owe this delightful surprise?"

Perfect, Kate thought. *Let's see how "delightful" you found the surprise when we hang up.*

"Mr. Gray, I represent Ms. Marcy Simpson. I understand that you will be representing the estate of Dr. Joe Dugan in the contested interpleader and declaratory judgment action involving a life insurance policy naming my client as the beneficiary. Am I correct on all that?"

After a slight hesitation Gray said, "Yes, that's correct. I must say I'm surprised to learn you're doing insurance work. It's a bit different from your normal celebrity representation, and you're . . . shall we say . . . a bit overqualified."

"Good, then there's no longer any fear that my client will be taken advantage of or intimidated, mentally or physically. Mr. Gray, neither you, nor anyone on your behalf will speak directly to my client again. Is that clear?"

"Of course, Ms. Muldoon. I had no idea Ms. Simpson was represented . . . "

"Obviously; otherwise, you wouldn't have tried to pressure her into signing that ridiculous, one-sided waiver. You know, Mr. Gray, when you make an agreement that unfair, and you pressure an unrepresented person, as you did, to sign without an opportunity to review or discuss it with an attorney, the possibility of your waiver being ruled invalid increases exponentially. Even if Ms. Simpson had signed your lopsided waiver, I'm almost certainly I could have gotten it set aside.

"Now, let me address the matter of Mr. Peters' assault on my client. I understand Mr. Peters was in your initial meeting with Ms. Simpson at *your* invitation. Yet, you didn't bother to keep him under control or invite him to leave when he caused Ms. Simpson to fear for her physical safety. I can hope, but I have serious doubts, that you did not intentionally include his near-physical attack on her as part of your overall intimidation ploy. Mr. Meardon was so concerned for my client's safety that he and Mr. Argyle felt the need to take steps to intervene because it looked as if Mr. Peters was going to *strike* Ms. Simpson. If Mr. Meardon, a man, and an attorney, felt Ms. Simpson was assaulted, one can only imagine how Ms. Simpson, the only woman in the room, must have felt in such an intimidating situation. I am certain a judge will agree that the circumstances of Mr. Peters' attack satisfy the prerequisites for an assault claim." Kate paused only briefly to let her words register with Gray before she charged ahead.

"I need to know if you will be representing Mr. Peters when I have him served with the restraining order and complaint for assault I'm preparing."

Ed was grinning as he took notes. He loved watching Kate in this mode. She was a true *tour de force,* and he had never seen anyone better—not even his drill sergeant in the Marines.

"I'm certain that won't be necessary, Ms. Muldoon. I can speak to him about his obligations."

"Yes, and we all know how well that worked out the last time. So, I'll take your response as 'no,' you will *not* be representing Mr. Peters, and I will have Mr. Peters served directly and wait to find out who *will* be representing him.

"Now," Kate continued, "you also need to know that when I spoke to Mr. Meardon, I requested several types of documents and other information that will no doubt help us all ascertain Dr. Dugan's reason for taking out—*and maintaining unchanged for nearly 20 years*—an insurance policy naming my client as the beneficiary. I have asked him to also send a copy of those documents to you. You'll be receiving them within a few days. You can also anticipate additional discovery requests from me shortly. After you've had a chance to review the documents from the insurance company, we can schedule a time to talk. Thank you for your time. Good day."

Kate hung up without waiting for a response. She sat back in her chair and grinned ear to ear.

"Ed, I need you to draft a complaint for assault against this Peters guy and a motion for a restraining order keeping him at least 100 feet from Marcy, her place of work, and her residence. No calls, mail, e-mail, texts, all the usual stuff," Kate directed as she turned toward her computer screen.

"I'll proof it tonight, and we'll discuss whether to file it when we meet with Marcy tomorrow. I want it ready in case she says 'go,' which she might not. In any event, we'll have it on hand in case this asshole Peters tries anything else. I might send a copy to Ronald Gray and ask him to share it with Peters. Maybe the threat of litigation will be enough to get him to back off, but somehow, I doubt it. There's more going on with this guy than we see on the surface. He's way too interested in the Widow Dugan's money. We need to get Terry Driver looking into him.

"I also want you to prepare two subpoenas for documents: one to Joe Dugan's medical practice, and one for the University of Miami Hospital. Request all employment records, including benefits and insurance policies, as well as health and medical records related to the good doctor himself, and any personal notes, letters, diaries, or calendars he might have kept. Give them two weeks to respond; that should be plenty of time. There's something going on here, and we need to figure it out."

Ed nodded and picked up his notes, "OK, Boss Lady." He gave her a mini-salute as he headed out the door and thought, *Yep, a real tour de force. I wonder what she's like in the sack.*

Ed's grin matched Kate's as he contemplated finding out.

Chapter 2

Later that evening, Kate walked down the hall to Ed's chaos-stricken office.

"Hey," she said training her eyes on Ed and away from the stacks of papers, books, and files covering everything but a small walkway leading from the office door to his desk. "I made a few edits to the Primary Paints response brief and sent it on to Fred Richards for his final review. I asked him to call us in a couple of days to give us his thoughts. I like the brief; I think Fred will too. It should be a winner, but you never know about the circuit court. It will depend on the panel we draw." Kate had her briefcase in hand and an "I've-got-to-get-out-of-here-before-I-scream" look on her face.

"Good to hear," Ed said. "It was mostly a rehash of our memorandum in support of the summary judgment motion, but I found a few new cases and put an additional twist on our *caveat emptor* argument."

"Yeah, I liked it."

Kate was ready to leave; the mess in Ed's office was beginning to make her anxious.

"I'm out of here for today. I've got to get a run in tonight, or I'll shoot someone tomorrow. And, as much as I love my funky neighborhood, it isn't the safest place to run after 9:00. So, I have to get home now."

"Want company?" Ed asked tentatively.

"On my run? Sure . . . if you think you can keep up," Kate teased.

"I'll take that challenge," he said reaching under his desk for his gym bag.

"OK, where shall we meet?" Kate asked. "I live in the heart of the

Old Cigar District. There's a park at Habana and Del Rio. Is that anywhere near your new condo?"

Ed was disappointed. He'd hoped Kate would suggest he come home with her to change, but he decided the park was a good meeting place—at least for now.

"Sure. I'm actually in the condos they made out of the old Cuesta-Rey factory. I know the park." Ed figured he'd reveal his residence and maybe she'd get the idea and reciprocate.

"Perfect. Meet you at the park in 45 minutes?"

Kate sensed what Ed was up to and decided to play dumb. The last time she let herself flirt with him, a near seduction had resulted, and that was three *long*, abstinence-filled months ago. She wasn't sure she still had that kind of willpower.

Ed agreed to meet her at the park's main entrance off Habana, and Kate headed out.

Kate was stretching when Ed showed up at the park, and he once again admired her legs, but this time from an athletic standpoint. Her calves and thighs were ripped, and her body was sleek and looked strong. They'd run together once before, briefly on the beach at the Breakers, but they had both been barefoot, and running in the deep sand had given him no real sense of her speed. He suddenly felt a pang of male ego as he worried whether he really could keep up with her.

Naw, Ed thought, *I've got nearly six inches on her and my Marine training. If I can't smoke her, I'll have to quit calling myself a Marine.*

Kate waved when she saw Ed walking toward her—shirtless. She felt a twinge as she recalled seeing him in his swim trunks at the Breakers.

Man, I need to get these hormones under control. He looks good enough to eat, she thought, and she felt the blood rush to her cheeks. She was trying to get her mind off Ed's body but having no luck. *Maybe the run will help,* she thought hopefully.

Kate explained she was planning on running six miles and had a good course she could recommend. Ed let her lead both in direction and pace—which was anything but slow, but still left him plenty of reserve in the tank.

As they ran they chatted about work—cases and clients, and then moved on to races coming up in the next few months. Kate wanted to run a half marathon in two months, and Ed was planning on running the full marathon in the same race. He suggested they train together a couple of nights a week. At the end of the run they were back at their meeting point in the park, and Kate began to slow for a cool down lap around the park.

"You don't mind if I blow it out on one more lap of the park, do you? I'll come back around and meet you on the next loop," Ed asked displaying more than a little male ego.

"Of course not. Knock yourself out," Kate smiled at him, and he took off.

She knew he'd been holding back on their run, and she was also pretty sure he was now trying to impress her. When he was about 20 yards ahead of her, she decided to see if she could maintain or close the distance between them.

There's no fucking way I'm going to let him lap me, Kate vowed as she took off after him.

She managed to keep the distance between them from growing, but she made no progress on him at all.

When they neared the point on the path where they'd separated, Ed began looking around for her. Finally looking directly behind him, he spotted Kate powering toward him. He laughed out loud and slowed a bit to allow her to catch up.

"Impressive gate you've got there when you let it all out. I should have known you were holding back earlier. I also should have known you wouldn't be able to just watch me run off. You're even more competitive than I am," he panted.

"How about that cool down lap now?" she panted back.

They both slowed their pace and circled the park one last time. As they were returning to their starting point, Ed noticed a very casual bar with outdoor seating across the street from the park.

"Want to catch a cold beer before heading home?" he asked, hoping to prolong their time together as he popped on the T-shirt he'd carried tucked into the back of his shorts.

"I look like shit, and I doubt I smell too great. Besides, the last thing I need is a beer. I'm trying to keep weight off not put it on," Kate replied.

"OK, then, how about some water and a salad. I doubt you've eaten much today. If you're going to train with me, you've got to keep your strength up," Ed said, crossing the street without waiting for Kate to agree.

"Who says I'm training with you?" she shouted after him, standing still with her hands on her hips.

She considered something to eat and decided she *was* hungry and crossed the street after him, knowing she should just head home.

"Besides, I only have my emergency $20 bill in my shoe, and I didn't bring a credit card."

"My treat then. God knows you've done enough for me to allow me to treat this one time," he responded, reaching the table the farthest from the restaurant door and signaling the waiter as he sat down.

What is it about guys? They seem impervious to sweat, it just doesn't stop them or even slow them down, Kate thought recalling the first time she made love to Bill; he had pounced her when she was in a full post-run sweat.

Kate followed him into the restaurant and sat across the table from him, attempting to keep her sweaty body to herself. Ed immediately changed to the seat right beside her. Her surprise apparently showed, because Ed flashed her his most mischievous grin. She could feel the heat pouring out of his body and found it oddly intriguing rather than repelling.

"I think we've thoroughly contaminated this corner of the courtyard," she said, trying to lighten the mood and resolving to keep herself from flirting with Ed this time.

They ordered drinks and looked over the menu of bar food. Kate found an omelet that looked reasonably light, and Ed ordered a hamburger and fries to accompany his beer.

"My condo is less than two miles from here. How far away do you live?"

Kate attempted to change the subject, but Ed was determined. He wanted more than a working relationship with Kate. Actually, he'd wanted more since they started working together. At first, he was too intimidated to initiate anything, plus, his prior screw up, getting involved with his first female boss, had also held him back. Until, that is, their weekend at the Breakers. He'd been certain he sensed interest emanating from Kate, and he went for it. Up to that point, Kate had always been very careful to keep things on a business level. It drove him crazy. He'd started to think he was getting old and losing his appeal. As he considered all this, Ed decided to take the direct approach.

"So, Kate, did you and Bill ever patch up your lover's quarrel?" he asked, staring directly into her eyes. He saw her flinch.

"It wasn't a lover's quarrel, Ed. Bill wants to remarry, and I do not. We want different things. And, his ideal mate is about 180 degrees different from me. So, no, I'm not with Bill now, if that's what you're asking. As a matter of fact, I haven't even heard from him since the night I turned down his marriage proposal."

Kate looked down at the tabletop and thought what a shame it was that she'd lost more than a fabulous lover when she told Bill she wouldn't marry him. What she'd really lost by getting sexually involved with Bill was an incredibly good friend—she vowed she wouldn't make that mistake again.

"Well, remember what I said," Ed broke into her thoughts.

"What's that?" Kate said, shaking off her momentary self-recriminations.

"Shit, Kate! You really know how to crush a guy's ego," he pouted, not entirely in jest.

"Don't you remember at the Breakers, after you stopped me from carting you off into my bedroom and having my way with you, you agreed you'd let me know when you were ready for a little 'no-strings-attached, rebound sex.' You'll kill my male pride if you tell me you can't remember that."

Kate laughed. "What I remember from that conversation is each of the reasons I gave you for why I said no. Do you want me to recap them for you?"

"I remember something bogus about you being a little older than me, and, of course, the whole Boss Lady, sexual harassment thing. But seriously, Kate, I would like to see you outside of the office. We get along so well and have so much in common. Don't you think it's worth a try?" he persisted.

"Ed, I've lost one of my best friends mixing sex with friendship. It's just a bad idea," she said, noticing the sexy pout on his face. "But, don't worry, sailor," Kate knew the Marine in him hated to be called "sailor." "You've still got your magic. You just need to find someone younger . . . and less damaged."

He really is quite hard to turn down. I must never let myself get drunk around this guy again. I'm not sure I'd have the same resolve if presented with that opportunity a second time, Kate thought as she continued to regard Ed appreciatively.

"Well, until this younger woman shows up, I think I'll just keep on sexually harassing you. After all, I have to keep up my skills," Ed teased.

"You really are totally incorrigible! I'm so glad you told me what your mom used to say about you being unable to take 'no' for an answer. She had you pegged—you really can't. Now stop badgering me. I think our food is coming." Kate needed to end this mild flirtation; she could feel herself beginning to yield.

"OK, fine. Let's talk running. I propose we work out together three times during the week and one time on the weekend. I think I can whip you into good enough shape to manage a personal best in the half marathon in two months," Ed said, deciding to take a less direct approach for a while.

"Sounds like a plan, but at least one of our weekly workouts has to be a hot yoga session. I can't wait to hear you whimper like a little girl after 20 minutes in the hot yoga room," she said, knowing most men have no idea what they're getting into with hot yoga.

"You're on," Ed said, full of male ego. "After all, how hard could a yoga class be? And hot is nothing new to me. Remember, I did an extended tour in Afghanistan."

Kate just smiled knowingly.

Chapter 3

Thursday morning, Kate's direct office line rang, and caller ID indicated it was coming from Phillip Bentley, the CEO of Square Foods, Kate's largest corporate client.

"Kate Muldoon. Good morning, Phillip," she answered.

"Morning, Kate. I've got a new one for you!" Phillip greeted her.

"Always good to hear from you," she responded with a laugh.

"Yesterday at five, one of our assembly line workers, Bob Gentry, went home with his lunch pail in hand. This morning, Bobbi Jo Gentry came to work with *her* lunch pail in one hand and a purse in the other! The guys who work on the line with him . . . er . . . her . . . are going nuts, and the workers from every other work area are strolling by to check out Bobbi Jo's makeup and hairdo. We need help, and fast. No work is getting done, and I'm afraid there's going to be a fight or an accident. Nobody's paying any attention to what they're doing. It's a circus over here!"

"Believe it or not, Phillip, this isn't the first of these situations to come across my desk. Let me guess, the chief issue right now is which bathroom she will be using," Kate said, briefly recalling her first such matter involving the 50-year-old CFO of another corporate client. The guy was married with three kids when he went on a family vacation. One week later, he returned as a woman getting divorced from her wife of 25 years—that one had been a doozy.

"How did you guess?" Phil replied.

"It's always the first issue. And often, once that issue is resolved, everything else falls into place pretty quickly," she informed him. "Josie Myers, your HR Director, is really terrific with your employees.

I think we should press her into service today. Have her give me a call and I'll walk her through my recommendations.

"But, Phillip, just so you know where this is headed, let me give you a quick overview. The law will protect Bobbi Jo's choice, whether it's to cross-dress or undergo a complete sex change—surgery, hormone therapy, and all. My best advice is to try to keep her employed and work with her as she makes this transition. It's the best way to avoid potential litigation. That said, she is *not* entitled to create a disruption in the workforce. Also, it's very likely she's already engaged legal counsel and knows her rights."

Kate was pretty sure Josie would be able to handle the first steps without Kate making her own trip out to the plant, and she would prefer to handle it that way. She knew if *she* conducted the interview, Bobbi Jo would think the company had "lawyered-up" on her.

"OK, I'll have Josie call you right away. I need to get this line back up and running at capacity as soon as possible," Phil said, making it clear his primary concern was profits—as usual.

As Kate hung up, she buzzed Ed's office.

"I've got a new issue at Square Foods that I'll need you on. Can you come to my office in a few minutes when the HR Director calls? My guess is you haven't handled a matter like this before," Kate said smiling. "It will be great experience."

"OK, Instant Message me when she calls," Ed suggested.

Five minutes later, Josie was on the line. Kate put her on speakerphone, and IM'd Ed.

"Hey, Josie," Kate greeted her. "I hope you weren't planning on doing anything important today. I think your hands will be pretty full managing the Bob becomes Bobbi Jo situation."

"I had a full day of employee evaluations and promotion recommendations planned, clearly that's all on the back burner now. What a zoo! My phone is ringing off the hook, women refusing to use the same restroom as Bobbi Jo, men refusing to work on the same line with her," Josie sighed. "I've read some articles online about this sort of situation, and, so far, our group of employees are proving the articles to be spot-on."

Ed walked into Kate's office and sat down at the worktable in the corner, opened his laptop, and began taking notes.

"I have confidence you can handle this without me there, but if you want me, I can be there this afternoon. It's actually better if you deal with Bobbi Jo without 'legal' becoming involved—unless or until we have to, that is. I do, however, want to send my male associate, Ed Evert, out to meet with Bobbi Jo's teammates and the foremen in her section. Ed is here with me in my office. He can easily be there later this morning," Kate said, shifting a questioning gaze toward Ed. He nodded.

"I know most of your line employees are male. Can you tell me the makeup of Bobbi Jo's team and the name of her foreman?" Kate inquired.

"The foreman is Gerry Black. He's not too bad. But, Kate, we only have seven women in the whole plant, none, of whom, are on her line. I just can't find women candidates with an interest in line work. I've been worrying about our lack of diversity in this division for some time," Josie responded.

"Well, this is one way to increase your diversity numbers!" Kate laughed. "But I don't think you're going to get many of your male employees to demonstrate this same level of commitment to diversity!"

"No kidding," Josie chuckled. "It would be great if Ed could come out this morning and handle the conversation with the coworkers," Josie said. "I've already fielded 10 calls just from women employees saying they nearly freaked out when they saw a set of feet in the stall next to them pointed toward the back of the stall instead of the stall door," Josie laughed. "Bobbi Jo must have a weak bladder!"

Kate glanced at Ed and saw his head jerk up from his notes as an incredulous look crept across his face. He IM'd Kate, "*ur conf calls r always the best.*"

"Hopefully, she's not just making a point," Kate replied. "I gave Phillip a heads-up that Bobbi Jo's decision is protected, and we need to work with her, if we can. I also told him she's probably already received legal counsel on her rights.

"The first thing I need you to do is go to the line where she's working and invite her to your office for a confidential conversation. Expect her to be defensive. You should have your assistant HR manager, Kathy, join you so you have a witness to the conversation. Ask Kathy to take notes. If Bobbi Jo asks for a union rep to join the meeting you should allow it, of course. But, if she asks to record your conversation or have an attorney present, you should tell her 'no' because taping is against company policy, and it's also your policy to have the first conversation on any personnel issue with the employee only, because it ensures an open dialogue about a workplace issue."

"OK, let me get Kathy in here so she knows what we're doing."

Josie placed them on a brief hold.

Kate looked over at Ed who was looking at her with a somewhat stunned look.

"Is this what I think it is?" he asked in disbelief.

"Probably. Stay tuned and take notes," Kate answered.

"OK. We're both here now," Josie said, and Kathy chimed in with her hello.

"Kathy, your role in the conversation with Bobbi Jo is mostly as witness and scribe," Kate began again. "This first conversation will be primarily fact finding. We'll need to talk again after your meeting. Let me give you the talking points you should cover.

"First, let Bobbi Jo know you recognized this is a big day for her and that she's probably excited and maybe a bit anxious. She needs to be told right up front that the company is ready to work with her to make her transition a smooth one *in the workplace*. You should encourage her to acknowledge that her coworkers haven't had an opportunity to prepare for this big event as she has. She needs to understand they might need help with the adjustment, and that you would appreciate her understanding.

"Second, you should remind Bobbi Jo that if she feels harassed or threatened by a coworker, she should come to you with any concerns. Inform her the company will be talking with her coworkers to explain her rights and protections.

"Then you should ask her a series of questions. What is her intention regarding the permanence of this change? Specifically, is she going forward with a physical sex change, or is she only going to dress and otherwise present herself as a woman? Is she looking for flexibility to move back and forth with her identity, or is she planning on remaining Bobbi Jo going forward?

"You should ask what she wants to be called. Can we consistently refer to her as 'her' or 'she'? Find out if she's gone public with her family and friends. She needs to understand if there are inquiries from outside the company, you will be referring them to her directly. The company should simply let her know if an inquiry occurs.

"Find out what stage her transition is in, and explain that you can't change her employee records to reflect a new name, etc., until it's legally changed, the same way we handle newly married women or divorcees who take their maiden name back. Ask her to keep you informed of her progress in that regard. Ask if she has an attorney to help her with the process, and if so, find out who it is. Also ask whether she will need medical leave for surgery, and, if so, when and how long."

Ed was eagerly taking notes but winced at the mention of surgery.

"Ask her about the restroom situation and explain some of her female coworkers have expressed a concern and ask for her thoughts. Also ask if she has a message for her coworkers and if she wants to have them ask questions or engage in some other form of direct dialogue.

"During this interview, you will be able to determine her willingness to work with us verses an intent to create a legal issue that could provide her a cause of action or create a platform for protests and press coverage," Kate concluded.

"OK," Kathy exhaled. "We've both taken notes on this, but I want to make sure our list of questions is complete. Would you mind sending us an e-mail of those talking points?"

"No problem. I'll have Ed e-mail you the list within 15 minutes. Read it through a couple of times so it comes across more as a conversation than an interrogation," Kate advised.

"Josie, I think you and Kathy can handle this without me there, and it's actually better if you do. The conversation will take on a different tone if I show up. Think you can handle it?"

"Yes, but I'm not sure we have much confidence the men here will take our message to heart. It will certainly help to have your associate come out and handle that aspect."

"I'll get him prepared and out to the plant this morning. Plus, I'm going to make sure Phillip attends the meetings. It will signal there's an expectation of compliance. Ed should meet first with all of the foremen, and then have a group meeting with the rest of the guys on her line. The message Ed will be delivering is that Bobbi Jo's transition is protected, and they are to treat her like any other coworker—with respect. They should treat her no differently than they did before today. And they must understand harassment, or any other form of abuse, will not be tolerated. Under your company policy, gender identity is protected, similar to an employee's race, ethnic background, national origin, religion, gender, age, or disability. They also need to know the company's complaint and dispute resolution policies and the union's grievance process apply.

"If Bob was on a company bowling, softball, or other team, Bobbi Jo should continue to be on the team unless the league is restricted by gender. In that case, we will need to see where Bobbi Jo is in the legal and medical process. You need to explain that the company will control those things it *can* and will work with her to try to reach the right result on those matters that are outside the scope of the company's control."

"This all sounds like a landmine field—lots of ways for us to screw up. I hope we can pull it off as smoothly as you make it sound," Josie said skeptically.

"Oh, there'll be problems, you can count on that," Kate told them. "We'll just try to make them as manageable as possible, and, frankly, a lot depends on Bobbi Jo's intentions. But, let's not borrow trouble. Call me when you're done talking with her and we'll discuss next steps."

"Also, send me an e-mail as soon as you have set up a time for Ed to speak with the foremen and the rest of her coworkers. I recommend there be no break between his discussion with the foremen and the crew. The foremen should remain with Ed and just have the crew come into the same room. We want to make sure the foremen don't have any unauthorized sidebars with their guys and stir up issues. Having Phillip there will set the expectation of what the company considers acceptable leadership behavior for the foremen," Kate warned.

"Finally, what sort of employee was Bob? Was he a good worker, any promotions coming up? How about performance problems?" Kate asked, trying to anticipate any difficulties that may arise in the future.

"That's the crazy part. Bob was a great employee. I just put him up for promotion to foreman, but he didn't know about it yet, and no action had been taken on our recommendation," Josie replied.

"Well, that could be a blessing. Bobbi Jo won't be able to complain that her transition has negatively impacted her career if we ultimately promote her after this. Hang tough, ladies. The fun is just beginning!" Kate loved her work.

She turned to Ed as Kathy and Josie said their good-byes and hung up—he seemed a bit shell-shocked.

"Kate, I've never handled anything like this before. I'm not sure I can pull this off," he confided.

"Yes, you can, and probably more effectively than I could. I'm a woman, but you're a big, strong Marine. Which one of us do you think a bunch of assembly line workers and their foremen will listen to better?" Kate wanted to challenge Ed to stretch outside his comfort zone. "I'll give you the talking points. There aren't as many as I gave Josie and Kathy, and you'll do almost all of the talking. But, there will be questions, and you have to be able to answer them," Kate directed.

"OK. But don't think for one moment you'll always get your way just by calling me a 'big strong Marine.' Though I have to admit I like it a whole hell of a lot better than 'sailor,'" Ed said, shooting her his best grin.

Kate smiled back, and then launched into the guidance he would be delivering to the plant foremen and Bobbi Jo's coworkers.

Later that afternoon, Kate heard from Josie and Ed that their meetings had gone well, but she knew they weren't out of the woods yet. The next three weeks would be the real test.

Bobbi Jo had been surprised by the company's response. She'd come into the meeting hostile, expecting to be fired. When she finally understood the company planned to help her with the transition, Bobbi Jo seemed to get on board with the idea of working cooperatively with the company and her coworkers. She decided during the meeting to make the transition permanent, at least at work, and would not switch back to her male personae. She acknowledged that switching back and forth would be harder for her coworkers to handle and could create confusion or an unintended affront.

She also confirmed that she wanted to be called Bobbi Jo and referred to as "her" or "she" going forward. She ultimately seemed to understand the reasoning behind the company's inability to change her name and gender on their records until she did so legally. At first, she'd wanted to make an issue of this point and said she'd be talking with her attorney about it. But, she seemed less defensive once Josie explained the company did not change women employees' names when they married or divorced until they brought in their marriage license, divorce decree, or some other legal document granting a name change.

The next few weeks would determine whether Bobbi Jo would truly give up her initial belief that she needed to sue the company to get what she wanted, or if she was looking for something to litigate. Kate had seen plenty of situations where the employee really wanted a fight and to garner cash or press coverage, rather than find a true resolution.

Ed's meetings had gone well for the most part. The foremen were surprised gender identity was protected and once that fact sank in, and they heard it reinforced by the CEO, they were more interested in whether Bobbi Jo was going to be "surgically altered" and "what the hell that would entail." Ed reported a number of the guys seemed to get quite squeamish when the topic of surgery came up but were relieved to hear they weren't expected to know or learn about the surgery unless they wanted to *and* Bobbi Jo wanted to tell them. Ed emphasized the employees were not to text, e-mail, IM, or Facebook about Bobbi Jo's transition, and, while they all seemed to understand this directive, human nature being what it is, Kate knew the story would eventually surface somewhere on social media.

Chapter 4

At 5:20 that same afternoon, Marcy Simpson arrived at the offices of Sterns and Gladstone. When Sophia led her back to Kate's office, Kate and Ed were seated at the circular worktable in the corner next to the window discussing Marcy's situation and discovery options.

When Marcy walked in, Kate quickly rose from behind the table without saying a word and hugged her in a long, warm embrace. Ed noted, although they were smiling broadly, both women had bright tears in their eyes. It was clear they meant a great deal to each other.

"Ed," Kate said when she finally pulled back slightly from Marcy, "I want you to meet my long-lost sister from another mother, Marcy Simpson."

Both women laughed at their inside joke.

"Marcy, this is Ed Evert. He'll be working with me on your matter. Ed, you should know, Marcy is one of the smartest women I've ever met. As a matter of fact, the only lapse in her intelligence I'm aware of is her temporary weakness for my brother, Sean Muldoon."

Ed scrutinized the women and decided they actually *could* be sisters. Marcy's hair was a slightly darker shade of auburn than Kate's, but they shared the same green eyes and slightly tawny skin tone. Both were about 5 foot 8 and athletically built. Marcy looked a little older than Kate, but otherwise, could have been her body double.

"Let's get down to work, kid, and then I'm taking you out for a catch-up dinner if you have time," Kate said as she led Marcy to the worktable.

"We've been over the insurance policy a number of times and done a bit of research on case law interpreting potentially ambiguous beneficiary designations in policies. So far, my initial gut reaction appears to be correct, and, while it's not certain how the court will view the wording in Joe's policy, we should be in excellent shape. I believe the two insurance attorneys, Meardon and Argyle, likely came to the same conclusion, and that was the reason they were hoping to pay the proceeds over to you so quickly.

"There was a recent U.S. Supreme Court decision, originating out of the Virginia courts, that I think is instructive here. Divorce or separation does not *automatically* exclude the former spouse from remaining the beneficiary under a policy, even when the insured remarries. In a nutshell, and without getting into too much legalese, I believe the specific listing of your full name should carry the day and win out over the more generic descriptive term 'my wife.' It's also significant that Joe kept the policy intact and current without any change, and paid an annual premium for each of the subsequent 19 years."

"Maybe," Marcy began, "but I wasn't his wife for so many of those years, Kate. Let me tell you what I remember about the day Joe first told me about the policy. It might help explain why he took it out in the first place, even if it doesn't help us understand why he kept it in place 16 years *after* our divorce."

"Perfect," Kate said. "We're all ears."

Kate picked up a pen and pad and Ed popped open his laptop. They were ready to take notes and start building their case in favor of making Marcy a multimillionaire.

Marcy stared out the window for a moment, her eyes focused at some distant point, as she began to tell her story.

"One night, shortly after Joe accepted the residency position in UM's cardiac department, he surprised me and took me out to dinner. He was finally starting to earn some money, after all those years of med school and internships." Marcy paused. Her voice had a wistfulness that revealed her fondness for that early, impecunious time.

"Joe came home from work a little later than usual that night, and he began telling me about all the administrative details he'd plowed through during his orientation as part of the 'new hire' process. It all seemed pretty mundane, but then he said he'd purchased a life insurance policy and made me the beneficiary." Marcy paused again and sighed heavily before continuing.

"Kate, this seems like a such a long time ago and almost like someone else's life. Anyway, I remember not wanting to even think about Joe not being around forever, much less talk about it, and I told him so. See, we had this 'master plan' that we'd been working on for years. It started when we were both in med school at UF. Joe was several years ahead of me, and we wanted to get married. So, rather than wait for both of us to complete med school, we decided I would work as an ER nurse and a medical transcriptionist and support us until Joe finished medical school and his residency. Then, we were going to trade, and Joe was going to support me while I returned to medical school. It was getting close to being my turn. I'd gotten my nurse practitioner certification along the way to increase my earning capacity, but also to close the gap on some of the medical school courses I would need when I finally got back to it. Joe told me the insurance premium was partially subsidized by UM as an employee incentive so we could afford it and, he emphasized, it would ensure I would get to go to medical school even if he wasn't there to support me."

There was a longer pause as Marcy fought back tears. Kate retrieved the box of tissues and a bottle of water from the credenza behind her desk and quietly placed them on the worktable next to Marcy.

"Well, you know what they say," Marcy sniffed and started again, "if you want to make God laugh, tell him you have a plan!" she laughed wryly. "God must have had a hearty laugh about our master plan. Obviously, the divorce broke our 'master plan' into a million pieces."

"Marcy, do you recall Joe saying the insurance policy was to ensure you'd get to go to medical school even if he wasn't there to support you? Do you remember those words?" Kate asked.

"Yep, I remember the conversation well. We hardly ever went out to dinner back then, we didn't have the money or time. It was just a little pizza place, but we each had a glass of wine. It was a real celebration for us. I remember telling him he couldn't die—it wasn't in the master plan! That made us both laugh. Kate, we never spoke about the insurance policy after that, and I never even knew the amount of the death benefit."She paused and drew a deep breath. "Just a couple of years later, Joe was divorcing me so he could marry Joan."

Marcy struggled a moment, and then continued, "I learned later that Joan was pregnant with their first baby when they'd gotten married. The little guy was born just five months after their wedding—and he wasn't early! He was a big boy; the birth announcement in the paper said he weighed 8 pounds 10 ounces—so much for the master plan and our deal.

"When we got divorced, Joe's divorce attorney threatened to seek alimony for Joe. He said because I had been the one with an earning history, Joe had a legal right to alimony from me. I couldn't believe they could do that, but I asked a couple of lawyers I knew if a man could be awarded alimony, and they all said it was possible.

"I was so deeply in debt then. I'd paid for my first two years of med school from some savings and student loans, but then I took on Joe's school payments when I started working full time. We wanted to keep our borrowing down to a minimum, but I did have to take out a personal loan to pay for part of his tuition, and I ran my credit cards to the max during that time. Anyway, I couldn't afford a lawyer. I think Joan's parents paid for Joe's—her dad was a bigwig attorney. He'd been one of the founders of Gray and Ferguson before he got into politics. They hired Ron Gray, the same guy I met with the other day, to represent Joe in the divorce. Gray told me if I agreed to waive any claim I might have for support from Joe and keep paying off our debts in my name, he would tell Joe to waive his claim for support from me. Seemed like a good deal at the time, especially since he also told me that if I waived support, we could be divorced within a couple of months. I ached every time we had to meet to discuss the divorce. Once Joe told me he didn't love me anymore I just wanted it over. What a nightmare. It all came on so fast. I couldn't believe I'd been so naïve and unaware of what was going on. Man, I was such a chump!" Marcy concluded, pulling another tissue out of the box.

"Hardly," Kate said with venom. "Joe and his attorney took huge advantage of you. Joe's future earning capacity should have been taken into account. He would have ended up paying *you* support and very likely supporting you during medical school. It's called rehabilitative alimony, and Florida judges love to award it. And, he should have taken responsibility for his debts from med school. That is what would have been fair. Joe must not have been as great a guy as you thought. It's reprehensible that he sanctioned his attorney's actions."

Kate was clearly steamed that Marcy was so shabbily treated by someone she had loved and so richly advantaged.

"Well, Kate, I'll admit, I loved him, but when someone doesn't love you back, it's sort of pointless. You just have to let go." Marcy sighed again. "So, did any of that help?"

"You bet," Kate replied. "Now, let me ask some questions. Is there anyone else who might have known about your 'master plan,' your deal regarding taking turns in medical school, or about the insurance policy? Did you or Joe ever talk to anyone about it?"

Marcy sat thoughtfully for a moment staring out at Biscayne Bay visible from Kate's forty-third-story window.

"Yeah, but I doubt she'll remember anything about it—not willingly anyway," Marcy said as she looked at Kate. "Joe told his mom, Grace Dugan, when we took her out to dinner after he started his residency. I remember she told me she was happy I would get to pursue my medical degree, but she wanted to know when we were planning on having her grandchildren! I guess she got them pretty quickly after that—just not from me. But, Kate, she'd never say anything that could potentially hurt those kids, regardless of how she feels about Joan. The insurance policy would give those kids a great start in life and replace some of the millions Joe would have earned if he'd lived. Grace Dugan will never remember our conversation, and if she does, she won't admit it."

"We'll see about that," Kate said emphatically. "The threat of perjury can be pretty persuasive. Besides, there are other people who could help us out. We've located the agent who sold Joe the policy. He's retired now, but he may recall the circumstances related to the original purchase. It was a lot of insurance for someone so young. And, we also know the identity of the other agent, the one who took over the account when the first agent retired. Both agents dealt with Joe each year when the premium came due. The second agent is still with Upton Insurance. We'll be interviewing the agents in a few days. Their testimony could be pretty significant in this contest."

Kate stopped to assess Marcy's state of mind before she went on. Marcy was getting a lot of information to process all at once. Kate wanted to make sure she wasn't too overwhelmed.

"We're also going to get some information from Joe's estate. If we discover he had a separate policy naming Joan and the kids as beneficiaries that could be helpful because it would show he was making separate provisions for them. And, we'll find out what account Joe used to pay the annual premium on this policy. Apparently, Joan was unaware of its existence, and apparently Joe intended it to be a secret. We've prepared a request for information from Joe's estate," Kate said, handing Marcy the legal papers listing the documents and information they were requesting from the estate.

Marcy's hands began to shake as she read through the discovery requests. "Can we really ask for this stuff? Do they have to give it to us?" Marcy asked tentatively.

"Yep. They're challenging the payment of the insurance proceeds to you, so they have to participate fully in the discovery process. You need to understand that they will likely come up with their own request for information and documents from you. And, Marcy, they will make requests they think will embarrass you. But, remember, whatever they ask for has to either be evidence they can use in court or could to lead to admissible evidence. Otherwise, we'll object to it, and they'll look like the jerks they are."

Marcy smiled weakly and said, "I'm kind of over worrying about being embarrassed by that group. They pretty much completely humiliated me the last time we met. There really isn't much left they can do to me that I couldn't take."

Kate looked at Marcy's face and saw resigned determination. She didn't want to raise Marcy's hopes unrealistically or fail to prepare her sufficiently for the oncoming fight. It was a delicate balance. Four million dollars is a lot of money, and people would do almost anything to get their hands on it. The legal battle was going to be a ferocious one, but Kate liked her odds.

"Marcy, we have another matter we need to discuss," Kate said, pulling out the complaint for assault and motion for a temporary restraining order against Zeke Peters. "What Zeke did in that conference room at Gray and Ferguson qualifies as assault. He physically and verbally threatened you and made you feel at risk. Hell, his actions made Meardon and Argyle think he was going to physically attack you. I don't know what the guy's game is, but he is way too interested in what happens to the insurance proceeds.

"I want you to think about filing a complaint against Zeke for assault and at the same time ask the court to enter an order prohibiting him from contacting you by phone, e-mail, or text, or coming anywhere closer than 100 feet of you. I want you to know what your rights are, and we want you protected. We've prepared the paperwork needed to start both of those actions, but whether we file them is your call."

Kate slid the complaint and motion in front of Marcy and watched as she read through them.

"Kate, Zeke would hit the roof if you filed these things," Marcy said lifting her head only halfway through her review of the pleadings. "You probably need to know a bit about him. He's a hothead, and his temper gets the best of him all the time—at least it used to. The run-in I had with him at the lawyer's office wasn't the first time he's physically threatened me. When Joe was in med school, Zeke used to hang around our apartment when he was back in the country. Joe had known him since they were kids—they grew up together here in Miami, went to private school together. They even went off to college together at the University of Florida. They were in the same fraternity. Joe's grades got him into UF Medical School, but Zeke had to go offshore to get his medical degree." Marcy looked out the window again and was silent.

Finally, she continued.

"Joe told me Zeke always had a problem with drugs and alcohol, so he wasn't the best student. He said Zeke had a few run-ins with the law in high school and college, but I never asked for the details. I really didn't like the guy at all and could never figure out why Joe gave him the time of day—Zeke was such jerk. When Joe wasn't around, Zeke would verbally harass me, tell me I wasn't good enough for Joe, not pretty enough, or rich, or smart enough. He was just a jerk. More than once he physically threatened me when Joe wasn't in the apartment. After the first time, I just blew him off, figured he was all bark and no bite. I never told Joe the details because when I complained about Zeke, Joe would take Zeke's side and tell me Zeke was like a brother to him, and that I was exaggerating." Marcy was quiet for a moment before continuing.

"Kate, when I heard that Joe gave Zeke a job in his practice group, I was stunned. I think Zeke's parents' connections here in Miami probably helped get the practice going. But Zeke always seemed like such a liability to me . . . anyway, that was years after our divorce, so it wasn't any of my business."

"Marcy, I understand your reluctance to file the actions against Zeke, but the guy sounds like a loose cannon, and I want to protect you. I have a suggestion. How about I send Ronald Gray a copy of these documents and tell him that I will file them in a heartbeat if Zeke contacts you in any way. We can see if that's enough to keep him away from you. But, you have to promise to let me know the minute you see or hear from Zeke again. In the meantime, I'm going to have Terry Davis, my PI, do a little background search on Zeke Peters. I don't trust him, and I haven't even *met* the guy."

Kate paused and waited for Marcy's reaction.

"OK, Kate. I agree it would be nice to have some protection and not have to deal with Zeke. And I promise I'll let you know if he contacts me again. It does seem odd that he's interjected himself into Joan's life—he must like her a whole lot more than he ever liked me," Marcy laughed as she said this and smiled, but she looked as if she'd been through hell and back.

"Look, Marcy, it's entirely possible that Joe was actually the good guy you thought he was—with the exception of the infidelity, of course. It's possible he purposefully kept that policy current with you as the beneficiary to, in some way, make up for his failure to keep his end of your master plan. It's an odd approach, since he'd have to die for you to benefit, but, let's wait and see what the evidence shows us."

Kate patted Marcy's hand. "Now, how about that catch-up dinner? Are you hungry?"

"I'd love that Kate. It's been so long, and I have missed talking to you."

"Great. Ed, could you call Terry and bring him up to speed on Marcy's situation and tell him I want him working on these items," Kate said, handing Ed a list of tasks she had jotted down as they'd talked.

"Marcy, my PI, Terry Driver, is great at digging up information that most people think has been buried too deep to be found. By the way, do you have an address for Grace Dugan?" Kate asked, hoping Terry could work his magic one more time. Kate's gut told her there was more to Joe Dugan's story than they knew at this point and she knew if anyone could dig up the whole story, it was Terry Driver.

Marcy supplied them the last address she had for her former mother-in-law, and Ed headed back to his office to bring Terry up to speed on their newest case and give him Kate's list of assignments. Terry was going to be very busy interviewing the insurance agents and finding out what he could about Grace and Joan Dugan, Zeke Peters, and Joan's father.

It's a good thing Terry loves his work as much as Kate and I do, Ed thought as he headed down the hall.

Chapter 5

The following morning, Kate met Ed outside her favorite yoga studio ten minutes before the 6:00 class.

"You ready for this, sailor?" Kate teased. "This practice isn't for everyone, and you might not be able to hang for the whole 90 minutes. Have you been drinking water this morning?"

"Shit, Kate, it's only yoga. How hard can this be? It's not like we'll be running around in the heat doing obstacle course training. Plus, no one will be shooting at me, so I think I can handle it!"

Ed fumbled with the yoga mat and towel Kate handed him.

"OK, if you think you're ready, let's do this. But take this bottle of water and drink half now before we start practice, and then some more when the instructor cues a water break. If you start to feel lightheaded, either stand still or kneel on your mat. If you still feel dizzy, lie down flat and stay there until the dizziness passes, and then get up very slowly. The more you get up and down, the dizzier you'll feel. And, your breathing will be your best aid. Remember to exhale completely through you nose and don't hold your breath.

"We do two sets of each posture. If you find you're struggling, just do one set and watch the other one. The first set is the longest. You might want to watch the first, and then join in on the second set. And, whatever you do, don't leave the yoga room. Just lie down if you can't continue but don't leave the room."

Kate continued her string of advice as they walked into the yoga studio and signed in for the class.

"Jeez, Kate, you make it sound like some sort of torture—it's just yoga. I'll be fine." Ed was embarrassed by Kate's attention. He knew he could hang with her—it was just yoga, after all.

"Hey, Kate, did you bring me a new victim?" the trim, young woman in bright yellow and orange yoga togs behind the front desk asked as Kate slipped off her warm-ups, revealing her own body-hugging purple and blue yoga outfit that left nothing to the imagination.

Kate turned to introduce Ed to Leah Sturgis, one of the co-owners of the studio and their teacher for the 6:00 a.m. class.

"Yep, this is my colleague Ed Evert. He filled out your new student paperwork online. We're training for the Habana Marathon in two months, and I suggested he add some yoga to his training regime. He's in decent shape, but needs to work on his flexibility."

Decent shape? I'm in fabulous shape. What the hell? And how the hell does she know what my flexibility is? I'd like to wrap her up and bend her in some interesting positions, Ed thought as he shook Leah's hand and took in the scene at the yoga studio. *One thing for sure, the women in this class are in great shape—and they all wear spandex extremely well. A 90-minute class here will fly by with this sort of scenery.*

Then they walked into the yoga room. Ed was immediately hit by the heat—over 100 degrees, he was sure of it. It took his breath away, and to make matters worse, the vents in the ceiling were *still* pumping out massive amounts of hot air. It was Afghanistan all over again—but without the sand and gunfire. His body automatically went into survival mode. He was instantly on alert and panting.

"Ed, relax. Breathe through your nose only. Match the length of your inhales and exhales. Surrender to the heat, don't fight it, and finish that first half of your water bottle. You're going to need to be sweating, and soon." Kate gave Ed these tips as she unrolled her yoga mat and placed the yoga towel over it. She then laid out Ed's mat and towel for him since he seemed stuck and unable to move.

Kate tapped his water bottle again, and then lay down on her mat and began to gently bend and stretch her legs. As she relaxed into her mat, she closed her eyes and started breathing rhythmically.

Holy shit! There isn't enough air in this room for all these people. My lungs are on fire! My head is spinning. I have to lie down before I fall down. How can all these people be so relaxed? Seriously? People really do this to themselves on purpose? Surely the heat will shut off soon. Ed's brain was whirling quickly as he tried to sort out why he was torturing himself.

He decided to lie down and try to surrender to the heat. Kate's inert body was stretched out next to him, and for once, he was not even interested in how great she looked. He was conserving his energy for survival.

Five minutes later, Leah walked into the room and said, "OK, early morning yogis, are you ready to get warm? We'll begin our practice standing, feet together, interlace your fingers, and bring your knuckles under your chin."

Is she fucking joking? Get warm? Seriously? I'm already beyond warm and standing may or may not be an option, Ed thought, already struggling to stay in the room. *This is insanity. These people are all nuts!*

Ed watched as Kate lithely sprang to her feet, and for a brief moment, he hated her. When he tried to stand with similar agility, he hated her again.

Fifty-five torture-filled minutes later, after contorting his body into positions he had no idea he could manage and spectacularly falling out of nearly every posture at least once, the instructor told them to stretch out on their backs, head to the front of the room, feet to the back. He was drenched in sweat. He couldn't have been wetter if he'd gone swimming.

Ed thought the class was over and was just getting ready to congratulate himself on surviving when the instructor said, "OK, the warm-up portion of our class is over, and now the real yoga begins. Spine strengthening!" like it was some great treat. Ed wondered if anyone ever died from spine strengthening.

After another 40 minutes of twisting, turning, and bending his body into pretzel shapes and knots, the instructor announced, "Great work, class. Final *savasana*! Please take at least two minutes to let your body absorb all the benefits of your hard work before you charge off into your day. This is where the magic happens! *Namaste*."

Why does she sound so fucking happy all the time? What is she, some sort of a sadist? Two minutes—is she kidding? I'm never moving again.

Ed lay still and began thinking of ways to kill the instructor. He heard Kate breathing softly next to him. No one moved, Ed began to feel sleepy and knew he was close to falling asleep—or passing out. Everything was stillness and silence. His body was a puddle of sweat . . . Then a sudden rush of cold air hit him. The sharpness of it felt like pinpricks all over his body, and his eyes sprang open.

Kate was sitting on her mat looking at him. He realized the cold air was coming from the hallway. The other students were beginning to stream out of the yoga room heading off to the showers.

Ed did a mental inventory. He wiggled his feet and hands and tried to sit up. He instantly felt dizzy but forced himself to remain upright. Kate grinned at him.

"What's the matter, sailor? It's just yoga!" Kate grinned triumphantly. "Need help standing up? We have to hit the showers and head to the office."

"I might need help standing *in the shower*. Are you volunteering?"

Ed hoped his voice sounded stronger than his legs felt.

"You did great for your first time," Kate said, ignoring his flirtation. "You didn't have to take a knee even once. You just burned some calories, and you have to keep your strength up if you're going to train with me!" she laughed. "Plus, I understand you have a bitch of a Boss Lady. You need to get to work."

Kate held out her hand to help him stand, but he wouldn't let himself take it. His male ego had survived the yoga ordeal . . . but just barely. At least he now knew the secret to Kate's beautifully trim body. As the cool air from the hallway revived him, Ed again found himself lusting after her as she walked off toward the shower room—spandex butt swaying seductively.

Over breakfast, Kate and Ed discussed their work in progress. The workload had been reasonable over the last two months and still was even with the addition of Marcy Simpson's matter. It was a good thing too, because they were looking at a potential weeklong jury trial starting on Monday in a products liability matter for her client Brighton Industries. The witnesses were all prepped, and the exhibits and exam questions had been completed since the case was first set for trial, nearly a month ago. Kate had wrapped up the Opening Statement and would practice it as she ran on the beach this weekend. She planned to get in one more weekend at the beach with her two beautiful golden retrievers before returning to the confines of their much-smaller quarters at Kate's city house.

During breakfast, Kate explained some of the specific areas of testimony she planned to elicit on cross-exam of the plaintiff and the import of each as it played into the comparative negligence argument she would be making in closing. The plaintiff had admitted some of the points during his deposition but had hedged on others. Kate hoped to trap him in a couple of his more implausible statements and give the jury additional reasons not to believe his testimony generally. It was going to be a game of cat and mouse, but Ed's money was on Kate the Cat.

"So, what do you have planned for this weekend?" he asked Kate, trying to not let his ulterior motives show.

"Not much, just head out to my beach house and get some sun and relax. *If* we start trial on Monday, and it's not all that likely we will, we won't have much time to exercise or relax. How about you?"

Ed hoped for more, but settled for this opening.

"So, where's your beach house?"

"Garrett Beach. It's about an hour and a half away, but the beach is wonderful and the little town is pretty, secluded, and sleepy . . . worth the drive. It's a great getaway." Kate knew Ed was fishing, but she was disinclined to take the bait. She really needed some alone time with her pups. "You should check out the club scene in the Old Cigar District. I have a couple of girlfriends who say it's the hottest scene this side of South Beach. Your former boss, Suzy Spellman, loves that area; the marina is her second fave."

Damn it, Ed thought, *I sure wish she'd stop trying to push me into looking for women*. Ed was sure he'd never met anyone quite as impervious to his boyish good looks and charm. *She has to know I'm trolling; she just refused to bite. Maybe I'm losing it.*

"I'll think about checking it out this weekend," he surrendered.

When Kate and Ed walked into the office together at 9:00, two hours later than either of them usually arrived, their secretary, Sophia Touche, gave them a wary look.

"Did you guys have a hearing this morning that I didn't know about? I've been wondering where you were. It was odd that *neither* of you were in at your usual early hour."

Sophia put her hands on her generous hips and gave them her best "disapproving-Italian-momma" look.

Kate laughed and simply said, "Sophia, we don't want to be too predictable. Where's the fun in that? We've got to keep you on your toes."

To herself Kate thought, *I'll be damned if I'm going to explain when I occasionally arrive around the same time all the other attorneys are drifting in!*

"That's all well and good, but Terry Driver is looking for you," Sophia said with a frown. "He wants to come by today to discuss the list of projects Ed gave him in the Marcy Simpson matter. I told him I thought you'd be in later this morning, maybe around 10:30, but I didn't know for sure because you hadn't bother to let me know. And, I told him I wasn't sure how long you'd be here this afternoon. I thought you might be headed to the beach for the weekend and want to get ahead of the Friday traffic." Sophia was pouting to let Kate know just how upset she was at not knowing her whereabouts and at the same time pumping her for more information.

"OK, Mom. I've got it. We'll call you next time we grab breakfast to work on trial prep. Jeez, it's like being a teenager again," she said, laughing at her secretary's pout.

"Yeah, well, that's what I'm afraid of. I've got teenagers at home, I don't need them here at the office too," Sophia said as she shot Kate a suspicious look and handed her the morning mail.

"Thanks, Mom. I'm going to my office now to work. Let me know when Terry gets here," Kate chuckled and walked down the hall toward her office.

Ed leaned in to Kate as they walked away and whispered, "Man, we're going to have to be more careful. We don't want Mom getting the wrong idea, now, do we? You know, breakfast is the most suspicious meal of all."

He winked. Kate shot him an evil glance but said nothing.

Just before noon, Sophia let Kate know that she was sending Terry back to her office. Kate IM'd Ed in case he wanted to sit in on the conversation. Both men showed up about the same time.

"Am I keeping you busy enough, Terry?" Kate asked with a laugh. "Seriously, unless I'm totally off the mark, I think there's a lot below the surface in the Simpson matter."

"Based on what Ed told me yesterday evening and what I've learned so far, I have to agree with you, Kate. I couldn't sleep last night, so I started looking up the Dugans on the Internet. It's amazing what you can find out for free just sitting in your living room having a cold beer and half-watching the Yankees kick the shit out of my Rays. Whoever is responsible for letting Madden leave should be shot!" Terry responded. "But, don't think for a moment that I won't be charging my full hourly rate for my time." Terry grinned. He knew Kate would pay him whatever he billed as long as he kept bringing her the results.

Kate laughed. "I agree about Madden, but then the Cubs really needed him—and his bag of tricks and miracles. That's what it took for the Cubs to finally win the Series! So, what have you got on the Dugans?"

"Well, the Joe Dugan story is your basic All-American Boy makes good, then proves the old adage that 'only the good die young.' Of course, I've always thought that was only because they didn't live long enough to get into any real trouble or be found out," he laughed. Terry turned serious as he began to give Kate and Ed the rundown on his late-night Internet search.

"Joe graduated at the top of his high school class at Holy Cross Academy here in Miami where he was also a standout soccer goalie; lettered all four years. He got an academic scholarship to Florida—UF still doesn't have a men's soccer team, and he needed the financial aid. From what I could gather about his parents, they probably didn't have a pot to piss in or a window to throw it out of back then. Dad was a reporter for the *Herald*. Mom was an elementary school teacher. He's got a younger brother too, Michael, who did OK, but nothing like Joe. The address Marcy gave you in St. Pete for the senior Dugans still seems to be good, and it looks like the brother and his family are also up there."

Terry paused momentarily and looked at some notes he'd brought with him.

"Not sure why they moved from Miami . . . probably for the lower cost of living once they retired. It looks like they followed the younger son up there, so maybe there was something else. Who knows? Perhaps they get along better with that daughter-in-law. Apparently, this Joan Dugan is a handful. She's your typical skin-and-bones society broad, but she's had some legal issues that they've tried to keep quiet. Speeding tickets, possession of marijuana, DUIs, complaints by her neighbors about minor property damage she caused on a couple of occasions when she came home drunk—took out some mailboxes, plowed through some front yards, crashed into someone's hedge . . . that sort of thing.

"She was also issued noise violations for loud parties that went on into the wee hours of the night and some loud fights out on their pool deck. So, again, who knows? Maybe she wasn't Mom and Dad Dugan's cup of tea. Joe's oldest boy, Murphy, seems to be following in his mother's footsteps. He's only 16, but he's already lost his driver's license due to speeding tickets, and he's been busted for underage drinking and possession of marijuana. So far, the two younger boys, 13 and 11, seem to have stayed out of trouble, but they're young, so there's still time."

Terry paused to review his notes.

"That's about it on the Dugans. I found an old write-up about Joe and Joan's wedding—it was quite the social event. From that article, I learned her parents' names, and I can see why Joan turned out the way she did. Her dad is our infamous former Senator Ferguson. As you might recall, he's had his share of legal peccadillos.

"Funny thing, Joe Dugan Senior actually wrote an exposé on Old Fergie's biggest scandal. I don't know if you remember that one, but it was what ended his political career. He was photographed with his hand in the wrong crotch at a party on his boat. Anyway, he didn't run for re-election after that and sort of slipped into the background politically."

Terry checked his notes again. "That's about it. I didn't start on Zeke Peters last night—I was just too disgusted with the Rays' play, so I went to bed."

"Not bad for a night at home, Terry. Thanks!"

Kate always appreciated Terry's deep background on the players in a legal drama, it made it easier to formulate her next set of questions and theories.

"Yeah, and while I've got you, let me give you an update on where I am with the two insurance agents that dealt with Joe Dugan. This morning, I interviewed the guy who originally sold him the policy, Johnny Sutton. It was a great interview; the guy is a real character. He remembered the whole transaction without any prompting at all—said he didn't sell many $4 million policies.

"According to Sutton, Dugan told him he wanted the policy, to quote Sutton, for his 'pretty, little nurse wife because she wanted to go to medical school and become a doctor.' Sutton even remembers seeing a photo of Joe's wife that he carried in his wallet. Sutton said she was 'a really pretty girl with auburn hair.' He asked Dugan why she wanted to be a doctor, since she'd married one and would never have to work again. Dugan told him, between the two of them, his wife was much smarter and would no doubt make a better doctor because she was so compassionate. Kate, I've got to tell you, this guy is going to be a great witness, but we need to nail down his testimony soon. He's 83 and already had two bypass surgeries."

"Damn! How's his health generally? Does he come across as a doddering old fool or does he have some credibility?" Kate asked.

"I'd say he's damn good for someone his age," Terry responded. "When I got to the retirement community recreation center where I met him, the old dude was playing duplicate bridge and flirting with every broad in the place. The guy's got quite the gig. There must be 15 to 20 little old ladies for each of the men there, and Sutton's much whippier, physically *and* mentally, than all the other guys put together. The dude is a riot to talk to. His memory seems crystal clear, but, Kate, like I said, he's 83. We need to get his deposition set, and soon."

"I'll have Polly work on it right away. We'll make it a video depo, just in case he doesn't make it to the hearing. I'll have her set it for next week. This is great news. Any word about the other agent?" Kate inquired.

"His name is Milton Martin. He's out of the country this week and due back the week after next. I'm already on his calendar for Monday the week he gets back. I hope he's as helpful as Sutton."

Terry looked through his notes again.

"One more thing on the Senior Dugans. Apparently, Mr. Dugan is quite ill. They have hospice at the house now. I think the best way to handle this is for me to go to St. Pete and interview some neighbors and friends, and then try to get in to see Mrs. Dugan. It's going to be tricky and sensitive with the old guy so ill."

"That's true, but if anyone can handle it, it's you. I think you should head up there and interview as many of the Dugans as you can." Kate was hopeful, and once again, grateful to have Terry on her team.

"I think I'll drive up the end of next week if that's OK with you. I want to see what I can find out about this Zeke Peters and follow up on some other leads on the Dugans that I have here in Miami, and, besides, I have plans for this weekend. And, the Rays are at home next weekend, maybe I can take in a game and bring them some good luck."

"Sounds good. You've already done a ton on this matter. Keep me posted on any new developments. Thanks."

Kate and Terry shook hands, and he took off, and Ed returned to his office.

As Terry was leaving, Kate's phone rang. It was Meardon calling to let her know they had pulled together the documents she'd requested, and he could either send them by mail or they could be picked up today.

Always curious and impatient, Kate told him she'd send a courier for the documents immediately. She wanted to have a quick look at them over the weekend. She wouldn't have much time to review them if they were in trial in the Brighton matter next week. Plus, if she was going to try to take old Johnny Sutton's depo sometime next week, she needed them for background. Kate called Polly and asked her to arrange a courier to pick up the documents and to set up Sutton's deposition. She literally rubbed her hands together thinking about what they already knew and how much more they would likely learn. She liked this new case more and more with every passing day.

"Thanks for the update, Kate," Marcy said when Kate finished bringing her up to speed on Terry's news. She hesitated briefly.

"Kate, I hate to bother you with this, but I had a troubling visit this morning. Tony Beltran, one of Sean's old buddies from the Miami homicide division, stopped by. He said there might be an investigation into Joe's death. Apparently, the hospital drew blood when Joe's body was brought in. The ME at the hospital couldn't believe Joe had died of a heart attack. Joe was such a health nut. Now, it looks like there might have been digitalis in Joe's blood. Tony said he just wanted to give me a heads-up, but I'm afraid it was more than that.

"When the detectives brought Joan in to ask about medicines Joe had been taking and to tell her about the digitalis in Joe's blood work, she immediately told the detectives about the $4 million insurance policy. She told them if they thought it was foul play they should be questioning me, because I had more to gain from Joe's death than anyone. Tony asked me all sorts of questions about why Joe would have a policy naming me beneficiary and why I didn't agree to waive any claim I might have to the insurance money."

"Marcy, why didn't you call me the moment he showed up?" Kate exclaimed.

"I didn't want to bother you, and, at first, it just seemed so ridiculous. How could I be suspected of anything? I didn't know Joe kept the insurance policy in effect. Why would I even suspect that? Hell, I didn't even know how much the policy was for, not even when he first told me about it. I just refused to let him talk about it. And, Kate, I hadn't seen Joe in over 10 years!"

"Marcy, in the future, if anyone—I don't care *who* it is—asks you about Joe, or his death, or the policy, you need to send them to me. You shouldn't be answering any questions unless I'm with you. How well do you know this Beltran guy?"

"I haven't seen Tony since Sean took off. We don't exactly run in the same circles anymore. I was surprised to see him this morning. Do you think he was trying to get info out of me, maybe trying to get me to incriminate myself? I'd hate to think that," Marcy groaned.

"I wouldn't bet against it. Cops are always looking for a lead. And they love to come up with theories, and then see if they can fit the evidence into their theory. I can't see them liking you for murder, but cops have been known to grab for the easy answer. And $4 million is a bunch of money, which is very likely what got the cops' attention. What did you tell Beltran?"

"Not much really. After all, I don't have much to tell. I said I hadn't seen Joe in over ten years and had no idea he kept that insurance policy after we divorced. I let him know the first I heard about it was from Ron Gray. But, he asked me a lot of questions about my job at the ER and the types of medications we have there. The questions made me very angry, but I tried not to let him know. Kate, what do you think is going on?"

"I don't know. But you say the cops are looking at Joe's death as a possible murder?" Kate asked.

"Yes. Apparently he didn't have a prescription for digitalis, and the EMTs didn't administer it. That's created suspicion of foul play."

"OK, thanks. I'll see if Terry Driver can follow up on this with both the cops and the hospital. And, Marcy, don't forget—speak to *no one* without me, and call me immediately if anyone else approaches you about anything related to this matter."

Kate didn't like where the new piece of the puzzle was pointing. She knew there was more to the Joe Dugan story, but she hadn't even considered the possibility of murder.

After she hung up with Marcy, Kate immediately punched in Terry's number. She wanted to tell Terry about this new development and get him working on learning what the cops and hospital might know. She also hoped he could subtly let Joe Dugan's mother know the cops were investigating her son's death as a murder. That news could shake some information loose, and Kate wanted to know whatever Grace Dugan was willing to share.

Later that afternoon, as Kate sat at her worktable reviewing the documents from Upton Insurance, Doug Bennett, Kate's least favorite partner at the firm, abruptly opened her office door and barged in uninvited.

"I need to talk to you," he barked.

"*Excuse* me?" Kate asked, incredulous at his rude interruption.

"I said, 'I need to talk to you.'" Doug's tone was only slightly less abrasive the second time, and he showed no signs of leaving her office.

Kate's experiences with Doug, who she had nicknamed "Doug the Dick," were all bad. Their interactions ran the gambit from Doug backstabbing her personally, to him attempting to poach her clients through numerous dirty tricks—all of which had failed so far. She could barely stand the sight of him, but she sat silently, trying to stay calm, fighting her desire to throw him out of her office.

"I just got an extremely angry call from Ron Gray. Apparently, you're representing an ex-wife of one of his clients who just died. He said your client is trying to jump on an insurance policy intended for the guy's widow and kids and interfering with the payout to the widow. He also said you were incredibly rude to him, and he's all kinds of offended—wants to talk to our managing partner to lodge an official complaint against you for lack of professionalism. I gave him Jack Hazard's name and number," Doug the Dick said with a smug smile; he was always happy when he could rain on Kate's parade.

"Is that so?" Kate responded after a lengthy pause. "True to form, Doug. Whenever you're involved in something I can be assured of two things. First, you're looking for a way to throw dirt on me, and second, you're sure to have the facts completely fucked up," Kate observed, continuing to glare at him.

"My cases are none of your business. But, just so you'll know how completely wrong you are *again*, let me fill you in on some of the *actual* facts. The insurance company was ready to pay the entire $4 million death benefit to my client, Marcy Simpson, because she is specified *by name* as the beneficiary on the policy that Gray's client took out nearly 20 years ago. Oh, and by the way, Gray's client continued to pay the annual premium on that policy each year, without making any change to the beneficiary clause—each and every year, Doug, even during the 16 years after they divorced. Also, your buddy, Gray, used physical and mental intimidation on my client in a sleazy attempt to pressure her into signing a ridiculously one-sided waiver and release. I've been considering reporting him to the bar for being involved in the physical assault that was made on my client."

Kate stood and took two steps toward Doug.

"So, don't come bursting in here trying to tell me what to do. Now, get the hell out of my office and let me get back to work. You're not in charge of me—or my work, or this firm. I'm sick of your sophomoric attempts to stir up shit. Get out of here and try to find something productive to do with your time."

Kate took another step toward him, and he began to back away but did not leave her office. She walked back to her desk and punched in Ed's office number, keeping the phone on speaker.

"Hey, Boss Lady, what's up?" Ed asked in his usual cheerful manner.

"I've got a bit of a problem in my office. Any chance you could pop down here?"

"I'm on my way," he responded and clicked off.

"Want to stay and listen to Ed's version of the phone call Gray's all up in arms about, while he escorts you out of my office, or are you ready to leave quietly on your own? My next call is to Jack Hazard and maybe security." Kate grinned at Doug who was now retreating toward the door.

The two locked eyes for several moments without speaking. Doug's eyes emanated pure hatred.

"You know, you're going to pay for being such an aggressive bitch one of these days," he growled in a low voice. "Someone's going to give you what you deserve. I hope I'm there to see it," he said, his voice laced with venom. He turned toward the open door and came face-to-face with Ed.

Without another word, Doug brushed by Ed and hurried down the hall.

"Did he just threaten you?" Ed asked in shocked disbelief, making a mental note to report what he'd heard to the firm's personnel committee.

"Yep, Doug the Dick at his finest," Kate responded. "Thanks for coming. I thought I might need some help getting him to leave. Evidently, Ron Gray called him to complain that I was rude to him when I called the other day, and he's pissed that our client is making his job difficult."

"Good to know you've managed to get under his skin. Sounds like you have him running scared. I wonder if he's started to review the documents from Upton. They're looking good for us and bad for the newly widowed Mrs. Dugan."

Ed smiled at Kate, noting that she looked like she wanted to throw a punch, and glad he got there before she did—he was pretty sure Kate could take Doug if push came to shove, but he saw no reason to find out.

Kate turned and took a lap around her office, breathing deeply, and then asked, "You have a few minutes to talk about these documents?" She pointed to the documents from Upton that she had spread across her worktable.

"Sure," he replied.

For the next half hour, Kate explained her thoughts about how each document could be used to prove Dr. Joe Dugan really did intend Marcy to be the beneficiary of the $4 million insurance policy.

Chapter 6

On Monday morning, Ed and Kate sat with about 50 other attorneys in Judge Kilmer's courtroom. They were all waiting to see which cases the judge was going to hear during his month-long trial docket. Kate had already prepared Ed for the fact that they would almost certainly *not* be reached. There were over 30 cases on the docket, and theirs was number 18 on the list.

Over the weekend, Kate had learned the first four cases had settled and would be removed from the docket. She also learned the next three matters were filing consent motions for continuances, and she knew Judge Kilmer would grant those motions.

Judge Kilmer didn't like to schedule more than four trials on his month-long trial dockets. He just saw no reason to work that hard; after all, he was the judge. All these facts made it highly unlikely their case would be reached this month. So, she expected their trial to be set over onto the judge's next civil docket—which was, unfortunately, at least a month away.

Kate hated this part of the process. You had to be ready for trial even when you knew you would never be reached, and that you would almost certainly be set over to another trial calendar, sometimes several months down the line. Consequently, much of the trial prep would have to be refreshed before the case could finally be presented—and you might not even be reached on the next docket, meaning your case would be set over yet again. The whole process was such an incredible waste of attorney time and clients' money, but it was the system they had, and they had to live with it. Clients struggled to understand why the system worked this way, especially when they were pushed from one trial docket to another multiple times as Brighton Industries had been.

At a leisurely 9:15, Judge Kilmer took the bench and began calling the docket. One after another, groups of attorneys leapt to their feet to announce a settlement or pled for more time. The judge kept reading down the docket and, when he got to the thirteenth case, two groups of attorneys jumped up, glared at each other, and declared, "Ready for trial, Your Honor."

The next two matters also reported, "Ready," but the plaintiff's lawyer on the sixteenth case begged for more time due to an unavailable key witness.

Kate held her breath. She was suddenly hopeful they might finally be reached.

But her hope was short lived. Case 17 reported, "Ready for trial." And Kate sighed unhappily as the judge announced, just as she'd anticipated, he was only taking these four matters given the estimated length of time the attorneys predicted their trials would take. Kate and Ed, and the other unlucky, passed-over attorneys, all packed up their briefcases and boxes and headed back to their offices. At least for Kate and Ed, there was a decent chance Judge Kilmer would reset them high on the next trial docket, and Brighton Industries would finally get its day in court.

In the hall, Kate heard her name called out, and when she turned, she saw Steve Sloan waving at her.

"Hey, there! If it isn't my favorite divorce attorney," she said, giving Steve a long, friendly embrace.

"Steve Sloan, meet Ed Evert, my A-Number-1 Top Associate."

Ed and Steve shook hands, and the three lawyers stood in the hall exchanging pleasantries for a few moments.

Eventually, Steve said, "Sorry the Bill thing didn't work out, Kate."

Kate was taken aback by the comment but recovered quickly.

"Well, you'll have that when a guy asks you to marry him and you turn him down. He's a great guy, but he wants to remarry, and I'm not walking off that plank *ever* again," she laughed.

As a second thought, Kate asked, "How'd you find out?"

"Oh, well, Pam told me. According to Pam, she and Bill have gone out *quite a lot* over the last several months. I thought you might know."

Kate just laughed wanly.

"Like I said, when you turn down a guy's marriage proposal, things aren't always smooth sailing afterward. I'm glad for Pam . . ." Kate faltered slightly before adding, "and Bill too. He's really a great guy, and I know getting married again is super important to him. Give Pam my best. And, you'd better start looking for a new paralegal, Steve. Bill isn't likely to want his new bride working your long hours!"

"I don't think it's quite *that* serious, but it has been going on a while, and she does talk about him a *lot!*" Steve replied.

After a few more minutes of casual conversation, they said their good-byes and Kate and Ed headed toward the stairs. Kate was silent until they reached the front door of the courthouse.

"Are you dating anyone yet?" she asked, looking over at Ed.

"Odd question, but no, not yet. I have this slave driver Boss Lady who forces me to work every waking moment!" Ed responded with a wink as he opened the door for her. "Why do you ask, Boss Lady?"

Kate continued, "Well, remember I said I'd tell you when I was ready for some 'no-strings-attached, rebound sex'?"

Ed stopped in his tracks. Kate turned around when she sensed he was no longer walking next to her. His eyes registered shock, and a huge smile slowly spread across his lips.

"You bet I do. I had almost given up hope, and I thought you'd forgotten!"

"Oh, I didn't forget," she said giving him a sexy grin and shaking her hair back over her shoulders. "Want to blow off the rest of the day and head out to my beach house?"

"Now?" Ed asked incredulously.

"Uh-huh. Now," she grinned again as she looked up into his very handsome face.

"Sounds perfect," he said as reality began to sink in that this could actually happen.

Kate whipped out her cell phone and called their paralegal, Polly McGuire.

"Polly, it's Kate. As we expected, we didn't get reached on the trial docket, and we're being set over to the next one. It could be as much as two more months, but would you check for us tomorrow to see if the new docket has been published?"

Then Kate added, "By the way, something has come up, and Ed and I will not be returning to the office today . . . and we may not be in tomorrow either, depending on how things go today."

Kate smiled at Ed, and he returned a lusty grin and turned a brilliant shade of pink.

"Can you call the Brighton Industries client representative and witnesses and let them know we aren't going to trial this month?" Kate directed. "And tell them I'll call within a week with the new trial docket dates. Thanks. See you tomorrow or Wednesday."

Ed just stared at her, and then started to laugh.

"Good to see you're taking charge, *as usual*, Ms. Muldoon."

"Well, somebody has to, Mr. Evert. Now, I'm going to drop you at the office so you can pick up your car, and then you can meet me at my beach house. I have to stop by my house here in the city and collect my girls."

"Your girls?" Ed said, looking alarmed and apprehensive. "You didn't tell me you have kids."

"Yep, Sadie and Phoebe, my two beautiful blond, three-year-old . . . *four-legged* girls. They're goldies, Ed, you know, golden retrievers. Dogs, Ed. They're dogs. Man, did you look worried," she said through her laughter.

On their way back to the parking garage under their office building, she gave Ed the address of her beach house and some simple directions. She told him to call her when he reached the town of Garrett Beach and she'd give him directions for the last part of the drive.

No second thoughts about setting up a date specifically to have "no-strings-attached, rebound sex" with her very fine-looking young associate had crossed Kate's mind until Ed got out of the car and closed the door of her Mercedes. As he headed to his car, the full import of what she'd just done hit her, and she felt the bottom of her stomach dropped two stories.

"What the fuck have you done, Katherine Mary Muldoon?" Kate said under her breath shaking her head. "*What the fuck?*"

Kate talked to herself the entire hour and 15 minutes it took her to get from the city house to the beach house. Sadie and Phoebe sat in the backseat with their ears cocked and heads turned toward her the whole way. They weren't sure *what* was going on, but they were positive it was something *big*.

She had quickly emptied the contents of the fridge and pantry of the city house into shopping bags and loaded them in the back of the Mercedes because the beach house had almost no food. Halfway through this exercise, Kate stopped.

Ed isn't coming out to the beach for the food, she reminded herself, *but then again, I can't just throw him on the bed and rip his clothes off—as tempting as that sounds. Besides, I know I'm going to need some wine even if he doesn't.*

Kate had never done anything like this before. In fact, she was amazed . . . and slightly horrified at her actions so far. It was almost as if someone else was in charge. She was suddenly seriously nervous.

Kate managed to get to the beach house, put the food away, take a quick shower, and changed into a blouse and skirt before Ed called to say he was in Garrett Beach. She took a large gulp of the glass of red wine she'd opened as she told Ed he was about 15 minutes from the house and when he saw the small grocery store on the left called *The Beach Specialty Shoppe,* he should turn left at the next street. It was a cul-de-sac called Palm Drive. She added he'd see her car in the driveway, the front door would be unlocked, and he should come on in when he got there. She'd probably be out back with the girls.

Kate ran back to her bathroom and put on a bit of makeup and pulled her hair up into a loose twist. She grabbed her wine and called to the dogs. As she opened the sliding door onto the back deck, she stood to the side so the dogs wouldn't knock her over as they burst through the door ahead of her.

Kate purposefully headed north on the beach—away from Bill

Davis' house. Running into Bill was a complication she hadn't exactly thought through, but she wasn't going to feel uncomfortable in her own house, on her own special beach. While she really didn't want to run into him, it would be all right if he was with Pam, she decided. Kate briefly wondered how serious they were, but then told herself it didn't matter and she wasn't going to think about it.

When Kate turned to head back to the house, she saw Ed standing on her back deck holding a glass of wine and watching her. The sight caused butterflies to again kick into action in her stomach. But then she noticed he was wearing the clothes Lance, the "Wonder Concierge" at the Breakers, had picked out for him. It made her giggle and brought back a little of the tingling she'd felt when Ed kissed her and nearly carried her off to bed. It seemed like years ago, but it was only a few months since they'd stayed at the Breakers and celebrated rescuing young Phil Bentley from almost certain doom.

Yes, I can definitely do this, Kate decided, thinking again of Ed's excellent kiss.

He was headed toward her now. When they met, she introduced him to the girls, and they all seemed to take to one another very well. Ed cemented their affection when he threw their slobbery wet tennis ball for them to chase.

"I see you're wearing your lucky pants. Ready to give them a second try?" Kate teased.

"I'm ready to lose them and take you right here and now, but your neighbors might call the cops." Ed's look told her he wasn't kidding. "What an incredible view," he said, changing the subject. "I don't see how you can ever force yourself to leave here."

"It's called a mortgage. It's great motivation to go to work every day. And, I'm sure you noticed the hour and a half drive out here. My house in the city is pretty nice too; small but nice, and really close to the office."

"Already planning our second rendezvous, Ms. Muldoon?"

Kate blushed slightly and smiled. "Let's take this one step at a time."

"I don't think you'll be disappointed, if that's what you're worried about," Ed winked and took her hand.

It was a simple but very intimate gesture and the shock of it hit her hard. It was the first time they'd actually touched since the Breakers. Kate's doubts started to creep back to the surface.

Shit! We're going from hand holding to sex at the speed of light, she thought.

They walked silently back to the house and sat on the deck finishing their wine, enjoying the warm breeze off the water, and talking about work. Kate went inside to retrieve the wine bottle, but when she turned around, Ed was standing right behind her in the kitchen. He placed their glasses on the table and walked toward her, and she backed up a few steps, feeling the sweet, low tingling beginning.

Kate laughed nervously.

"I thought we could grill some steaks for dinner since we didn't eat any lunch."

"Sounds good, we can do that . . . later," he said stepping closer to her and pinning her against the counter. He took the wine bottle from her hand and set it on the counter. Placing his hands on either side of her, he leaned against her.

"Kate, I want you now. I don't want to wait or play any more games. I've wanted you practically from the first day I met you and every day that we've worked together I've wanted you more." He slipped his hands to her waist, and then her hips, pressing her closer to him. She could feel her heat rising and his desire swelling.

"Promise you won't sue me for sexual harassment, Ms. Muldoon," Ed chuckled and kissed her long and hard, his mouth nearly devouring her.

Kate's knees felt weak. Ed's lips and tongue wandered down her neck as he drew her closer and lifted her slightly off her feet and sat her on the kitchen counter. He pressed his forehead against hers as he unbuttoned her blouse. In a sudden motion, he reached down and picked her up in his arms, turned, and walked toward the bedroom, closing the door with his foot as he walked in to ensure they wouldn't be interrupted.

"I think this is where we left off," he whispered.

Kate said nothing. She wasn't sure she could. But she knew she didn't want to tell Ed "no" this time. Her need was simple and primal. She needed this, she needed him, and she needed him *now*.

Ed set her down at the foot of the bed and slipped her blouse off over her shoulders and let it fall to the floor. He gently laid her back on the bed, running his fingers down her chest finding the front closure of her bra. He released it. She moaned as he gently caressed her nipples and pushed the bra away.

Ed pulled his shirt over his head and lowered himself between her legs, brushing her pelvis with his own, now rock hard and aching. He cupped her breasts in his hands and buried his face in her, nipping gently at her nipples making her wiggle hard against him. He hooked his thumbs under her bra in the back and pulled it up over her head, twisted and held it in one hand, pinning her arms above her head. Then he began kissing her neck and breasts again as she struggled against him.

She came quickly with an explosion so hard and long that the sound of it alone nearly made him come.

"Again," he said as he released her arms and began to work his way down her stomach, kissing and nipping as he went.

"Again and this time with me," he said as he pulled off her skirt and panties.

Ed untied his swim trunks and pushed between her legs, finding her hot, wet, and ready for him.

"With me now," he gently ordered as he pushed further up and into her.

She gasped and wiggled as he pressed higher. Her fingers dug into his shoulders and biceps as she writhed against him. He felt himself nearing the top and unable to hold out much longer.

"Now, damn it, now. I want to feel you explode with me inside you."

Grasping his biceps tightly as she felt herself begin to shudder, a low moan crept out from deep in her throat. Ed felt himself exploding, thoroughly consuming her and being consumed by her.

When the wave of pleasure stopped, he pushed up to keep from crushing Kate, and he saw a small tear running down from the corners of her eye.

"God, Kate, did I hurt you?"

Her eyes fluttered open and she whispered, "No."

She lay beneath him breathing slowly and deeply, wrapping her arms around him, pulling him closer, and burying her face in his shoulder.

You didn't hurt me. Knowing Bill is truly gone from my life has hurt me, but you didn't hurt me, Ed, Kate thought. *And now, I've just made things incredibly complicated.*

She felt confused, but satiated; conflicted, but content. She knew she would have to sort this out, but for now, she just wanted to enjoy it. Somehow she felt she deserved it after so many wasted years with Adam. Bill had awakened her need, but she knew she couldn't be what Bill needed, and he'd clearly moved on. It was time for her to move on too.

Ed rolled to her side so his weight would not be directly on top of her. "I don't want to crush you; you're surprisingly small. It must be that take-charge attitude of yours that makes you so imposing. You seem to grow when you're giving orders," Ed chuckled and lifted her chin so he could look into her eyes. "You know you're quite beautiful."

Kate looked steadily into Ed's eyes and considered what had just happened. There was no going back from this, and she had no reference for how they would go forward. She desperately worked to block thoughts about anything past today and tomorrow, and her mind refused to think about anything from her past. So, she just rolled toward him and lay still, relaxing in his strong arms as he began to stroke her back.

Kate woke after only a few minutes and slipped into the bathroom while Ed snored softly. She looked at herself in the mirror and shook her head.

"What the fuck are you doing, girl?" she asked her reflection. "You have created one hell of a mess here, and you have no one to blame but yourself. Now, you're going to have to figure out where you go from here."

When she returned from the bathroom, Kate carried a warm washcloth. She gently wrapped the cloth around Ed's now-wilted manhood. He murmured appreciatively and reached for her. She pulled away gently.

Good God, he's beautiful, Kate thought with pleasure.

She began gently stroking his chest and legs. He cracked open one eye and looked at her quizzically.

"What are you up to?" he said, smiling at her slyly.

"Well, you know how much I like to be in charge, and you certainly didn't let me be in charge *at all* the first time, so, now, it's *my* turn."

Kate looked down at her handiwork and saw that he was beginning to peek out from under the washcloth. Adeptly, she pushed herself between his legs, placing her thighs over his and hooking her calves around his shins, pinning his legs out straight. All her yoga was paying dividends. At the same time, Kate pulled away the washcloth and gathered his now revived manhood up in her right hand and began to stroke him with her left.

Ed tried to grab her arms and pull her upward to him, but she drew away still holding and stroking him.

"Hey, what do you think you're do . . ." Ed's words cut off as Kate slipped him into her mouth and began to suck rhythmically.

"Oh God, oh God . . ." was all Ed could manage for the next few moments. He tried again to pull her to him, but after only a few seconds, he simply surrendered to her and came again with magnificent force.

When he was relaxed, Kate released his legs and crept catlike up his body to sit on his now again limp member. Ed slowly opened both eyes like he was looking into a bright light.

"I should have known you wouldn't let me keep the upper hand," he said softly. "And man, do you look self-satisfied! I think I'm going to like our little competition."

Kate laughed and looked out the window.

"It's such beautiful weather, and we only have today and maybe some of tomorrow. I suggest we make the most of our surroundings."

From the deck Kate's dogs suddenly started barking wildly. Kate arched an eyebrow, then sat up, looking toward the beach.

"Ed, this is all going to be a problem, or at least terribly complicated, but I'm choosing not to think about it today. I'm headed out for a walk on the beach and a dip in the ocean. Want to join me?"

Kate walked naked into her closet, grabbed a bikini, and returned pulling up the bottom and slipping on the top as she walked out of her bedroom. Ed watched her leave the room and thought he had never been with such a confident, sexy woman. He wondered if he would be able to keep up but was determined to try.

He bounced off the bed, retrieved his swim trunks, and headed out of the bedroom tying the drawstring as he walked.

He found Kate on the back deck kneeling down petting a basset hound while talking to a very tall, well-built man. Ed walked out the back door and waited for an introduction. Kate stood.

"Bill Davis, this is my colleague, Ed Evert. We're playing hooky today because our trial got passed over to the next docket. We've had a hell of a couple of months and decided we were due a day off at the beach."

Bill's stare was nothing short of a challenge. Ed held his gaze without a word, and then reached out his hand to shake Bill's. Bill's grip was overly firm; Ed returned the pressure.

I can play this game, Billy Boy. Your loss is my gain, and I don't intend to relinquish my recently won territory, dude, Ed thought as he stood staring back at Bill.

"Nice to meet you, sir."

Ed knew there was at least 10 years between them, and he figured the 'sir' would have just the right impact on Bill's ego.

You'd have to be deaf, dumb, and blind to not figure out what Kate and I were just up to before you barged in, Ed thought smugly.

"I remember when you played for the Dolphins. That was a terrible, cheap shot Gunter laid on you. You were a key component of that team. My dad and I used to love watching you play when I was a kid." Ed congratulated himself on another zinger, and all very respectfully delivered.

"Yeah, kid," Bill grinned. He was playing the game too, calling him kid. "It *was* a cheap shot, but my life didn't end, and I can't really complain about how it's going." Bill's eyes were still locked on Ed's. "I think I saw you sitting at the defense table with Kate at the hearing about the Bentley kid, didn't I?"

Bill gave Ed the once-over stare, thinking, *I could take you if it comes to that.*

"I stopped by the hearing to catch up with Kate, but it was too crazy with all the press," Bill said, looking at Kate who was registering her shock to learn Bill had been in court that day.

He smiled shyly, looking a bit regretful, and then looked back at Ed.

"Kate's a piece of work in the courtroom, isn't she? I'm sure it's a real benefit to be able to watch a master at work. She's a pretty complicated woman and loves to be in charge."

"Not always," Ed said even though he knew he was getting close to the edge, but his manly territorial nature had taken over.

Kate watched the two men taking each other's measure and bandy not-so-thinly veiled barbs.

"I'm right here, gentlemen," Kate said gently. She'd decided it was time to break up the cockfight.

She moved closer, crashing through the laser-lock glare between the men.

"So, Bill, how's Pam? I ran into Steve Sloan in the courthouse today, and he told me you two have been dating."

Ed looked at Kate and smiled broadly. *Score!* he thought. *Ballsy move, Kate.You totally knocked Bill on his back foot with that one comment.*

"Yeah . . . Well, we've gone to dinner a couple of times," Bill stammered.

"She's a great person and a hell of a paralegal. I'd love to steal her away from Steve, but she's pretty loyal to him."

Kate was secretly congratulating herself for remaining so calm and holding her own in the conversation, but she wanted to move to another topic. "It sure is good to see Howie. How's he doing? Does he miss my beautiful girls?"

"I think he does. Whenever we run by here he comes up to the house and barks. When I saw the girls on the deck today I figured you were here."

Bill looked back at Ed, and the stare down began again.

"We were just going to take the girls for a walk and a swim," Ed said reaching down to rub Phoebe possessively behind her ears.

He really wanted to put his arm around Kate, but her vibe said *NO* loud and clear. It was obvious she wanted to handle this on her own.

"Well, Howie and I were just headed home." Bill almost sounded defeated. Then he turned to Kate, kissed her on the cheek, and said, "I'll call you tomorrow."

Bill headed down the stairs and back toward the beach with Howie trotting after him.

Phoebe and Sadie looked up at Kate quizzically, confused that their friends were leaving.

Ed walked up behind Kate as she watched Bill walk away. He touched her shoulder lightly. She was shaking very slightly, it was more like a vibration. "You OK?"

"Yep, but like I said, this is going to be very complicated. And, this encounter was probably the easiest part."

Kate turned and placed her hand gently on Ed's chest.

"Sorry about that. Now where were we? Let's go for a run and a swim, and then I'm going to fix you the best meal you've had since the Breakers . . . *and* I have something very special in mind for dessert," she grinned seductively and ran off to the beach.

Chapter 7

As Kate drove back into the city Tuesday afternoon, she ran the events of the last 24 hours over and over in her head. She still couldn't believe she'd invited Ed out to the beach house for "no-strings-attached, rebound sex." It had been a bit over three months since the night she told Bill she loved him but would not marry him. When Bill didn't call or reach out to her for three weeks, Kate tried to tuck away the part of her Bill had opened up. After a month, Kate thought she had managed to slip effortlessly back into her former, sexless life—all work, no play.

Now, she'd learned Bill had been seeing Pam Logan all the while she'd been keeping a secret hope in her heart that he'd eventually call her. Learning that for the last three months Bill had been seeing the beautiful, and much younger, Pamela Logan, had set off all of Kate's insecurities.

Well, you just learned that he did stop by to see you at the Bentley hearing, Kate told herself.

But, she immediately argued back, *he sure didn't try very hard to talk to me. He could have called me some time over the last three months. But no, instead, he shows up on my doorstep the moment I step out of character and go for some randy sex. Jesus, talk about bad timing.*

Kate was full of self-recriminations, doubts, anger, and remorse as she drove toward Miami.

She had to admit she'd felt jealous and discarded when she learned Bill was dating Pam—even though, technically, she was the one who had done the discarding. Well, not really discarding. When Bill asked her to marry him after their one-month whirlwind affair, she'd tried to explain that she loved him but wasn't ever going to marry again—not ever, no matter who asked her. In fact, she'd told him he was perfect, and if she ever were to marry, it would be to him.

But, hell, I wasn't even completely divorced from Adam when Bill proposed. And just because I turned down his marriage proposal, it didn't mean that I didn't want to continue to see him, or at least remain friends. Turns out that was a pipe dream! In fairness, it was good we realized we want different things. Bill just needs to be married, and I definitely have had enough of marriage to last a lifetime. But, damn it, why did we have to discover that so soon? I really wanted the fun, and especially the sex, to go on for a bit longer, Kate thought and sighed heavily.

But it was more than just sex Kate had enjoyed while she was with Bill. He'd seemed proud of her and interested in her life. They'd shared the events of their days and made each other laugh. Kate knew she had never been happier with anyone, and doubted she ever would be that happy again.

And now, I've just had a delightful romp in the sack with my young associate—several romps, as a matter of fact, Kate thought, feeling the tingle between her legs. *I've crossed all kinds of lines, and things are bound to be much more complicated at the office. This situation has so many ways it could go wrong,* Kate sighed once again.

Part of her regretted her decision to surrender to her newly discovered "inner slut," but another part was still tingling from the experience.

He certainly has stamina, she thought of the double hat trick in under 24 hours. *Not sure we should reprise this, but it definitely was fun. After all, it was just "no-strings-attached, rebound sex." We both know that, so it will likely be a one-time event now that we have it out of our systems.*

It was nearly 3:00, and she was about an hour from the city when her cell phone rang, interrupting her review of her recent sexual adventure. She hit the call button on her steering wheel.

"Bill?" she asked, not believing the caller ID on the heads-up display.

"Yep. How are you, Katie?" Bill's voice was soft.

Oh, damn, why did he have to call me Katie? She cringed.

"I'm fine, Bill, just fine. How about you?" Kate tried to make her voice sound strong and matter of fact. *Well, this isn't awkward at all, now is it? Jeez!* she thought.

"Surviving, hanging in there," Bill responded.

Quick, think of something to chat about, she thought.

"How are the twins? Are they still enjoying college life at UF?"

"Yep, they're totally into it. They rarely even come home for a weekend anymore. And they're starting to develop a few degrees of separation from each other too. Aniston is doing a semester abroad in France next term, and Ashley is doing an internship with a marketing firm in New York City. I guess they are really starting to grow up now." Bill sounded a little wistful. "But, that's the way it's supposed to be, I guess."

"Yes, it is, and you have a lot to be proud of in those daughters of yours."

I wonder how the twins are handling their dad dating someone only a little older than they are. They were none too pleased when he told them he was seeing me, Kate's mind was wondering.

"Hey, did you open that Ferrari dealership you were talking about?" she forged ahead, filling the conversation void with another topic.

"We're in the process. It will be opening in two more months. I hope it's as successful as the business consultant predicts. We'll see." Bill paused and the awkward silence set in again.

"Katie, I didn't call to talk about the girls or my business. I wanted to tell you that I miss you. I've been trying to sort things out after . . . after you told me you didn't want to marry me. I miss talking to you . . . I miss my friend . . ."

"I miss you too, Bill," Kate's voice wavered slightly, and she found she couldn't speak momentarily.

"I've been following your ever-exciting career in the paper. I've even attended a few hearings in addition to the Bentley matter. Watching you in court is like watching a pro athlete," Bill said.

Kate laughed, "Well, you would know, Mr. Pro."

Kate wondered which hearings he'd attended. She hadn't seen him, but she knew she was extremely focused and blocked out her surroundings when she was in court.

"I've noticed you bring the kid with you a lot . . . Ed," Bill said.

"He's my associate. I finally found someone who wants to work hard and can keep up with my pace and meet my deadlines. He does good work. I'm lucky to have him backing me up. He's made a big difference in my work life. I no longer have to do it all myself, and I'm not at the office until midnight every night."

Kate noted that she sounded defensive and decided to stop talking.

"Kate, I'd like to get together sometime this week, maybe grab dinner somewhere in Miami. I'm going to be at the main Mercedes dealership for sales promotions this week. Any chance you could work me into your schedule?" he asked abruptly.

Bill's question took her by surprise, and she was at a loss as to how she should respond. Finally, she decided to just say what was on her mind.

"Bill, do you think that's a good idea?"

"Why wouldn't it be?" he asked.

"I don't want to complicate your life or get in the way of you . . . sorting things out," she fumbled.

"It's just dinner, Kate. Don't overthink it," Bill said with a little laugh.

"Yeah, well, that didn't work out so well for me the last time," she said against her better judgment. She was remembering how Bill had constantly told her not to overthink things, and then sprang a marriage proposal on her.

After a lengthy pause, Kate said, "How about Thursday? I could meet you somewhere in town around 7:30."

"Sounds great. I'll call Thursday and give you the details. Thanks, Kate. I'm looking forward to it. See you Thursday. Bye." And just like that, he was gone.

"Yea, bye . . ." Kate said, knowing Bill had already hung up.

"Now what?" Kate said out loud to herself and the two dogs in the backseat. "Now what?"

Maybe he just wants to tell me that he and Pam are engaged and he's decided he should do it in person. In any event, he's involved with someone else now. No way he's looking for anything other than just dinner with an old friend.

And what are you doing with Ed—for heaven's sake. Jesus, Kate! You have done an outstanding job of fucking up your life. It's not like you're walking around looking for some drama to fill up your empty hours.

Kate's phone again disturbed her reflections.

"Hey, there, Suzy. What's up? You're not going to believe my news . . ." Kate began when she saw her friend's name come up on caller ID. She was immediately interrupted.

"Where the hell are you and why aren't you in your office today?" her friend demanded.

"Well, hello to you too, and how is your day going, Ms. Spellman?"

"Yeah, hi. But seriously, where are you? I stopped by your office and learned you weren't in yesterday or today. I'm in a fucking mess, and I need help," Suzy replied.

"The girls and I are on our way back into the city. I just spent two days out at my beach house—with a man, I might add," Kate laughed.

"What? OK, you *do* have to tell me all about that. But, I think for a change, I may have topped your news. Mine is pretty odd—even for me." Suzy sounded stressed.

"What's up?" Kate asked concerned.

"Well, you know I broke up with Jimmy—my neighbor's contractor. So, I was feeling the need to blow off some steam and engage in some meaningless partying at The Angler, the bar I like down at the marina."

Oh, good God, not again, Kate thought.

The Angler was a total dive, populated by fishermen, dockworkers, day cruise captains, and dive masters. If ever there was a place to get in trouble, it was The Angler. Suzy loved it.

"What happened? I thought you turned over a new leaf and swore off The Angler," Kate asked anxiously. The one good thing about Suzy's affair with Jimmy had been it kept her out of The Angler. There was never a good story that began at The Angler.

"I just needed to get my groove back, sweetie," Suzy replied. "But I think I might have gone a bit over the line this time. See, I brought this guy home with me on Saturday night . . ."

Kate groaned loudly.

"I know," Suzy sighed. "But it had been *two whole weeks*, and I really needed to get back in the game. Anyway, when I woke up on Sunday, he was still there. I checked his wallet while he was asleep because I couldn't remember his name . . ."

Kate groaned loudly again.

"I know . . . don't say it . . . But, well, he doesn't have a driver's license or any other type of ID. No money either, by the way. I'm pretty sure I paid for our drinks Saturday night," Suzy sounded sheepish.

"Jesus, Suzy! What were you thinking? This is just dangerous," Kate admonished her friend.

"Tell me about it," Suzy said. "Now, I can't get rid of him. He was still there this morning when I left for work. He was there all day yesterday too. I asked him if I could drop him off somewhere on Monday, and again this morning, but he said he'd call a cab."

"Oh my God, Suzy. The guy could be a criminal. He could rob you blind—or worse. You cannot go back home today."

Kate was alarmed now. This *was* over the top, even for Suzy.

"I know, I know. So, what do you think I should do? I'm too embarrassed to call the cops." She sounded uncharacteristically perplexed.

"Meet me at my house in the city. I'll be there in half an hour. If you get there before me, let yourself in, you know where the hidden key is," Kate directed. "I'll call Terry Driver, my investigator. He used to be with the Miami PD. I'll have him meet us at my house, and we'll give him your house key. He can head over to your place and remove this guy—forcibly, if necessary. You are not going home until this guy is gone. As a matter of fact, you should stay with me tonight, just to be on the safe side. There is no telling what sort of lunatic he might be."

"Great plan. I'll see you at your place in the city."

Suzy paused, and then added, "Thanks, Kate. I realize I was totally over the line this time. But I was just feeling so alone after breaking up with Jimmy, and kind of old. I hate that."

Holy shit! This is her worst escapade yet! Kate thought as she hit the call "end" button.

"Call Terry Driver," Kate commanded. The connection went through.

When Kate arrived at her house, Suzy and Terry were already there. As she walked in, she heard them laughing and chatting happily. Stepping into the kitchen, Kate watched her friend as she flipped her jet-black hair over her shoulder and looked at Terry with her big, chocolate brown doe eyes.

Good God. Now she's flirting with my PI. This woman is insatiable, Kate thought in amazement.

"Leave my PI alone. He's here on a mission. You can flirt with him later!" Kate laughed.

Terry looked perfectly content to be the object of Suzy's flirtation, and Suzy looked equally content to be engaged in her favorite pastime.

Kate gave Terry the details of his new mission as Suzy listened, looking only a tad sheepish. When Kate finished, Suzy suggested that Terry should come back to Kate's when he finished extracting her unwelcome houseguest and she would take them all to dinner. Suzy smiled lustily as she winked at Terry. Terry grinned broadly and said he'd be back in a couple of hours.

As Terry walked out the door, Kate looked at Suzy and said, "*Seriously*, girlfriend? You need to give that thing a chance to cool down."

Over dinner, Terry related the tale of his meeting with Suzy's "accidental houseguest." When he got to her house, the guy had been sprawled out on one of Suzy's deck chairs by the pool sunning himself in his underwear. Terry had thrown his clothes at him and told him he had three minutes to get dressed or he was taking him as is. The guy seemed totally unfazed by Terry's sudden appearance and laughed as he got dressed. He also steadfastly refused to give Terry his name.

Terry drove the guy back to The Angler because that was where he asked to be taken. Terry had taken a circuitous route to the marina. He not only wanted the stranger away from Suzy's neighborhood, but he also didn't want him to be able to find his way back. Terry then returned to Suzy's house and did a thorough inspection of doors and windows to make sure everything was secure. Before leaving her house, he dusted the lounge chair and the door handle of his car for fingerprints and collected a good set. He was planning to talk his buddies on the force into running the prints to see if they could identify the guy.

When she learned this, Kate asked him to also have Beth Anderson, her friend in charge of the Miami FBI office, run the prints. Suzy protested mildly. She didn't want their friend Beth to know about her latest bonehead move. But Kate told her she was going to have to suck it up. They needed to know who this guy is, and the FBI has access to a much larger bank of prints than the local cops.

Suzy thanked Terry profusely and proceeded to reinitiate her flirtation. Kate was pretty sure Terry felt fully rewarded for his efforts. For the rest of the evening, Kate simply sat back and watched the maestro at work as Suzy played Terry like a Stradivarius.

Chapter 8

When Kate walked into her office early Wednesday morning, she noticed Ed's office light was on. She'd given her next step a great deal of thought. How do you reclaim your old boring but totally orderly and predictable life after tossing everything up in the air all at once? She'd come to terms with the fact that she had given in to her insecurities and primal urges and violated an internal code of conduct.

But, damn, it was fun! she thought. *And now, it's time to pay the piper.*

Kate decided there was no reason to put off the inevitable, and besides, she wanted to be in control of the circumstances of this discussion. *As usual,* she chided herself, *you always need to be in control.*

Setting her briefcase down next to her desk, she picked up her extra large Starbucks mug and walked down to Ed's office.

As she walked in, she took in the clutter and chaos that surrounded him, wondering again how he could think in the midst of such a mess. But, over the three and a half months they'd been working together, she had almost gotten used to the chaos.

"Good morning, beautiful," Ed said with a charming grin.

"Yeah, we need to talk about that," Kate said, closing his office door.

"You look like a woman with a guilty conscience. I have just the cure for that," Ed said, pushing back from his desk and starting toward her.

"Stop right there, sailor. Not one step closer," Kate ordered.

Ed stopped but kept smiling. Kate really wished he wouldn't. He was just so damn gorgeous, and she couldn't help but remember how great he'd looked in her bed—naked. Kate felt her cheeks flame up and knew she was blushing.

This is going to be harder than I thought, she decided.

"Look, Ed," Kate said, sitting down on the arm of the side chair piled high with legal volumes from the library, "we need to talk."

"Yep. Definitely a guilty conscience at work here," Ed laughed and sat back down behind his desk. "OK. Let's talk, Boss Lady. Do you want to start, or shall I? No, wait. I know the answer to that. You certainly want to start because you want to control the conversation. So, please, ladies first," he said, smiling at Kate in an all-too-knowing way.

She sighed. Her resolve was rapidly dissolving. She decided to charge ahead quickly with the words she'd planned.

"Ed, the last two days were fun, but they were a mistake. *My* mistake. I am *totally* to blame. I shouldn't have asked you out to the beach. I was feeling weak, and mad, and insecure, and . . . well, frankly, old and rejected. I had no business involving you in my own little personal drama. It was a mistake, and I'm sorry."

Kate stopped and looked at Ed. His smile was gone now. He just sat silently staring at her.

After a minute, Ed finally said, "Is it my turn now?"

Kate nodded.

"Good, because I've got a lot to say. From my perspective, making love to you was *not* a mistake. It felt right, *very* right."

Kate started to speak, but Ed cut her off.

"You said it was my turn, so you can just sit there and listen to me like I listened to you." Ed's voice had a stern edge to it that Kate had never heard before, and it surprised her into silence.

"That's better. Now, as I was saying, I'm *glad* we made love—*repeatedly,* I might add. You certainly seemed to be enjoying yourself and me, and God knows I was enjoying myself . . . and you. From my point of view, it was about damn time. We have been sexually attracted to each other for a while now. Hell, it's been from the beginning, as far as I'm concerned." He flashed her a grin, and then continued.

"Kate, I have no regrets, even if you do. I also don't care what motivated you to be ready now as opposed to two or three months ago. I'm just really glad you got there—finally. And, news flash, Kate:

I want to do it again! I want to do it again right now, if you'd let me."

"Don't you even think about that, Ed Evert! That's *not* happening," Kate said sternly, causing Ed to break out laughing.

"What? Not here? Not ever? Not now? Or not today?" he asked. "Kate, we are two very well matched people. I respect you more than you can imagine. We work well together, and now we know we make love well together too."

"We *made* love well together. Made. Past tense, Ed. It was a one-time thing. Remember? 'No-strings-attached, just a rebound thing.'"

Ed chose to ignore her comment. "Kate, I'm a grown-up. I know we'll need to watch ourselves at work. I get that. But, I do not see any reason we can't have a relationship outside the office."

"What? Like we're going to hang out at clubs, take in a movie, go to the symphony? Plays? Ed, do you have any idea what a small town this can be?" Kate threw up her hands in exasperation. "This is just *not* going to work. There is no way. And I need to end it now before I fuck things up worse than I already have."

"Kate, this is not just about you. You don't always get to dictate and direct. We are in this together. *I* do *not* want to stop seeing you, and *I* do not *intend* to. And I don't believe you really want that either."

Kate was silent for a few minutes and just stared at Ed. Finally, she sighed deeply and said, "I need to meet your mother."

"What? You won't have sex with me again unless you meet my mother? Kate, that's just weird," he said in amazement.

"No, silly. You told me she used to say you'd grow up to either be a salesman or a lawyer because you can't take 'no' for an answer. I just want to know how the hell she managed to live with you without strangling you. Did you *ever* give up on an argument?" Kate asked and started laughing. Ed quickly followed.

"All right. We need some ground rules if this has even a prayer of succeeding. And we have to stick to them; otherwise, we are looking at a fucking train wreck!" Kate decided.

"OK, Boss Lady. Lay down the law," Ed said knowing he had won the battle, but also knowing he needed to give her a concession or two.

"Well, to begin with, no touching in the office. And, after this conversation, we won't talk about anything other than work in the office," Kate began.

"So, you think our offices are bugged or what? Kate, that's silly." Ed was already pushing back on the rules even before he could tell himself to quit while he was ahead.

"Damn it, Ed. I don't want us to be overheard. There are people in the firm who would love to get some dirt on me, Doug the Dick for one. And besides, it will be easier to keep our minds on our work if we don't let ourselves talk about personal stuff."

"OK. OK. You get that point, I concede," Ed said recognizing she might be right, but damn if he didn't want to violate the new rules even before the ink was dry.

"And we can't be seen in public together," Kate said, pushing hard now that she'd won a point.

"Oh, for fuck's sake!" Ed exploded. "We're seen in public together all the time *now*. How many working dinners and lunches have we had? Hell, we've even had breakfast together in public. We're also seen together at Bar meetings. We work out together. We've even gone out for a drink after work. It would look worse if we suddenly stopped doing those things."

"OK. You win that point. We will keep doing those things, but nothing else—and no touching or talking about it in the office," Kate cautioned.

"You know, I should probably tell you that my mom discovered the more she told me I couldn't do something, the more it made me want to do it just to prove her wrong. And right now, I want to wrestle you to the floor of my office and have my way with you." Ed was smiling mischievously now.

"That figures!" Kate huffed. "But don't even think about it. Besides, we'd be crushed to death under an avalanche of books and papers."

"OK. Anything else, Boss Lady? Or are you done laying down the law?" Ed continued to smile at her. It was making her twinge and ache deep down.

"For now. I'm done *for now*. We'll see how this goes." Kate paused momentarily as she shifted gears.

"We've got to get down to work. Any chance you can come to my office in a half hour? We need to discuss our pending matters," Kate said, easily moving on to the next point of her agenda. "With the continuation of the Brighton trial, we actually have some breathing room. For the first time since you got here, we don't have six matters all on fire at the same time. It feels good, but I don't want to let things slide. You never know when the next onslaught will hit. And, Ed, you don't fall behind in cases at the last minute, you fall behind at the beginning when you don't start soon enough," Kate said as she stood to leave his office.

"One more thing," Ed said as Kate put her hand on the door handle preparing to leave.

She turned back around. "Yes?"

"What did Bill say when he called yesterday?"

It was a left field shot and caught Kate completely off balance.

"What?" was all she said, feeling her face redden.

"The man said he would call you, and I'm guessing he did. He still has it bad for you, Boss Lady. I know the look. So, what did he say?"

"He wants to have dinner on Thursday," she said as she considered how much of this topic she was willing to discuss with him. "I'm guessing he wants to tell me in person that he's proposed to Pam."

"Maybe," Ed shrugged. "But he didn't look to me like a man who was asking someone else to marry him any time soon. Let me know what happens."

"Ed, Bill and I were really good friends before I screwed up and slept with him. He and his first wife were casual friends of ours when I was married to Adam. Then his wife was diagnosed with breast cancer. She died about two and a half years ago. Bill and I became closer during the time he was watching her die. It was exceedingly tough on him. I tried to be a good friend. Now, he wants to be married again. It's who he is, and he knows it's not something I want. Does that answer your question?"

"Yeah, sure," Ed said and looked around awkwardly. "Just let me know if that status changes. I at least want a heads-up—if not a fighting chance."

Kate realized her tone was a bit harsher than she'd intended.

"Ed, I just thought of a new rule." She softened her tone. "My intent is that this relationship, whatever it is or becomes, is exclusive and if that intention changes, I'll tell you. I promise." Kate watched as Ed's eyes softened. "Can I ask you to do the same?"

"Of course," he responded.

Kate turned to leave but stopped again.

"Ed, we're at different places in our lives. You need to keep your options open. There are a few life decisions I've made that you have not, like getting married and having kids. I don't want to stand in your way. OK?"

Kate looked at Ed's fresh face.

"Got it, Boss Lady. But don't get confused, because I'm not. Your life isn't over. I intend to keep reminding you of that," he said, and there was that mischievous grin again.

Kate smiled wanly, feeling old and completely out of her element.

"OK," she said. "See you in 30 minutes—my office."

As she walked back to her office she thought, *Well, that didn't go the way I planned. He's clearly far better at this 'no-strings-attached' sex than I am. Probably has a lot more experience at it . . .*

Ed showed up in Kate's office exactly 30 minutes later with a stack of files on his laptop and two cups of black coffee from the deli in the lobby of their building balanced on top of the files.

"I figured we'd need some stimulation to get us going this morning since you already vetoed my first suggestion," he said as he winked at Kate and set the coffee on the worktable in the corner of her office.

"Jesus, Ed! It hasn't even been an hour, and you're flagrantly violating the rules already!" Kate threw up her hands and glowered at him.

"Sorry, sorry. I'll stop. I promise." He held up his hands in surrender.

"But sometimes it's just hard to pass up a great line. So, which matter do you want to start with: Marcy Simpson, Bobbi Jo née Bob, the Fisher trial, the Goodman and Prior summary judgments, or the Primary Paints appeal?" he asked, popping open his laptop and spreading out the files on the table.

"Primary Paints. It'll be easy to knock this one out. Fred Richards is going to call this morning at 10:30 to discuss the response brief we sent him last week. He sounds like he's happy with the draft, so I suspect we'll be able to file it tomorrow. It will be good to get that one put to bed finally. You should plan on sitting in on the discussion with Fred. If editing is needed, you're doing it." Kate's voice was stern, and her eyes were fixed on Ed.

"I wonder if the circuit court will grant the appellant's request for oral argument. It's been way too long since I've had a chance to make an appellate argument. It's a lot of prep for a short, but very important, 20 minutes, and it's a total rush. As much as you love to argue, you should think about getting some appellate court experience—you could ask your mom to come watch you argue so she can see how you've put your skills to good use!"

"She'd like that. But I'm not letting you get anywhere near her. She knows entirely too much about me, and I don't want her giving you any ammunition!" Ed said, laughing.

"Fair enough. OK, let's talk about where we are in the Fisher trial prep. I think there's a better than 50 percent chance that we'll be reached in two months. If we try Fisher in two months, we could have back-to-back trials because Judge Kilmer put us on next month's docket for the Brighton trial. We need to plot out our internal deadlines for the pretrial steps in Fisher."

With that, Kate began outlining each step of her standard trial prep, setting completion dates for each, and then assigning each task to one of them.

For the next hour, Kate and Ed worked through their pending civil matters ending with Marcy Simpson's.

"The Johnny Sutton deposition is set for Friday. We're going to his place, rather than making him come here. I'm headed out right after yoga in case you want to come along. I know you're looking forward to your second hot yoga class, right?" Kate smiled wickedly, and Ed groaned.

"Maybe I'll be sick that morning, or perhaps I'll oversleep. Unless you want to give me a personalized wake-up call," he shot her his own wicked grin.

"Watch it, Mr. Evert. You are not following the rules."

Kate stood up and stretched.

"I'm hoping Terry managed to get a reading on the reason one of Miami's finest paid a visit to Marcy last Friday. Apparently, there is evidence of foul play; the good doctor had digitalis in his blood when he was brought into the hospital. Digitalis can cause your heart to stop and display all the signs of a heart attack if a sufficient dose is administered. The cops are looking for someone with access to the drug, motive to kill, and opportunity to drug Dr. Dugan. In their eyes, Marcy scores high on points one and two, but she didn't *know* she had motive because she was not aware that the insurance policy still existed. Plus, she hadn't seen Joe Dugan in years, so she didn't have opportunity. The cops are barking up the wrong tree if they think our girl was involved. I'm considering paying Mike Taylor a visit and disabuse him of such thoughts. Besides, I haven't harassed him in a while."

Later that afternoon, Terry Davis showed up at Kate's office unannounced. From his face, Kate could tell his news was troubling.

"Kate, Beth called me earlier this afternoon to let me know we've got an ID on Suzy's unintended houseguest. The FBI matched the prints I pulled. They belong to a man on their top 20 most wanted list. The feds have been tracking the guy up and down the eastern seaboard. They're always a day or two behind him. He's got quite a trail of warrants—everything from B&E to murder. Beth said the feds have profiled him as a sociopath. He's got a couple of aliases, but they think his real ID is Gary Cook, born in Seattle, a 38-year-old college grad." Terry shook his head. "God, Kate, to think Suzy let this guy into her home. She's so fucking lucky. He could have killed her."

"I know, Terry. It's serious. She's never been this reckless before. We've got to get her to understand the enormity of the risk she took. I could strangle her myself every time I think about it." Kate sighed, sitting back in her chair and shaking her head.

"Yeah, she was totally nonplussed about it. I went back to her house with her yesterday to check the place out, see if anything was missing and make sure it was locked up. I've convinced her to get a better alarm system and stressed that she should use it all the time. You just never know.

"I thought I'd head over to her office and tell her exactly who she brought home and try again to impress on her just how fucking lucky she was to get away with this one. The guy is still on the loose, but there's an APB out on him. The feds are crawling all over the marina area. I hope to God they find him. No telling if he'd be able to find his way back to Suzy's place, but there's a chance, and I want to make sure she's taking precautions."

Kate detected real concern in Terry's voice, and she wondered if her friend Suzy had cast her spell on yet another unsuspecting male.

"Please do and when you talk to her, tell her from me she owes us another dinner. Seriously, Terry, do you think Suzy should come stay with me for a few days? At least until the feds find this guy, or they think he's moved out of the area?"

"I had the same thought. I'll see what I can do and let you know." Terry looked away, and Kate decided he might be planning on offering Suzy alternative shelter himself.

"Thanks, Terry. You're the best," she said, certain Terry's interest was more than professional concern.

Suzy has that effect on men, Kate thought. *I just hope she doesn't break his heart—but even if she does, he'll have a hell of a ride while it lasts.*

"I also wanted to let you know that I talked to a couple of guys down at the precinct about Marcy," Terry said, shifting topics. "As we thought, Tony Beltran's visit wasn't a random social call. He went there to see how she'd react to learning Dr. Joe might have been murdered and that she might be a person of interest in the murder investigation. The cops and prosecutor are pretty sure they've got the evidence to prove he was poisoned, but they don't have a clue who poisoned him. Apparently, they're looking at anyone with access to pharmaceutical-grade digitalis—that's what they found in his blood. The stuff is pretty fast working, so whoever did it would have been with the good doctor no less than an hour before his death. That's a pretty short window. Hopefully, our girl has a solid alibi for that time period." Terry paused and looked at some notes. "It would have been Wednesday night two weeks ago, around 9:00 or 10:00."

Terry continued his briefing, "When the cops brought the Merry Widow in to tell her the news about the blood work, she went bat-shit-crazy on them—screaming and crying and throwing things. Ranting on and on about how could they ask her such questions, didn't they know who she is and who her daddy is. Evidently, it was pretty ugly. The widow immediately pointed to Marcy, saying she's a nurse and has access to all kinds of drugs. Apparently, her big cheese father was pretty pissed when he found out they hauled his little girl down to the station for questioning. *He* even pointed to Marcy as a suspect." Terry shrugged.

"I gotta tell you the cops find the whole insurance policy piece very suspicious. Most of those guys would take out a hit on their ex-wives before they'd take out a life insurance policy naming them as the beneficiary! And the size of the policy isn't going to help our girl."

"So, evidence no longer matters at all?" Kate asked sarcastically. "You know, sometimes I just want to remind the cops and the prosecutor to follow the evidence, and when there isn't any, find some; don't make shit up!" Kate shook her head disgustedly.

"Marcy hadn't seen or talked to Doctor Dugan in years, and she didn't know the life insurance policy was still current. So, where's the motive and opportunity? If the only qualifier to becoming a suspect is access to the drug, they need to look at Zeke Peters. That dude is way too interested in the Dugan estate and the lovely, newly widowed Mrs. Dugan. Something stinks there. If the cops are looking for someone to shake down, they ought to try Zeke."

"Don't shoot the messenger, Boss Lady. I just report the news, I don't make it." Terry lifted his hands to signal surrender.

Kate sighed. Since Ed had started calling her "Boss Lady," it seemed like everyone was picking up the habit.

"Yeah, I know," she sighed. "I guess I'll have to go see my favorite state attorney and Chief Jordan. I've left them messages, but they don't seem to want to return my calls. First, however, I'm going to call Marcy to give her an update—and find out where she was, and who she was with Wednesday, two weeks ago, from 9:00 to 11:00 p.m."

Chapter 9

Thursday afternoon, Kate's cell phone rang, and the caller ID announced Bill Davis was on the line without any acknowledgment of the potential significance of his call. That always seemed wrong to Kate. She felt her "smart" phone should be able to detect incoming calls that carried potential danger. Warning bells should go off or something. She had resisted the trend toward linking certain numbers with specific ringtones. That seemed too campy and frankly insufficient to truly provide the type of advanced warning Kate wanted. Besides, what ringtone would say "the great love of your life, who you refused to marry, is calling"?

"Hello, Bill." Kate tried to keep her voice calm and lacking inflection.

"Hi, Katie," Bill said, chipper as usual. "How's your day going? I know you've been there since the wee hours . . . unless, of course, you have something or someone delaying you in the mornings these days."

"I got here a little before 7:00 this morning, Bill," Kate responded, not wishing to answer his implied question. "How's *your* morning?"

Two can play this game of innuendo, Bill. And, please don't call me Katie again, Kate thought. *I can barely do this as it is.*

"Pretty interesting so far. I just got back from a quick overnight test cruise with the sales rep for Monte Carlo Yachts. They wanted some feedback on their new 86-foot model. I'm sure they're hoping I'll consider upgrading. Anyway, it's a supercool boat. You'd love it."

"I'm sure I would! Your life is definitely more glamorous than mine!" Kate laughed wistfully.

"Doesn't have to be . . ." Bill responded, and his words hung heavily in the air.

After a brief lull in the conversation, Bill finally said, "I wanted to let you know I've made reservations for our dinner tonight at The Pelican. I've heard it's nice, but I haven't had a chance to try it." Bill seemed to hesitate.

No doubt he's trying to figure out how to tell me he and Pam are engaged. Maybe I should save him the price of an expensive dinner, Kate thought.

"You know, we don't have to do dinner. If there's something you want to tell me, you can just tell me over the phone. An expensive dinner isn't really necessary," Kate said, trying to keep them out of an awkward situation. She couldn't imagine anything more uncomfortable than going to dinner with someone else's fiancé who was once your lover.

"What are you talking about? I *want* to see you and thought we could try a new restaurant." He sounded surprised. "Can I pick you up about 7:00? Our reservation is for 7:30."

Kate's reaction was visceral. *No, you can't pick me up. The sight of you in my house where we were so happy will be too hard to take,* she thought.

"How about I meet you at the restaurant at 7:30," was all Kate could manage for a minute. And then she added, "If you're sure you don't want to just tell me what's on your mind now. In case you've forgotten, I'm not really the kind who needs to be wined and dined."

"No, I haven't forgotten. Nor have I forgotten that you like to be in charge and control the timing and setting of everything. We can do it your way, if you don't want me in your house. I'll meet you at the restaurant." His voice had a decided edge to it now. "And, Kate, I am looking forward to seeing you. I've missed you, even if you find that hard to believe."

Bill hung up without saying good-bye.

Kate sat at her desk looking out the window wondering if she sounded as bitchy to Bill as she did to herself.

Her phone rang and interrupted her latest session of self-recrimination. It was Terry.

"Kate, I've gone about as far as I can go with my investigation of the Dugans and Zeke Peters here in Miami. I'm going to head up to St.

Pete this weekend to see if I can talk to Dr. Dugan's brother, at least."

"Sounds good. Anything new on Zeke, and how he fits into the story?" Kate inquired. "He's such an enigma in this mess, and I just can't get over the feeling that if we could figure out his angle, we'd learn a lot about Joe and Joan Dugan."

"Nope, nothing yet, but I agree with you. I think there's something rotten here, and I believe Zeke has a hand in whatever it is. I'm hoping Dugan's brother can shed some light on the issue."

There was a slight pause before Terry went on.

"Kate, would you mind if I brought someone along with me on my trip to St. Pete this weekend?"

"Hell, it's your weekend. I'm thrilled you're willing to work through it. If you want to take someone along, have at it."

Terry usually kept his personal life to himself, and Kate was more than mildly interested in this new development.

There was a lengthy delay. Finally, Terry said, "You sure? Even if it's Suzy?"

"What? *My* Suzy? Oh Jesus, Terry! I hope you know what you're doing. I love Suzy, but the girl's love life is . . . legendary, and not always in the good sense of the word." Kate was laughing, wondering how wrong this liaison could go. She decided she wasn't going to think about it. "Have fun, dude, and don't say I didn't warn you."

"Yeah, I know. But . . . I thought I'd go for it," Terry laughed nervously. "Anyway, I'll let you know what I learn. Bye."

Kate was still chuckling as she hung up. She considered her next move. Neither Mike Taylor nor Chief Jordon had returned her calls, so she knew she would have to pay them a personal visit. She decided she'd start with a surprise visit to the chief. The only question was whether she would take Ed with her.

She'd told him Bill wanted to have dinner tonight and she really didn't want to have to field his questions about it in case he remembered. On the other hand, she wanted him along as a witness to her meetings. Ultimately, she decided she'd take him with her, but they'd drive separately. That way, she would limit his opportunity to question her, and, when they were done, she could head directly home to change for her "dinner date with destiny" as she'd decided to call it.

"Want to go harass the chief of police and state attorney with me?" Kate asked when she walked into Ed's disaster area office later in the day.

"Always a pleasure with you in the lead, Boss Lady. What have they done this time?" Ed asked, looking up from his computer.

"Well, in fairness, they didn't do it on purpose, but the chief had one of his officers talk to Marcy without coming through me," Kate responded as she watched Ed shut down his computer and hunt for the shoes he'd kicked off under his desk.

"Marcy?" Ed inquired.

"Yes. Apparently the police have decided she looks like a suspect in Joe Dugan's death. Stupid really, but there you go."

Kate sighed as Ed pulled down his sleeves, buttoned his top two buttons, straightened his tie, and slipped on his jacket.

Damn, I wish he was taking those clothes off—not putting them on. I'm beyond horny, and it's only been two days, Kate thought as she tried to look away from Ed but found him irresistible.

"Ready," Ed said as he looked at Kate. "What?" he asked when he caught her staring at him. "That's a funny expression, Ms. Muldoon. I'd almost say it was lecherous if I didn't know you would *never* be so bold as to break your own rules. We're in the office after all, madam."

Ed was laughing now, and Kate knew she was blushing again.

"We're taking separate cars," she informed him. "I'm not coming back to the office when we're done."

"Hmm, sounds like someone needs to go home and get ready for her big dinner date tonight." Ed grabbed his backpack and slung it over his shoulder. "Don't forget our deal, Kate. I want fair warning and a fighting chance. I think we should plan on a little dinner date of our own this weekend." Ed had decided to play it aggressive.

"Ed, please, can we just do this and try to remember our rules? This whole thing is hard enough. My mind needs to be on Marcy's predicament, not having sex with you." Kate spun on her heels and walked toward the elevator with Ed following along chuckling.

At the precinct, Kate announced to the desk officer that she and Ed were there to see Chief Jordan.

"No, we didn't call ahead. No, we don't have an appointment. And, no, he doesn't know what we want to talk to him about. We'll wait as long as it takes, but we'll only need about 15 minutes of his time, so we're sure he can work us in."

Kate set her briefcase on the floor and stood staring at the desk officer, waiting for him to let the chief know she was waiting.

When he did nothing, Kate said, "Are you telepathic? Do you have some new signal you can send the chief without using the phone or computer?"

The desk officer glared at Kate but reluctantly picked up the phone and called the chief.

"Chief, Kate Muldoon and one of her associates—"

"His name is Ed Evert, sir," Kate interjected.

"Yeah, Ed Evert. Ms. Muldoon and Mr. Evert are waiting here to see you—they don't have an appointment."

There was a pause.

"No, sir. I don't know, and she didn't say."

Another pause.

"Yes, sir. She's standing right here."

Another pause.

"Sir, she says she'll only need 15 minutes . . ." the desk officer was avoiding eye contact with Kate. "No, sir. She already said that she'd wait . . ."

"Tell him I can get a court order if that is now necessary for a defense counsel to talk to the chief of police," Kate said loudly with biting sarcasm.

"Yes, sir. Like I said, she's standing right here in front of me."

There was a short delay in the desk officer's conversation. Kate could hear Chief Jordan cursing on the other end of the line, the desk officer cringed, and then said, "OK, I'll send them back."

To Kate and Ed he said, "I think you know your way," and he reached under the desk and hit the button that unlocked the security door separating the lobby from the squad room.

Kate smiled victoriously.

"Thank you for your prompt, courteous, and professional service to the public," Kate said, mocking their professional law enforcement motto.

As they walked back toward the chief's office, Kate and Ed were the targets of numerous scowls, frowns, and piercing stares. She knew she was not the most popular person in the room, and that was just fine with her. Her lack of popularity had been won by exposing a group of narcotics detectives who were running their own drug ring. Those former detectives were now in federal custody awaiting trial.

"Chief, it's good to see you. Thank you for taking the time to fit us into your schedule on such short notice." Kate always thought it was important to say the right words even if your sentiment didn't always match.

"We won't take up much of your time, but I was having trouble reaching Mike Taylor to give him notice of representation of a new client. So, I decided I would *hand deliver* it to him, and I thought you should receive the same courtesy."

Kate pulled out a letter stating she represented Marcy Simpson and requesting any further contact with Marcy by the state attorneys for the Miami-Dade area be made through her office.

"I've recently been engaged by Marcy Simpson in an interpleader and declaratory judgment action regarding payment of insurance proceeds relating to the death of Dr. Joseph Dugan. I understand your office is now investigating his death as a possible homicide. Good call by the hospital to run a tox screen when Dr. Dugan was brought into the emergency room. I heard they found digitalis in a quantity sufficient to stop his heart."

Kate watched Chief Jordan closely and gave him a B+ for keeping a poker face. Only the small tick in his left eye gave him away. She knew he was wondering how she had learned so much about his investigation.

"Anyway, I understand one of your officers decided to pay my client a visit to try to shake her up. There are several things you need to know so you can redirect your investigation in a more profitable direction. First, my client had not seen or talked to Dr. Dugan in over ten years. Second, she had absolutely no idea she was still the beneficiary on an insurance policy on Dr. Dugan's life and was stunned when the attorneys for Dr. Dugan's estate and the insurance company told her about the policy. Finally, she has an alibi for the time frame that the lethal dose of digitalis would have been administered. So, if you have seriously targeted the ex-wife of 16 years, you are barking up the wrong tree."

"Thank you, Ms. Muldoon. It's always good to hear your version of the facts. Have you thought for a moment that Ms. Simpson could have hired a hit man to do her dirty work? Four million dollars is a lot of money. She could afford some serious professional help with that kind of dough."

"Look, Chief, she would still have to know about the insurance policy to have a motive. Do you have any evidence that proves she knew about that policy? Or anything linking her to obtaining that quantity of digitalis? Or hiring a hit man, for heaven's sake?" Kate asked point-blank.

"Not yet, Kate, but we're looking at every possibility," Chief Jordan responded frankly.

"Well, I hope so, but you might want to look a little closer to home. Have you found out whether Dr. Dugan had a separate policy on his life running in favor of his wife or boys? Have you looked into how happily married they were? From *my* brief investigation, I can tell you Mrs. Dugan was quite a handful. I wonder how much her well-known and well-respected husband liked her outrageous conduct sullying his reputation.

"And then there's the whole Zeke Peters mystery. That guy is just way too interested in the affairs of Dr. Dugan's estate and his attractive young widow. So, here's what we'll do. You proceed with your investigation, and I'll do the same. Let's see who finds the rat first. I've given you a heads-up. I know you'd like to be first to solve this one, and I promise I'll be a gracious loser if you are. Oddly, I just can't bring myself to promise to be a gracious winner," Kate smiled innocently at the chief.

"Got it, Kate. And despite what you might think, I really do appreciate and value your insights. I'll tell you what: I promise we'll contact you before asking Ms. Simpson anything further, not that we have to, you know. But understand, we *will* be talking with your client. Four million dollars is motive in everybody's book."

Kate appreciated the chief saying he valued her insight, and his comment did seem genuine, but she worried that he was being blinded by the size of the insurance policy. She wondered if he really would look at others who might also have sufficient motive to murder the good doctor.

"Great, Chief, and thanks. OK, we'll get out of your hair. We're walking over to spread a little joy in the state attorneys' office now. Feel free to call ahead and warn him we're coming," she said, still smiling.

"No. I think I'll let it be a surprise. I owe him one."

The chief rose to shake their hands as they said their good-byes—something he had never done before.

On their walk to the state attorney's office, Kate kept Ed engaged, talking about the law as long as she could. She was trying to keep his mind—and hers—off of her "dinner date with destiny."

As they entered the office, the receptionist's head snapped up, and Kate was sure she detected a hint of fear on her face. "Ms. Muldoon, this is a surprise," she said through clenched teeth. "Does Mr. Taylor know you're coming?"

"No, Claire," Kate said, reading the young woman's desk nameplate, "it's a surprise," she said and winked. "Could you tell him that I really need to see him? I have something I want to hand deliver, and we need to have a quick conversation. Tell him it won't take more than 15 minutes."

"Sure, Ms. Muldoon. I'll be right back," Claire said, trying to find an escape. She knew her boss would not be happy to learn Kate Muldoon was paying a visit.

"No need to leave your desk, Claire. I'm sure you can call him. If he's busy, you can leave a voice mail," Kate said, knowing that if he answered he couldn't use the excuse that he was in conference.

"OK," Claire willingly agreed, not wanting to face her boss with the news of his visitor's identity. "Sure, I'll call him."

"Thanks, and tell him Mr. Evert is here too," Kate added nodding to Ed, who smiled handsomely. Claire immediately succumbed to his grin and quickly called her boss. Moments later, Mike appeared at the security door.

"Kate, I was just going to return your call. It's been a busy couple of days. Hello, again, Mr. Evert. I hope you are enjoying working with Kate. I hear she can be a tough taskmaster."

Kate shook Mike's hand as she walked through the security door.

"Yes, sir. Very much," Ed said with a grin. "We're actually a very good fit. We work very well together, and I enjoy working under her. I'm learning a lot," he said walking in behind Kate.

Ed's obvious double entendre stunned Kate, and she threw him a nasty glare over her shoulder. Ed was grinning ear to ear. Kate struggled hard not to blush as she tried to stifle her anger.

When they entered Mike's office Kate sat in one of the side chairs and pulled the letter of representation from her briefcase while Mike and Ed continued to chat. Mike joked that Ed's military training must be why he was able to meet Kate's tough work expectations.

"This isn't a social call, Mike, and I know you'd rather talk to the devil than to me," Kate interrupted the boy talk. "I'm trying to play square with you. You may not have known, but I am representing Marcy Simpson in the interpleader and declaratory action related to an insurance policy Dr. Dugan took out—*and maintained every year for nearly 20 years*—specifically naming his ex-wife, Marcy Simpson, as the beneficiary. We know the cops are now investigating Dr. Dugan's death as a murder, and we understand that the widow and her politically well-connected father seem to be making unfounded accusations about Ms. Simpson's involvement. I couldn't help but notice that you and the chief have already bought into Senator Ferguson's theory, and I don't appreciate the stealth visit by Tony Beltran to my client. You want to talk to Marcy, you call me and we'll come in together."

"Actually, I had no idea you would be involved in an insurance matter—although, I have to say if I had $4 million riding on a matter, I'd want you in my corner." Mike sounded genuinely surprised and only a little obsequious.

"Thanks, Mike. Looking for my vote when you run for state attorney?" Kate laughed. "Seriously, don't approach her again without notifying me. Here's my written notice of representation. I just delivered a copy to Chief Jordan, just so there's no misunderstanding or confusion in the future," Kate warned.

When Mike said nothing further, Kate continued. Handing Mike the representation letter, she said, "Can I give you a helpful hint? No charge. If you're looking for someone to blame for Joe Dugan's death, you're in the wrong ballpark if you're coming after Marcy. As we just informed Chief Jordan, Ms. Simpson had not seen or talked to her ex-husband in over ten years, and she was completely unaware that he maintained an insurance policy naming her as the beneficiary after the divorce. In fact, she was stunned when she learned about it. She thus lacks motive or opportunity. More to the point, she has an alibi for the time immediately preceding Joe Dugan's death. Marcy was at work during the window of time the digitalis would have had to be administered. If you want to avoid another embarrassing incident like the Bentley hearing, you may want to start looking at other possible suspects. And I suggest you'll find more likely targets much closer to home. In any event, you must come through me to speak with Ms. Simpson in the future." She waited to see if Mike would respond. When he didn't say anything, she continued.

"That's all we needed to tell you," she said standing up. "I figured an in-person visit was more difficult to ignore than a phone call. I hope next time I'll get a prompt return call. It is, after all, still required in our professional code of conduct."

She extended her hand to Mike, Ed followed suit, and they walked out of Mike's office and through the security door.

Kate kept walking briskly out of the building, pausing only briefly just outside the building to turn to Ed.

"You will never again make a comment like that. I've worked hard to earn a reputation as a credible attorney, and I won't allow your double entendres to undermine me."

Kate's eyes glistened with anger, and Ed knew he'd crossed a line.

"I'm sorry, Kate. I really am. I promise I won't do that again," he said, astounded at the ferocity he saw in her eyes.

Kate just glared at him, and then turned and quickly walked toward the public parking garage where they'd both parked.

Damn, I really shit in my mess kit this time, Ed thought. *And of all the terrible times to fuck up! Just before she has dinner with Bill. Shit, shit, shit. Mom said my smart mouth would be my downfall. I've got to learn to walk away from great set-up lines.*

Ed thought briefly about running after Kate to catch up and apologize again. But he decided instead to let her leave without further irritating her. She needed time to get over her anger, and he needed time to dig himself out of the mess he was in.

As she walked to her car alone, still fuming at Ed, Kate realized they'd wrapped up their meetings early, and she would have time to take the dogs for a walk when she got home, and still be able to change clothes and make it to dinner on time. She'd promised herself she was not going to this meeting with Bill looking worn out from her day and feeling anything but dazzling.

After all, it's not every day you dine with the man you love as he tells you he's going to marry someone else, Kate thought smiling wanly.

Chapter 10

Kate valeted her car when she arrived at The Pelican because she was wearing, by her own estimation, "stupid shoes." The heel was a tiny, five-inch long spike. They made her legs look totally hot, but they were meant for sitting, not walking. The short, black cocktail dress barely came to her mid-thigh; the plunging V-neckline revealed that no bra could possibly be worn underneath. The dress clung to Kate's body and shimmered as she moved. When she stepped out of her car and handed the keys to the valet, every head, including the women, turned to assess her. No one seemed disappointed.

Good, Kate thought, smiling to herself. *If I have to listen to the man I love tell me he's marrying someone else, I'm going to make him, and every other man in the place, and maybe even some of the women, at least want to take me to bed.*

The maître d' became an instant fan the moment Kate approached his station. Perhaps he recognized her, or he might just be really good at faking it—it didn't matter to Kate. She desperately needed to be treated as if she was the most special person in the room tonight, even if it was by a complete stranger paid to make her feel good. Kate's insides were in turmoil. She hoped she was fooling the gawkers with her calm exterior.

As she followed the maître d' into the dining room, Kate instantly spotted Bill at his table in the bay window. He looked positively gorgeous. His perfect tan against the classic dark suit and white shirt, opened at the neck, was stunning. A wide, boyish grin broke across his face and melted her heart. She fell in love with Bill all over again. She was dying on the inside and just wanted to fall into his arms and never let go.

As the maître d' pulled out her chair he whispered, "If there's anything, anything at all, that you need this evening, all you have to do is just ask."

I want my heart to not be broken tonight. Think you can manage that? Kate thought cynically but simply thanked him as she looked deeply into Bill's face—and held her breath.

"That was quite an entrance, Katie." Bill stared into her eyes and smiled. "You making a statement? If you are, you've got a ready audience. There's not one person in this entire room not ogling you." He grinned appreciatively.

"I don't know what you're talking about, Mr. Golden Boy. I think they're all looking at *you*. I have to work hard just to keep up with you." Kate found herself smiling back at him, exceedingly happy to be back in his company.

"I know this probably doesn't fit into your agenda for dinner tonight Big Boy, but I sure have missed you. Missed looking at you, talking with you, and seeing that beautiful smile. Thanks for asking me out for dinner. No matter what you're planning on telling me tonight, I'm really happy to be here." Kate knew they could at least be friends again, and she was realizing just how much she'd missed her friend.

"I don't know what you're talking about, Katie. I truly don't have an agenda or a message or anything in particular to discuss, but I will tell you, I miss you more than I should. Besides, I thought we'd both taken long enough to think about what you said when you told me you weren't going to marry me. Aren't you curious what I've been thinking about in the intervening three months you gave me to decide what I want?" Bill asked mysteriously, turning to the waiter who'd appeared, ready to take their cocktail order. Bill waited for Kate to order first.

She knew she needed the courage a martini would give her to face this dinner and ordered one. Bill ordered the same, and the waiter magically dissolved into the background.

"Well," she said after a pause, "I never said anything about three months. You were the one who made the decision to wait three months. Anyway, I've been told what you've been doing, or maybe that's *who*."

Kate noted that Bill's grin faded slightly. She felt instantly guilty.

"Look, Bill, you seem really happy, and I *want* you to be happy. I suspect you've figured out that most women would call me crazy for turning you down. I understand Pam Logan is among them. She's beautiful and smart; I know she will make you very happy," Kate blurted out, deciding she couldn't stand waiting for Bill to make the announcement she was convinced was coming.

Who knows, she thought, *maybe if we can get this part over, I won't need to stay for dinner*, Kate thought dejectedly.

"Katie, I don't know what you've been told or by whom, but let me set the record straight. In the last three months, I've gone out to dinner with Pam Logan exactly twice. I invited her to the symphony once, and she took me to a charity ball. She's a nice person, but our interest levels are . . ." Bill struggled for the right word, "lopsided," he decided summed it up.

"I've also had dinner with other women during these past three months. But mostly, Katie, I've been thinking about you, what we had, and why you're so damn scared of it."

Bill's grin was completely gone now.

Kate sat motionless and thinking, *Is it possible Bill isn't going to tell me he and Pam are engaged? Could I have read this whole setup so wrong?*

The waiter appeared with their drinks.

After several sips, Kate said softly, "So, you didn't ask me to dinner to tell me you and Pam are engaged?"

Bill stared at her in disbelief.

"Jesus, Kate, you really do overthink things. Where in the hell did you get that idea?"

"I know you want to get married, and I know you and Pam have been dating. Hell, you and Pam have been dating longer than we did! Steve Sloan seemed to think it was pretty serious when I ran into him at the courthouse last week. He said Pam talks of little else. So, it was just a logical conclusion that, well, you found someone you wanted and she wasn't averse to the entire institution of marriage. I don't know, it seemed logical to me . . . and I really do want you to be happy, Bill."

Kate was fumbling now and decided to stop talking.

Bill continued to stare at her. She could feel her cheeks heating up, she knew the color was rising, and oddly, she felt tears starting to sting her eyes. She looked away, took another sip of her drink, and several deep breaths, determined not to let the tears come.

"Please say something, Bill," she pleaded after a few more minutes as she continued to fight back tears.

"Why couldn't I pick you up at your house tonight?" Bill finally asked.

"What? Honestly?" Kate's head snapped up from her drink, surprised by his question.

"No, I want you to lie to me." Bill raised his eyebrows and looked at her in angry disbelief. "Yes, *honestly*. Is it because Ed's there?" When Kate didn't answer immediately, he said, "Well, is he?" He was not backing down.

"No. He is not there. He's *never* been there. It's crazy to think that," Kate blurted out.

"Not any crazier than thinking I asked you to dinner to tell you I'm marrying someone else," Bill retorted indignantly.

Kate considered his statement for a moment and conceded, "Yes, you're probably right about that."

She slipped him a small smile. He was having none of it. She knew she'd have to answer his question.

"The truth: I knew I wouldn't be able to take seeing you in my house again. You're the only man who ever seemed to fit in that house. I wasn't up to seeing you there, knowing you wouldn't be staying."

"And why did you assume I wouldn't be staying?"

"Because you were going to tell me you were marrying Pam . . . Oh shit, what a mess."

Kate went silent.

"OK, let me ask this . . ." Bill hesitated before going on. "How serious are you about this Ed fellow?"

Kate fell silent.

"I know he is quite interested in you. It was written all over him when I saw the two of you at the beach. He couldn't have made his intentions any clearer—he practically oozed protectiveness. Frankly, I was surprised you put up with it. So, I'm asking how serious is it?"

Kate was thrilled to see the waiter hovering in the background trying to gauge when would be a good time to take their order.

"Do you want to order dinner, Bill? Our waiter looks like he'd like a sign that we're ready. Do you still want to have dinner with me? I seem to have made a complete mess of things so far."

"Yes, I want to have dinner with you, and, yes, I'm starved, so let's order." Bill turned slightly and nodded to the waiter.

They both ordered from the evening's specials because neither had opened their menus. Kate wondered if she would even be able to taste her food.

I've totally fucked this up, she thought. Her head felt like it would explode. *What was I thinking? Why did I succumb to my insecurities and have rebound sex with Ed? That isn't even like me. Was I that hurt by the fact Bill was seeing someone else, or was I that attracted to Ed? I'm a fucking mess!*

The self-recriminations flew through Kate's head as she looked at Bill across the table. A heavy silence filled the space between them.

Finally, Kate said, "I want to start this whole evening over . . . No, I want to start this whole month over."

Kate could barely look at Bill, but she forced herself, and she drew a deep breath as she began to answer his question.

"Bill, Ed and I work together every day. We're work colleagues, and, very recently, we've started working out together. We've become friends. The day you stopped by the beach house was the day I saw Steve Sloan at the courthouse. The day I learned you were dating Pam Logan. I understood you'd moved on. I was feeling hurt by that—I know it was irrational, but I was. I'd been sitting around waiting for you to call, and I found out you'd moved on. I was also profoundly hurt that you hadn't called, or stopped by, or even sent me an e-mail or text before that day. It was as if you'd ceased to exist.

"I figured, since I couldn't give you what you wanted, you'd found someone who could—and logically so. I certainly didn't blame you. I just felt left behind, and hurt, and stupid, and old, and lonely. That day was the first time . . . Ed has ever been there . . . It was the first time I let myself do anything other than rebuff his flirtation."

Kate looked into Bill's eyes and saw hurt and pain.

There was a long silence between them. Kate wanted to flee. She couldn't stand seeing the pain on his face.

Finally, Bill sighed deeply and said, "I'm sorry, Katie." He reached out and took her hand. "I'm sorry I didn't call you the day after you told me you wouldn't marry me. I wanted to call. Hell, I wanted to storm down to your house, take you to bed, and tell you that you had to marry me, and I wouldn't let you out of bed until you said 'yes.' I wanted to call you every day, and I did come see you in court—you're amazing, by the way—but I didn't feel like I could reach out to you then."

Bill looked away as he struggled to keep his composure. "You seemed to have put me aside and moved on with *your* life, *your* career. It seemed to be what you wanted. I felt I was in the way. So, I did start dating. I probably should have talked to you about it before I did. I'm sure it was upsetting to learn about it as you did."

"Bill, you don't owe me an explanation—" Kate began.

"Yes, I do," he interrupted. "Look, we both screwed up. But, I know I miss you terribly and, now that I've tried to date other women, I miss you even more. I miss my friend, as well as my lover. And I can't help it that I want to be married, that I want you to be my wife. I don't think I'll ever stop wanting that."

Kate was unable to speak, and they sat holding hands for a long time.

Their salads came and when the waiter left, Kate said, "Any chance I can have a mulligan? A do-over? You owe me one you know." They both laughed as they recalled Bill's first request for a mulligan.

"Yep. But let's just be friends tonight. We were that first, and we know we can do that without getting in each other's way," Bill said rationally.

"And that right there, Bill Davis, is exactly why I really do love you," Kate laughed. "Yes, let's have dinner and talk about all the things we haven't been able to tell each other for the last three months."

Their moods brightened as they regaled one another with the news of their lives. Bill told Kate about the progress on the new Ferrari dealership in Palm Beach, and about his twins' adventures and misadventures at college. Kate told Bill about Suzy's latest disaster, Terry and Suzy hooking up, and Beth and Melissa's wedding plans.

Toward the end of their evening, over the last glass of wine, Bill dropped a significant piece of news.

"Kate, I'm thinking of taking a trip in the *Leona,*" he said, referring to his 76-foot Monte Carlo yacht named after his late wife. "Actually, I've been thinking about doing this for years . . . island hopping through the Caribbean for a couple of months. I've had the trip completely charted for the last two years. Before she was diagnosed with cancer, Leona and I talked about making this trip as soon the girls went off to college. After she got sick . . . and we both knew she probably wouldn't recover, we never talked about it again. I probably should have insisted that we just do it then. But now, I think maybe it's what I need to do." Bill's face reflected both the sadness of his recollection and the importance of his decision.

Kate was silent as she remembered their idyllic weekend in Bimini aboard the *Leona*.

"For a while, I'd hoped *we* could do the trip together, Katie. But, I've come to realize I need to do this trip on my own. Actually, I'll be taking Howie as my first mate. I don't know how much longer the old dude has, and he loves being on the boat."

Kate found that she was uncharacteristically speechless. She took Bill's hand in hers and pressed it to her lips.

"What a wonderful idea, Bill. It's perfect," was all she could choke out.

Bill requested the check, and Kate asked if they could at least split it.

"Absolutely not, Katie. You can buy me dinner next time—maybe when I get back from my trip, if 'Captain Protective' will still allow you to have dinner with an old friend," Bill said with a wry smile.

Kate opened her mouth to protest but decided to let it go. Who knew what would happen in the next several months?

As they walked outside, Kate handed her valet slip to the young man at the door. After an appreciative ogle, he ran off to retrieve her Mercedes. Bill reached down and unexpectedly wrapped his arms around Kate, pressing her hips to him as he firmly grasped her bottom. He bent down and kissed her sensuously and passionately enough to make her knees weak. The kiss twanged all of Kate's deepest feelings.

"Damn you, Bill Davis," Kate managed breathlessly when he finally let her up for air. "That was unfair," she gasped as she smiled and melted momentarily into his arms.

"No more unfair than you wearing this outfit to dinner and expecting me to keep my hands off," he said, running his hands up her sides, caressing the outer edge of her nearly naked breasts.

Expecting, but not necessarily hoping, Kate thought to herself.

She knew she had to leave him here because she had no other option, but it was not what she wanted; it was not even in the universe of what she wanted.

Chapter 11

"Do you swear or affirm to tell the truth, the whole truth, and nothing but the truth?" The court reporter held the Bible out for Johnny Sutton as he solemnly laid his hand on it and swore that he did, "so help me God."

The videographer was capturing the scene. Sutton looked like a "kindly little old man" straight out of central casting; lots of gray hair, stylishly combed to the side.

No comb-over here, Kate thought. *And, look at how his remarkably glasses-free blue eyes sparkled mischievously. He even looks like he's got his own teeth! I can understand why all the little old ladies at the Happily Ever After Retirement Village are lusting after him. And what a flirt!*

Johnny had asked Kate out to dinner five minutes after Terry Driver introduced them. When Kate remarked on the speed of his invitation, Johnny replied, "Well, at my age, young lady, you have to act fast. You just never know," and then he'd winked at her in a surprisingly lusty way.

I'd definitely go for him if I were 40 years older!

Marcy sat next to Kate, Ronald Gray and his paralegal sat across from them. Johnny Sutton sat at the head of the table, with the court reporter to his right, and the videographer stood at the other end of the table with his camera mounted on a tripod pointed directly at Mr. Sutton. Mr. Meardon, the insurance company attorney, sat two-thirds of the way down Kate's side of the table.

Kate quickly took Johnny through all of her normal deposition preamble regarding being under oath, telling the truth, listening to her questions carefully before answering, and asking her for clarifications if he didn't understand a question. Then she walked him through his educational and professional history before jumping into the heart of the reason for the deposition.

"Mr. Sutton, do you remember a man named Dr. Joseph Dugan?"

"I sure do, honey. What a great guy . . ." and with that, Johnny was off to the races. He volunteered nearly every detail Terry had learned when he'd first met the old man. Kate barely needed to say a word; she simply asked a few follow-up and clarification questions.

When Johnny reached the point in his story about Joe pulling out a photo of "his pretty little nurse wife," he turned to Marcy and said simply, "You're still just as pretty as you were in that picture, honey. You don't look like you've aged a day. You could tell Dr. Dugan loved you so much by the way he talked about you. He was so proud. He said you'd be a better doctor than he ever could be."

Marcy's breath caught, and she choked back a sob. Kate touched her arm gently as she handed her a tissue and asked if she needed a minute. Marcy shook her head no, but held the tissue to her mouth and stared down at the table.

"I'm sorry, sweetie. I don't mean to make you sad, but you should know how much he loved you," Johnny said, looking as if he wanted to put his arm around her himself.

"Objection!" Ronald Gray erupted.

"Really, Mr. Gray? What is the nature of your objection? There wasn't even a question, so it really can't be to the form of the question. And the information is exactly on point. Perhaps you just don't like what Mr. Sutton said, but that is hardly a basis for an objection," Kate said, smiling broadly.

"Well, then, move to strike!" Gray shouted.

"Duly noted, Mr. Gray. We'll let the judge sort it out. Don't worry about the interruption, Mr. Sutton, it's just lawyer talk. Let me redirect you to your testimony . . ." Kate started to ask another follow-up question, but Sutton interrupted her.

"Thanks, but I don't need to be redirected. I know exactly where I was. Dr. Dugan was applying for the policy, and we were discussing his reason for taking it out in the first place."

"Objection! Mr. Sutton couldn't possibly know what Dr. Dugan was thinking. That's pure supposition. Move to strike again!" Gray bellowed indignantly.

"Well, I'll tell you what, sonny. How about I just tell you what Dr. Dugan said, and what he wrote down on the policy application."

Johnny glared at Ron Gray as he leaned forward in his chair and directed his response specifically to Gray.

"Dr. Dugan said, 'My wife has worked hard to put me through medical school, and we have a deal: she'd worked while I went to med school, and then I'd work to put her through med school. I want this policy so she gets to go back to med school no matter what happens to me.'"

Johnny Sutton continued to glare at Ronald Gray daring him to object again.

"Because of the size of the policy," Johnny continued, "I asked him to be specific on the application about the reason he was taking it out. If you have the application somewhere you'll see what I'm talking about."

With that, Johnny sat back in his chair again looking very self-satisfied.

"As it happens, I do have a copy of the application and a few other documents from Upton's records. I'll show them to you now and ask you if you can tell us what they are." Kate was having fun. Johnny's testimony couldn't be going better if it had been scripted.

She directed him to carefully review each of the three documents she handed him, and then she asked him to explain each one, beginning with the policy application.

Johnny slowly looked through the application, and when he got to the last page, he pointed to the line that responds to the question, "*Why are you requesting this insurance coverage?*"

"See right there, sonny boy, just like I remembered it." Johnny looked straight at Ronald Gray who was now beet red.

"See, Dr. Dugan wrote, 'This policy will ensure that, no matter what happens to me, my wife, Marcy Anne Simpson Dugan, will be able to go back to medical school. She deserves this.' Dr. Dugan was a good man, and he loved his Marcy."

Marcy dissolved into tears and excused herself from the room.

Kate pressed on.

"Thank you, Mr. Sutton. Can you identify the next document?" she asked as she pushed the policy toward Johnny.

"I sure can. That's a copy of the policy we issued Dr. Dugan. I delivered the original to him personally. I asked him if he wanted a copy for his wife, and he said that wouldn't be necessary. He had taken Marcy out to dinner to tell her about the policy after he applied for it, and she told him she didn't want to talk about it . . . She said something like, 'You can't die, it's not in our master plan.'"

Next, Kate slid the premium payment records in front of Johnny and asked him to explain what they were.

"Well, this is the record that Upton keeps on annual premiums. See here," he pointed at the document, "Dr. Dugan renewed every year. When I was servicing the account, about two weeks before the premium was due, I'd go out to his office and ask him if he wanted to renew the policy. I also talked to him about the death benefit amount, and beneficiary, and all that, to make sure he didn't have any changes. Since he was the owner of the policy, he could have cancelled it at any time or changed the beneficiary. I sort of expected one of those years he might say they had a baby who he wanted to add as a beneficiary. But he never wanted to change anything."

"Objection! Again, Mr. Sutton couldn't possibly know what was in Dr. Dugan's mind," Gray interrupted again, but he was looking more and more dejected with each objection.

Johnny again sat forward in his chair, and this time pointed an accusing finger at Ronald Gray.

"You're right again, sonny. So, I'll tell you what I said and what Dr. Dugan did. I said, 'Dr. Dugan, do you want to change anything in this policy? You can reduce or increase the amount of the death benefit, change or add a beneficiary, or even cancel the policy if you want.' And every year Dr. Dugan said, 'No, Johnny. I want it to stay just the way it is.' And then he'd take this big business-style checkbook out of the bottom drawer of his desk, and he'd write a check for the premium."

Johnny again sat back in his chair and turned to Kate.

"Any other questions, young lady?"

"Mr. Sutton, thank you. I think you've answered all my questions. I'll turn the questioning over to Mr. Gray." Kate turned her gaze on Gray and sat back in her chair, grinning like the Cheshire cat.

"Thank you, Kate. I only have a few questions, Mr. Sutton. I don't want to wear you out."

"Don't you worry about wearing me out, sonny. I could do this all day," Johnny replied.

"Fine. Let me ask you how many times you've met with Kate, Ms. Muldoon, before today?"

"I never met her before this morning, and for that I am truly sorry. She certainly brightens up a room," Johnny said as he turned to Kate and winked.

"So, it's your testimony that you never met with Ms. Muldoon to go over the questions she was going to ask you, or what you remembered about Dr. Dugan."

"Nope. Like I said, sonny, I never saw her before today," Johnny repeated.

"Tell me, how many policies did you write while you were employed by Upton?" Gray asked.

"Wow, I never really thought about that. Let me think a minute and I can give you an estimate. Let's see, I worked for Upton 12 years, and on average I probably wrote . . . maybe 25 to 30 policies each year. But only about 10 or 12 of those were life insurance policies. So, probably between 120 and 144 life insurance policies would be a good estimate, but you can ask Upton. I know they keep records on everything on those computers," Johnny responded succinctly.

"Thank you. How is it, Mr. Sutton, that you remember this one policy out of those 144 policies? And remember it so clearly?" Gray asked, violating the first rule of cross-examination: never ask a question on cross that you don't know the answer to or can't prove to be what you want the witness to say. Gray had no idea what Johnny would say, and yet, he asked the question anyway. Johnny obliged Gray by proving the reason for the rule.

"Well, you see, sonny, it's this way. I had never before sold a policy with a face value of even a million dollars, and I never again sold one for four million. It was the highlight of my professional career. My wife and I, God rest her soul, celebrated the sale by taking our first trip to Europe. It was a cruise, and every night at dinner, we toasted Dr. Dugan, and I told everyone sitting at our table the story of how Dr. Dugan was going to put his wife through medical school even if he died before she was finished." Johnny leaned back in his chair again and smiled directly into the camera.

Kate could scarcely keep from laughing. She had to look down at her notes as she tried to wipe the enormous smile from her lips.

"Mr. Sutton, how many years were you the agent on this account?" Gray asked trying to recover something from this deposition.

"I was Dr. Dugan's agent for six years. The last year, I told him I'd be retiring soon and he'd have a new agent. Dr. Dugan took me to lunch that year. He asked me an odd question at lunch. He asked if Marcy was no longer his wife whether that would prevent her from remaining the beneficiary as long as he kept the policy current."

"That's enough, Mr. Sutton. I didn't ask about that. You answered my question. I don't need to hear any other details."

Gray was in a panic now. He had no idea where Johnny was headed, but he knew he was not going to like it.

Kate arched one eyebrow as she looked at Gray. *Does he really think I won't ask about that on redirect?*

"Mr. Sutton," Gray said after a significant pause, "how old are you?"

"I am 83 years young, sir. And my memory is good enough to allow me to play two hands of duplicate bridge at the same time. I'm not bad at chess either, just in case you wanted to know. Stop by my place anytime you feel up for a game."

Johnny was in his element now and having fun at Gray's expense.

Gray scrambled again for composure, "What's the state of your health?"

"Pretty darn great. Especially since I had that last bypass surgery three years ago. My doctors say I could live to 100 and the ladies at Happily Ever After sure hope I do."

Johnny looked directly into the camera again and winked.

"I have no further questions," Gray said in defeat, and he started to put away his notes.

"I have a few questions on redirect, Mr. Gray."

She could see Gray's chest fall even further as he looked down at the table and took out his notepad again.

"Mr. Sutton," Kate turned toward Johnny again, "you started to say something about a question Dr. Dugan asked you regarding what would happen if Marcy was no longer his wife."

"Objection to this line of question. Move to strike," Gray said halfheartedly.

"Would you care to elaborate on your objection, Mr. Gray?" Kate asked, knowing Gray had no legitimate basis for his objection.

When Gray said nothing, Kate continued.

"Before you answer that, Mr. Sutton, let me ask you something else. Mr. Gray asked you if we have ever met before today, and you answered we have not, is that correct?"

"Yep, and that's my loss," Johnny said smiling broadly now.

"Thank you, Mr. Sutton," Kate smiled at Johnny, and then continued. "Mr. Gray did not ask you whether you've ever talked to someone else from my office before today, however, did he?"

"Nope, he should have, but he didn't," Johnny smiled.

"Have you met anyone from my office before today, Mr. Sutton?" Kate asked.

"I sure have. I met Mr. Driver, the man sitting there at the back of the room. He came out to my place a week ago," Johnny replied.

"Can you tell us about that meeting?" Kate probed.

"Well, let's see. He came out during our weekly duplicate bridge tournament. He'd called earlier in the morning to see if I would be available to meet with him. He said he had some questions about an insurance policy I had written. I told him to come ahead. When he got there, we were just finishing up the tournament, and he said he'd just watch until it ended—I won, by the way; I had great cards that day." Johnny flashed his winning smile.

"I asked him what policy he was interested in and when he told me it was Dr. Dugan, I told him pretty much everything I just finished telling you and Mr. Gray, except I didn't tell him about Dr. Dugan's question the last time we met. He didn't ask, and frankly, I didn't think to mention it."

"Mr. Sutton, can you remember any questions Mr. Driver asked you?" Kate asked.

"Well, the poor guy didn't get much of a chance to ask me anything. I just started telling him about Dr. Dugan and what I remembered about the day he bought that policy and our meetings at premium time. I've been told I'm a bit of a talker, Ms. Muldoon, and I guess I am. It was nice having an audience that day, and especially nice to have one with good hearing. We don't have too many of those at Happily Ever After!" Johnny laughed.

"Did Mr. Driver tell you how to answer any of the questions I would be asking you at your deposition?" Kate inquired.

"Nope, he didn't even tell me about you, or that I'd be giving a deposition. Besides, Ms. Muldoon, nobody puts words in Johnny Sutton's mouth," Johnny nodded toward Gray and said again, "nobody."

"One last question, Mr. Sutton," Kate paused, and then said, "can you tell us about Dr. Dugan's question and what you told him regarding Marcy remaining the beneficiary if she was no longer his wife?"

"Objection. Move to strike. Calls for a legal conclusion," Gray said weakly.

"Not really, Ron. I'm simply asking Mr. Sutton what he told Dr. Dugan. You can answer the question, sir."

Kate looked at Sutton and waited.

"I told him that the policy named Marcy specifically, and it shouldn't be a problem, but if he was worried, he could always make a change to the beneficiary. I even told him, since he had the original policy, all he needed to do was scratch out the words 'my wife' and leave her name in place and initial the scratched out part. Or, he could make a written request to the insurance company to change the way the beneficiary is worded."

After a moment, Johnny added, "Do you have the original policy, Ms. Muldoon?" he asked innocently.

"Not yet, Mr. Sutton, not yet," Kate responded. "I have no further questions," she said and closed her notepad.

Chapter 12

As Kate drove back to the office following Johnny Sutton's deposition, her cell phone rang. The caller ID announced it was Bill Davis. Kate's heart immediately began to ache as she hit the answer button on the steering wheel.

"Hey, this is a treat—getting to talk to you two days in a row. Better be careful, I could get used to this," Kate said trying to sound lighthearted to mask her true feelings. "Not sure I thanked you enough for the great dinner last night. The restaurant was amazing."

"Hey, yourself. Actually, I'm calling about last night. I haven't been able to think about much else. It was wonderful talking to you."

"Yeah, and the good night kiss wasn't too bad either," Kate said trying to keep it light, which was the opposite of how she really felt.

"Well, you had that coming. Trust me, I wanted a lot more, but that will have to keep me for a while."

Bill paused, and Kate said nothing, because she was struggling not to tell him how much she wanted him.

"Katie, being with you last night just reinforced what I had already decided about trying to date other women. It's not the same. My feelings for you are just different . . . and more . . . Listen, I'm not great with words, but I want what we had . . . maybe what we still have? And I want it with you."

Kate remained silent as she pulled off the road and into a parking lot and put the car into "park." Her eyes were misting over, and she needed every bit of concentration to keep from crying.

"Katie, you still there?" Bill asked.

"Uh-huh," Kate murmured because she was unable to talk.

"Katie, I think we both need a bit more time to sort things out. Anyway, I know I do. And I'm hoping that you may not be as settled into this Ed thing as you think . . . I mean . . . I don't really know how you feel about Ed. But, you know what I want, and you've told me you can't be . . . my wife . . . and I respect that, Kate, I really do. I admire who you are, and I would never want you to think I wanted to change you. But, I'm 44, and I know who I am too. So, I need to figure out where I . . . go from here."

"Uh-huh," Kate said again as she choked back a sob.

"Kate, are you OK?" Bill asked finally realizing his usually talkative friend was not speaking.

"No, Bill. I'm not OK," she managed to get out.

"Listen, I didn't call to make you feel bad. I had a great time last night. I want to have that, and more, and I want to have it with you. But, I don't know if that's possible for me. And I don't know if that is something you want under the current circumstances . . . you know, with Ed in the picture and all . . ."

Kate's forehead was on the steering wheel, and she was sobbing softly. Regrets were running wild through her head.

"So, Kate, I've decided that I need to take this Caribbean cruise I told you about. I need some time alone on the boat, time to sort out this mess from my perspective. Maybe when I come back in a month or so we can see where we are and . . . well, just see where we are." Bill's voice cracked a bit.

"Oh God, Bill, what have I done? Why can't I just be a normal person? Why can't I just be what you want?" Kate was in full sob now, and she didn't care if he knew it.

I've fucked up the best thing that ever happened to me. I'm hopeless, Kate thought as she fumbled for the tissues she kept in the glove box of the car.

"Katie, I'm sorry I made you cry. I wanted to do this in person, but I didn't really trust myself. You didn't do anything wrong. I understand why you reacted to the news of my dating. I was stupid to not tell you, but, Kate, I kept thinking I could get over you, and then I'd tell you when I was. But none of those women were you; they just made me miss you more. I'm not over you, I'm not sure I can get over you. I have to figure this out, so I don't hurt you anymore."

"Bill, stop. What we had was different for me too. It was a whole different quality than anything I've ever felt. But, I'm me . . . I'm not Leona . . . and I respect what you want too," Kate said struggling to regain her composure.

"Kate, I called to tell you I'm leaving tomorrow morning at first light on the *Leona*. I'll probably be gone at least a month. I'm going to do a lot of thinking. I'd like to know I can call you when I get back. Would that be OK?" he asked.

"It's a date," Kate said. "Please be careful. It worries me that you'll be out there by yourself."

"Don't be. I'm a pretty good captain, and if I need to hire a mate to make any lengthy crossings, there are always guys available for hire at the marinas."

After a pause Bill continued. "Listen, I probably won't call, e-mail, or text. That's all too much like 'real time.' It would be like a crutch for me and wouldn't give *you* the distance and time *you* need. But I'd like to drop you a postcard from time to time. Just to let you know . . . I didn't cease to exist. Would that be OK?"

"I'd love that. Please be careful. And, Bill, know this, whatever else comes out of this, I want to thank you for helping me see what love is. I love you, Bill Davis," Kate whispered into the air.

"And I love you, Katie Muldoon," he whispered back.

They hung up at the same time.

Kate arrived back at the office two hours later than she'd planned. She refused to go the office with red-rimmed eyes and a stuffy nose. So, she went home, walked the dogs, took a quick shower, and changed into jeans and a casual blouse, something she'd rarely wear to the office. But it was Friday, and most of the office wore jeans *every* Friday. Besides, after her phone call with Bill, what she wore to the office seemed insignificant.

When she finished reviewing her notes from Johnny Sutton's

deposition, Kate called Ron Gray. To Kate, the deposition testimony, along with the documents from the insurance company, was all she really needed to make her case at the interpleader hearing. But, she still wanted the documents and information she had requested from Joe Dugan's estate.

"Gray & Ferguson, how may I help you?" the English-sounding receptionist inquired.

Why do people think a receptionist with a British accent is so great? Kate wondered as she gave her name and asked for Ronald Gray.

"Calling to gloat?" Gray asked gruffly as he answered the phone.

"Hardly, but you have to admit, if there was ever any question about Joe Dugan's intent regarding the purpose of that insurance policy, I think today's deposition cleared that right up."

Kate loved the fact that Gray was feeling the pinch now. He'd been such a prick to Marcy, she wanted him to be feeling the pressure.

"What I want to know is when we can expect the documents and information we requested the day after the interpleader complaint was filed. As soon as I have your responses, I'll be ready to set the hearing date. There's no sense dragging this out."

"I don't agree. Now that there are questions about the circumstances surrounding Dr. Dugan's death, I think we need to proceed very cautiously. After all, Ms. Simpson would not be legally allowed to profit from Dr. Dugan's death if she turns out to be the one who slipped him the fatal dose of digitalis. And, having $4 million will make her a huge flight risk," Gray responded smugly.

"You can't be serious, Ron! Marcy had no idea that policy was still in place or that she was still the beneficiary—what ex-wife would? And how exactly do you think she managed to slip Dr. Dugan a fatal dose of digitalis when she had not seen him in over ten years and was working miles from his office where the EMTs found him the night of his death?" Kate asked as her dislike of Ronald Gray tripled.

"That's for the police and prosecutor to find out. Not me. We won't be agreeing to a hearing any time soon. I don't care what that old man said. Joe Dugan couldn't possibly have meant for his ex-wife to have $4 million, his kids only receive three million, and his wife of

16 years get *nothing*. No judge will believe that," Gray said, tipping his hand regarding the other insurance provisions Joe Dugan had in place at the time of his death.

"Oh, I don't know about that," Kate said probing further. "It seems to me he wanted to cut the current Mrs. Dugan out altogether. Ever think of that? I wonder why that might be. I really can't wait now to get the documents and information I requested. The Dugan estate is getting more and more interesting by the minute." Kate was totally fed up with Gray's pompous style.

"Well, you'll get the information exactly when it's due and not a moment before. Now, if your client wants to finally be reasonable, I may be able to convince Mrs. Dugan to put more money on the table. Say $100,000, if Ms. Simpson takes that money now and drops her claims to the insurance proceeds. Plus, I think Mrs. Dugan's father could be persuaded to stop pressuring the prosecutor and chief of police to arrest Miss Simpson, and maybe even encourage them to entirely drop their investigation of her."

Gray is revealing himself to be a true piece of shit, Kate thought.

"My, my, Mr. Gray. If I didn't know better, I'd say that you're threatening criminal proceedings in order to get your way in this civil action. And you're implicating our dear old philandering Senator Ferguson in your threat. I guess he might not care about such things any more, but you might want to check the ethics rules. Last time I read them, making such a threat was deemed a violation." Kate paused to let Gray absorb her words but then hurried on.

"As you should know, I have an ethical obligation to pass along your offer to my client. I'll do that and will let you know if she's interested. Have a good weekend, Mr. Gray." Kate hung up without waiting for a response.

People like him are what gives lawyers a bad name, she steamed as she picked up the phone to call Marcy.

"Have you recovered from the depo, kiddo?" Kate asked when Marcy answered the phone.

"Yes, I think so, but that was rough. It's sort of nice to find out that Joe really did love me at one point. I just wish I knew why he kept that policy current or why he didn't change the beneficiary to Joan. None of this makes any sense, Kate." Marcy sounded exhausted.

"Well, it just got more bizarre, I'm afraid. Marcy, I called Ron Gray to find out when to expect the documents and information we requested over two weeks ago. He let slip that Joe had another insurance policy, one for three million naming his boys as the beneficiaries, but he did not have one in favor of Joan. For some reason, I think your ex-husband was trying to cut his current wife out of his estate as much as he could. I'll know more when I get the information from Gray, but in the meantime, Gray's not in a hurry to set the hearing on the interpleader." Kate waited while Marcy digested her news before going on.

"And, Marcy, Gray offered you $100,000 if you drop your claim to the insurance policy, but he also sort of threatened you. He said if you took the money he's now offering, he'd convince Joan and her dad to stop pressuring the cops and prosecutor to investigate you as a suspect in Joe's death."

Kate knew this was not news Marcy was prepared to hear. There was a lengthy pause on the line.

"Kate, are they seriously looking at me as a suspect in Joe's death? How can that be? I hadn't seen Joe in forever and, as God is my witness, I had no idea that insurance policy was still current—why would I even suspect that? Joe told me he didn't love me anymore. He had a new wife and family. I moved on because I thought he had. This is a nightmare. Is Gray trying to blackmail me? It sure feels that way to me." Marcy was getting angry. "Kate, I'd rather not receive one cent than let that bastard blackmail me. Maybe I should just walk away like I did the last time. I can't even imagine going through this legal fight—they think I'm a *murderer*? Holy shit!"

Marcy was fuming, but she was also starting to panic.

"Marcy, stop for a moment. I need to ask you some questions. First, I assume you have access to digitalis in the ER at Jackson Memorial, right?"

"Of course, it's one treatment for heart attack patients. But, it's under lock and key, like all other drugs, and access is highly regulated. There are records, both a written log next to the cabinet and an electronic log, that show who's been in the cabinet and when. But, Kate, I'm one of the four ER employees who has a key to the cabinet. One of us is on duty at all times."

Marcy calmed a little as she explained these facts to Kate.

"OK, next question: how can we prove where you were two weeks ago, the night Joe died, specifically from 7:00 p.m. to midnight?"

"Like I told you, I was at work in the ER. I'm always at work somewhere—thank God in this case. I took an extra shift for a friend so she could have a long weekend with her husband and kids. The hospital records will verify that," Marcy sounded reassured.

Kate thought for a moment, and then followed up.

"Here's the thing. I think Gray and our former Senator 'Philandering' Ferguson plan to make trouble for you, put pressure on you in an attempt to make you take their offer. I've been to see the chief of police and the state attorney to let them know I am representing you, and if they have any questions for you, they need to come through me. But, that only gives us a bit of a heads-up. We need to be completely ready to *prove* your innocence—contrary to what the law is supposed to be.

"The cops really should be looking for evidence of motive, means, and opportunity. Right now, they think they have motive: $4 million worth. So, we have to think of ways to prove you did not have the means or opportunity to slip Joe a fatal dose of digitalis. Your work records and the medicine safe records will help. But, they could suspect you of hiring someone to dose Joe. So, I need to get your bank and phone records, and have a forensic review done on your computer, iPad, and phone . . . all of your electronics."

"Kate, you can have the damn things and do whatever you want. I didn't kill Joe, and I didn't hire anyone to kill him, and I'll be damned if I'm going to let Ronald Gray and 'Philandering' Fergie push me around again. Kate, I want to fight this." Marcy had worked up a good mad now.

"OK, I'll fight with you, but you probably already know this—they're going to fight dirty, and it could get really ugly," Kate warned.

"As far as I'm concerned, they're already fighting dirty, and it's way past ugly. That all started 16 years ago!" Marcy replied.

Shortly after 5:30, Ed knocked on Kate's office door; she waved him in.

"You've been behind closed doors all afternoon, but I wanted to see how Johnny Sutton's depo went, if you have a minute."

"Sure, no problem, come on in. I missed you at yoga this morning, dude."

"Yeah, about that, I thought I'd take this week off—that shit nearly killed me last week. But, I'll give it another shot next week, I promise. You know you could ensure that I make it to class on Friday morning if you just happen to spend Thursday night with me."

"Not today, please, Ed. I'm not up to it." Kate looked down at the top of her desk and worked at staying composed.

"The depo went great, Ed. But, Gray and Ferguson have taken off the gloves. Things are going to get really ugly before they get better," Kate said.

She related the statements made by Sutton during the deposition, and Gray's comment during their brief phone call.

"So, Marcy thinks she's ready to fight, but I don't think she has a clue just how awful things are going to get for her. Next week should be pretty telling." Kate looked at Ed's face; he seemed a bit stressed.

"You OK?" she asked.

"I'd like to ask you about some other stuff, but it's against the rules to do it here. Can we grab a drink or dinner this evening?" Ed's eyes seemed to plead for attention.

Kate didn't feel up to any more emotional turmoil. She considered telling him no but decided that wouldn't be fair, plus, she suddenly realized she hadn't eaten all day.

"How about a big grouper sandwich and a beer?" Kate surprised him by asking.

"Wow, I didn't think those words were even in your vocabulary!" he laughed. "Great idea. Where shall we go?"

"There's a wonderful little bar and bistro in my neighborhood, it's called 'The Shack,'" Kate said.

"I've seen it; I know right where it is," Ed grinned. "So you live around there? Are you in one of those old Miami-style, single-family homes that miraculously didn't get torn down?" he inquired, still hoping to figure out where Kate lived and for an invitation to Casa Muldoon.

"Yep, just around the corner."

Kate knew what he was up to, but she was too tired to care.

"Look, this has been an emotional butt-kicking day. I'm ready to call it and start my weekend early. Want me to tell your Boss Lady to let you get out of here? We can grab a nice corner booth at The Shack and watch the comings and goings on a hot Miami Friday?"

"I sure would appreciate that, ma'am. I've been working pretty hard this week," he laughed. "And if you're a good girl, I'll tell you the latest Bobbi Jo Tales from the Wild Side."

"It's a deal. I'll meet you there," Kate said as she reached for her bag. "You headed home to change? Needless to say, I'm good to go as is."

"No kidding. I almost didn't recognize you. I don't think I've ever seen you in jeans, and certainly not in here. You rock those Sevens, by the way—totally hot!" Ed smiled seductively.

"Enough rule breaking; stop talking. I'll see you at The Shack." Kate shut off her computer and headed for the door. For a change, she was leaving her work behind. Of course, she knew she'd be back in the office early the next morning—right after watching her ship sail.

When Kate arrived at The Shack, Ed was already in a booth toward the back of the restaurant with a great view of the action. She couldn't help but notice two young women sitting on bar stools turned in Ed's direction. They were tossing their hair and crossing and uncrossing their legs. Ed had noticed too. He tossed them an occasional smile as Kate stood watching.

What am I doing with him? I should be shot! Kate's guilt and self-recriminations started chasing across her mind again. She inhaled deeply and walked back toward Ed.

When he saw her coming, his smile widened, and he rose to greet her with a kiss that she wasn't expecting.

"Well, I hope there isn't anyone in here who knows us!" Kate said as she slipped into the booth.

Ed followed her in, sliding very close and placing his arm behind her on the back of the booth.

Maybe he is Captain Protective, Kate thought, and then instantly hated herself for everything.

"I just wanted to discourage the two barflies over there. They've been inviting me to join them with their not-so-subtle signals for the last ten minutes. I see you went home and changed shoes before heading here. I like them a bunch!" Ed said, as he looked down at her four-inch wedge Salvatore Ferragamo sandals with ankle straps.

"Yep, my house is just around the corner, and these are one of the few pairs of shoes I have that both look hot and I can actually walk in. Thanks for noticing."

Kate glanced toward the bar and received eye daggers from the barflies. She laughed.

"Man, you broke their hearts big time—don't let me go to the girls' room unless we can see both of them. I might get bumped off in there!"

Ed laughed as he signaled the waitress who had apparently also enjoyed her view of their booth much more before Kate arrived.

"Amstel Light for me and a grouper sandwich with fries," Kate said.

"Fries? I've never heard that word come out of your mouth before," Ed said as he allowed his arm to drop down off the back of the booth and around Kate.

"I'll have the same," he said to the waitress, who shot Kate an evil glance as she walked off.

"Wow, tough room to play if you're sitting with a hunky Marine type," Kate said, easily slipping into a slightly more flirtatious mood against her better judgment. It felt good, and she was so tired of emotional turmoil. For some reason, she needed to feel attractive and wanted, just the way she was, no alterations needed.

Mike, the owner of The Shack, saw Kate and waved as he started to walk over.

"Mike Prescott, meet Ed Evert," Kate introduced the men. "Mike is the owner of this fine establishment, and his food is one of the reasons I can't give up running or hot yoga."

Mike reached over and shook Ed's hand as he said, "So, all this time I've been worrying about this beautiful young woman sitting alone at my bar. I now know the reason. Great to meet you, Ed. You're one lucky dude. Kate here is oblivious to the come-ons she gets from my male customers. Nice to know she's not spending her nights alone."

Mike stood back and grinned at Kate.

"You're full of shit, Mike, and that's why you're the perfect bar owner!" Kate said laughing.

"Enjoy yourselves, kids. You two just increased the ambiance of my restaurant 100 percent. Your next round of beers is on the house."

"Like I really need two beers!" Kate laughed again and saluted Mike as he walked back to the bar.

"I'll help you out, if it comes to that. Never let a free beer go to waste," Ed said.

Kate could tell he was in his element.

"Do you want to hear about Bobbi Jo's latest adventures?" he asked with a twinkle in his eyes.

"Regale me," Kate replied as she sat back into his arm and exhaled deeply, relaxing for the first time all day.

"Well, it's like this . . . What do you think happens when a new single guy is hired to work on a line with a pretty, and as far as he can tell, unattached woman?" Ed began.

"Great. This is new. Tell all," she grinned.

"So, the new guy, James Bell, thinks Bobbi Jo is hot. Plus, he discovers she's really good at her job. She's been assigned as his mentor for the first month; that pushes them together on the job quite a bit. None of the other dudes on the line tell James anything about Bobbi Jo's transition. According to them, they thought they weren't supposed to. Plus, I think they were enjoying watching James and Bobbi Jo flirt. James decides, after a week on the job, to ask Bobbi Jo out for a beer after work, just to say thanks for all her help getting him up to speed."

Ed paused to take a sip of the newly delivered beer before continuing.

"And as often happens, one beer led to another, and then another, and finally, they decided to do shots. Always a good idea when taking a female coworker out for drinks, right?" Ed said and winked at Kate.

"Several hours later, James slides his arm around Bobbi Jo, and they start kissing and making out. James thinks Bobbi Jo is especially interested, so after a little while, he decides to try for third base, and he slides his hand up Bobbi Jo's skirt—and what do you think he finds?"

"Oh Jesus. This is not going to end well, is it?" Kate said laughing.

"Nope, it certainly didn't," Ed grinned and took another sip of beer.

"So, James pulls his hand back really fast and looks at Bobbi Jo who is, in his words, 'grinning like she just won the fucking lottery.' James does the only thing he could think of; he punches Bobbi Jo in the mouth. Bobbi Jo decides to let James know that she can still punch like a man, and she punches him in the nose."

Ed took another drink and thanked the waitress who just delivered their grouper sandwiches.

"The bartender takes exception to a man striking a woman and comes over and accosts James. James starts shouting, 'She's no woman' and Bobbi Jo starts screaming 'Yes, I am.' Then James shouts, 'Well, how come you've got a dick, and for fuck's sake, it's bigger than mine.' At that point, the whole bar joined in, and there was a bar fight to end all bar fights. James, Bobbi Jo, and several other customers end up being hauled off to jail."

Ed and Kate howled with laughter and both took big bites of their sandwiches and ate a few fries.

"Josie and Kathy called me this morning while you were at Sutton's deposition and related the whole tale, between giggling fits, that is. Apparently, Bobbi Jo and James both called in sick the day after their arrests. When they came into work today, they looked, not surprisingly, like they'd been in a bar fight."

Ed took another bite of his sandwich, and then a big drink of his beer.

"But the fun isn't over yet. James filed a race discrimination claim with the union and HR. His position is that the other guys on the line didn't tell him about Bobbi Jo because he's African American. Not to be outdone, Bobbi Jo filed a sex discrimination claim with the union and HR, saying James sexually assaulted her and the company should have known he was likely to sexually attack her, though she doesn't say why. Her position is the company never should have placed him on the same production line as a woman, but again, she doesn't explain that either. Her attorney has followed up. He says he expects the company to take disciplinary measures and compensate his client. It's a fucking mess," Ed concluded, smiling broadly at Kate, "our kind of mess. It should keep me busy for a while."

Two more beers showed up at their table, compliments of Mike Prescott. Ed had finished his sandwich and first beer and most of his fries. Kate was halfway through her sandwich and about a quarter of her fries. She slid her plate toward Ed and asked if wanted to finish her meal. He dug in.

Kate gave Ed an overview of their next discovery steps after Sutton's deposition, and then sipped her beer, nibbled on an occasional fry, and looked out at the bar.

When he finished Kate's meal and half of his second beer, Ed looked up at Kate. She was deep in thought. He reached over and pulled her closer and kissed her. Kate did not respond.

"You're deep in thought, Ms. Muldoon. What's up?"

"Ed, please don't do that again. Not here. We don't know who could be watching."

Ed pulled his arms away from Kate and looked at her, his eyes intense.

"Kate, are you going to tell me about your dinner last night? Remember, you told me you would let me know if things changed—I get a heads-up and a fighting chance. Remember? So what happened? Did he tell you he's engaged to Pam Logan, or was I right and he's still got it bad for you?"

Kate sighed deeply. *What the fuck are you up to here, Kate? You know you don't feel the same way about Ed as you do about Bill.*

"Ed, Bill is leaving town. He's taking his yacht to the Caribbean and island hopping for at least a month. It's a trip he's wanted to take since before his wife died. They had hoped to take the trip together when their girls went off to college. He said he needs time to think about what he wants. He's been dating and . . . I guess he didn't find what he's looking for. So, for the next month or so, Bill is not a factor—at least not physically. I'm not going to lie and tell you I'm over him. But, Ed, we're still the same two people, and those two people want different things out of life. I'm not going to marry him, and he's not going to give up wanting to be married."

"Does he know we're involved? Sexually, I mean. I don't know how he could have missed it."

"Is that what we are, Ed? I thought we just had 'no-strings-attached, rebound sex.' And, yes, he knows, and, yes, it hurt him. Now, we aren't going to discuss Bill Davis anymore."

Kate looked into Ed's eyes trying to read what she saw there. He opened his mouth to say something.

"Please, no more," she sighed. She was emotionally exhausted.

"OK. No more on that topic."

Ed took Kate's hand again and raised it to his lips. "You look beat. Shall we get the check? I can make you forget how tired you feel, if you'll let me."

"Not tonight, Ed." Kate shook her head.

I'm not up to 'no-strings-attached' sex tonight, she thought. *Maybe I never was.*

Chapter 13

At 4:15 a.m., Kate's eyes snapped open. For some reason, she felt certain Bill would be leaving the Miami marina within a few hours—she didn't know what Bill had meant by "first light", but it sounded early. A plan had been brewing in her brain since her telephone call with Bill yesterday. She'd decided she needed to watch him sail off on his Caribbean adventure. She didn't want him to know she was watching, but she wanted to be there as the *Leona* sailed. The marina was a little less than four miles away from her house, and she figured she could run there and back and count it as her long run for the weekend.

As quietly as she could, she dressed in her running clothes, but there was no fooling Sadie and Phoebe. The minute she reached for her running shoes, they ran down the stairs to stand excitedly by the front door, ready for a run.

"Not today, girls. Sorry, this run's too long for you, and you would make me too conspicuous. Come on, let's go out to the backyard, you can romp around there while I'm gone."

Kate bent down and rubbed both dogs behind their ears. They gazed up at her with sad eyes not understanding why they weren't going with her, but knowing they were being left behind—and milking her guilt about leaving them. She succumbed and gave them an extra helping of kibbles in their bowls on the back porch.

Kate's pace to the marina was a good one, and she was there a little after 5:30. Sunrise was supposed to be at 6:15, and she decided she had a few minutes to waste. She could see the *Leona* still in her usual slip; the lights were on in the main cabin. Kate stood watching the boat's details come into focus as the sky grew lighter, but soon, the smell of coffee wafted to her from The Angler, now serving breakfast and bound to be packed with fishermen, day cruise captains, and the occasional holdover drunk from last night.

Kate decided she needed coffee.

Inside The Angler, it smelled of stale beer, grease, coffee, and bacon. It was dark and the few lights that were on only made the room seem darker. Most of the tables were full, but the customers were all pretty quiet—perhaps out of courtesy for those who were hung-over, which would be at least half of them. Kate's appearance drew stares from every table. She walked to the bar and ordered a coffee to go, and paid for it with her emergency twenty that she always carried in the ID fob on her running shoes. A couple of the customers in the booths in the back wolf whistled when she propped her foot up on the bar stool to retrieve the twenty. A couple of others asked if she wanted to go fishing, or on a day cruise because they had the boat that "could get it done."

Kate decided this wasn't the time or place to discuss sex harassment or take a stand for woman's liberation. She just smiled sweetly, picked up her change and coffee, and headed out the door.

In the parking lot, Kate noted the sky had grown pink in the east, and she knew the sun was about 20 minutes from rising. The *Leona* was still in her slip, but now lights were on in the main cabin and the fly bridge. She was pretty sure she saw the silhouette of a man on the bridge. Diesel fumes were rising from the engine; Bill was warming up his yacht.

In the far corner of The Angler parking lot, a dome light came on in an older model, dark Mercedes. The back passenger door opened and a bleary-eyed, scruffy-looking man with dark hair and about a four-day beard stumbled out of his car. Kate watched as he shuffled toward The Angler, pulling bills and coins out of his jeans pockets.

Probably seeing if he has enough for breakfast, Kate decided. *At least he had the good sense to sleep it off in his car rather than try to drive home in what was no doubt a seriously fucked-up condition last night*, she thought as she watched the man stumble past her.

Kate noted that under the scruff, he was reasonably good looking, about six foot one or two, and in reasonably good physical condition. The guy nodded at her and smiled. She felt an inexplicable chill as she looked into his eyes.

Shit, there's more there than meets the eye. I wonder what his story is? Kate shuddered and decided it was time to move on. She didn't care for The Angler's clientele in the morning any better than at night.

Kate walked out on the pier to the building that housed the harbor master's office. She leaned up against it looking out at the *Leona* and drinking her coffee. She spied Howie running up and down the deck, and then charging down the gangplank, followed by Bill. They both headed down the dock toward the office.

Crap! I should have remembered he would check in with the harbor master before taking off, Kate realized as she turned and looked for a place to hide, stepping behind the office building. *Trapped like the rat I am*, she thought, pretty sure Bill hadn't seen her.

But Kate hadn't counted on the basset hound's nose, and no sooner had she assured herself that she was safe in her hiding spot than Howie kicked up a terrible howling. He came charging around the corner of the office building and jumped up on Kate, pushing her into the trash can she'd been standing next to, knocking over both Kate and the trash can, and spilling her coffee down the front of her T-shirt.

"I love you too, Howie, but seriously, you're going to blow my cover," Kate whispered to him and tried to urge him back to Bill without saying anything more.

"HOWIE, get back here!" Bill called out. "What the heck are you doing back there? You'd better not be getting into the garbage. I don't have time to give you a ba—"

Bill stopped midsentence as he came around the corner and saw Kate sprawled out on the dock amid the trash that had tumbled out of the can, with his large, friendly basset hound licking her face. It took him a minute to make sense of what he was seeing, and then he started laughing so hard it doubled him over.

Kate was mortified but could still see the humor of the situation and started giggling too.

"Please tell me you've come to stow away on my trip!" Bill said as he extended Kate a hand up and pulled Howie off her with the other.

"Not exactly. I thought I'd come and *quietly* watch you leave this morning. I guess that worked out about as well as everything else I've tried to do lately."

Kate brushed off her butt and started picking up the trash and righting the trash can.

"I'm sorry, Bill. I didn't want to intrude. I didn't want you to know I was even here. I fucked this up splendidly." Kate continued berating herself and apologizing to Bill as Howie started chasing around madly with his nose to the ground, clearly looking for Sadie and Phoebe.

Bill gently took Kate's arm and pulled her into his arms and kissed her gently again and again.

"This is why I *called* you yesterday. I knew I couldn't see you again and keep it under control. Jesus, Katie, please come with me. We can run away from here—just leave everything behind us . . ." He kissed her again.

Kate rested her head on Bill's chest and melted into his arms. It felt so good, so natural.

Why am I struggling not to give in? Kate wondered. *Because you're afraid you'll lose who you are*, she answered her own question.

Kate looked up at Bill. He wiped the tears from her eyes.

"OK, sorry." He kissed her cheeks where her tears had been. "I know you can't come with me—at least not now, not like this. But, I'm glad you came to see me off. Come on, no need to lurk in the shadows anymore," he said, taking her hand, leading her around to the front of the office building. "The jig is up. You should have known Howie would find you—what part of basset *hound* did you forget?" he laughed.

"I forgot you always check in with the harbor master right before taking off. I would never have come out on the dock if I'd remembered that," Kate said, sniffing back the last of her tears.

"Well, come out to the slip and wave good-bye properly," Bill said, handing the confused-looking harbor master a handful of papers, shaking his hand, and telling him he'd call a couple of weeks before he returned.

Together, Kate and Bill walked down the dock toward the *Leona* holding hands with Howie trotting along beside them. When they reached the gangplank, Howie continued up to the ship's deck and turned to bark at Bill.

Bill pulled Kate in for one last kiss. "Last chance to stow away—I'll close my eyes and you can scamper up the gangplank," he said with a smile and a kiss.

"Bill, I'm sorry to complicate things for you this morning . . . Please be careful. I'll help you cast off—I'll get the lines . . . Bill, I love you."

"I love you too. I'll be back. Maybe we can figure out a way . . . anyway, I love you. Take care of yourself . . . but I know you will . . . you're the most independent person I've ever met." He kissed the top of her head and turned and walked up the gangplank.

Kate stepped to the back of the boat and watched him winch in the gangplank. Then she untied the stern line, and Bill pulled it up onto the ship's deck. As she walked toward the bowline, still tied to the dock, Bill walked with her on the deck of the boat.

Kate untied the bowline and held it as Bill took the helm. She threw the line onto the deck. Bill powered up the engine and began backing out into the main harbor channel.

She turned, walked onto the main dock, and watched the *Leona* back out and turn toward the ocean. As the boat motored out, she walked along with it as far as she could, and then stopped and waved good-bye. Howie barked one last time from his spot on the deck, Bill raised his hand to wave, and the *Leona* left the harbor.

Kate watched as long as she could, but finally the tears in her eyes made it impossible to see clearly. The *Leona* drifted away on her adventure.

As she headed back up the dock, Kate noticed the scruffy man who had been sleeping in his car walking out of The Angler with a cup of coffee. He shuffled to his car and drove off. Kate noted the license plate was from New York and the dealer's decal on the back looked like it said Buffalo.

"No doubt about it, there's a story there," Kate said aloud as she kicked into a run.

The sun was up, and it was time to get her day started—throw herself into her work the way she always did when she needed to forget about the dull ache in her heart.

Saturday mornings at the office were always quiet, and this morning Kate was the only attorney on her floor. By noon, she was deep in thought as she edited the final version of the jury instructions Ed had left on her desk for review. She cursed vigorously when her cell phone rang. She liked to read through jury instructions without interruption because that is the way the judge would read them to the jury. Indeed, the judge would have the doors of the courtroom locked just before he started reading the jury instructions to ensure there would be no interruptions.

"Kate Muldoon," she said tersely, upset that she'd have to start again, and that her phone simply said "caller unknown."

"Kate? It's Steve Jordan. I'm calling from a payphone, and I'll deny ever making this call, so it will do you no good to tell anyone."

"Good morning to you too, Chief. What's up?" Kate wondered what in the world the chief of police was up to—this had to be the oddest call she'd ever gotten from him, and it had only begun.

"I'm calling to tell you Mike Taylor is working on getting an arrest warrant sworn out against your client, Marcy Simpson. I'm going to be expected to execute on that warrant as soon as Taylor delivers it to me. I wanted to give you a heads-up."

"You're kidding, Chief! Pardon my French, but what the fuck is Taylor using as evidence that would be sufficient to justify this?" Kate was furious.

"That's why I'm calling. It's a very thin thread, all circumstantial, but he has taken it to Judge Crawley, and you know Crawley's never met a warrant he won't issue the state attorney."

"That's for sure. But, seriously, Chief, what evidence is there in the arrest warrant?"

"Marcy has access to the drug used to kill Dr. Dugan, and she stands to gain \$4 million as a result of his death. Taylor says that's all he needs, and in front of Judge Crawley, he's right. Plus, he's been told you clobbered Ronald Gray at the deposition of that insurance agent who issued the policy, and Gray is terrified you'll get a hearing on the interpleader before we finish our investigation into Dugan's death. He's going to claim Marcy is a flight risk and needs to be incarcerated to prevent her from profiting from her crime or fleeing the jurisdiction."

"This is just crazy. Marcy was at work the night of Dugan's death, it had been years since she'd seen him, and she had no idea the insurance policy was in place," Kate huffed unable to hide her nearly overwhelming exasperation. "I don't suspect Taylor checked out the evidence showing Marcy was at work that night, or the evidence from Jackson Memorial's ER that would show she didn't remove digitalis from their drug safe."

"Mike says she likely hired someone to handle the actual murder, but, of course, there's no *evidence* of that yet either. Kate, this is going to be beyond embarrassing to the department if it turns out we've rushed to arrest her, and she isn't our killer," Chief Jordan said, stating the obvious.

"Well, you can count on some major embarrassment then, because you've got the wrong person, and I'm going to shove that arrest warrant up Mike Taylor's ass before I'm done. He's being played, and there's probably some sort of political payoff because that's how Mike functions. Just yesterday, that asshole Gray threatened to have Joan Dugan's father, 'Philandering' Fergie, put pressure on the prosecutor's office to issue an arrest warrant against Marcy. He said if Marcy would accept their latest offer of \$100,000 to waive her claims to the insurance proceeds, he'd back off. We didn't accept his offer, and you see where we are now. That sounds like blackmail to me. It's certainly an ethical violation. What a sack of shit!"

Kate was struggling to regain her cool. She took several deep breaths before continuing.

"OK, listen, Chief, I really appreciate the heads-up. I'll do what I can to keep the shit from hitting *your* office. But it's going to hit the prosecutor's office hard when I prove Taylor, Gray, and Ferguson are pursuing this prosecution for their own personal gain. But, for now, I think I'd like to get Marcy to come in on her own. Can you give me a chance to do that?" Kate asked.

"Yes, but you're going to need to get her here by 3:00 this afternoon. I doubt I can hold them off beyond that. I'll be at the station myself and handle the processing. But, Kate, you need to know Taylor is going to press for no bail. And depending on the judge you draw, he might be successful."

Kate knew Chief Jordan was right.

"Kate, I can hold her here at our facility for a few days while you see what you can do about bail. She'd be in a cell by herself here, and that will be better than county—at least for a few days."

Again, Kate knew Jordan was correct.

"OK, I'll try to explain that to her. I appreciate everything you're doing, Chief. What can we do to help your investigation? I've got Terry Driver working on a couple of angles. Can we coordinate with you? I know it would have to be on the down-low, but can't we pool our resources to bring this miscarriage of justice to a quick resolution?" Kate asked, already planning the next steps in her investigation.

"I promise we will take a serious look at anything you bring us, Kate, but you know I can't bring you in on our end of the investigation. I promise we'll pursue all leads."

Chief Jordan hesitated, and then said, "Besides, Kate, you always seem to know what's going on in my department—sometimes better than I do. I know Terry Driver is a great investigator, but sometimes, he seems damn near clairvoyant, if you know what I mean."

The chief chuckled; Kate briefly smiled.

"Yeah, well, we may all need a little supernatural power before this one is over, Chief," Kate sighed. "OK, thanks again for the heads-up, and I'll see you shortly."

"FUCK!" Kate shouted loudly into her empty office as she hung up, and immediately picked up her cell phone and punched in Marcy's number.

Kate continued to talk to Marcy as she drove to her condo. She wanted to make sure Marcy didn't run, which is precisely what Kate knew her own impulse would be if faced with the same circumstances.

During the 15-minute drive, Kate explained what was happening and what their options were. At first, Marcy was frantic. She couldn't conceive of being in jail. She was panicking and threatened to take off. Kate continued to talk to her about the burden of proof the prosecutor would need to convict her of murder and how running would only make her look guilty of a crime she didn't commit.

Kate tried to explain that purely circumstantial evidence wouldn't be sufficient. The prosecutor would need to be able to explain how Marcy managed to slip Joe the digitalis while she was at work miles away, that she *knew* the insurance policy was current, that she *actually* accessed the drug safe at her ER and withdrew digitalis, or that there was *evidence* of her hiring someone to kill Joe Dugan. Kate stressed the police chief was committed to doing a thorough investigation, and that her own PI was working the case even now.

Marcy grew silent, and Kate said, "You know, Marcy, this is just another underhanded fear tactic Gray and Ferguson are employing like they did when Joe filed for divorce."

"Well, it's working," Marcy said simply. "I'm terrified, but I know now that they'll stop at nothing. I don't want any of their damn money. I never did. I just want to be left alone. Kate, make them leave me alone."

"Marcy, the best way to do that now is to help the cops solve Joe's murder, or at least prove *you* didn't do it. I know it's not the way the system is supposed to work, but unfortunately, it is the way it works far too often," Kate informed her terrified friend.

"Marcy, I'm pulling into your condo parking lot. I'll be up to your place in three minutes."

She jumped out of the car and bolted into the condo's elevator lobby. Jamming her foot in the elevator door just as it was about to close, she quickly got in and punched Marcy's floor.

"Sorry, guys," Kate said to the startled couple on the elevator. "I'm going to make you stop on the fifth floor."

When Kate knocked on the door to Marcy's condo it immediately flew open. Marcy's face crumbled when she saw Kate, and she fell into her arms. Kate held her tightly, and, as Marcy wept, Kate promised whatever bail amount the judge might set, she'd make sure it was satisfied and she'd have her out of jail as soon as humanly possible.

Eventually, Marcy stopped crying, and they sat on her small balcony for several minutes in silence as Marcy breathed in the air and soaked up the view she knew she would soon lose the freedom to enjoy.

Finally, Marcy said resolutely, "OK, I'm ready. This is just the first step in our beating the shit out of Gray and Ferguson. Let's do this."

Together, they headed to Chief Jordan's office. On the way, Kate explained what she was about to experience and how she should act.

As the two women approached police headquarters, Kate spotted the press contingent waiting at the front door.

She quickly turned to Marcy, took her arm, and said, "Marcy, there's press. I have no idea how they knew to be here, but I seriously doubt Chief Jordan tipped them off; he doesn't want any press on this arrest. So, it probably means the chief has a leak in his department. My guess is someone tipped Mike Taylor's office, and Taylor notified the press. He's always looking for PR opportunities."

Marcy gasped as one of the reporters shouted that he saw them coming, and the entire mob turned and rushed toward them in one large, angry swarm.

"Hold tight, Marcy, and let's pick up the pace. Let me do the talking. We aren't going to provide them with a statement until we have you released. Try not to even hear what they say."

Kate put one arm around Marcy's back and wrapped her free arm around her front to shield her. They pressed forward quickly, as all manner of ugly, accusing statements were hurled at Marcy. Kate repeated several times, "No comment at this time" as she shouldered her way through the crowd.

Suddenly, they were in the door; Chief Jordan greeted them with a grim smile and ushered them into his office.

"Kate, I have no idea how they knew when you were coming in. Please believe me, *I* didn't tip them off," he assured them once they arrived in his office and he closed the door.

"I believe you, Chief. My guess is you have a leak, and it drains all the way to Mike Taylor's office. He uses the press as often as he can to help his political aspirations. I hope this time I can break it off in him so far up that he gets fired, and his career as an attorney is in tatters," Kate answered, barely able to keep her temper under control.

"Well, the judge who issued the arrest warrant has left for the day and that means Marcy will automatically be held in custody, at least overnight."

With that, Chief Jordan turned to Marcy and said, "Marcy Simpson, you are under arrest for the murder of Joseph Dugan. You have the right to remain silent, anything you say can, and will, be used against you in a court of law. You have the right to an attorney. If you cannot afford an attorney, one will be appointed to you. Do you understand your rights?"

Marcy's breath caught, and she grasped Kate's arm. "Yes, I do. Kate Muldoon is my defense attorney." And then, just as Kate had instructed her, Marcy said nothing further—not one thing.

Chief Jordan stood by his offer to keep Marcy in one of his holding cells, he said he thought he'd be able to hold her there for at least three days. Kate told him it wasn't going to take that long.

After saying good-bye to Marcy now sitting forlornly in the holding cell, Kate called the clerk of court to find out who was on duty for emergency motions on Sunday. It turned out to be Judge Blumquist.

Finally, a small break, Kate thought. Judge Blumquist was a tough but fair judge who Kate had appeared before numerous times. She set an emergency hearing for the first thing Sunday morning, and then called Ed to bring him up to speed.

Chapter 14

Kate arrived in Judge Blumquist's courtroom at 8:00 Sunday morning, ready for Marcy's arraignment. Ed joined her a few minutes later and sat quietly with her at the defense table. At 8:30, Chief Jordan personally brought Marcy into the courtroom from her holding cell at police headquarters. Marcy looked worn out, but defiant. She wore a bright orange jumpsuit and flip-flops, and her hands were cuffed behind her. Chief Jordan took the handcuffs off, and Marcy sat down heavily at the defense table. Kate put her arm around her, holding her closely for a few moments until Marcy's breathing slowed and became regular.

"How are you doing?" Kate asked, knowing the answer would be anything but good.

"Awful. This is a nightmare. I keep waiting to wake up," Marcy managed to whisper.

"OK. Let's see what we can do to get you out of here," Kate patted her arm.

Chief Jordan leaned forward and asked if he could speak with Kate alone for a moment. She rose and walked with him toward the empty jury box.

"Kate, I'm going to see if I can get a moment with the judge before the hearing," Jordan whispered. "I want to let him know we have not completed our investigation and feel the arrest warrant was rushed."

"Thanks for the heads-up, Chief. That should intrigue Judge Blumquist."

In her heart, Kate knew the chief's motives were likely less about preventing a miscarriage of justice than protecting his own butt.

Jordan wanted to create distance between his office and Taylor's in the event the judge found the arrest warrant was improvidently issued. After being caught up in Taylor's grandstanding in the Bentley matter, and getting a major ass chewing for it from Judge Blumquist and the press, Chief Jordan didn't think his office could take the political fallout if it happened again.

As Kate walked back to the defense table she saw two reporters entered the courtroom and take places at the back where they began snapping photos and taking notes.

Kate leaned in toward Marcy and said, "There's press in the courtroom. Just keep looking forward toward the bench. When the judge comes in, we'll all stand up until he tells us to sit. Then the prosecutor will present his case first. I'll address the court after that." Kate was trying to keep their discussion low key. She hoped giving Marcy an idea of what to expect during the hearing would help her stay calm.

"Marcy, I want to suggest to the court that we will agree to wait until the criminal investigation is over before we press for a hearing on the interpleader. The prosecutor will have a difficult time arguing you're a flight risk if we take away the possibility of you having $4 million at your disposal."

"That's fine. I'm not going anywhere, even if I do get out of jail. In fact, I'm pretty sure I won't even be going to work. I bet I'm going to be suspended from my job, if not fired outright. After all, the hospital can't employ an ER nurse with access to digitalis after she's been accused of murdering someone by overdosing them with the drug," Marcy smiled wanly. "And, I doubt any of my friends will want to include me in our usual bridge games, shopping trips, or exercise classes. God knows, I wouldn't want an accused murderer hanging around me. So, I'll have very few places to go even if I'm released on bail. I'm sure my neighbors won't want to see me either." Marcy shrugged, and then continued. "But the view at my condo would be far better than the jail cell, so I hope you're successful."

Marcy's dejected tone broke Kate's heart.

"Hang tough, Marcy," Kate said as she patted her arm.

A man in a suit entered the courtroom and walked toward Kate and Marcy.

"Excuse me, Ms. Muldoon. Are you representing Ms. Simpson?" He did not extend his hand. "I'm Dr. Dan Jenkins, the head of the ER department at Jackson Memorial. I'm Ms. Simpson's supervisor. I'm here to ask you to inform Ms. Simpson that she is suspended pending the resolution of this criminal matter."

Dr. Jenkins refused to even look at Marcy; instead, he directed his words and eyes to Kate only.

"Dr. Jenkins, you can tell her yourself. She's sitting right here." Jenkins snubbing Marcy had pissed Kate off, and her voice was icy.

"Don't worry, Dan," Marcy said turning to face Dr. Jenkins. "I'd do the same thing in your shoes. But, Dan, I didn't do this, and I hope you know that in your heart of hearts."

Jenkins simply turned on his heels and took a seat in the back row of the courtroom as close to the door as he could get.

A few minutes later, another man in a suit entered the courtroom from the back and walked toward Kate and Marcy. Marcy turned to look at him when he said hello.

"Hello, Mr. Meardon. My, how the circumstances have changed since I first met you," Marcy smiled weakly at her former champion.

"Ms. Simpson and Ms. Muldoon, I came because I want to make sure you understand the insurance company will not be paying for Ms. Simpson's criminal defense," Mr. Meardon responded.

"Of course not," Kate replied. "But I'm glad you're here because we're going to assure the court Ms. Simpson won't seek to have the interpleader and declaratory judgment hearing until she's completely cleared of all charges. I'm assuming you will assist us in coordinating that. By the way, you need to know that she's innocent and we'll prove that. But, as soon as that's done, we'll be seeking release of the entire $4 million. You were at Mr. Sutton's deposition, and it couldn't be any clearer that Marcy is the intended beneficiary of Dr. Dugan's insurance policy. You also should know, this criminal charge is being used by Gray and Ferguson to pressure Marcy into waiving her claims to the insurance money."

"I hope you're right, Ms. Muldoon." Meardon turned to Marcy.

"Good luck, Marcy. I knew you were going to need a strong attorney, but I had no idea things would get this ugly. At least you're in good hands." Meardon walked to a row midway back and sat down.

"The rats can't get off this sinking ship fast enough," Marcy murmured under her breath to Kate.

Kate put her arm around Marcy again. "Don't sweat this stuff. Things always look bleak at this point."

Mike Taylor and an associate from his office who Kate did not know walked in from the side door and took their seats at the prosecutor's table. Taylor didn't even look toward the defense table.

Guilty conscience, Kate concluded.

"All rise." The bailiff called the courtroom to order a few minutes after 9:00, as Judge Blumquist entered.

"You may be seated," Judge Blumquist said as he looked out at the relatively small number of people in the courtroom. "Madam Clerk, call our first case."

"State of Florida vs. Marcy Anne Simpson," the clerk said, and then read the case number.

"Mr. Taylor, you're up. I must say, I'm surprised to see you here on a Sunday morning."

"My appearance for the State underscores the gravity of the charges before you, Your Honor," Taylor began pompously and without introducing his associate.

"Your Honor, Marcy Simpson is the ex-wife of Dr. Joe Dugan, the prominent Miami heart surgeon who recently died. Blood tests done on Dr. Dugan when he was brought into the ER at the University of Miami hospital showed a high level of digitalis—a drug that will stop a person's heart if administered in high enough doses. Notably, Dr. Dugan had not been prescribed digitalis, nor was he under a doctor's care for any known heart condition. Dr. Dugan's death was not from natural causes as first thought. It was murder."

Taylor paused for dramatic effect.

"Ms. Simpson has been charged with Dr. Dugan's murder because the evidence shows she had motive and means. First, she has access to the murder weapon, the drug digitalis. Ms. Simpson is an ER nurse at

Jackson Memorial and one of only a handful of employees there with access to the locked drug safe where their supply of digitalis is kept." Again Taylor paused. This time he looked at Marcy.

"Even more importantly, Your Honor, Ms. Simpson is the *only* person who stands to benefit from Dr. Dugan's death. Due to what can only be a scrivener's error she is the named beneficiary on a *$4 million* insurance policy that Dr. Dugan took out 19 years ago. Based on this evidence of motive and means, an arrest warrant was issued by Judge Crawley yesterday, and Ms. Simpson has been held at police headquarters pending her arraignment today." Taylor checked his notes before continuing.

"Your Honor, Ms. Simpson, Dr. Dugan's *ex*-wife, is a substantial flight risk. She is currently fighting to have the insurance proceeds—all $4 million—released to her rather than paid to Dr. Dugan's widow and children. Ms. Simpson could potentially be awarded that sum, and it is doubtful she would remain in the country after receiving such a payout. The State asks that Ms. Simpson be remanded to the county jail and held there, without bail, pending trial on the charge of first-degree murder. Thank you, Your Honor."

Taylor sat down and turned smugly toward Kate.

Kate glared at him as she stood.

"Kate Muldoon and Ed Evert for the defense, Your Honor. The State's so-called evidence is pure speculation and circumstantial drivel. Mr. Taylor is once again rushing to judgment without allowing the Miami Dade police force to complete its investigation into the serious charges he's laid against my client," Kate said as she again glared at Taylor.

"Marcy Simpson is innocent of the charges pending against her, as a *thorough* investigation will prove. Ms. Simpson has never been arrested on any charge prior to yesterday—as a matter of fact, she has never even had a speeding or parking ticket. She has been a model citizen and has faithfully served as an ER nurse practitioner at Jackson Memorial for over 20 years. Contrary to the State's assertion, Marcy Simpson had neither motive nor means, and, as the *actual* evidence will prove, she also did not have opportunity to kill Dr. Dugan."

Kate picked up a copy of the insurance policy and asked to approach the bench. As she walked toward the bench, she tossed a copy of the insurance policy onto Taylor's table, and she continued.

"Until nearly a week after his death, Ms. Simpson was entirely unaware Dr. Dugan had maintained the insurance policy I just handed the court. As you can see, the policy *specifically* names Ms. Simpson as the beneficiary. Dr. Dugan maintained that policy for 16 years *after* he divorced my client, secretly paying an annual premium of just under $4,000—even *after* filing for divorce from Ms. Simpson. Dr. Dugan's motive for maintaining the insurance policy is a mystery—and one that deserves to be thoroughly investigated. We are doing just that in the pending declaratory judgment and interpleader action relating to the funds the insurance company has placed in the court registry.

"On Friday last week, we took the deposition of Mr. Johnny Sutton, Dr. Dugan's original insurance agent. Mr. Sutton's testimony provided evidence of Dr. Dugan *intentionally* maintaining Ms. Simpson as the beneficiary well after he divorced her—a divorce he obtained in order to marry the current Ms. Dugan, who was pregnant at the time of their marriage."

"Objection," Taylor said jumping to his feet.

"Do you have evidence that she wasn't, Mr. Taylor? Do you have evidence of *anything?*" Kate asked sarcastically.

"Overruled, Mr. Taylor. Sit down," Judge Blumquist said sternly. "The circumstances surrounding this mess are unusual, to say the least, and it is difficult to say at this point what is, and what is not, germane. Since you've brought this charge so early in your investigation, we must allow the defense to present their side of the case, just as you have, Mr. Taylor."

Judge Blumquist looked back at Kate. "Please proceed, Ms. Muldoon."

It pays to have the judge's confidence and the chief of police whispering in the judge's ear, Kate thought.

She asked to approach the bench again, handed the judge and Taylor copies of the waiver Gray tried to pressure Marcy into signing when she first learned of the policy.

"From the moment Ms. Simpson was told about the policy, the lawyer for Dr. Dugan's estate, Ronald Gray, and a man named Zeke Peters, have attempted to physically and mentally intimidate Ms. Simpson into waiving her claim to the insurance proceeds.

"The document I just handed the court is a copy of the extremely one-sided waiver Mr. Gray attempted to get Marcy to sign under duress at their first meeting. Mr. Zeke Peters attended that meeting at Mr. Gray's invitation, and Peters verbally berated, and then physically assaulted Ms. Simpson when she refused to sign the waiver. In fact, Mr. Peters was so intimidating that the two attorneys from the insurance company present at the meeting jumped up to protect her. One of those men is in the courtroom today and can testify as to the truth of that last statement if necessary, Your Honor. Could you please rise, Mr. Meardon?"

Meardon rose and nodded to the judge, then sat back down.

"Mr. Peters is neither a family member, nor an attorney, and, as far as we can tell, had no purpose for being at that meeting other than to berate and physically threaten Ms. Simpson."

Kate paused and watched the judge page through the waiver—his heavy eyebrows shooting up, and then down, as a look of distaste spread across his face.

"My office has prepared, but as yet has not filed or served, a complaint for assault and a motion for temporary restraining order against Mr. Peters. Just this last Friday, following Mr. Sutton's deposition, Mr. Gray, the attorney for the current Mrs. Dugan and the Dugan Estate, again threatened Ms. Simpson."

Kate's eyes shot daggers at Mike Taylor, daring him to object again.

"Your Honor, Mr. Sutton's deposition testimony was *devastating* to Mr. Gray's case. Shortly after the deposition concluded, Mr. Gray threatened to have the widow's father, former Senator Ferguson, press the prosecutor's office to bring criminal proceedings against Ms. Simpson unless she agreed to waive her claim and accepted a settlement of $100,000. That offer was turned down, and, as you can see, Mr. Gray and Mr. Ferguson appear to have followed through on their threat."

Kate set the waiver document down and placed her hand on Marcy's shoulder.

"My client has now been arrested, charged with first-degree murder, and jailed overnight. Just this morning, Dr. Jenkins, Marcy's supervisor at Jackson Memorial, seated in the back of the courtroom," Kate gestured toward Jenkins, who appeared to want to shrink into the floor, "came to this courtroom to inform Ms. Simpson that she has now been suspended indefinitely from the job she has held for nearly 20 years. All of this has happened because the State has filed charges against her prematurely. It looks like Mr. Gray has managed to enlist the assistance of the prosecutor's office, and possibly even Marcy's employer, in his intimidation tactics—exactly as he threatened he would.

"Significantly, Your Honor, all these actions have been undertaken despite the fact that my client had not seen or talked to Dr. Dugan in well over ten years, nor can the State come forward with a shred of actual evidence to the contrary. Moreover, on the night of Dr. Dugan's death, Ms. Simpson was at work at Jackson Memorial, miles away from the site where the emergency technicians picked up Dr. Dugan. Indeed, Ms. Simpson was at work from 4:00 in the afternoon until midnight, an hour *after* Dr. Dugan was declared dead at the University of Miami Hospital. According to the medical evidence, the fatal dose of digitalis was administered sometime within an hour, two at the most, of Dr. Dugan's death. Dr. Dugan was not at Jackson Memorial that evening and rarely saw patients there. The time of his death, according to the hospital records, is 11:07 p.m. Numerous witnesses, as well as Jackson Memorial's timekeeping records, can attest to the fact that Ms. Simpson was at work during her *entire* shift that night."

Kate looked at Taylor in disgust.

"In addition, the records from the ER's drug safe at Jackson Memorial will show that Ms. Simpson has not accessed the cabinet in order to remove digitalis in a number of months. And that drug was used by Ms. Simpson to *save* a man's life.

"Significantly, Your Honor, Ms. Simpson has informed the insurance company, who is represented here today by Mr. Meardon, that she will not proceed with the interpleader hearing until this criminal matter is cleared up. Therefore, the State's argument that she is an alleged 'flight risk' is as ridiculous as the rest of their so-called evidence. Marcy Simpson has every reason to stay in Miami until her name is cleared—indeed, she has four million reasons."

Kate glanced back at Meardon, who nodded.

"Finally, Your Honor, the defense requests that Dr. Dugan's body be exhumed so that a complete autopsy can be performed. An autopsy should have been performed immediately upon his death. But Dr. Dugan's death was, remarkably, ruled 'natural causes, heart failure' by the ME's office. Nevertheless, the State has filed a murder charge without the benefit of a death certificate ruling Dr. Dugan's death a homicide."

At this news, Judge Blumquist's heavy dark eyebrow again danced on his forehead as he turned a sharp stare toward the prosecution's table.

"In light of the dearth of any *real* evidence against my client, the charges against her should be dismissed and she should be released immediately. Thank you, Your Honor." Kate voice registered complete disgust, which hadn't been difficult since that was exactly what she felt.

"Mr. Taylor, what evidence do you have that a fatal dose of digitalis was administered to Dr. Dugan?" Judge Blumquist inquired.

"Unbeknownst to the State, the hospital drew blood when Dr. Dugan was admitted. That blood work showed signs of digitalis when it was analyzed," Taylor replied.

"Is Ms. Muldoon correct when she states the medical examiner did not complete an autopsy, and instead, listed 'nature causes, heart failure' as the cause of death?" Judge Blumquist pressed.

"Well, Your Honor, the official cause of death was listed as heart failure, but, Judge Blumquist, a high dose of digitalis can *look* like heart failure," Taylor explained.

"So, you're telling me you've arrested Ms. Simpson for a murder the ME hasn't yet found to be anything other than death from natural causes?"

The judge's eyebrows were hard at work again as he stared at Taylor.

"Well, yes, but the news of the digitalis in the blood sample is kind of new to the State," Taylor began to explain.

"Mr. Taylor, you will have the body of Dr. Dugan exhumed by the ME, and his office will do a complete autopsy and enter the appropriate findings regarding the cause of death *before* Ms. Simpson can be charged with anything."

Judge Blumquist looked at Marcy.

"Ms. Simpson, please rise. I have some questions for you. Bailiff, swear in Ms. Simpson."

Marcy stood next to Kate and held her elbow for support as the bailiff brought the Bible to Marcy, who solemnly placed her hand on it and swore to tell the truth.

"Ms. Simpson, were you at work in Jackson Memorial's ER from 4:00 p.m. until midnight the evening of Dr. Dugan's death?" Judge Blumquist began.

"Yes, Your Honor. I actually didn't get off until 12:45 that night because of the number of patients coming in from a multiple car crash," Marcy answered meekly.

"At any time during your shift that night, did you leave the hospital?"

"No, Your Honor. Jackson Memorial's ER is a constant flow of patients needing urgent care. Once you're on duty, you remain on duty until you're relieved. Usually, there isn't time for a meal break, and sometimes it's even hard to find time to go to the bathroom!" Marcy said, warming to the judge's questioning.

"Mr. Taylor, how do you expect to prove Ms. Simpson managed to give Dr. Dugan an overdose of digitalis while she was at work?" The judge's eyebrows were arched high now.

"Your Honor, she could have slipped out, or she could have paid someone else to give Dr. Dugan the fatal dose . . ." Taylor stammered a bit.

"But you have no *evidence* to support either of those theories, do you, Mr. Taylor? You could just as credibly argue Ms. Simpson cloned herself or suspended time," Judge Blumquist interrupted. "Mr. Taylor, 'opportunity' usually means that the suspect actually was physically present or had access to the victim. It sounds like Ms. Simpson has a pretty decent alibi. Until you have something that will disprove her alibi or shows she hired someone else to kill Dr. Dugan, the charges against her will be *dismissed*."

The judge looked down at his notes.

"Mr. Taylor, did you speak with Ronald Gray or anyone else representing Dr. Dugan's estate before you decided to have Ms. Simpson arrested?"

Judge Blumquist's eyebrows rose high on his forehead again.

Taylor hesitated and looked down before answering.

"Yes, Your Honor. Yesterday, I talked to Ron Gray and the widow's father, Senator Kenneth Ferguson. They've been understandably concerned since they learned Dr. Dugan was murdered, and they are anxious to bring this matter to a conclusion. Ms. Simpson is the only person with a motive to kill Dr. Dugan, and she could easily have gotten her hands on digitalis. We are trying to keep a felon from fleeing the country while we finish our investigation. We also want to make sure she doesn't profit from her crime and collect the $4 million."

Taylor recognized his position was not being enhanced by the judge's questioning. He was getting desperate and slinging as much mud as he could.

"Mr. Taylor, Dr. Dugan could have gotten his hands on digitalis too—he was, after all, a heart surgeon. How do you know he didn't commit suicide?" Judge Blumquist's question hung in the air unanswered.

"Mr. Taylor, I have warned you in the past about bringing charges before the police have completed their investigation. Now, Ms. Simpson will be released immediately, and you will get back to work. And, Mr. Taylor, I expect you to work this one by the numbers. I want every 'i' dotted and every 't' crossed. Do you understand?"

Taylor said nothing; his face was pulled tight with tension.

"I will admit the insurance policy piece of this is, shall we say, unusual, but unusual circumstantial evidence does not prove murder, Mr. Taylor. It may give you a line of inquiry, but it is not proof of anything." The judge looked back at Marcy.

"Ms. Simpson, you are free to go. The charges against you are dismissed for now. However, we will hold you to your promise not to seek a hearing on the declaratory judgment relating to the funds in the court registry until the mystery surrounding Dr. Dugan's death is solved, or at least until it is clear you were not involved."

Judge Blumquist sat back in his chair.

"Your Honor, can we at least get Ms. Simpson to turn in her passport?" Taylor couldn't resist trying to inflict one more inconvenience on Marcy.

The judge looked at Marcy and said, "Ms. Simpson?"

"Your Honor, I don't have one, I've never had one. I don't go on vacations, can't afford them, and so I've never needed a passport," she replied shyly.

Judge Blumquist glowered at Mike Taylor and said, "Call the next case, Madam Clerk."

Kate wrapped her arm around Marcy and whispered, "We'll meet Chief Jordan back at the station; you're riding with me. We'll head to the station to pick up your personal belongings."

At the last minute, Kate said, "Ed, can you meet us there?"

"Sure," he replied as he tried to fully appreciate the miracle his boss had just pulled off.

As they walked out of the courtroom, Meardon smiled at them and turned to leave.

Dr. Jenkins again approached Kate.

"Please inform Ms. Simpson that she is still suspended until the investigation into Dr. Dugan's death is complete."

With that, he quickly turned and scurried out of the courtroom.

Marcy was silent on the ride from the courthouse to the police station. Once there, she silently changed into her own clothes and collected her purse, watch, and earrings. She stood next to the discharge desk, still silent, as she was processed. Kate watched her carefully.

Ed showed up just before it was time to leave. He observed the women warily; he sensed their emotions were running high. His were too. Kate had nearly ignored him in court, and she had refused to spend the night with him last night because she was too wrapped up in Marcy's situation. While he understood Kate felt the pressure of Marcy's case, he felt she was avoiding him, and he was pretty sure it had to do with her dinner with Bill.

The dude's out of the country, and I don't get why she would moon over him after the way he's treated her, Ed thought glumly.

Finally, Marcy's release was complete. When she turned toward Kate, she had tears in her eyes.

"Thank you, Kate. I knew you'd come through for me. But, Kate, what do I do now?" she whispered. "I don't have a job, and finding a new one is going to be impossible in this town, even when this criminal charge is resolved. News of my arrest was all over town yesterday, my neighbors and friend aren't going to want to see me. I'm a total pariah." Marcy's shoulders shook as she started to sob.

"Marcy, you're coming with me to my beach house. You can stay there. We're close enough to the same size you don't even have to bring much in the way of clothing. Besides, it's the beach, and it's pretty laid back. My goldies will love having company."

Kate had already thought through the situation, and she had a plan.

"Plus, my PI, Terry Driver, gets back in town this evening from St. Pete where he was trying to see what he could find out from Grace Dugan and Joe's brother. I'm going to text Terry and ask him to meet us at the beach house. We can discuss what he learned over dinner. Are you up to that, Marcy?"

"Oh, Kate, getting away to the beach where no one knows me would be a relief, a very welcome relief, if you're sure I won't be a nuisance," she sighed deeply.

"Ed, you're coming too, if you have this evening free," Kate directed.

Ed nodded.

Well, at least she still includes me in the work meetings, but the last time we were at the beach house, we fucked our brains out, and it's going to be hard to keep my hands off her. Ed's thoughts plainly were not on his work.

"I'm sure Chief Jordan intends to investigate Joe's death, but it's not his only case," Kate said brightly. "We are going to help him with his investigation, because, as of now, it *is* our only case.

"Let's run by your condo, Marcy. We can pick up a few things and you can get your car. Then we'll swing by my city house and collect the dogs, if you wouldn't mind keeping them with you at the beach this week, that is. I'll head back to the city later tonight. I've got an early meeting tomorrow with the FBI that I can't reschedule," Kate said as she ushered Marcy out the door and toward her car.

"Ed, do you want a ride to the beach, or do you want your own car?" Kate asked solicitously.

She'd sensed that he was feeling irritated because she'd been so preoccupied.

"I'd rather ride out and back with you, and leave my car at your place," Ed readily agreed.

And I'm going to see if I can't convince you to invite me to spend the night with you tonight, Ms. Muldoon, Ed thought hopefully.

Chapter 15

At the beach house, while Marcy showered away the taint left from spending the night in jail, Kate, with Ed's help, made an enormous pan of lasagna to feed everyone for dinner. Not only was Terry joining them, he was bringing Suzy Spellman with him. Kate had already let Marcy know that Suzy was now part of her legal team—you never know, Marcy might want to sue Jackson Memorial for firing her. In any event, Suzy was now arguably privy to attorney-client communications and work product, so it was important to have her officially on the team.

Around dinnertime, Kate's house was full of noise and people. Marcy set the table on the back deck, made a salad, and opened some red wine. The five of them huddled around the table drinking and eating as Terry gave an account of his weekend in St. Pete—at least the *work* aspect of the weekend. Kate was pretty sure she didn't want details on the rest.

"I started by canvasing the older Dugans' neighbors," Terry began. "All of them knew the Dugans had recently lost their son who lived in Miami, and they all knew the senior Mr. Dugan is gravely ill and hospice is at the house on a regular basis. Unfortunately, that was about all the neighbors could tell me. Apparently, Mrs. Dugan has been keeping to herself since her husband grew so ill." Terry ate a large forkful of lasagna before continuing.

"I decided to follow my gut and try the brother, Michael, before barging in on the mom. He's a doctor at the VA hospital at Bay Pines in St. Pete. He carries the rank of Major in the Army, joined through ROTC—apparently he used military scholarships to put himself through med school at USF."

Terry grinned with another forkful of lasagna halfway to his lips.

"I'm glad I listened to my gut."

Terry stuffed the fork in his mouth.

"You know, Boss, now that we all know you can cook, we might expect dinner invitations more often."

Terry winked at Kate. She saluted him with her wineglass.

"So, the brother was very informative. Turns out no one in Joe's family can stand Joan. According to Michael, Joan is, and I quote, 'a spoiled, rich bitch, who throws a tantrum when she doesn't get her way, and manipulates everyone around her.' Apparently, they rarely saw Joe or the boys except when Joan wanted to take a trip somewhere without them or agreed to check herself into rehab—which, from what Michael said, happened at least once a quarter."

Terry took a drink of wine, and then continued.

"The last time Joe came for a visit—about two months ago—he told Michael he couldn't take it anymore and he'd begun divorce proceedings against Joan."

Upon hearing this news, Kate stopped eating and laid down her fork.

"Joe felt Joan was an unfit mother on top of everything else—drugs, alcohol, public indecency, and destruction of private property—generally a bad egg. When the oldest boy lost his driver's license within 3 months of getting it because he was high on pot and alcohol, Joe decided to divorce Joan and try to get sole custody of the boys. He'd asked Michael about good private schools in the St. Pete area."

Terry casually took another break to eat the rest of his lasagna.

"My God, Terry!" Kate said happily. "This is spectacular news! Did Michael know who Joe hired as his divorce attorney?"

Kate was literally sitting on the edge of her chair now, already thinking about calling Chief Jordan to let him know there was someone who *actually* had motive to murder Joe Dugan.

"No, Michael didn't have any specifics. From what he said Joe had only recently made up his mind to get the divorce. But if he took any steps at all, we should be able to find out either from the legal community or from his checkbook. I'll start looking for leads tomorrow."

Terry finished his wine, and then said, "I told Michael the police are looking at Joe's death as a murder and asked if he knew any reason Joe would be taking digitalis. He didn't. I also told him the Miami police had arrested Marcy. He nearly exploded, said Marcy wouldn't hurt a flea, and asked what evidence they had. I told him they were relying on the fact that Joe maintained a $4 million life insurance policy with Marcy as the beneficiary. Michael was dumbstruck by that news. He finally said, 'I guess he *did* still love her. Always said he did.'

"Joe's family was furious with him for divorcing Marcy, and they didn't speak to him for months—didn't even attend Joe's wedding to Joan. Then they found out about the baby and tried to patch it up. But it never took. They never could tolerate Joan's behavior."

Marcy stood up from the table and walked into the kitchen. Kate followed her.

"I'm OK, Kate. I only need a tissue. This is all just so much at once. I feel like I'm in a bad movie. Shit, what a mess Joe made of his life. He didn't deserve all that, infidelity or not, he didn't deserve all that anguish."

Marcy pulled out several tissues and blew her nose. She picked up the tissue box and said, "Come on, Kate, let's go back out and see what other horrors await us tonight."

When Marcy and Kate returned to the table, Terry said, "Sorry, Marcy, I guess this is all pretty upsetting to hear. I asked Michael about this guy Zeke Peters—you know, how he fit into this whole picture. Michael said, 'If you find out, let me know, because I sure could never figure it out.' Michael said Zeke was always the polar opposite of Joe, and nobody could understand why Joe let him ride around on his coattail. Evidently, the friendship began when the two were juniors in high school, but it had taken a turn for the worse within the last several months of Joe's life. According to Michael, Joe switched the personal representative named in his will and the trustee named on a trust he'd set up for the boys from Zeke to Michael. Joe didn't give him a reason for the switch, but said they'd all find out soon enough.

"After talking to Michael, I finally decided to bite the bullet and go visit Mrs. Dugan. I took Suzy with me because I thought Mrs. Dugan might be more relaxed around a woman." Terry winked at Suzy who smiled back flirtatiously.

"I told Mrs. Dugan that I was investigating their son's death because the hospital had taken a blood sample when he was brought in by ambulance the night of his death. I told her the sample revealed a high dose of digitalis. I asked if she knew whether Dr. Dugan took digitalis for any condition, or if she had seen it anywhere around his house. I also asked her if she knew of any heart conditions Joe might have had. She said Joe was extremely healthy and took great care of his body, and she couldn't imagine why he would take digitalis."

Terry helped himself to a second serving of lasagna and poured another glass of wine before continuing. Not to be outdone, Ed followed suit.

"She asked me if the digitalis caused Joe's death. I told her we didn't know yet, but the idea had come up, and that Marcy was being held in connection with Joe's death."

Terry reached over and patted Marcy's hand when she tensed.

"Grace Dugan is a fan, Marcy. Her words were, 'Well, that's just the stupidest damn thing I've ever heard. Marcy could no more hurt someone, let alone kill Joe, than I could fly to the moon.' I told her about the insurance policy, and she just laughed and said, 'They should arrest that floozy he married and that deadbeat Zeke Peters.' Mrs. Dugan didn't know her son was thinking of divorcing Joan, but then, with all she has on her plate with her husband right now, Joe might not have wanted to tell her."

Terry dove into his second plate of lasagna, but came up long enough to add, "I also asked Mrs. Dugan about Zeke Peters. Her words were, 'May he rot in hell.' She said, although they had both played soccer, Joe never had anything to do with Zeke socially until midway through their junior year in high school. Then the boys suddenly became inseparable. Ms. Dugan said she always felt Zeke had something he was holding over Joe's head, but she didn't know what it could be."

"That's how I felt too," Marcy said in a loud whisper. "Joe cut Zeke slack for everything and always took his side. He'd say, 'You just don't know Zeke like I do. He's really a great person, and he'd do anything for me.' I could never figure out how Joe could be so blind where Zeke was concerned."

Marcy looked out at the ocean, now dark and wild as a storm approached.

"Anything else to report, Terry? I'd say you earned your keep this weekend." Kate smiled at her PI and again thought how lucky she was to have him on her team.

"Nope, that's about it. I'll start working on the divorce angle this week. I planned to run by the good doctor's office and the hospital on Monday to pick up the documents they said they would have ready for me in response to our subpoenas. I hope Zeke isn't in the medical offices. I doubt he will be. I'm going early in the morning and from what the receptionist said when I stopped in last Wednesday to make sure the documents would be ready, it doesn't sound like Zeke is an office regular. I'm hoping I can talk to some of Dugan's coworkers. They might know something about his plans regarding divorce. I'll let you know what I learn,"Terry said, polishing off his second plate of lasagna.

"Great, and I'll let the chief know what we've learned. We'll see if he really intends to investigate these leads, or if former Senator Ferguson has scared him off," Kate said, picking up her plate and heading to the kitchen. "Looks like the weather is going to get nasty. Ed, we need to get back to the city before it gets too much later."

Ed smiled as he thought of his plan for their evening.

Marcy followed Kate out to the kitchen and insisted she clean up so they could all get on the road. Kate asked again if she was sure she'd be OK alone at the beach house with the dogs. Marcy assured her she would be and was actually looking forward to some time to sort through the events of the last several days.

The women hugged each other, and Kate said, "Marcy, stay strong. This is all going to make sense. We just need to unravel the mystery, one layer at a time."

Kate was silent on the drive back into the city. The car seemed empty without her dogs, even though Ed was sitting next to her in the passenger seat.

"You going to talk to me, Kate?" Ed asked after 20 minutes.

"Sure, sorry. I'm just thinking about the information Terry gave us. I wonder what Zeke Peters, aka 'Devil Spawn,' could have had on Mr. All-American, Joe Dugan. They seem like such an unlikely pair. And I am intrigued to learn Dugan was about to divorce his wife and try to get sole custody of the kids. If Joan Dugan is half as unstable as she seems to be, I can easily see her killing Dugan if she learned about his plans."

Kate fell silent again. The wind had kicked up and rain was beginning to fall in torrents on the windshield, making visibility difficult.

"Kate, you seem distant. I'd really like to spend some time with you. I know you're deep into Marcy's case, but I feel totally shut out. I want to spend the night with you tonight. I want to hold you and take your mind off work for a while. I want to help you relax." Ed slid his hand over to touch Kate's shoulder and gently caressed the back of her neck. "Please."

Kate tensed.

"Oh God, Ed, I think I've led you to see me as something I'm not. I don't mean to hurt you, but apparently I'm not really someone who can have 'no-strings-attached' sex. It just isn't in my makeup. Last weekend with you at the beach was the first time I've ever done anything like that," Kate glanced to the side at Ed. "I am so sorry I involved you in that aspect of my life. It was wrong. I used you to make myself feel better. It was incredibly selfish of me."

"Kate, give me a chance. Just stop thinking of me as someone you work with or someone you cheated on Bill with. You didn't cheat on him. Hell, he went on without you way before you and I had sex. If anyone is being unfair here, it's Bill. He wants to keep you hanging around, feeling guilty if you move on, while he's moved on just fine and is out there sampling other options. Don't you owe yourself a chance to find out whether there might be someone else who could make you happy? Maybe even me?" Ed was speaking softly, but his words were sharp and direct, and they hit home.

Kate drove on in silence.

"Look, I know I'm not Captain America, ex-Pro Football Star, and I sure as hell don't have a big-ass, fancy yacht and a string of luxury car dealerships. But, damn it, Kate, I make you laugh, I treat you as well as you'll let me, and we have a lot in common. Let me in, Kate, let me help you."

To Kate, he sounded genuinely interested in something beyond sex.

"Ed, Bill's money is entirely beside the point. If I gave a flip about those things, I'd have married him. Look, until Bill came along, I'd never known what it was to love someone, or to actually be loved by someone." Kate stopped herself. She was only getting in deeper with Ed. She knew she needed to just end this. "Ed, there's a lot you don't know about me—a whole lot."

"I want to learn all those things. It isn't just sex with me, Kate, in case you thought it was. I find you captivating. I think about you when we're not together. There're all sorts of things I want to talk to you about. When I see something interesting during the day, the first thing I think about is telling you. Don't get me wrong. I want to have sex with you too." He smiled and Kate looked sideways at him and laughed a little.

"I find you incredibly hot—so sue me. I'm physically attracted to you. But that is not the only thing I think about." Ed had turned in his seat and was looking straight at her as she tried to keep her eyes on the rain-drenched road.

She fell silent as Ed continued to look at her.

I should end this now. I don't love him the way I love Bill, she thought. *Oh really?* she responded to herself. *Since when did you become so wise in the ways of love? You just admitted you were 36 years old before you experienced it the first time. How do you know whether you love Ed, or whether there's more than one way to be in love? Bill wants the "marriage and kids, house in the suburbs, little wife at home cooking dinner" type of love. That's not you. Do you even know what Ed wants? What you want? You've shut him down before finding out.*

Kate shot Ed another sideways glance; he was still looking at her intently. She sighed and said, "OK, tell me about your family, and I'll tell you about mine. We can start there."

For the next 45 minutes, Ed told Kate about his mother and father, both teachers, and his younger sister who had gotten caught up in the drug culture and is still trying to straighten herself out. He described growing up in the middle class in the Upper Peninsula of Michigan, joining the Marines at 18, and putting himself through undergraduate and law school on loans and scholarships. Kate then told Ed about her four siblings, her father leaving them when she was only four, her mother dying of breast cancer because she waited too long to see a doctor and couldn't afford proper care because she didn't have health-care insurance through her employer. And she told him about Adam.

Ed listened quietly, and when she was finished, he said, "Kate, it's no wonder you have difficulty trusting men. Between your father, your brothers, Adam, and the asshole males you work with, it is a wonder you talk to men at all. I'll give Bill credit. He must have been pretty great to break through that barrier."

Her head turned abruptly to look at Ed; he smiled.

"Yep, I can say something nice about Captain America. I suspect if we didn't want the same prize we could be decent friends. Of course, I'd tell him he's an idiot for ever leaving you available to potential raiders like me." Ed winked at her when she glanced in his direction. "But, Kate, now that you've been liberated from your belief that all men are basically pond scum, how about giving yourself a chance to get to know us a little better . . . starting with me."

Kate glanced over and caught Ed's winning grin and just laughed.

"So, Mr. Not-Pond-Scum, how about a nightcap?" she asked as they pulled on to her street and into her driveway where she parked her car next to Ed's.

As she shut off her car, she turned to Ed.

"We're just going to talk, got it?" Kate gave him a stern look, and he raise his hands in surrender, but continued to smile broadly.

"I just wish we didn't work together, Ed. It complicates everything . . ."

"OK, I quit . . . but just for tonight," he quipped.

They walked from the car into the backyard and entered the house through the kitchen.

"The bar's in here," Kate said walking into her small pantry. "What's your pleasure? Last time I let you drink hard liquor, I got you drunk."

He walked into the small pantry behind her and placed his arms around her waist. "I don't need liquid courage," he said stroking her arms and turning her around to face him. He kissed her with great intensity and pressed her close.

Kate pulled back slightly and rested her head on his chest. She was suddenly overwhelmed with how exhausted she was. She didn't want to fight it any longer; she wanted to give in.

"How about a nice, big red wine, and I'll show you the house and my before, during, and after pictures," she suggested, still trying to keep them out of the bedroom.

"Perfect."

Ed released her, and they walked back into the kitchen where she pulled a bottle of wine from the cooler. As she opened it, she began to tell Ed about the house and what it looked like when she first opened the front door. They walked into the living room, and Kate turned on a few lamps and pulled out her photo album of her house renovations. Sitting side by side on the sofa, Kate tucked her feet under her and leaned toward Ed to point out specific photos, and she began to tell the tale of her tiny, jewel box of a house.

"This is what it looked like when I first walked in. All the windows on the first floor were boarded over because the house had been standing vacant for a couple of years. The only thing holding the house up then was the thousands of termites in the walls, standing shoulder to shoulder! I swear, you could hear them chewing away on the studs and latticework. The first project was having the house tented, then getting the boards off the windows and replacing the glass in many of the windows on the second story." Kate looked at the photos and smiled.

"Whatever possessed you to tackle this house?" Ed asked, totally bemused by the idea of a single woman renovating a house alone with the assistance of a few tradespeople.

"I had promised myself a house—a real house with a yard—after law school . . . This was the only way I could make that happen. I had huge student loans from undergrad and law school. So, this house was the only thing in my nonexistent price range. I bought it for a song at a tax auction, literally on the courthouse steps."

For another half hour, they perused Kate's photos, and she regaled Ed with tales of her renovation. They had finished their wine, and Kate asked if he'd like a tour of the rest of the house.

"I sure would," he smiled slyly at her. "Can we start upstairs?"

Kate laughed and looked into his eyes. There was depth there, something more than lust. He seemed to genuinely care for her.

Maybe this isn't just sex for him. And I'm a grown woman, for heaven's sake, so even if it is, where's the harm? Why should I pine away for Bill when he's out having the adventure of a lifetime? And why should he get to decide what he wants after tasting what else is available, and I shouldn't? Kate debated, locked in heavy deliberation with herself.

She stood, took Ed's hand, and led him up the stairs.

At the top of the stairs, Kate turned left, into her room, and stopped to look up at Ed, placing her hands on his face, pulling him down to kiss her. She gently unbuttoned his shirt and pushed it off his shoulders and laid her cheek against his chest.

"Hold me for a moment," she whispered.

Ed caressed her back and ran his fingers through her hair as he kissed the top of her head. Lifting her chin, he kissed her again. She moved to the bed, and slowly turned down the covers and undressed. Ed stood watching as she slipped under the sheet, and then he walked to the bed and undressed. He slid in next to Kate and pulled her to him, stroking her gently as she ran her hands over his chest and arms, and then down his back. Slowly and gently they explored each other, letting their hands linger when they found a spot that caused the other to shudder or sigh with delight.

Finally, Ed whispered, "Kate, I can't hold out much longer. I want you so much."

Kate responded by gently pulling him on top of her and running her hands over his muscular back and shoulders. As Ed's pace quickened, Kate's hands traced down his back and grasped his buttocks as he began thrusting; she responded with pulsating of her own. Together, they came with force and energy, and then collapsed, kissing each other as Ed rolled to the side.

When they had relaxed, he said, "Kate, you do something to me no one else ever has. Thanks for letting me in tonight; thanks for sharing yourself."

Kate snuggled into his chest and willed her mind to be empty. They both fell deeply into sleep.

Chapter 16

Kate woke to the unusual feeling of someone lying awake in her bed, staring at her. She opened one eye and immediately saw Ed's smiling face, fully awake and slightly puzzled.

"You know, I don't think I've seen you asleep before. You woke up first when we were at the beach. Hell, you were up, making coffee and dressed for a run by the time I crawled out of bed. That's how much you wore me out," he smiled, brushing a strand of hair out of her face.

"What time is it?" Kate asked quickly, sitting up and looking at the clock on the nightstand; it said 6:23. "I need to get going. I've got a meeting with Beth this morning at 8:30." Kate started to swing her legs over the side of the bed, but found herself unable to move. Ed's arm was around her waist, and then suddenly she was lying under him.

"Not so fast. You have time, though a morning run is probably not in the cards. You must have been exhausted, Kate. You were sleeping so soundly." He kissed her lips, and then began kissing her neck. Kate squirmed, and Ed's kissing became nipping.

"Ed, I really need to get going," Kate lied; she had plenty of time. All of her doubts from the night before were flooding back in on her.

Why do I feel so damn guilty about sex with Ed? Kate wondered and she relaxed slightly. *We really are two consenting adults; we aren't doing anything wrong,* she tried to reassure herself, but immediately added, *Except that he works for me, and then there's that whole being in love with someone else.*

Her body stiffened again.

"Kate, I'll let you up if you really want to get up now, but promise me it won't be another week before we can do this again." Ed had pushed up, holding his torso over hers, pinning her to the bed with his hips. He looked down at her with pleading eyes.

He's certainly perfected that look and clearly knows it's effective. Damn, just look at those arms and that chest.

Kate's thoughts were not under control, and her hands reached up to caress his chest. She could feel herself begin to tingle, and she knew she wanted him.

He rolled onto his back and pulled her on top. She kissed him, and as she sat up she felt him getting hard.

"Ummm, morning wood," she wiggled, and Ed groaned with desire.

In one swift motion, he wrapped his arms around her, sat up, pressed his face into her breasts, easily overpowering her as he pushed her backward, and quickly slid inside.

"That will teach you not to play with a loaded weapon if you really want to get out of bed. And, now, I get to have my way with you," he grinned down at her, gently pinning her arms to the bed as he began to rock higher inside her.

Kate wrapped her legs around his waist squeezing him inside and letting him control the pace of their movement. She watched his eyes intently; there was fire and need. He came quickly, but remained hard inside her and continued stroking until she came.

"I can't get enough of you," he whispered.

"Well, that will have to hold us for a while, Mr. Evert—maybe even a whole week!" she laughed, and tried to push him off of her, to no avail.

"I'll let you up if you promise we can do this again *very* soon," he said, kissing her neck and making her squirm.

His rapidly withering manhood was no match for Kate's wiggling, and soon, they were headed for the shower.

When Ed took off for his apartment, Kate headed to the FBI's beautiful new Miami Field Office Building for her meeting with Beth. The agenda was the identity of Suzy's unintended houseguest.

She arrived with a Grande Mocha Latte for Beth and a Grande House Dark for herself. It never hurts to grease the wheels when the FBI is doing you a favor, even when the top dog is a close friend.

"You look bright-eyed, happy, and very well satisfied this morning, Kate. I thought your love life was on hold. I don't suppose it's that fine-looking young associate I see you with *all* the time, is it?" Beth inquired as she gratefully took the latte from Kate.

"Don't get me started, we won't get to our business if I begin that tale," Kate sighed with a smile.

"Any chance you and Melissa could grab dinner with Suzy and me sometime this week? It's been awhile. I want to beat up on Suzy about her most recent stupid trick, and I think I need FBI backup."

"Actually, I think we're free *tonight* if you are," Beth said checking the calendar on her smart phone.

"OK, I'll call Suzy. She may resist since she's in heat with my PI right now, but she owes me, so I'll insist."

Kate briefly wondered if Terry's heart was broken yet as she sat back and sipped her coffee.

"So, let's talk about our friend Suzy and her out of control libido," Beth said growing serious. "It's downright scary to think she had this guy in her house. Just look at him, Kate, he even *looks* scary. I think our girl needs glasses and a way better 'creep detector.'"

Beth handed Kate a wanted poster featuring Gary Cook.

"Oh my God, Beth!" Kate said grabbing the poster. "I saw this guy just the other day, Saturday morning about 5:30. He was at The Angler. I saw him crawl out of a car parked in the back corner of the lot and walk right past me on his way into The Angler. He came out about a half hour later with coffee and drove off!"

Kate suddenly felt sick, just knowing she'd been so close to someone wanted for so many crimes.

"Kate, don't tell me you're hanging out at The Angler all night now too. What has gotten into you? It was bad enough when it was just Suzy, but you too? I swear, you both should switch to my team. It's a lot safer," Beth laughed.

"No, it's not like that. I ran down to the marina to watch Bill Davis take off on a Caribbean trip—it's a long story, I'll fill you in at dinner tonight. The important thing is I can tell you about the car he was driving. A dark blue older Mercedes with New York plates and a dealer decal that I'm pretty sure said Buffalo," Kate hurriedly told her friend. "Can't you put out an APB or something like that to see if you can pick him up if he's still in the area?"

"We can do that and better," Beth said excitedly. "We've got CCTV cameras throughout the city, plus, we'll send out alerts to all the local law enforcement officers in the area. With any luck at all, we'll grab him, if he's still driving the same car, that is. This is a great break, Kate. Let's hope we get him before he does something worse than embarrassing our friend Suzy."

On the way to her office, Kate called Suzy to let her know Beth had shown her a photo of Gary Cook, her sociopathic houseguest, and brought her up to speed on their discussion.

"So, if you see a dark blue older Mercedes, you need to keep away from it and call the cops—especially if it's in your neighborhood," Kate instructed.

"Don't worry. I've learned that lesson, and I will most certainly do that—of course, I sort of have my own bodyguard right now," Suzy actually giggled.

Oh God! Poor Terry. This is bad; she's giggling! Kate groaned to herself.

"Yeah, well, about that, you're going to let your libido cool off and give Terry the night off tonight, or at least meet him after you have dinner with Beth, Melissa, and me tonight. Our usual place at 7:30." Kate's tone indicated Suzy had no other option.

"But, Kate, we're in that really great stage where we do it all the time, and you may not know this, but your PI is *very* inventive!" Suzy giggled again.

"Stop talking! I work with the man. You can't tell me about this. Enjoy it, but keep it to yourself, and please don't break him—I need him. And I'm not taking 'no' for an answer on dinner. You're coming to dinner—end of discussion. You owe me," Kate insisted.

"Please tell me you and Beth aren't going to spend the *entire* night ganging up on me about how stupid I was. I got it. I've learned that lesson, I promise," Suzy whined.

"It won't be the only thing we talk about. But, we get a couple of shots so we can get it out of our systems, and you're just going to have to take it. Jesus, Suzy, every damn time I think about that creep in your house I want to scream," Kate said emphatically.

Suzy finally acquiesced and promised to meet them at 7:30.

Next, Kate called Marcy to see how she was doing. Not well was the answer. Marcy had made the mistake of buying a *Miami Herald* when she ran to the grocery store to restock Kate's nearly bare beach pantry and fridge. There was a large story about her arrest and release. She was still in tears.

"Marcy, I have a feeling the story about the arrest of Joe's real murderer is going to run on page one, and I will personally make sure they print a retraction of all the supposition and exaggerations they have written about you." Kate was furious that Marcy's name and reputation were being dragged through the mud—all because Mike Taylor is a publicity-seeking hack with enormous political ambitions.

"It won't matter. I will always be known as the nurse arrested for murder. I don't think it will even help if I leave Miami . . ." Marcy sobbed.

"Marcy, take the girls for a walk on the beach. It always cheers me up when I'm in the dumps. I know it's easy to say, but you have to give this time, and you can't be beating yourself up every day. I've got a pretty good library of escapist reading out there. Get lost in a book. But let me know if you need company, you can always come stay with me in town." Kate knew Marcy was dying inside.

"I'll be OK. It just hit me hard seeing my *photo* in the paper under that headline, *Killer Nurse?* What a nightmare. I wish I'd never even heard about that stupid insurance policy!" Marcy sniffed back tears. "Don't worry about me, Kate. I'll read all the books in your library if I have to—you just do what you do best. Prove me innocent and speak up for Joe—someone has to speak for the dead."

I hope I can do that, Kate mused as they hung up. *I just wish I knew what the hell Joe Dugan would say.*

When Kate arrived at her office around 9:30, Sophia greeted her. Using the suspicious tone Kate was sure she reserved for her teenage children, Sophia grilled her about where she'd been, pointing out it was two hours after her normal arrival time, and there was nothing on her calendar.

Kate tried to be patient in her response, but she found Sophia's questions irritating this morning.

Someone else trying to control me, she grumbled to herself.

Kate explained she had a meeting with Beth at the FBI office, and she would be in her office the rest of the day, "long after you've gone home," Kate couldn't help adding under her breath as she walked down the hall.

Kate settled into the mundane work of sorting through mail and e-mail, but Ed appeared at her door about 40 minutes later, looking very self-satisfied.

"You need to work on your poker face, Mr. Evert. You look like the damn cat who ate the canary," Kate laughed.

"That's next," Ed said with a wicked grin.

"*Close the door*, Ed!" she sighed with exasperation, kicking herself for not keeping her comments strictly work related.

"So, what brings you to see me?" she asked, trying to recover some decorum.

"Actually, I just wanted to see if you were in and to tell you I think we should plan a date night maybe Thursday—it would be one way of assuring I'll make it to yoga on Friday morning," he winked.

Damn, he's incorrigible. I've created a monster—hell, maybe I'm the monster, Kate reflected as she considered her options.

"That's true," Kate said wearily. "Or it could ensure I *don't* make it to yoga, if this morning is any indication."

Kate did her best to shoot Ed a disapproving scowl, but based on his reaction, she decided he was immune.

"OK, we can plan on Thursday but only if you can manage to not break the rules between now and then. Think you can do that?"

"With you as the incentive, I'm sure I can manage it!" he chuckled as he left her office.

Later that afternoon, Terry Driver called to report on his interview with Milton Martin, the second and most recent insurance agent on Joe Dugan's life insurance policy.

"Hey, Boss," Terry said when Kate answered her phone.

"Hey, yourself, and my name's Kate," she responded. "So what's the word?"

"The word is someone's gotten to Mr. Martin. He said he didn't remember Joe Dugan, or his $4 million policy, and he never had any conversations with him. Martin was incredibly nervous the entire time I was with him. He was sweating profusely and wouldn't make eye contact for anything. Of course, I asked him if he'd talked to Ron Gray, Joan Dugan, or her dad, Senator Ferguson, and he denied talking to any of them. I explained the deposition process and how it would be important for him to tell the truth; otherwise, he would face potential perjury charges. But, I couldn't get him to open up at all."

Terry was obviously disappointed; he wasn't used to striking out.

"Do you remember if Johnny Sutton said anything about Milton when you interviewed him?" Kate inquired, trying to think of ways to persuade Milton to tell them what he knew.

"Nope. Johnny didn't say anything about him, but I didn't ask him. I'm planning a trip back out to Happily Ever After tomorrow to ask him about Milton. I'll let you know what he says, but I'll turn in my PI license if it turns out Milton is telling the truth. Kate, he's a terrible liar."

Terry shifted to a new subject. "So, when I went to Dugan's medical practice today to pick up the documents, the office manager asked me to come back to her office. She seemed agitated and said they weren't done with their review and wouldn't be ready to produce the documents we requested until tomorrow. I told her I'd return. But, because she was acting strangely, I reminded her the subpoena you sent to the medical practice is a court order, and they are required to provide all documents requested, and even to allow me to see how and where the documents were maintained.

"She said she knew that and planned to comply, but she wanted the attorney who represents the practice to be there when the documents are produced. It's not someone from Gray and Ferguson, thankfully. It's Larry Lewis—he's with Smith and Fields. I used a little charm and learned they found some interesting documents in a locked drawer in Dr. Dugan's desk when they cleaned it out over the weekend.

"They'll have the documents copied while I'm there tomorrow. I'll ask them to make two sets, one for us, and one for Ron Gray. But, Kate, I wouldn't be surprised if Gray is there tomorrow when I show up for the documents."

"Thanks, Terry. As Alice in Wonderland would say, 'curiouser and curiouser . . .' I think I'll go with you tomorrow morning. What time are you planning on being there?" Kate asked.

"We set the meeting for 8:30, but I'm planning on being there at 7:30 at the latest. It's always good to know who wants to be there before us," he replied.

"Great, I'll be there no later than 8:00," Kate responded and was about to hang up when Terry spoke up again.

"So, I hear you're jumping my claim tonight. Suzy says you insisted she have dinner with you, Beth, and Melissa. I guess I'll get leftovers when you're done with her," Terry laughed.

"Did she tell you we're going to chew her out for being so stupid bringing that sociopath into her home?" Kate asked.

"Yep, she was looking for sympathy, but I didn't give her any. I hope between us we can harass her enough she'll think twice before ever doing such a stupid thing again," Terry said grumpily.

Or maybe she'll just figure out a way to enlist you as her permanent watchdog. I think I'd actually like that—as long as you both agree not to talk to me about it, Kate thought as she and Terry said their good-byes.

At 6:30, as she was packing up to head to dinner with the girls,

Kate's cell phone rang; caller ID told her it was Suzy.

"You are *not* backing out of our dinner. We will hunt you down if you don't show up, Ms. Spellman. I mean it," Kate said sternly.

"I wouldn't think of it. I'm really looking forward to having three mother hens tell me what a fuck up I am," Suzy laughed. "But, that's not why I'm calling. Kate, I just got a very interesting piece of news that you need to hear, and I didn't want to bring it up at dinner. There's a junior partner over at Gray and Ferguson who I dated for a couple of months—one of the most boring lays in the world, but he was good for great dinners and generous gifts. Anyway, he just called me, looking for a hookup. I had to engage in some minor phone sex and the promise of a date in the near future, but during the call, he was trying to impress me, and he let some info slip. Philandering Fergie promised Mike Taylor he'd throw the whole weight of his well-oiled political machine into Mike's run for state attorney general in exchange for Mike pursuing criminal charges against Marcy. Can you believe it? That's got to be an ethical violation for both of them. Too bad we'll never be able to prove it."

"Don't be so sure. The Bar Ethics Committee can be pretty persuasive. What's this guy's name? I bet he'd be happy to talk anonymously, especially if he thinks his own ticket is at stake."

Kate was angered by the audacity of Ferguson's dirty tricks and Mike Taylor's unfettered ambition.

"William Greene, but please try not to get my name linked to any of this—although it might keep William from calling me in the future, and that wouldn't be all bad," Suzy laughed. "By the way," she added, "Ferguson also put pressure on the administrator of Jackson Memorial. Fergie told the administrator he'd make sure their funding was cut if he didn't fire Marcy. What a scum! I hope she does decide to sue them."

"You're the best, Suzy. This is great information; I just have to figure out how to use it. I promise I'll go a bit easier on you tonight, and I'll even buy the first round of drinks as a way of saying thanks! See you shortly," Kate chuckled, and they hung up.

Kate and Suzy were the first ones to arrive at the restaurant, but Beth and Mel soon followed, and the roast of Suzy began in earnest. She took it well and answered every comment with "You are *absolutely* right, I don't know what I was thinking," or "You don't need to worry. I'll *never* do anything like that again, I promise."

When there was a lull in the scolding, and after they'd ordered their dinners, Suzy asked if she could have the floor for a few minutes to tell them about Terry and how in lust she was. Despite Kate's protests, Suzy couldn't be dissuaded from giving some details about Terry's inventive ideas involving his handcuffs and the tray of ice cubes from their minibar at the hotel in St. Pete. As usual, Suzy's tale of her sexual adventures was highly entertaining, and the women were laughing so hard they forgot to be cross with her.

When Suzy's tales were told, Beth and Melissa informed them they'd set a date for their wedding, but were still looking for the right place. They had wanted a small outdoor wedding, only about 50 people, and had hoped to find a hotel on the beach, but everything was booked for the next six months. They didn't want to wait that long. Kate asked if they would consider her beach house as the wedding venue. It was quickly decided her place at the beach would be the perfect location.

When it was Kate's turn, she told them about her most recent dinner with Bill. She then regaled them with the story of her run to the marina to "secretly" see him off on a cruise to the Caribbean, only to be discovered by his basset hound. When she finished they all were laughing so hard tears were rolling down their cheeks.

"So, you see, now Bill is off somewhere in the Caribbean trying to find himself and figure out what he wants," Kate concluded.

All three of her friends instantly asked what *she* wanted.

Kate sighed heavily. "I'm trying to figure that out, but I think I've sort of complicated things. You see, I recently started seeing someone—well, it isn't really 'seeing someone.' Frankly, it's really mostly sex . . . I mean it started out as 'no-strings-attached, rebound sex' . . . but now, I'm not sure what it is."

Kate was stammering now, and her friends were looking at her in stunned disbelief.

"Wow, Kate, this is totally unlike you. First, you have an affair with Bill, and now you've got someone new. So, who is it?" Suzy asked with interest.

"Well, actually, you know him," Kate replied. "As a matter of fact, he used to work for you." Kate giggled in spite of herself.

There was silence at their table for the first time that evening.

"What? Ed? *Your associate, Ed?* The guy who *works for you?*" Suzy asked, horrified. "Are you out of your fucking mind? I mean, the guy's a hunk, and you just know someone that age wants to fuck *all* the time. But, for Christ's sake, Kate—he *works* for you!!! Even I wouldn't do that, and *didn't* do that, or him! And, it wasn't because I didn't want to. Holy fuck, Kate! Even I know better than to have sex with someone who works for me! He could seriously sue the firm and create all kinds of hell for you once you grow tired of him or he of you." Suzy stared incredulously at Kate.

Kate squirmed silently, feeling properly chastised.

Finally, Suzy continued, smiling a bit now. "OMG, Kate, I can't fricking believe you! You are no better than *I* am when it comes to *your* newly awakened libido!! Actually, I can't believe I'm going to say this, but you're *worse* than I am!"

Suzy looked at Kate, trying to figure out if she was ashamed or proud of her.

"I know, I know. I can't believe I did it either," Kate stammered. "In my defense, I didn't succumb until I heard from Steve Sloan that Bill was seeing Steve's beautiful, young paralegal. According to Steve, it sounded like they were pretty serious. I found out about it when I was with Ed. We ran into Steve as we were leaving the courthouse. I just felt so old, and left behind, and needy . . . So, I asked Ed out to the beach house for what he called 'no-strings-attached, rebound sex.' It sounded great, and the sex *was* great—*is* great. He stayed over again last night."

"Holy crap!" Suzy snorted, nearly spilling her drink.

"But, I really don't think I'm the 'no-strings-attached' sex type. And to make it worse, Bill stopped by the beach house right after we did it the first time. I know he knew immediately what we'd been up to . . . Oh shit. This sounds so bad . . . And it is, but it seemed like a good idea at the time . . ."

Kate's face was scarlet, and she was faltering. She looked around the table at her friends' astounded faces.

Finally, they all started laughing at once.

"Kate Muldoon, welcome to life. It's *complicated!*" Beth said, and reached over to pat her friend's hand.

"Yeah, I can't decide if I'm mad at you or proud of you. I think what I am is insanely jealous! One of the reasons I told Ed to find another job was I was hoping I could tap that if he was working for someone else!"

Suzy's confession caused them all to start laughing again, and Kate ordered another round.

Chapter 17

At 7:50 Tuesday morning, Kate drove past the parking lot at the Heart of Miami Cardiology Clinic, the prestigious cardiology practice Joe Dugan had built. When she didn't see Terry's black Grand Cherokee, she kept going, but as she rolled past the clinic's driveway, she glanced farther up the road and saw Terry's car parked in the lot next door.

Kate pulled in and parked next to him, walked over to the driver's door and tapped on the heavily tinted glass. Terry powered the window down a few inches and said, "Hop in the passenger side," and powered the window back up. Kate walked around and heard the door locks clink as she put her hand on the door handle.

Terry does love his cloak-and-dagger stuff, she thought, smiling to herself.

"What's happened so far?" she inquired sliding in next to Terry who was looking out the front windshield through a long-range telescoping camera lens. She took a sip of her Grande Extra Bold.

"So far, I've seen the office manager arrive, and one of the doctors in the practice. According to DMV, the doctor's name is José Perez. He's a cardiologist like Joe Dugan, and about as well known. Dual certified in the U.S. and Mexico." Terry smelled the fresh coffee and finally looked over at Kate, appreciatively accepting the double espresso she offered.

"I also discovered they have on-site, 24/7 security with a company called Discrete & Secure Protection. But, they haven't had the service long, just started about three weeks ago. Before that, they only had a burglar alarm. Not sure why the change in their setup. Interesting that it started up right after Joe Dugan's death."

"Jesus, you're a sneaky bastard. I never want you investigating me!" Kate said admiringly.

"Who says I haven't already?"

Terry glanced at Kate again and winked.

"And about this thing with the kid. What's up with *that*? I thought Suzy was kidding when she told me last night!" Terry laughed.

"Damn it! She wasn't supposed to tell anyone. Now I'll have to kill her next time I see her, so you'd better enjoy your dalliance while she's still alive. And, just in case you plan on harassing me about this, or telling anyone else, I have plenty of ammunition for reprisals, Mr. Handcuffs and Ice Cubes!" Kate countered.

Terry choked on his coffee, and Kate laughed.

"So, I suggest we just don't go there ever again, agreed?" Kate arched her brow as she looked at him.

Terry nodded in agreement, and said, "You got it, Boss Lady."

"Other than Dr. Perez, the office manager and the current security detail, anyone else at home next door?" Kate asked.

"Nope, and I suggest we pop over as soon as we've finished our coffees. It's always good to show up early—it tends to put the target off balance," Terry explained.

Kate agreed. She'd used the same ploy with witnesses and opposing counsel to great advantage.

After another ten minutes, the two of them walked to the clinic and tried the front door. It was locked, so Terry knocked heavily. A large, surprised-looking security guard opened the door only as far as the chain would allow.

"Hello, there, I'm Terry Driver, and this is Kate Muldoon. We have an appointment this morning with Shirley Warner, the office manager, and an attorney, Larry Lewis. I guess we're early."

Terry's tone was friendly and yet assertive, letting the security guard know he had no intention of waiting outside until the appointment time.

"I guess you can come in and wait inside," the young and extremely well-built security guard said.

"I'll tell Ms. Warner you're here early, but I don't know if she'll be able to meet with you until Mr. Lewis arrives."

"Thanks, we appreciate your hospitality, Allan," Terry said reading the young man's name tag, working to build rapport. "You know, you look kind of familiar. Ever serve on the Miami police force? I was there for about 10 years."

He's smooth, Kate thought, again grateful he was on her side.

"Nope, I was thinking about applying when I left the Rangers, but this gig came along first. Private security sure pays better than public service, I'll tell you that."

"You got that right!" Terry responded, and, just like that, Allan and Terry were instant friends.

"So, what caused the clinic to go with live, on-site, 24/7?" Terry asked as casually as if he was asking for the time. "They have a break-in or something?"

"They have drugs here and noticed some missing about a month ago. They're also getting rid of one of the doctors in the practice—turns out that can be pretty contentious. Who knew, right?" the loquacious security guard continued.

"Yeah," Terry said, "who knew."

"Well, let me go tell Ms. Warner you're here," Allan said as he walked through the waiting room door.

"It's a pleasure to watch you work, Mr. Driver," Kate said softly. "I think we're going to need to find out what drugs went missing, but I bet digitalis is one of them. And I'm also betting our friend Zeke Peters is the doctor being given the heave-ho."

"Right there with you on both counts," Terry replied.

Before the guard could return, there was another knock on the front door; Terry opened it.

"Hi, you must be Larry Lewis. I'm Terry Driver. I think you know my colleague, Kate Muldoon," Terry said nonchalantly as he held out his hand.

A somewhat befuddled Larry Lewis shook Terry's extended hand and turned toward Kate, finding her hand extended too.

"Larry, we worked together on the local grievance committee

about four years ago. You probably don't remember me."

Kate knew full well he remembered her. They had fought over a number of charges Kate had found far more egregious than Larry—plus, he had asked her out only to discover she was married at the time.

"Of course, I remember you, Kate. It's great to see you again. Sorry to hear about your divorce," Larry blurted out with a smile.

"Those things happen," she replied. "We got here a bit early to pick up the documents we subpoenaed. I understand the practice has decided to sever its relationship with Dr. Peters. I know terminations can be sticky. I don't envy your job on that," Kate said knowingly, as she began engendering her own instant rapport.

Kate saw Terry smiling approvingly behind Larry.

"Don't you know it," Larry said with a sigh. "The practice is in chaos right now. Between Dr. Dugan's death, the missing meds, and terminating its relationship with Peters, there hasn't been a boring moment for the last three weeks. All we need now is a tax audit and life will be perfect."

"Ouch, sounds like a mess—but good for the billable hours, right?" Kate winked at Larry; he smiled and nodded in agreement.

Allan walked back into the waiting room to find the three visitors chatting happily.

"Ms. Warner said she wanted to wait for Mr. Lewis, but since he's here now, I guess you can all head back. Mr. Lewis, you know where the conference room is, don't you?"

"Sure, could you tell Shirley we're all here and she should come in as soon as she can? No reason this should take longer than necessary," Larry said and led off through the door and down the hall to the right.

"Dr. Perez will be joining you too," Allan shouted after them.

Dr. Perez and Shirley Warner entered the conference room only moments after Kate, Terry, and Larry had made themselves comfortable at the large conference table. Introductions were accomplished, and Kate and Terry fell silent, waiting to see how Larry planned to proceed.

"As I mentioned, everything's been chaotic and nothing's gone as we might have hoped the last several weeks. Kate, I'm actually glad you're here. When we started collecting documents to respond to your subpoena, we decided it was time to clean out Joe's, Dr. Dugan's, office. The office staff didn't want Mrs. Dugan to participate. She can be difficult to work with and has always been pretty insulting to the staff. Mrs. Dugan wanted Zeke Peters to go through the office for her, but because he was being . . . asked to separated from the practice, we weren't comfortable with that idea. So, over the weekend, a couple of our nurses worked on it with Shirley. Everything was pretty standard stuff. Dr. Dugan was very meticulous; there wasn't much junk to clean out. But, there was one drawer in his desk that was locked. We never found the key, so we had to get a locksmith out to open it for us."

Larry stopped talking and looked down at the tabletop.

"We just got it open a couple of days ago," he continued. "And I now wish we'd opened it sooner. Somehow, though, it just didn't feel right to start rifling through his things until last weekend. I guess we weren't ready to accept the fact that Joe was gone." Larry looked up at Kate and Terry. "Anyway, when we got the locksmith out here, he said it looked like someone had tried to jimmy the lock. There were also some fresh chips in the wood at the top opening of the drawer. Now that we have it open, I can certainly understand why someone would have wanted to get into that drawer."

Larry paused again searching for the right words.

"When they called me to tell me what they found, I told them to leave it just as it was. I figured you'd want to see the contents as Dr. Dugan originally organized them. We looked at the documents, but didn't take them out of the drawer or rearrange them. Oddly, it all seemed so intrusive. Anyway, let's move to Dr. Dugan's office so you can take possession of the documents, including the ones we collected from our general files. We've stacked those on top of Joe's desk."

Larry stood and led the way.

Kate tossed Terry a sideways glance, raising her eyebrows, and he responded in kind.

This is going to be far more interesting than I'd imagined, Kate thought.

When the group reached Dr. Dugan's office, Shirley unlocked the door and stood to the side as they all trooped in. The office was empty except for some pieces of furniture. There were no books on the built-in shelves, and no art or diplomas on the walls. Even the floor was empty. An area rug was rolled up along one end of the room. All that remained was a small sofa, a coffee table, a couple of side chairs, a small table, a desk chair, and a large old wooden desk. There was no sign that a well-known and highly respected doctor had worked here for years. It seemed to Kate as if the man's existence had been wiped from the earth.

Talk to me, Joe Dugan. If I'm going to speak for you, you have to talk to me, Kate thought. But, standing in the empty office, Joe Dugan's voice seemed to have been silenced forever.

Larry Lewis led the way to Dr. Dugan's desk. As Kate and Terry watched, he pulled open the drawer. On the top of a pile of documents about four inches deep, was a legal-sized envelope with the words, *"For Marcy Anne Simpson, My One True Love"* written in large block print.

"Don't touch another thing," Kate said as she pulled out her cell phone and dialed Chief Jordan's number. "I'm contacting the cops. The police should have investigated this whole office. This was after all where the EMTs found Dr. Dugan the night he died. I take it no cops have been here?" Kate asked.

Lewis and Warner shook their heads.

"There's an allegation of murder being made against my client, Marcy Simpson. There's every chance these documents will provide evidence that will help prove her innocence and possibly help identify Dr. Dugan's murderer," Kate said.

"Yes, this is Kate Muldoon," she said into her phone when the chief's office answered. "It is absolutely imperative that I speak with Chief Jordan immediately. I'll hold," Kate said with authority to the receptionist on the other line.

There was silence in the room as they waited for the chief to pick up his phone.

"Chief, Kate here. You and your most trusted detectives need to come to Dr. Dugan's office at his clinic immediately. There is evidence here that may bear on Marcy Simpson's innocence and help you identify Dr. Dugan's murderer. I'm not entrusting it to anyone but you, for obvious reasons. I'll wait for you to get here."

Kate stayed on the line just long enough to hear Chief Jordan agree to meet her.

I guess when you talk, Dr. Dugan, you shout. Thanks for speaking up. Your "One True Love" needed this, Kate thought, as she sat down in Dr. Dugan's desk chair and tried to restrain her hands from diving into the contents of the desk drawer.

She could see legal documents, letters, and what looked like an insurance policy among the documents in the drawer.

While they waited for Chief Jordan, Kate and Terry interviewed Dr. Perez and Shirley Warner. They learned the practice had decided to sever its ties with Zeke Peters the day after Joe Dugan's death. Every single doctor in the clinic had wanted Zeke out of the practice almost from the moment he joined them. Zeke consistently saw the fewest patients and added the least value, both monetary and otherwise. But, for years, Joe Dugan had fought to keep Zeke in the practice. Once Joe was gone, the other doctors couldn't get rid of Zeke fast enough. The day they voted to kick Zeke out, they also changed the locks.

Several days later, when a routine audit was done of the drugs on-site, they discovered they were short a large quantity of digitalis and some oxycodone.

Dr. Perez told them that for the last two months of his life, Joe Dugan hadn't been himself, and he'd confided in Perez that he was going to be filing for divorce soon. Dugan had said he hoped the divorce wouldn't be too disruptive or negatively impact the practice, but that he couldn't continue to watch his wife's abysmal conduct damage his boys. Unfortunately, Perez didn't know who was representing Joe in the divorce or how far along he was in the process. Joe also told Perez he'd recently sent away three samples for paternity testing because he was almost positive he was not his oldest son's biological father.

As they were finishing up their interviews, Allan walked into Dr. Dugan's office with an awestruck look on his face. He let them know the chief of police had arrived and was asking for Kate. Kate asked Allan to escort the chief back to the office. She thanked Dr. Perez and Ms. Warner for their time and told them the chief would no doubt be interviewing them shortly.

"Hello, Chief. Fancy meeting you here. This case is certainly not short on surprising twists and turns, is it?" Kate said.

"You can say that again. Kate, this had better be good; we left a department meeting. By the way, these are my three best homicide detectives, Luis Porrello, José Diaz, and Maria Diageo. Folks, this is the infamous Kate Muldoon you've heard so much about. And this is Terry Driver, one of the good ones that got away from us," Chief Jordan said making the introductions.

As they shook hands, Kate brought the chief and three detectives up to speed on their conversations with Dr. Perez, Shirley Warner, and Larry Lewis. When she got to the part of the story about the desk drawer, Kate pointed to the still-open desk drawer and said, "According to Dr. Perez, after the locksmith opened the drawer, they didn't remove anything. You'll notice the lock looks like someone may have tried to jimmy it open, and the desk drawer has marks around the top edge in the front, and the back looks like someone tried to pry or pound it open. Unfortunately, a number of people have had their hands on the desk and drawer since Dr. Dugan's death, so I'm not sure you'll find any helpful prints, but it's worth a try."

Chief Jordan and his three detectives pulled on evidence gloves, and the chief looked as if he was about to start looking through the documents in the drawer.

"Chief, I have to ask a favor," Kate said, reaching out her arm to stop him from diving into the contents of the drawer. "I'd like to inventory what's in the desk drawer and get a copy of everything before it leaves here with you. I trust you, Chief. If I didn't, I might not have called you until we'd made our copies and photos. But, after Mike Taylor's rush to have a warrant issued for Marcy's arrest, and knowing who's aligned against my client, I have concerns about the safety of this evidence once it leaves here. I have a valid subpoena for these records, and I know that doesn't matter since they're evidence in a criminal case, but I have a legal claim to at least copies."

Chief Jordan looked up in surprise at Kate and hesitated. Finally, he said, "That's reasonable under the circumstances. Larry, you can serve as a witness to this too. OK, folks, let's get this investigation started. We should have done this as soon as we learned about the digitalis in the doc's blood. Porrello, start taking your photos; Diaz and Diageo, start looking for trace evidence. Kate, Larry, and Terry, we'll work our way down through these documents one layer at a time, taking photos, and making our inventory and copies as we go. Diageo and Diaz, get the investigation kit out of the car. I don't hold out much hope for helpful prints—the office looks like they've cleaned it up pretty thoroughly."

Back at the office, Polly made three additional copies of the documents they'd retrieved from the clinic. Pam would create an inventory and hand deliver a full set of the documents to Ronald Gray, along with a receipt for him to sign with the inventory attached. Kate drafted a quick letter to accompany the documents explaining how and when they were discovered and referring Gray to Chief Jordan if he had any questions.

Kate and Ed pored over the set of documents Kate had designated as their "working set," making notes as they studied them. The papers found in the desk drawer were, of course, the most interesting. The letter that had rested on the top of the pile was handwritten, from Joe Dugan to Marcy, dated a month after their divorce. In it, Joe explained that he didn't know if she would ever read the letter since she'd return the others he'd sent her, but that he wanted this letter hand delivered to her in the event of his death.

Joe's letter was an obvious effort to set the record straight with Marcy, who, in addition to returning Joe's previous letters, apparently wouldn't answer his telephone calls. Those unopened letters were also among the documents found in the drawer. The envelopes had remained unopened until Chief Jordan slit the tops and pulled out the letters. Each envelope was marked with a handwritten "Return to

Sender" across the address.

The letter on top of the documents looked like it had been opened and re-read numerous times; the creases of the folds were worn thin from refolding. The letter spoke poignantly of Joe Dugan's loved for Marcy, but he also explained how he'd gotten drunk at a holiday party she hadn't been able to attend because she couldn't get the time off from work. He wrote that he'd blacked out and woke up in bed with Joan in a motel room. Until that night, Joan was just one of the young women in the hospital administration office who flirted with Joe and the other doctors, many of whom, like he and Zeke, were married but played along for the fun of it. He hadn't even known who her father was at the time. The only other person who ever knew about this slip was Zeke, because Joe had called Zeke to come get them at the motel and take them back to their cars. Six weeks later, Joan told him she was pregnant, and the baby was his. Joan refused to have an abortion, and Joe had done what he considered the honorable thing: he divorced Marcy and married Joan. The letter ended with a promise from Joe that he would "find a way to make it right someday."

Also in the drawer was the original insurance policy with handwritten changes to the beneficiary line that now read, *"Marcy Anne Simpson* ('Dugan' was crossed out), *my* ('first' was added) *wife."* In addition to these changes, Joe had written a note just above his signature line on the last page stating, *"It is my specific intention that this policy remain in place even now that Marcy and I are divorced. She doesn't know I've kept the policy current. I hope she will use the proceeds however she wants, but I pray that she will have the opportunity to go to medical school someday. I love you, Marcy. You are my one true love, Joe."* All of the interlineations on the insurance policy had been initialed and dated by Joe Dugan, and he'd taken the extra step of having his changes notarized.

Under the insurance papers were draft copies of a petition for dissolution of marriage, prepared by none other than Kate's favorite divorce attorney, Steve Sloan. The allegations in the child custody section of the papers were a scathing attack on Joan, highlighting her drunkenness and drug addiction, as well as a number of incidents of child abandonment and neglect. If even half of what was alleged in the petition was true, there was no way Joan was going to get custody of the boys. The divorce would have been sensational in all the horrible, tawdry sense of the word.

I guess I'll be calling Steve first thing tomorrow morning, Kate mused.

At the very bottom of the drawer was an opened envelope addressed to Dr. Dugan, inside was a report from a genetics lab. There was a lot of medical terminology Kate didn't understand completely, but there was no missing the fact that Dr. Dugan had submitted three samples of DNA for paternity testing. There was a less-than-1-percent-probability samples A and B were related, and a 99 percent probability samples B and C were. The report was dated a little over four months ago.

Now, all I need to do is figure out who A, B, and C are, and I think I have a pretty damn good idea, she smiled sadly.

The documents from the clinic's administration office held little information except for the life insurance policies that Dr. Dugan had taken out through work. He had purchased a $1.5 million policy on his life naming a trust set up for his sons as the beneficiary. The trustee was now his brother, but, until four months ago, the trustee had been none other than the "Devil Spawn" himself, Zeke Peters. Joe had also maintained a second $1.5 million policy naming Joan as the beneficiary, but that also changed four months ago when Joe changed the beneficiary to the trust for his boys. No other insurance policies had been purchased as far as the newly discovered documents indicated. A recently executed will was also among Dugan's papers; his brother was named as his personal representative.

Looks like you'd had enough of her shit. Sorry you didn't get the satisfaction of divorcing her ass, Kate's thoughts were spinning as she sat back in her chair after her review of the documents. *But, at least now, I'm sure Joe Dugan has finally begun to tell me what he wants.*

Kate said good-bye to Ed, and without further explanation, told him not to expect to hear from her until noon the next day. She picked up a set of the documents and drove out to the beach.

Phoebe and Sadie raced to greet Kate the moment she opened the door of her beach house, nearly knocking her down as she tried to pet them both at the same time, while balancing the large stack of papers.

"Kate, what a great surprise!" Marcy said when she saw Kate wrestling with the dogs.

"Why didn't you call? I would have made you my world-famous Chilean Sea Bass. You can get some totally awesome fish at the market in town . . ."

Marcy stopped talking when she saw the look on Kate's face.

"Oh shit, Kate, is there more bad news? I can't imagine anything worse than what I've already experienced. It *is* bad news, isn't it? That's why you're here in person."

Marcy sat down abruptly on the sofa and buried her face in her hands.

"No, sweetie, it's not bad news," Kate said, sitting down next to Marcy and putting the documents on the coffee table in front of them and her arm around Marcy's shoulders.

"It's actually incredibly good news, but it *is* significant, and it *will* knock you on your ass. So, I came to pick you up and dust you off. I'm also going to make you my best comfort food dinner, and we're drinking one of my very best wines—the whole bottle, maybe two.

"You sit here and read these documents we found in a locked desk drawer in Joe's office at the clinic," Kate said, tapping the stack and placing the letter that had been on top of the pile on Marcy's lap, along with the copy of the envelope addressed to *"Marcy Anne Simpson, my one true love."*

"I'll get the wine—you're going to need it."

Marcy's entire face quivered.

"Oh my God. Oh my God. Oh my God," was all Marcy could say for several moments as she rocked back and forth with tears pouring down her face. Kate patted her on the shoulder and went to fetch a box of tissues.

"Here you go; you'll need all of these, I think," Kate said as she handed Marcy the box. "You'll be OK. Just read. I'll get the wine." Kate walked into the kitchen.

Before she could even get the cork out of the bottle, the keening began in earnest in the living room. Sadie and Phoebe immediately ran back into the living room to sit on either side of Marcy with their chins on her knees—providing their very best doggie support.

Dogs always know when you need to be consoled, and all they need are their big beautiful brown eyes to get the job done, Kate thought as she recalled all the times her girls had been there for her with their own special version of consolation.

Chapter 18

The morning sunlight poured through the sliding glass doors that made up the back wall of Kate's beach house.

She reluctantly lifted her head from the sofa's armrest, and found she wasn't as hung-over as she should be. The remains of their comfort food dinner—homemade mac and cheese, two pints of ice cream, an empty bottle of Joseph Phelps Insignia, and a half bottle of Armagnac—littered the coffee table.

Marcy was still very much asleep at the other end of the sofa. Sadie and Phoebe were curled up on the floor next to them.

It had been quite a night.

Kate rested her head back down on the sofa, knowing the minute she put a foot on the floor the girls would be ready for a run on the beach. She had to work up to that.

She lay very still, contemplating the events of the previous night. Marcy had read every piece of paper three times. During the first time through, she'd cried so hard Kate wondered if she was going to need to call 911. Marcy had barely been able to breathe between sobs.

The second time through the documents, Marcy asked tons of questions, and Kate was able to explain the significance of the documents and the fact that Joe changed his life insurance beneficiary from Joan to the boys' trust and the trustee from Zeke to his brother, Michael. The hardest questions were about the lab report. Kate just didn't have the answers, not yet anyway . . . but she would.

The third time through the documents, Marcy was no longer crying. Instead, she was getting mad. She knew someone had duped her ex-husband and destroyed her life just because they could. Marcy wanted revenge.

Slowly, Kate sat up and carefully placed a foot on the floor. Sadie's eyes opened, and she lifted her head. Phoebe followed suit.

"Come on, girls," she whispered, heading toward the back door.

She picked up a bottle of water, a tennis ball, and her cell phone on the way. There was no beach run in her immediate future, but she knew a walk would clear her head.

As she walked along the beach and played ball with her dogs, Kate called her office. She left a message for Sophia saying she would be in later that afternoon and could be reached on her cell phone until then.

Next, she called Steve Sloan's direct office line and left a message for him to call her cell phone at his earliest opportunity. Then she called Ed's office—as she'd suspected, he was already in the office and picked up on the first ring.

"Good morning. Are we going to see you today?" From the tone of Ed's greeting she knew he was irked. "I've got a couple of things I need to talk over with you. We can do it now on the phone if you like," he snipped.

Yep, he's got his nose out of joint about something! How tedious! I've got enough on my plate without having to deal with "relationship" issues, Kate thought.

"Good morning to you too, Mr. Evert. Yes, I will be in about midafternoon. I just left a message for Sophia letting her know. And, it's only 7:30, so no need to get pissed off that I'm not there. I really don't need the hassle right now. Besides, we have a ton to do." Kate's tone was tense and perhaps a bit harsher than she intended. On the other hand, maybe it was exactly as intended.

"Sounds like someone got up on the wrong side of the bed," Ed countered.

"I could say the same for you, so don't start down that road, neither of us wants to go there. Believe me."

Kate's own attitude was now decidedly testy.

"I'm out at the beach," Kate started over and tried to soften her tone.

"Really? Sounds like fun," he sniped.

"Not really, Ed. Marcy had a hell of a night last night, but the bottom line is she wants blood from the people who ruined her life. I want to talk about what I need you to do for me on that score, but first, tell me what work issues have *you* so spun up."

"OK, Boss Lady," Ed said in an attempt to reduce the tension in their conversation.

"Both the Goodman summary judgment brief and the Fisher motions in *limine* are done and ready for your final approval. You've been so tied up in the criminal issues lately you haven't been available on the pending civil docket issues, and things are backing up," he said, walking close to the edge again. Kate struggled hard not to rise to the bait.

When she failed to respond, Ed continued, "*And finally*, Bobbi Jo's attorney called and wants to talk settlement."

"OK. Tell Bobbi Jo's attorney the only points we'll discuss are ways in which we can coordinate efforts to accommodate Bobbi Jo's transition. There will *not* be any money on the table. Then make sure the final versions of the Goodman summary judgment brief and the Fisher motions are on the system. Send me an e-mail to confirm that, and then I'll review them online. If they're ready to go, I'll let Polly know. She can take it from there," Kate said, succinctly responding to each of Ed's concerns.

"And, *finally*," Kate said, mimicking Ed's tone, trying, with increasing difficulty, to keep her irritation in check, "I need you to do two things for me this morning on Marcy's case—*if* you have the time, of course," she added pointedly, and then paused, waiting for her anger to subside before continuing.

"Please call Chief Jordan and see if there's a time today or tomorrow that we can have a conference regarding the material we found in Dr. Dugan's desk. I have some discovery ideas, but the cops are more likely to be successful in getting the info than we would be. Then please call Judge Blumquist's office and see if we can get an in-chambers hearing either at the end of this week or the beginning of next. I want to let him know we think we're going to be ready to request the interpleader hearing within a week. Since we told him we'd wait for the criminal matter to be resolved, I want to give him a heads-up that we now think we have the evidence to show our girl is totally in the clear."

Kate had finished her list of to-dos but couldn't help herself as she added, "Let me know if you're too busy—I'll ask Polly to do these things for me."

"I have the time, Kate," Ed responded, sounding wounded.

"Great," she replied acerbically. "By the way, I have also placed a call with Steve Sloan this morning. I'll let you know what he has to say about Joe Dugan's divorce—*if* you're still interested in my *criminal* cases, that is."

Ed knew now that he'd step over a line—*again*. He realized he shouldn't have pushed Kate. She never reacted well to that. But he was feeling brushed to the side and wanted to get her attention. Now he had it, but not the way he wanted.

"I'm interested, Kate," he sighed with resignation.

"Nice to know," she said as she hung up.

Kate turned her phone to vibrate and headed back to the house. She wanted to hear from Steve Sloan, but at this point, she wasn't sure she wanted to hear from anyone else. She was pissed at Ed, probably unreasonably so, but she couldn't talk herself out of it.

When she got back to her house, she left the wet, smelly dogs on the back porch and fed them. They'd have to stay there until she could get them in the outdoor shower under the deck. Next, she sneaked back inside to make a pot of much-needed coffee. Her phone vibrated while she waited for the coffee to brew.

"Hey," Kate whispered as she stepped out on the back deck so that her conversation wouldn't wake Marcy who was still asleep . . . or passed out on the sofa in the living room.

"I've been wondering when I'd get your call," Steve said by way of greeting. "It's a hell of a mess. We've got a bunch of issues to address, the attorney-client communication privilege for a starter. That's the reason I didn't feel I could bring this to your attention and waited for you to discover it yourself." Steve sounded defensive.

"I understand, Steve. Have you done any research on the

attorney-client privilege post-death of the client? I did when I sat on the ethics committee, about four years ago, but I haven't updated it. We can do that for you, if you'd like. Let me tell you what I recall to be the case, and then I'll get Ed to update the research and make sure I'm right. Sound good?"

"I did a bit of research myself knowing you'd find the divorce papers eventually," he replied. "Generally, the attorney-client communication privilege survives the death of the client and can't be waived by the attorney, but there may be a relevant exception. When the issue involves ascertaining the intent of the client in a testamentary situation, the privilege can be waived. I'm just not sure we can use that exception here. There are also some ethical rules on point, and that's why I was reluctant to come forward, Kate," Steve said, explaining his position.

"Steve, I think we have a couple of other points to consider. First, regarding the ethics rules, it's well established they're not intended to override the rules of evidence. But, more to the point, for the privilege to be applied in the first place, the communication between the attorney and the client has to be *intended* to be confidential. Otherwise, the communication simply isn't protected. Joe Dugan told you about Joan's conduct and his suspicions regarding paternity expressly so you would include those facts in the petition for dissolution. He never intended for that information to be kept confidential. On the contrary, Steve, Joe *intended* for you to publish the information in a document filed in the public record," Kate said, providing Steve the benefit of her analysis of the situation.

"That makes sense. Can you get Ed to spend some time on it and have him shoot me an e-mail explaining his research?" Steve asked. "I'd really appreciate that. As soon as I have it in hand, we can have a conference and decide how to proceed. But, Kate, you can anticipate strong opposition from Joan's attorneys, so we need to have our ducks in a row. Gray won't hesitate to file an ethics complaint against me. I don't mind a fight; I just want to be on the right side of the fight."

"Yes, we'll get on it right away. I have some information you may find interesting, even though you aren't involved in handling Dugan's estate. And as soon as we have the research done, I want to talk to you about the paternity blood test report we found in Joe's desk drawer."

"I knew you would. We'll talk, just as soon as we get straight on the attorney-client privilege. Call me later today." Kate told him she and Ed would be in touch soon and Steve said good-bye.

Reluctantly, Kate called Ed back and gave him his new assignment. The conversation was brief and frosty.

Kate walked back into the house for a cup of coffee. As she poured it, she heard a groggy voice from the living room.

"I smell coffee. Thank God, there's coffee," Marcy mumbled as she tried to sit up.

"The elixir of life. How do you take it, kiddo? You need about three cups of this to counteract our overindulgence of last night," Kate responded.

"Black, please; black, no sugar. I just need to mainline that stuff for a while."

Kate walked into the living room carrying two cups of hot, strong, black coffee and handed one to Marcy. "How are you feeling?"

"Drained, empty, mad, hung-over," Marcy smiled. "And a little bit happy, Kate, I have to admit it. He loved me, Kate. It doesn't make it perfect, but it sure makes it better, and it heals a part of me I didn't think would ever heal," she said resting her head on the back of the sofa. "How do I ever thank you, Kate?"

"We aren't out of the woods yet, not even close, but we will be. Just a little while longer. You have to keep hanging tough," Kate said, patting Marcy's hand.

"Now, I have to give my dogs a quick shower. They've been in the ocean this morning and smell really bad. Then I need to get ready for work. How about breakfast in the village in about an hour? Think you can pull it together by then?"

"I'll give it a try. I'm not sure I'm ready for a public appearance just yet. Let me see how I feel after a hot shower and more coffee," Marcy said as she took a big gulp and headed to the guest bath.

"OK," Kate said, standing up and heading toward the back deck.

On her way back into the city, Kate thought through her conversation with Marcy over breakfast at the Village Café in Garrett Beach. Marcy had been concerned about showing her face in a public place. She was sure everyone would have seen her photo under the "*Killer Nurse?*" headline. Kate had tried to reassure her that the public's memory is a short one, but Marcy had, nevertheless, worn a ball cap, sunglasses, and flipped up the collar of her jacket to hide her identity as much as possible. Happily, no one seemed to notice.

Marcy's vehemence about pressing forward as quickly as possible had only increased overnight. She wanted to clear her name once and for all. Kate again assured her the case was priority number one for her team right now. She also told Marcy about her call with Steve Sloan, and how the attorney-client privilege would most likely be dealt with, meaning the allegations in Joe's petition for dissolution of marriage and for sole custody of the children would likely get a full public airing.

Kate explained she'd be talking with Chief Jordan later in the day to request the coroner provide information regarding Joe's DNA, and to ask him to find a way to obtain the DNA of Zeke Peters as well. Whether they could obtain a sample of Joe's eldest son's DNA remained doubtful, but with the sample from the two adults, the son's was almost unnecessary. Finally, Kate informed Marcy she was already taking steps to let Judge Blumquist know they would be seeking a hearing on the interpleader as soon as possible given the evidence that had now come to light.

When Kate asked Marcy what she would do with $4 million, if and when she received it, Marcy responded, "I have no idea, but something I learned a long time ago is don't spend money you don't have—not even in your head. I guess I'll figure that out if it actually happens."

Kate's cell phone rang through the Bluetooth connection in the car. Caller ID let her know it was Ed. That information did not fill her with warm and fuzzy feelings. She wondered briefly if that should worry her.

"Yeah," Kate said abruptly into the car's microphone.

"Hello, Kate, how's your day going?" Ed asked cheerfully, making an obvious effort to overcome the distance created by their earlier conversations.

"Fine, Ed. How's yours?" Kate decided to play along.

"Not too bad. I wanted to let you know Chief Jordan said he could talk to us this afternoon around 4:00. He'd like to do it in his office. Also, Judge Blumquist has an opening late Friday afternoon if we want to swing by his office around 4:30. What do you think? Shall I set up both meetings?"

Ed was being overly solicitous now, but Kate preferred it to his earlier bossiness. She wondered again if she should be concerned.

"Sounds good. I'll be in the office in an hour, and we can head over to the chief's office together."

"OK. Let me know when you get into the office. I'll call Chief Jordan and set up our meeting, and I'll let the judge know we'll be there at 4:30 on Friday and give Ron Gray and Mike Taylor notice of the hearing," Ed said efficiently.

When they'd hung up, Kate wondered again whether she should tell Ed their brief dalliance was over.

It's exhausting having a relationship with someone you work with. They're always around, and it's especially tiring when you have to sneak around and worry your workmates will find out. Guilt is just so damn exhausting.

Ed and Kate walked into Miami PD's headquarters at 4:00. Kate asked for Chief Jordan and when she saw the cop at the desk flinch, she added, "He's actually *expecting* us—this time."

Kate smiled her warmest and friendliest smile in the hope the young cop would believe her. When the officer on the desk called the chief, she looked surprised when he told her to "send them on back—they know the way."

As they walked through the security door, a number of cops lifted their heads to watch them pass. They were used to Kate's fiery entrances and found her current docile demeanor odd. In the chief's office, handshakes were exchanged, and Kate and Ed settled into the side chairs in front of his desk.

"Thanks for seeing us today, Chief. I'm hoping we can bring you up to date on what's happening in our investigation of Marcy's case, and maybe convince you to coordinate efforts on some things you will be able to accomplish far more easily than we could."

"Happy to help, if I can, Kate."

"I've shown our client the documents we recovered from Dr. Dugan's desk drawer. Also, we sent copies of everything by hand delivery to Ronald Gray yesterday, so I expect you and the prosecutor are going to start getting pressure from him, if you haven't already."

Chief Jordan smiled and nodded.

"You need to know that neither Joe Dugan's brother, nor his parents, have any love for Joan, or Zeke Peters, for that matter. Apparently, Joan was a terrible wife and mother, and Zeke is the unexplainable 'Devil Spawn.' I highly recommend you talk with Dugan's mother and brother in St. Petersburg. I know you aren't going to want to just take my word for any of this. You could talk to Terry Driver too and get his report from his meetings with them, but ultimately, you'll need to talk to them personally.

"Also, I've talked to Steve Sloan about the divorce papers we found in the desk drawer, and we've looked into the question of whether his information might be privileged; it isn't. The allegations in the divorce papers about Joan, as well as what Joe told Steve about Joan and Zeke, and his other suspicions, were never intended to be treated as privileged. On the contrary, Joe Dugan provided that information exactly so it *could be* made public when he filed the divorce papers in the public record. I recommend you question Steve about the allegations and the other information he might have. Joe Dugan felt Joan is an unfit mother, and, frankly, he had the evidence to prove it," Kate said, summarizing their investigation for the chief.

"Sounds like you've been pretty busy, Kate. I'm not surprised. My team is just getting started. We'll follow up on those points, and I appreciate your spadework on these leads. So, what do you need from me?" he asked.

"Chief, when the coroner does his autopsy, I would like a complete copy of his findings, and he should look into whether Dr. Dugan's DNA matches one of the samples in the DNA testing report we found in his desk drawer. I'm guessing it will, and I'm guessing Dugan is sample A and neither of the other two samples will be related to Dr. Dugan's."

"That's easy enough. Send me the formal request for the information and I'll get it to you as soon as I can," the chief answered amicably.

"Thanks, but that's not all I'd like you to do," Kate interjected.

"Funny, I didn't think it was," the chief laughed. "Let me guess . . . I bet you want us to get a DNA sample of Zeke Peters and have that compared to the lab report too."

"You guessed it, Chief. What do you think?" Kate said, overjoyed the chief already saw the issue.

"Well, I don't think I'd be doing my job very well if I passed up an opportunity to get a sample of the 'Devil Spawn's' DNA. I doubt he will give it to us willingly. We'll get him in for questioning and see if we can pull some DNA without him knowing it, and if we can't, we'll get a court order. I'm pretty sure we have enough for Judge Crawley, especially after I explain how badly Mike Taylor used him when he issued the arrest warrant for Ms. Simpson. By the way, we discovered blood and other trace evidence of interest on the rug left in Dugan's office. We're running tests now. I'll keep you posted, but again, submit a formal request and we'll comply."

Chief Jordan was smiling broadly now. Kate could tell he was going to enjoy stuffing this one down Mike Taylor's throat.

"You're the best, Chief!" Kate said, laughing. "I bet you never thought you'd hear me say that, did you?"

"Actually, you're right. I didn't," he chuckled.

Walking back to Kate's car, Ed said, "Our meeting with Chief Jordan couldn't have gone better. I wonder how Taylor and Gray are going to react to the drastically changed circumstances."

"Not well is my prediction," Kate responded.

"Kate, how about we meet for a run in an hour? I haven't gotten in a 10-miler this week, and if I don't do it today, I'll fall off my training schedule. I've found a great route that runs down to the marina and back. I could meet you at your house. It's on the way."

Kate eyed Ed suspiciously and nearly declined, but she remembered she had not gotten in a long run this week either, and she needed it after her night of excessive drinking and eating with Marcy.

"I could use a long run. Marcy and I ate and drank way too much last night. I'll drop you at the office to pick up your car. What time will you be by my house?"

"Between 5:30 and 6:00. I'll run up the driveway and come in the back door," Ed replied.

"Or I can be on the front porch warming up and watching for you." Kate wasn't completely over her irritation with Ed, and she knew she didn't want him inviting himself to just 'walk in the back door.'

"Sure that works, too."

Ed knew Kate was still miffed and hoped the run would settle her ruffled feathers.

On the way to the office parking garage, they chatted pleasantly about the ramifications of the treasure trove of documents found in Dr. Dugan's desk drawer. But, when Kate stopped behind Ed's car in the garage, and he prepared to hop out, she said, "And, Ed, we're not getting together after the run for a roll in the hay. I'm tired and need a good night's sleep. Got it, Mr. Salesman? You can save your persuasive charms for another evening."

Ed looked surprised but grinned and simply said, "We'll see."

He closed the door and walked to his car.

"Yes, we will," she said watching him walk away.

Chapter 19

Ed stopped by Kate's office around noon on Thursday with two fresh coffees and some sandwiches from the deli in the lobby of their building. He'd been at Square Foods all morning, first meeting with Josie Myers and Kathy Long, and then in an initial negotiation session with Bobbi Jo and Jeff Graff, her attorney. Over their sandwiches, Ed filled Kate in on the events of his morning. Bobbi Jo's attorney was only interested in a monetary settlement and decidedly *not* interested in trying to figure out how to help Bobbi Jo transition to her new gender without entirely upending her work life.

"That's because if there's no monetary settlement, Jeff isn't going to get paid," Kate explained. "The whole sex harassment claim is bogus, and Jeff is simply being an opportunist. In the South, we call that 'bird-dogging,' but up North, they'd call it 'ambulance chasing.' What did you tell him?"

"I said the company isn't giving Bobbi Jo any money because the company hasn't done anything except try to work with her to ensure a successful transition in the workplace. Bobbi Jo's lascivious desire to try out her newfound sexuality was the reason for the drunken, after-hours, sexual encounter she had with her coworker. Of course, I didn't say it quite like that, trust me. I was far more 'understanding,'" Ed smiled. "But, after a while, I got tired of listening to her attorney beat his chest about how traumatized Bobbi Jo was when she found herself drunk in a bar, making out with a coworker.

"When I couldn't take the attorney's drivel any longer, I encouraged Bobbi Jo to try to explain why she felt the company owed her money. At first, she got all tangled up saying the company knew James was going to sexually harass her, but she was unable to explain why she felt that way. I think she was trying to imply that, as an African American male, James would be more inclined to sexually harass a white, female coworker. Happily, neither Bobbi Jo nor Jeff actually *said* that. You know, Kate, sometimes it seems we haven't progressed much beyond the 1950s. Anyway, after listening to them beat around the bush for a while, I decided to call their bluff.

"I asked, 'Certainly you're not implying all black men are sexual harassers, are you? That would be a *racist* comment, and the company has a very strict antidiscrimination policy. Such a claim would not only be extremely offensive, it could also be grounds for disciplinary measures, up to—and including—termination.' That seemed to quickly close down that line of attack. Both Bobbi Jo and Jeff immediately denied implying any such thing," Ed said laughing.

"Great job defusing that one. What was their next tactic, once the race thing was put to bed?" Kate inquired, nibbling on her sandwich.

"Well, finally, I think I got to the core of the issue. Bobbi Jo doesn't have enough money to pay for the surgery she wants to make her transition permanent. Apparently, she recently found out the company's health insurance carrier considers gender reassignment surgery an elective procedure, and it's not covered." Ed stopped talking to take a few more bites of his sandwich as he reflected on these facts.

"You know what, Kate, I think that's an incorrect conclusion. I don't think reassignment surgery is like breast augmentation or a facelift. I doubt any man—or woman, for that matter—would undergo such major surgery as a lark. There's something deeper at issue than appearance with someone like Bobbi Jo."

"A very enlightened view! People for whom sexual identity has never been a question tend to see gender transition, or reassignment surgery, as purely superficial; for appearance only. But the fact of the matter is, for someone who has never truly felt they were a male or a female, even though their body parts told them they were, their disconnect is at the very core of who they are. I'm proud of you for figuring that out," Kate grinned at her associate.

"Well, I've been doing some reading online about gender identity issues and what the surgery entails. I figured I needed to approach this from an intellectual perspective rather than emotional. I'm glad I did. The surgery is actually fascinating."

"So, where did you end up with Bobbi Jo and her 'bird-dogging attorney'?" Kate asked.

"I explained the company doesn't really have much say in what the insurer will and won't cover, but that we'd strongly ask them to reconsider their position. I also suggested Bobbi Jo look into that GoFundMe Web site and see what she can raise there. Plus, I told her that her time off for surgery would be medical leave under the company's FMLA policy, and she could use her accrued vacation time, so very little of her time off would be unpaid. In any event, when she returns from surgery, her job would still be there.

"Then I told her the company had just submitted her name for final approval for the line supervisor position that opened lasted month."

Ed took another couple of bites of his sandwich. "That's when I knew we had her. Bobbi Jo sat back in her chair and started to cry."

Ed's grin filled his face, "We really surprised her with that news. Josie and Kathy told her the paperwork had been in process when she made her announcement about the transition, and no one at the company thought there was any reason not to proceed with the promotion. I guess Bobbi Jo didn't think it was even a possibility. Her attorney didn't say much after that," Ed chortled.

"Sounds like you did a first-rate job. I'm sure the company is pleased."

"Yep. We saw Phillip Bentley in the hallway after our meeting, and Josie couldn't stop talking about the negotiations. I think they're all pretty pleased," Ed said with a self-satisfied smile, and then finished off his sandwich.

"Bobbi Jo said she'd get back to me in a couple of days, but at this point, she said she wanted to take a run at the GoFundMe site and challenge the health insurer's position on gender reassignment surgery. I told her I'd forward the articles I've been reading to the insurance company, along with a copy of Square Food's strongly worded recommendation for a review of their policy and a different outcome.

Bobbi Jo was very grateful, her attorney not so much. But, as you said, he may not be getting paid if Bobbi Jo decides she doesn't have a monetary claim against the company.

"I tried to help out on that score too," Ed continued. "I suggested Jeff might want to work on the insurance appeal, and he should consider mentioning the 'bad faith failure to pay' section of the Florida insurance code, and the similar section in the federal ERISA law. In any event, they seem to have lost interest in suing Square Foods for now."

"What about James' race discrimination claim?" Kate asked. "That seemed fueled by pure speculation."

"Yeah, you're right, speculation and embarrassment. I managed to use the embarrassment angle to our advantage. Turns out James decided not to pursue the grievance once he realized he'd have to admit he'd had his hand firmly wrapped around another man's penis—even though it was unintentional." Ed beamed, and added, "By the way, Bobbi Jo is rather pretty as a woman, and she dresses well. I hope she gets to have her surgery soon. I can see how a guy could be attracted."

"Sounds like you had a pretty great day."

"Yes, I have so far. Do I get a reward, Boss Lady?"

"Sure, I'll give you some more work. How's that?" Kate replied, sidestepping Ed's obvious come-on.

"Not what I had in mind, Boss Lady. How about we head over to The Shack for a couple of those delicious grouper sandwiches tonight, and then go to bed early so we can make it to our hot yoga class at Zero Dark Thirty tomorrow morning?"

Ed looked at Kate, pleading his case with his eyes.

Why do I find him so damn appealing? I shouldn't want him so much, I know he's not good for me, and yet I do, Kate lamented silently. *What the hell, I might as well enjoy myself . . . at least once more.*

"Sounds good," Kate told him, and registered the shocked look on his face when she capitulated so easily.

"But we need to huddle this afternoon and do some serious trial prep. The Brighton Industries trial will soon be staring us in the face. I've decided you're going to play a major role in the trial presentation, so your plate is going to be full."

"Wow, that's great news. What time do you want me back in here to talk trial prep?" Ed asked as he rose to collect their lunch things and headed toward the door.

"How about 3:30? I need to get organized so we have a profitable meeting—that way, we can get out of here early enough to secure a good booth at The Shack."

"Sounds wonderful. See you then, Boss Lady."

It was nearly 3:00 when Kate's cell phone rang, she saw her beach house number displayed on the caller ID window.

"How's it going, Marcy? Are the girls keeping you company or just getting on your nerves?" Kate asked, surprised to hear from Marcy in the middle of the day and hoping nothing had gone wrong at the beach.

"Everything is fine here, and the girls are marvelous company. But, Kate, you'll never believe who just called me." Marcy sounded out of breath and possibly close to tears. "Grace Dugan, Joe's mom. It nearly blew me away. I didn't even know she still had my cell number. What is it about my new life? Nothing can remain fixed for even a couple of hours. Anyway, Grace called to tell me Joe Senior died last night. I knew he was sick from what Terry said the other night at dinner, but I didn't realize the end was so close," Marcy sniffed and blew her nose. She'd definitely been crying.

"Joe Senior was a good guy. A bit old school, but his values were beyond question. I hadn't talked to either of Joe's parents since Joe moved out. Anyway, Grace called to tell me she'd learned Joe's death is being investigated as a murder. She said, and I quote, 'I can't believe those dumb-ass Miami cops actually thought you might have something to do with it. What idiots.' She offered to act as a character witness for me if I need one. When I told her we were pretty sure Joan's father and the estate's lawyer were behind my arrest, she said several words I didn't even think she knew! Then she said something like, 'that miserable, philandering, old cocksucker.' Kate, I think it was the first time I've laughed in weeks," she giggled.

It thrilled Kate to hear her friend sound so relaxed.

"That's great, Marcy. Just hang in there and soon you'll be laughing all the time," Kate said, hoping her prediction was correct.

"Well, I told Grace what you found in Joe's desk, and we had a good cry. She was really wonderful and supportive. She said she could tell Joe hated himself for divorcing me. Anyway, that's not the reason I wanted to tell you about her call. I mentioned to Grace that Zeke Peters and Joan seemed to be very close, and that Joe had divorce papers in his desk with some scathing allegations against Joan. Grace said Michael had told her Joe was planning on trying to have Joan declared an unfit mother. Grace would like to talk to you, Kate. Apparently, she has always wondered about the paternity of Joe's first son.

"You know, Zeke married before Joe and I, and he had his first kid five months after their wedding. When Joe divorced me, Zeke already had four kids all under the age of seven and he was in hock up to his eyebrows to his father-in-law.

"Kate, I believe Grace thinks Zeke got Joan pregnant and tricked Joe into thinking the baby was his. I know that seems pretty farfetched, but I just can't help wondering . . ." Marcy fell silent.

"I'll call Grace today. Are you going to St. Pete for the funeral?" Kate inquired.

"I don't know. I think I'd feel like an intruder. I haven't seen any of them in so long. Besides, maybe Joan will be there with the boys. No, I don't think it's my event. Anyway, please call Grace when you have the time," Marcy said, and then gave Kate Grace Dugan's cell number. "I'll let you get back to work. I'll call if anything else odd happens in my life." Marcy gave a wry laugh. "It seems to be happening on a daily basis lately," she said as she hung up.

Kate looked at the time on her computer screen, it was 3:15. She decided to call Grace Dugan immediately rather than wait until after her trial prep meeting with Ed.

"Mrs. Dugan, this is Kate Muldoon," Kate introduced herself when Grace Dugan answered the phone. "We've never met. I'm Marcy Simpson's attorney. I just got off the phone with Marcy, and she said you wanted me to call. But, first, let me tell you how sorry I am for your loss. Marcy told me your husband just passed. I understand he'd been ill for a while, but I know from experience that doesn't make it any easier."

"Thank you. Joe was barely holding his own against the emphysema when we learned Joe Junior had died. My husband's health really declined after that. He ended up with pneumonia within a few days. When I told him last week that Joe's death was being investigated as a murder, and that Marcy had been arrested, I think he just gave up. He didn't even talk much after that. One of the last things he said to me was, 'Grace, there is no way in hell Marcy had anything to do with Joe's death, but I wouldn't put anything past that demon he married.' Joe didn't think much of Joan. None of us do, and we could never figure out why Joe had anything to do with her. But, then we found out Joan was pregnant. We decided Joe was taking ownership of his mistake. But as Joe's first son, Murphy, got older, we just didn't see any of our Joe in him. Now, at 16, he's a dead ringer for that creep Zeke Peters.

"I understand Joe was in the process of filing divorce papers when he was killed. I sure hope the Miami cops have finally started to look at Joan and Zeke as suspects, I think they're both perfectly capable of killing someone if he got in their way. They're so self-absorbed and egotistical."

"Yes, ma'am. I've spoken with the chief of police here in Miami about redirecting his investigation," Kate assured Ms. Dugan. "I expect he'll be expanding his list of suspects soon. Unfortunately, he's a bit hesitant to take on Senator Ferguson's family without an ironclad case behind him, so it may take a while to reach a resolution. In the meantime, Marcy is out of jail, and the charges against her have been dropped, at least for now. But her life is far from back to normal. She's been suspended from her job, and she's afraid to even be at home. Ever since she learned Joe maintained a $4 million life policy naming her beneficiary, Marcy's world has been in turmoil. She was very sorry to hear about Joe Senior's death, and she was extremely glad to hear from you. I think your call gave her a much-needed boost."

"Glad to hear that. I was hoping she'd come up for the funeral. I would love to see her again. She was like a daughter to me, and I've missed her."

"I'm afraid she'd feel like an intruder at the services, at least that's what she said. And she's worried there'd be a problem if Joan is there with the boys."

"Oh, Joan won't be here. When I called to tell her Joe had died, I told her point-blank she wasn't welcome at the services. I simply wanted her to tell the boys their granddad had died—they used to be close. Tell Marcy to come if she wants to. It would be really nice to see her, and I could use her help.

"But that's not what I wanted to talk to you about, Ms. Muldoon. The last time Joe was up here in St. Pete with the boys, he and his brother, Michael, got to spend some time together. I just learned from Michael that Joe told him he'd recently had a paternity test done, and it was confirmed that he isn't Murphy's biological father. Murphy is Joe's oldest boy. Joe said he'd suspected as much for quite a while, and now, with the paternity test result, he was moving forward to divorce Joan. Given the physical resemblance between Murphy and Zeke, I'd bet my last dollar that Zeke is Murphy's biological father. Apparently, Joe planned to try to take all three boys away from Joan and enroll them in school up here. I didn't want to tell Marcy all this because I didn't think she needed anything more to worry about.

"Joe also said something to his brother that I thought might be helpful to you. Joe made some comment to Michael about how Murphy was probably the second time he'd been 'tricked' and that the first time was in high school. Michael said Joe didn't really explain much about his suspicions. But that got me to thinking. I remember both Joe and Zeke dated this one girl in high school. Her name was Miranda West. When I talked to Michael last night, he remembered there'd been a rumor that she'd gotten pregnant in high school and had an abortion—quite the scandal at their Catholic high school. That made me wonder, because Joe only went out with her once, but she and Zeke, on the other hand, had dated for months before she went out with Joe. It was around that time that Joe and Zeke became best buddies. None of us could understand that friendship—they were so different. I know it probably sounds like just the suspicions of an old lady, but I wonder if Zeke got that girl pregnant, and then used Joe in some way to put the blame on him.

"Last night, Michael told me, when they were in high school, Joe had confided that he'd only dated Miranda because Zeke promised she'd 'go all the way,' and Joe was looking for the experience. I guess Joe wasn't very proud of himself," Grace sighed. "That all seems like a hundred years ago. I guess I'm glad I didn't know about it at the time. I would have been so disappointed in Joe, but now it doesn't seem so bad, given the rest of this awful, sad story."

At 3:30, Ed walked into Kate's office, took a seat at the worktable in the corner, and listened to Kate's side of the conversation.

"Thanks for the information, Mrs. Dugan. I'm not sure if, or how, we'll be able to use it, but it certainly does shed some light on the mystery of Joe's ongoing relationship with Zeke. They did seem an unlikely pair.

"I'll tell Marcy you'd like to see her at the funeral service. Maybe she'll change her mind and head up to St. Petersburg. I'd love for her to take a little time off from worrying. We'll keep you posted on any new developments down here. Thanks again."

Kate hung up and looked at Ed momentarily before speaking. "Well, now that Joe Dugan has decided to start talking, he's gotten pretty damn enlightening. I'm not sure what I'm supposed to do with some of the information, but I'm glad to have it."

"So, now you're talking to the dead, Boss Lady?"

"Nope, I'm just listening, but Joe Dugan is sure talking."

Before they started their pretrial strategy discussion in the Brighton matter, Kate called Terry Driver and asked him to see if he could find Miranda West and interview her regarding her abortion in high school, and any connection she might have with Joe Dugan. It was a long shot, but stranger long shots had paid off in the past when Terry was involved.

They were seated side by side in their favorite booth at The Shack;

it was in the back and dark. Over their grouper sandwiches and beers, Kate and Ed continued their discussion regarding Joe Dugan's poor choices in best friends and second wives. They also hashed out whether Chief Jordan would find the new information useful enough to push him to investigate Joan or Zeke for Dr. Dugan's murder. Kate felt if the chief brought the two in for questioning, he might be able to use the new information to push Zeke into making an incriminating statement.

Ed then peppered Kate with follow-up questions about his trial prep projects and the part he'd play in the Brighton trial. He was clearly excited by the substantial role she'd handed him and thanked her repeatedly.

"Thank me after you experience the amount of work it takes to get this matter tried. Even though much of the written work was done when we put the case on the shelf the first two times we were rescheduled for trial, we still have hours and hours of prep time ahead of us.

"The good news is, after being pushed to new dockets twice, I'm fairly certain we'll be called this time. Brighton's CEO has mentioned an interest in having a mock trial run-through two weeks before the new trial date. If the mock jury doesn't buy our defense, we'll be scrambling to start serious settlement discussions. I'll give you my opening statement file, I want you to handle our opening, and I'll handle the closing argument. You've written the motions in *limine* so you'll be ready to argue those and the Rule 56 motion at the close of the evidence. But, you need to get up to speed on the deposition testimony of all the witnesses, not just the ones I've assigned you.

"If you're going to trial with me, you're going to have an active role, and we need to split the work basically in half. Otherwise, the jury will think one of us is the 'junior' lawyer, and they may not pay attention unless the 'senior' lawyer is presenting. Be forewarned, for me, presenting a case at trial is always like entering a tunnel. The rest of my life gets put on hold. All I do is prepare and present—I don't usually eat or sleep much. You'll earn your keep."

Kate took another bite of her grouper sandwich and thought back to her first jury trial nearly ten years ago. She loved the work. It was both the single most exhilarating—and terrifying—thing she could name, and it was exhausting. She hated to lose and took no shortcuts—not ever. She'd only ever lost two trials, and both were civil matters, one nonjury and one jury. She'd bitterly hated the experience and had vowed it would never happen again.

After a while, Kate noticed Ed had fallen quiet. She knew something was on his mind.

"So, what are you thinking about so intensely? Taking in the new info? Already planning your opening statement? What's got you so quiet all of a sudden?"

"Are we going to spend the night together tonight?"

"Well, that's a topic I didn't expect." She shrugged. "I suppose I should have. Listen, Ed, we were together a couple of nights ago. I don't think we should make a steady diet of it."

Kate registered Ed's disappointed look and wanted to change the subject.

Ed fell quiet again but finally said, "Why *not* make a 'steady diet of it,' to use your words?" His face was thoughtful, and Kate could see he didn't understand her position. She looked at him intently preparing to explain her views.

Ed's eyes twinkled. "Besides, you know it's the only way I'll make it to that crazy 6:00 a.m. hot yoga class tomorrow. And you said yourself it would be good for me to go to yoga at least twice a week. I'll make you a deal—sleep with me again tonight, and I'll make it to yoga tomorrow morning and twice next week."

"Ed! Damn it, sex isn't a bargaining chip."

"Oh, come on, Kate, I was just trying to be funny. Lighten up," he said, and his face broke into a broad smile. "The truth is, I want you, and I refuse to believe that you don't want me. When you let go and relax, I can tell you enjoy being with me."

Ed pulled Kate closer and kissed her with more passion than he should in this very public setting.

Kate pulled away.

"Ed, I'm just not as good at casual, 'no-strings-attached, rebound sex' as I thought I would be. I'm having a hard time figuring out why having sex with you makes me feel so damn guilty. I keep thinking about my ex-husband and wondering if I'm becoming more like Adam than I would ever care to admit."

"Kate, you're nothing like Adam. Admittedly, I don't know him, but from what I've heard, he has no principles. You have far too many scruples to be like him. Come on, we're simply two consenting adults who like having sex with each other. There's nothing wrong with what we're doing. And, if you're worried about Bill, you shouldn't be. Have you even heard from him since he took off on his Caribbean cruise? I'm guessing you have *not*. And, Kate, he knows I'm here *every day* and *very* interested in you. Besides, you *know* every hot chick in the harbors where he drops anchor is pursuing him. He's a good-looking, rich, single dude—he's a high-value target. Do you think he's pining away for you?"

"Ed, please stop talking about Bill. I get it. You've made your point. Bill isn't here, and that's his choice. I have choices too. I get it. I just want to feel good about my choices, and I don't do casual sex well, apparently."

"I never said it was *casual* sex—it's not casual to me. You're the one who said that. We've agreed to be exclusive, and I am. I know you are too. So, where's the harm in 'making a steady diet of it'? I want to, don't you?"

That's the problem. I want to, but I don't always like the way I feel about that. I still feel like I'm cheating on Bill, and I know I'm seriously complicating my life.

Kate's thoughts were a jumble as she gazed at the handsome young face in front of her.

"You really are a salesman, aren't you? You simply will not take 'no' for an answer! OK, let's not talk about it anymore. Let's finish our dinners and hit a few galleries, and then we'll see how we feel."

"I know how I'll feel, I'll want you even more. But, if that's the way you want to play it, I'm warning you, I'm going to be working hard at seducing you the entire time. I'm going to convince you to go back to your house and have outrageously magnificent sex with me."

Kate sighed. She could feel herself giving in.

Well, why not? she thought.

She signaled the waitress and ordered a martini—maybe a little liquid courage would banish her self-doubts and thoughts of Bill and Adam.

The house was dark and silent. Kate lay in Ed's arms listening to his rhythmic breathing.

It *had* been "outrageously magnificent sex," and most of her was glad she'd surrendered to Ed's persistent pursuit. Maybe she needed to finally say good-bye to Bill and let her heart find a new resting place . . . but was it Ed? And in a small corner of her mind, Kate wondered again whether she wasn't acting like Adam, even just a little bit.

Chapter 20

It took all of Kate's resolve to get them out of bed and into their yoga togs in time to make the 6:00 a.m. class. Kate had insisted Ed drive himself to the studio so he could head to his condo to get ready for work right after class. She knew he'd be a "distraction" if he came home with her, and they wouldn't get to work before 10:00. Nevertheless, she was feeling late when her cell phone rang as she jumped out of her car and headed toward the elevator of her office building.

She glanced at the caller ID before hitting the talk button, determined only to answer if it was someone she wanted to talk to.

"Good morning, Marcy. What can I do for you this morning?"

Kate got into the elevator and hoped her connection would hold during the ride to the forty-third floor.

"Hey, I won't keep you, but I wanted to let you know, I just heard from one of my neighbors at my condo. Apparently, someone broke in last night and totally ransacked the place. The front door was standing wide open this morning; the lock was broken. The superintendent finally came up to investigate, and then he called the cops. Of course, they have no idea what was taken, if anything, and they want me to go home and inventory the contents. But, I'm not really up to that right now and told them to just lock it up. I don't have much worth taking, so I'm not too worried. But I *am* concerned about the other piece of news I got from my neighbor. She also said there was a man lurking around the parking garage, asking if I was home. Apparently, he's telling people in my building he's looking for me because he had some 'critical legal news.' My neighbor gave him my cell phone number, but I haven't heard from anyone. And don't worry; I won't talk to him if he calls. I'll give him your number.

"Also, I'm thinking about heading up to St. Petersburg for Joe Senior's service. It's on Sunday afternoon, and I probably won't be heading back until Monday or Tuesday. Is that going to inconvenience you, I mean with the girls and all?"

"Good heavens, no," Kate replied. "I'll head out to the beach this afternoon after work. I probably won't be able to get there until well after 6:00. The girls will be OK in the backyard. They have the shade from the deck. Just make sure there's plenty of water and food before you leave. They'll take care of themselves. But, Marcy, can you give me the names of the neighbors who talked to this man. I'd like Chief Jordan to give them a call and get a description. The fact that someone was asking about you, and then there's a break-in at your apartment can't be a coincidence. This all makes me very glad you've been staying at the beach and out of harm's way. And it's great you've decided to attend Joe Senior's services, Marcy. Grace sounded like she truly wanted to see you. Give her a call and tell her you're headed up there."

"I did, and she asked me to stay with her. I feel odd about that, but she said it would actually help her deal with all the things she has on her plate related to Joe's service and burial. Do you think I'm doing the right thing, Kate?"

"Absolutely, kiddo. You'll be a great help. She said you were like a daughter to her while you and Joe were married. Go, you just need to be back by Thursday afternoon so we can do some prep for the hearing on Friday. Let me know when you're headed back. I'll keep the girls with me this week, and you can have the beach house to yourself whenever you get back. You need the break—treat it like a vacation. And don't worry, I'll let you know if something happens here."

"Thanks. I'll see you next week. Have a great weekend."

Marcy gave Kate her neighbors' names, phone numbers, and addresses. Kate told Marcy to drive carefully, and they said good-bye.

Kate realized she was actually looking forward to a weekend at the beach with her girls, just the three of them hanging out. She needed a rest from the hectic pace of the last several weeks.

Ed met her at her office door. She was glad he was there and hadn't gone back to bed after yoga, but she needed a little time to call Chief Jordan about Marcy's break-in.

"What's up?" Kate asked as she settled into her desk chair and clicked on her computer.

"Does that class ever get easier?"

"Yes, of course. It's just like anything else, it improves with practice," she grinned at him. "You seemed more into the postures this morning. I believe you were listening to her instructions and doing only as much as your body tells you is appropriate. That's how progress happens, by letting your body tell you how far and fast you should go."

"OK, well, I owe you two more practices this coming week, but I work best with lots of *reinforcement*," he smiled seductively.

"We'll see," Kate demurred. "Give me a minute, I need to call Chief Jordan."

Kate punched in the chief's number and left a message explaining Marcy's condo had been broken into last night and that a man had been hanging around her parking garage asking her neighbors about her. She requested the chief have a couple of his detectives call on Marcy's neighbors and show them photos of Zeke. She urged him to let her know if Zeke turned out to be Marcy's stalker.

Ed looked concerned when Kate hung up. "We may have to file that motion for restraining order after all."

"Yep, it doesn't sound good to me. She's decided to head up to St. Pete today, so I don't have to worry about her safety for now, but I'm concerned," Kate agreed.

"So, what's on your mind?" she asked as she turned back to Ed.

"Can I ask you a quick question about Beth?" Ed asked.

Kate eyed him suspiciously. "Sure what is it?"

She hoped Ed wasn't going to ask about Beth's sexuality, because she'd have to tell him it was none of his business, and she'd be disappointed in him.

"How long has she been with the FBI?"

Relieved, Kate responded, "About ten years. They recruited her out of law school, but she wanted to try the big law firm route first—law school debts are a strong incentive to sign on with the highest bidder. After a year, she realized it wasn't for her. I got the impression she was more inclined to shoot the male chauvinist law firm pigs than try to find a way to work with them. She says a lot of people think of the FBI as a bunch of macho men, and they are, but if you can match them on the practice range and in hand-to-hand martial arts training, they accept you and tend to look beyond your gender. Why do you ask?"

Kate was curious now. She wondered if her young associate was looking for a new career path that would provide some of the physical work he'd gotten used to in the Marines. She'd hate to lose him; she'd come to rely on him over the months they'd been working together. But, Kate had learned years ago, people need to find their own comfort zone in a legal career, and she would never try to discourage a career change just because it inconvenienced her.

"Well, I know you said you two were in law school together, and I was curious why she went the investigator route rather than the lawyer route."

"You should ask her sometime. I'm sure she'd be delighted to talk to you about it. Unfortunately, a government job doesn't pay all that well, but she loves it."

"I'll do that. Maybe I can get her to meet me for a drink sometime."

"Maybe, but I'd tell her what you want to talk to her about before you ask her for a drink. She's getting married in a few months, and you don't want her to get the wrong idea and turn you down."

"Thanks for the heads-up on that," he grinned.

After a slight pause in the conversation, Kate said, "You know, of course, I'd have to kill you if you decided to leave the firm. Either that, or I'd just retire!"

Ed blanched visibly. She instantly knew he was actually interested in a potential career change.

"I'm just kidding, Ed. Everybody gets to figure out where they want to land. Law firms are not for everybody. But just wait until after the Brighton trial. That might give you a taste of some of the *fun* we get to have. And, if you decide to leave, please give me a lot of notice. You'll be impossible to replace."

"Kate, stop worrying. I'm just interested in finding out how she ended up an FBI agent, that's all. And besides, if I did leave the firm, it *would* solve one problem," Ed said cocking an eyebrow at Kate. "You'd no longer be my boss. Maybe that would make your life a little less conflicted, Kate."

Kate's head snapped up.

"Don't go making any decisions on that basis, OK?"

That afternoon, Ed and Kate were sitting in the anteroom of Judge Blumquist's chambers, waiting for Mike Taylor to join them so they could see the judge together. When the door to the anteroom opened, Mike Taylor *and* Ron Gray walked in looking harried and irritated.

"This had better be good, Kate. I've already wasted too much of my day on the Simpson matter. You have certainly stirred this shit pot," Mike said by way of greeting.

Gray just glowered at her.

"Thanks, Mike. I always feel especially gratified when the prosecutor appreciates my work," Kate said smiling her sweetest.

The judge's secretary buzzed through to Judge Blumquist and informed him all parties were now present and ready for the conference.

"He says you can go on in," she told them, nodding toward the door to the judge's office.

"Thank you for seeing us on such short notice, Your Honor," Kate said as she walked into his office and took a seat across from Judge Blumquist. "I think you remember my colleague Ed Evert. And, Mike and Ron, we appreciate you being here so quickly too. I know how busy you are."

Kate grinned, Mike Taylor grumbled, and Ron Gray continued to scowl.

"Your Honor, there have been a number of important developments in the Marcy Simpson matter, and I thought it would be a good idea to bring you up to speed and explain why we will be moving to have the final hearing on the declaratory judgment as soon as possible." Kate hurried to seize the floor as Taylor was getting settled into his seat.

Taylor's head jerked up abruptly, and he started to speak.

"I don't think Mr. Taylor will have any serious objection to me briefly summarizing the meaningful changes in the case since Ms. Simpson's precipitous and improvident arrest and subsequent release," Kate glared at Taylor and quickly continued. "Some very important documents were found in a locked desk drawer in Dr. Dugan's office at his medical clinic. Among those documents were unopened letters to Ms. Simpson from Dr. Dugan dating back 16 years, right after they divorced. We also found the original insurance policy with handwritten, notarized changes, as well as divorce papers showing Dr. Dugan was planning on divorcing his second wife, Joan Dugan, and making some extremely negative allegations against her. Finally, we also discovered a lab report comparing DNA from three different blood samples for paternity determination.

"When we discovered these items, we immediately sent for Chief Jordan and did not touch the papers until he was present. The documents were responsive to my subpoena to the clinic, and Chief Jordan gave us copies as he was taking custody of the originals. We immediately sent a complete set of the documents to Mr. Gray, the attorney for Dr. Dugan's estate who happens to be here this afternoon.

"We've also learned that, about a month ago, Dr. Dugan's medical clinic experienced an unexplained loss of several drugs they keep on-site, including a large quantity of digitalis. And, we've learned the clinic has moved to sever its ties with one of its doctors, Zeke Peters."

Kate neatly summarized much of their investigation for the judge as she watched his eyebrows shooting up and down. She decided she wanted to play poker with Judge Blumquist. His bushy eyebrows were the best tell she'd ever seen.

"The chief of police informed us his department will be investigating each of these new developments, and they no longer consider my client a person of interest. Your Honor, there is simply no evidence showing Ms. Simpson knew the insurance policy was still valid. Moreover, we have documents proving she was at work during the time the digitalis would have had to be administered, and other documents proving she didn't take any digitalis from the Jackson Memorial drug safe. In short, we can prove she did not have motive, means, or opportunity to murder Dr. Dugan.

"Because we told the court we'd delay our request for a hearing on the interpleader and declaratory judgment until the investigation into Ms. Simpson's involvement in Dr. Dugan's death was settled, I wanted to let you know our intention is to schedule the final hearing as soon we can get it on the judge's calendar."

"Mr. Taylor, anything you want to add?" Judge Blumquist turned a sour look in his direction. "It sounds like Ms. Muldoon has done a superb job of ferreting out *actual* facts, as opposed to supposition and speculation. Have you uncovered any actual facts that would link Ms. Simpson to Dr. Dugan's alleged murder?"

"Your Honor, we are still working on that. The coroner has not finished his autopsy yet, but will soon. We're hopeful the results will aid our investigation," Taylor stammered.

"Mr. Taylor, I suggest you and the police broaden your investigation, if you haven't already. It sounds like making a case against Ms. Simpson will be very difficult indeed. Perhaps one of the leads Ms. Muldoon has unearthed may prove more profitable."

Judge Blumquist frowned at Taylor again, and then turned to address Kate. "I appreciate the courtesy of this information, and I certainly understand why you are ready to move forward with the interpleader and declaratory judgment hearing. As far as I'm concerned, the warrant for Ms. Simpson's arrest was unsupported and was properly dismissed. It does not sound as if another is likely based on *actual* evidence. My involvement in this matter is over. Thank you, Ms. Muldoon and Mr. Evert."

"Thank you, Your Honor, and thanks again for your time," Kate said, gathering her papers and standing to leave. Ed quickly rose to join her.

"But, Your Honor, we don't even have our autopsy report yet . . ." Mike Taylor protested.

"Mr. Taylor, you can take that up at the interpleader and declaratory judgment hearing in civil court. My involvement in this matter is concluded. Good day," Judge Blumquist declared as he glared at Taylor.

Driving toward her beach house, Kate replayed the events of the week over in her mind. Just when it looked like Marcy was in the clear and other suspects may be surfacing, Marcy's condo was broken into and a suspicious man was seen lurking about asking questions. Kate didn't like any of the possible reasons someone might be trying to find Marcy.

She hadn't heard back from Chief Jordan, but Kate was certain Zeke was behind this most recent attack on Marcy. It sounded like something an underhanded bully would do.

Or a sociopath, Kate thought suddenly. She hit her call button on the steering wheel and said, "Call Beth Anderson, cell."

Beth's phone rolled to voice mail and Kate left a message asking her to get in touch with Chief Jordan and send him a copy of Gary Cook's wanted poster. She briefly explained about Marcy's break-in and the man her neighbors said had been asking about her.

"It probably has nothing to do with Cook. It's much more likely it's that sleazy Zeke Peters, but just in case there's a connection, I'd like Chief Jordan to have Gary Cook's photograph. Call me on the cell if you have any questions. I'm out at the beach this weekend."

Kate was almost at her house, and when she cruised by Bill's place, she slowed down to look at his dark house. It was odd knowing he was not there if she needed to talk, and that she wouldn't be running into him on the beach or in town. She truly hoped he was getting himself sorted out, and she wondered if she was going to be able to do the same. Kate sighed heavily as she pulled into her driveway and saw her own dark house.

But my girls are waiting for me, and I owe them some quality time, Kate thought as she hopped out of the car and headed inside.

Her welcoming committee didn't disappoint. There were joyful barks, tail wags, and wiggles as she let her girls into the house from the back deck.

Chapter 21

Saturday morning, Kate woke a little after 8:00, really late for her. She lingered in bed reading the novel on her nightstand and listening to the news until the girls began barking at the back door, indicating they were ready to get their day started. She let them out into the backyard while she put on her shorts, a T-shirt, and running shoes, and set up the coffee machine so there'd be a fresh pot when she returned from her run.

Kate's pace was slow, just a nice easy jog. The girls were a bit out of shape since she hadn't run with them for a while; she wanted to take it easy on them, and herself. She ran toward Bill's house, a route she'd been avoiding for the last several months. She knew he was gone, but she felt drawn in his direction. When they reached Bill's section of the beach, Kate glanced toward his house. She was pretty sure she saw movement in the kitchen windows that ran along the back of Bill's huge beachside home. Kate slowed briefly and noted there were beach towels and bikini tops and bottoms hanging on the rails of his back deck. Either Bill *was* home and entertaining or his twin daughters were home from the university for the weekend. Kate figured the twins were the most likely scenario and smiled to herself as she wondered if the girls were entertaining gentlemen friends.

Wonder if Daddy knows his babies are home taking advantage of his absence. The cat's away, Kate smiled to herself and jogged on.

Bill's girls had not been pleased when he told them he was seeing Kate. They had lost their mom to breast cancer only a couple of years before, and they were having trouble accepting the fact that their dad was still very much a young man with an interest in women. According to Bill, his girls also thought Kate was too young for him. Kate wondered again how they'd felt about Bill's fling with Pam Logan, easily seven or eight years younger than Kate. She wondered if he'd even told them about Pam.

At the two-mile mark, she turned and headed back. On her way past Bill's house, she again looked toward his back deck and saw one of the twins and a young man lounging on the sunny deck. She waved, and the young girl waved back.

When she got back to her own beachfront, Kate plopped down in the sand, took off her shoes, and headed into the water with the girls barking and jumping beside her. The three of them swam out to a small sandbar a short distance from the shore before returning to the shallow water where Kate entertained her dogs by throwing pieces of driftwood into the water for them to return. She was glad to spend this time with them. She'd been feeling very neglectful over the last several weeks and had totally taken advantage of Marcy as chief dog sitter.

Next, the three headed to the outside shower under the back deck of Kate's house where she stripped down and shampooed both the dogs and herself. Taking a towel out of the small outdoor cabinet, she wrapped up her hair into a turban and grabbed another towel to dry her dogs. Kate loved the fact that she had a line of shrubs providing privacy from her neighbors on both sides and the Atlantic Ocean across the back of her house. Shaking out her hair, she draped her towel over her shoulders, and picked up the dogs' towel. She was heading toward the stairs to the back deck until Sadie and Phoebe unexpectedly started growling in the ferocious manner they used when feeling protective or scared.

"What is it, girls?" Kate asked as she walked out into her backyard to look around.

"I guess they smell me," Adam said, stepping out from the side of the house. "They never really liked me all that much, you know."

"Well, if you'd treated them better they might have. But, to you, they were just an inconvenience. What are you doing here, Adam?"

Kate stood naked except for a towel around her shoulders, hands on her hip, and two dogs standing next to her growling in a protective manner.

"Right now I'm looking at your amazing body. I never grew tired of that view, you know." Adam leered at her but came no closer. He knew Kate had trained Sadie and Phoebe to attack on command, and he figured she wouldn't need much provocation to speak that command now.

"You're trespassing, Adam."

Oddly, Kate felt no embarrassment standing naked in front of her ex-husband, and she didn't feel threatened—but she had no intention of telling the dogs to stand down.

"You don't live here anymore, and I have nothing to say to you other than get the hell off of my property." Kate did not move, and the angry tone in her voice caused the dogs to increase the volume of their growls. Phoebe barked ferociously.

"Well, I was in the neighborhood, and thought I'd stop by to tell you my news. Maybe have a cup of coffee, bury the hatchet, as they say."

"I'm not interested in burying the hatchet. You actually did me a favor, and I thank you for that. Now get off my property before I tell the girls just how unhappy I am to see you."

"Don't you even want to hear my news? I guarantee it will make you happy." Adam didn't wait for a response; he knew one wasn't coming. "I'm moving back to Iowa in two weeks. I've decided to return to my hometown and hang out a shingle. I've reactivated my Iowa Bar license and picked out the office space already. Can't you just see me as a country lawyer in Iowa? Pigs, corn, tractors, and all," Adam laughed. "I can't afford to live in Miami any longer. Besides, my reputation here is a tad bit tarnished."

A long pause followed before Kate responded. "You know what, Adam? I actually *can* picture that, and I hope you'll be very happy there. It may do you some good to get back to your roots. Besides, you always did like being a big fish in a little pond. Returning to Iowa could be just the thing for you."

"That's my plan." Adam paused again, and then said, "That is, unless you'd like to give me another chance. I think I've learned a great deal these last several months."

"Are you fucking kidding?" Kate laughed out loud. "You know there's no way that would ever happen. You had your chances, and I couldn't be happier being single. So, good luck and safe travels. Now take a hike."

A momentary flicker of anger passed over Adam's face, and he clenched and unclenched his fists several times.

"OK. I guess I knew the answer, but figured I'd ask to be sure. See you down the road, Kate, and if you're ever in Iowa—"

"Or Mexico City?" she said.

"What?" Adam looked surprised at Kate's comment.

"I said 'or Mexico City.' I understand you have a very nice place there, though exactly how you managed to afford it I have no idea—and frankly, I'm not sure I want to know. However, there is one thing I *do* want to know, Adam. Did you ever replace the gun I found in the BMW and gave to Steve Sloan? I understand he turned it over to the police when you disavowed any knowledge of it. The fact that it was unregistered, with no readable serial number, coupled with the fact that you didn't have a carry permit, could have been a huge problem for you."

Adam did not respond for several minutes. Finally, he grinned and said, "Well, sometimes a man needs protection from his business partners."

"That's what I thought. Now please leave immediately or I'll let Sadie and Phoebe give you a very special send-off."

At the sound of their names, the dogs began to bark angrily.

Adam turned quickly and retraced his steps around the side of the house and up the gentle incline to the driveway.

"Stay, girls, stay. Sit."

Kate wanted to give Adam a moment to get out of range before she headed up the outside steps to the deck, glad for once she'd remembered to lock the back door on her way out for her run. She'd be doing that on a more regular basis she decided.

Kate walked inside with the towel now wrapped around her as

she looked out at her front yard in time to see Adam pulling away in a black Mercedes C class.

"Good riddance. I certainly wish I'd seen the back of you years ago—better yet, I wish I'd *never* seen you at all."

Kate noted she was shaking and had a sudden urge to check the locks on all the windows and doors and take a quick inventory of the house to make sure Adam hadn't gotten inside.

She fed the dogs on the deck while she quickly changed and then brought them inside with her. She felt the need for some canine security.

Kate took her girls with her when she went into the village just before noon to buy a few fresh fruits and veggies and some fresh fish for the weekend from her favorite markets. She decided on a quick lunch and placed her purchases carefully in the cooler in her trunk, and then took the girls across the street to the Village Café where she sat at one of the outside tables with her dogs at her side.

As she was finishing her lunch, Kate heard a young voice call out, "Ms. Muldoon?"

Kate looked up and saw Aniston Davis (or was it Ashley? Kate could never be sure. Bill's twins looked so much alike).

"Hello," Kate replied. "Did I see you out on the deck when I ran by this morning?"

"Yes, and it's Aniston. I know we look alike and it's hard to tell, although Ashley just got her hair cut much shorter. She's got an intern gig in New York City coming up, and she decided she needed to look more businesslike."

"So I've heard, and you're going abroad for a semester. Sounds like you two are making the most of your college experience."

A young man walked up beside Aniston.

"Ms. Muldoon, this is Jake Frederickson. We met in Gainesville. Jake is a senior, and he's been accepted into UF's law school for next fall."

Kate shook hands with the young man and told him she was a

Florida law grad and, of course, thought highly of the school.

"Dad said Ms. Muldoon finished first in her class," Aniston said with a note of awe in her voice.

"Wow, that's very impressive," Jake smiled broadly at Kate. "I actually know who you are. We've all heard of the 'Defense Counsel to the Stars.' Who are you representing these days? I guess you can't really tell me, but I know I'll be reading about it in *People,* or one of those Hollywood gossip rags Aniston reads. Don't be surprised if you see my name on a résumé one of these days. I'd love to practice litigation, and I really want to return to Miami when I'm out of school."

"I'll keep watch for it," Kate smiled amicably.

Turning to Aniston, she asked, "Have you heard from your dad since he started his Caribbean cruise?"

"Yep, he's called four times, and we receive daily e-mails. I think he's afraid Ashley and I will self-destruct if he doesn't hover. I've also gotten three postcards from him, though they all came at once. I guess it depends on what port he's in and how regular the mail service is. The last I heard he was in Port Royal, Jamaica—you know, where the pirates used to hang out, but that was a day ago. He's taking his time and enjoying himself. He's even thinking about going to Cuba. I'm not sure he's got the appropriate clearance for that, but he's looking into it."

"That's great. Tell him I said hello when you speak to him again. I'm so glad he's having a wonderful time. And it was great meeting you, Jake. I'll watch for your résumé in three years!" Kate's tone was very upbeat, but her heart had sunk to her feet.

The young people walked into the café as Kate returned to her salad.

Bill was in constant communication with his girls, and she had not heard one peep, not even a measly postcard.

I guess that should tell you something right there, Katherine Mary Muldoon. Don't be a chump. The dude's not even thinking about you. Accept it and let it go. You're just friends now and nothing more will ever come of it. Get fucking over him. Maybe Ed has a point.

Kate spent the rest of the day doing chores around the house. It was good to get back to her little slice of heaven. She made dinner for one—grilled grouper and asparagus—and settled in at the table on her deck. As she ate, she checked her e-mails and texts for the first time all day. She noticed Ed had texted her three times. Twice about work and once to say he was going out for a ten-mile run in the morning and asking if she would like to join him. She noticed he'd also left her a voice mail. She listened to it.

"Hey Kate, haven't heard from you, but I know you said you needed to be alone, so I'm going to respect that, but I just want you to know I miss you. Let me know if you want to run with me tomorrow. I can go any time."

What is the matter with you, Muldoon? You've got a hunky younger man lusting after you, and you're treating him like dog shit. Bill isn't coming back to you. If he'd wanted you, he would have stayed here and fought for you. After all, he knows Ed's right here every day. It would have been an easy fight too, but not now. Get some self-respect, Kate. And, just because you're sleeping with your associate, you're not like Adam. If his 'visit' this morning told you nothing else, it should underscore that you are not like him.

Kate picked up her cell phone again and hit "call back." Ed answered on the first ring.

"Glad you're not dead. I was starting to worry. I don't think you've ever been radio silent that long before!" Ed sounded truly worried.

"Sorry about that. I actually haven't looked at my phone all day. I just gave myself some time to think. Now, I've had enough alone time, and I've done all the thinking I need to for a while. I'd love to run with you tomorrow, but I'm at the beach. Why don't you come out here for a run tomorrow morning? I'll even make us dinner, and we can head back to town on Monday morning if you'd like."

"I'd love that, Kate. How early can I get there tomorrow? I can't wait to see you. I could head out there now if you'd like."

"Tomorrow will be fine, Ed. I'll be up before 7:00, and we need to get started early because it gets hot really fast on the beach."

"OK, I'll be there. Thanks for the invitation, Kate. It means a lot to me."

They said good-bye, and Kate stared out at the ocean.

Talk about a major contrast. Kate, even you should see Bill is done, and Ed wants more. Let yourself enjoy life a little.

After cleaning up from dinner, Kate decided to retire early. She read in bed for nearly an hour, and then turned off the light and fell into a deep and peaceful asleep.

Hours later, Kate woke to the sound of her dogs' fierce low growling. She looked out into the dark room and saw their white teeth, bared and snarling, reflected in the moonlight.

"What is it, girls?" she whispered.

The dogs settled and stopped snarling.

The three of them listened intently as they stared into the dark night.

The sound came again a few moments later, and the dogs again began to growl softly. The noise sounded like someone coming up the backstairs to the deck. The dogs stood up when they heard the next noise, the low rumble in their throats continued, and Kate could see the hair on the back of their necks standing on end. She suddenly realized her Sig Sauer was in the gun safe on the other side of the house.

Reaching for her cell phone, she dialed 9-1 and held her finger over the 1 key.

Sadie and Phoebe took a couple of steps toward the bedroom door, ears cocked, tails low and bristling.

Kate saw the dark shadow on her deck at the same time the dogs saw it. They began barking wildly. Kate could see the dark shadow was a man about Adam's height and build, but that was all she could make out. He appeared to jump when the dogs started howling at him.

Surly even Adam isn't stupid enough to try to break into the house, Kate thought as she slipped out of her bed and quickly walked toward the French door that filled the back walls of her bedroom.

A shot hit the sliding glass doors in the living room, followed by another, and then another until the glass began to crack, and then shatter. Kate sprinted across the living room and into the den, unlocked her gun safe, jammed a clip into the butt of the gun, and racked the slide.

She raced back into the living room in time to see Sadie and Phoebe attacking the man who had entered the house through the broken back door. She raised her gun aimed for his chest and shouted, "Get out of here! I'm armed, and I know how to shoot."

The man looked toward Kate, hastily retreated through the door, and sprang off the back deck.

Kate called her dogs back as they started to sprint down the stairs after the man.

"Down Sadie, down Phoebe! Come here! Leave it!"

The dogs stopped and came back up the stairs. Kate found her phone and pressed the last 1.

"A man just shot out my sliding glass doors and got inside. I think he ran off, but I need the police immediately."

Kate gave them her address and the operator said she would stay on the line until the police arrived. Almost immediately, Kate heard a distant wail of the siren.

Kate walked to the front door, turned on the security lights, and looked out the glass side panel, but saw no sign of the intruder. She flipped on the living-room lights and turned back to survey the damage to the house.

To her horror, she saw her dogs on the ground panting . . . and bleeding. Sadie had a piece of cloth in her mouth and there was blood coming from her front left leg. Blood was coming from Phoebe's mouth and chest.

"Oh my God!" Kate shouted into the phone. "He's shot my girls. Send the EMS. Please send medical help."

Kate dropped the phone and rushed to her dogs, then ran to the kitchen for towels and her first aid kit.

As she worked on the dogs, Kate prayed out loud, "Please, God, not my girls, please, God."

Chapter 22

As Ed headed up Kate's street the sun was just lighting up the eastern sky. It was going to be a beautiful day, and he was feeling great. Kate had asked him to come to the beach and spend the day—and more importantly, the night—with her. He was getting there before she would be expecting him, so he hoped she'd still be in bed. Maybe he could convince her to stay there for a little while.

Rounding the last curve before Kate's house, Ed noticed several police cars parked on the side of the road, along with a number of other vehicles, making it difficult to thread his way the last 50 yards to her driveway.

As he began to turn into her drive, he slammed on his brakes and stared. A glass repair panel truck and the FBI Crime Scene Investigation van were parked in Kate's driveway. Kate's front door was standing wide open and police officers were milling about.

Ed jammed his car into park, turned it off, and leaped out, not even pausing long enough to close the door. He raced to the front door and pushed past the cops who shouted for him to stop.

Inside Kate's house was chaos. There were at least 25 people walking around, and they all seemed to be talking at once. Ed's eyes were instantly drawn to the back wall that *used* to be made of oversized glass sliding doors. One door had a huge crack in it, and the other was completely blown out. Glass shards littered everything.

Then he spotted the bright red stains on Kate's soft white carpet. The two big stains were suddenly the only thing he could see. He stood like a statue staring at them as the cops from outside caught up to him and started dragging him back outside.

"You can't be in here."

"Who are you?"

"What do you think you're doing?"

"Can't you tell this is a crime scene?"

Four cops grabbed Ed and lifted him off his feet as he fought to get loose.

"What happened? Where's Kate? Was she hurt? How bad? I want to see her."

Ed struggled with the cops until a familiar baritone voice interrupted the mêlée.

"You can let him go, boys. But, Ed, stand still. Do *not* move. This is a crime scene, and you don't want to destroy evidence. Calm down and I'll tell you everything. What the hell are you doing here, anyway? Do you live out here on the beach too? Shit, they must be paying you associates more than I thought. Should have listened to my momma when she told me to go to law school."

A meaty hand had clamped down on Ed's shoulder.

Ed turned to face the voice and saw Chief Jordan.

As calmly as he could manage, Ed said, "Where's Kate? Is she all right? Is that her blood?"

"She's all right, Ed. That's not her blood; it's from her dogs. She's with them at the vet's in town. Now tell me what you're doing here." Chief Jordan's voice was soft but stern, and he didn't remove his hand from Ed's shoulder. The four cops who'd been dragging him toward the front door didn't move away either.

"Kate and I were going for a run on the beach. We arranged to meet here this morning. What the hell happened and how badly injured are Sadie and Phoebe?"

Ed couldn't get up to speed fast enough, and he was trying to quash an overwhelming desire to race out the door and into town to find the vet. He needed to see Kate, and he needed to see her fast.

"A man tried to break in last night. He shot out the glass doors and came in through the hole in the glass. Kate's dogs attacked him. They got a couple of good pieces of him too." Chief Jordan paused to look up and down Ed's body, obviously looking for dog bites. Finding none, he finally removed his hand from Ed's shoulder and nodded toward his cops.

"You guys can get back to work outside. Mr. Evert will be fine with me until he leaves, which will be shortly." The chief looked pointedly at Ed, then back to his men as he spoke. "I'd like to get this scene cleared by this afternoon. The glass guy says he can be done by then, and I imagine Kate is going to want to bring the dogs back here if they're up to it."

"Ed? What are you doing here?" a female voice asked.

Ed turned to see Beth Anderson walking in the front door.

"We were supposed to go running this morning. Chief Jordan just filled me in. Are you sure Kate's OK? How bad are the dogs?" Ed accepted Beth's hug, grateful for a friendly face.

"She's fine, or she will be as soon as the dogs are out of surgery. The 911 operator dispatched the EMS crew because Kate said her 'girls' had been shot." Beth's eyes sparkled. "But in the end, it was probably a good thing she did. I don't think Phoebe would have made it without emergency treatment. Besides, they had quite a bit of evidence in their mouths and on their bodies. The EMS guys preserved it, and that's going to give us a leg up—or maybe that's eight legs up." Beth laughed at her own joke, and then grew serious again.

"Kate managed to get to her weapon by the time the man broke through the glass, but she didn't have to take the shot. I'm glad for that."

Beth looked Ed up and down, noting his running shorts and T-shirt.

"You're not going to get that run in this morning, but I know Kate would be glad for the company at the vet's."

"What are you two doing here anyway?" Ed asked, finally starting to put the scene together. "This isn't your jurisdiction, Chief. How did you guys find out about this? Did the local cops call in reinforcements?"

"I'm sure they would have, but Kate preempted them," Beth smiled at Ed. "You know how she is, always taking charge. She called me around 3:00 this morning and told me what happened as the EMS team was working on the dogs. I talked with them about collecting evidence from the dogs, and told them I'd be out to collect the samples for our lab to process. They didn't argue—I don't think they see this sort of thing very often out here in their sleepy beach community. I called Chief Jordan. I don't believe in coincidences. Kate has her hands in enough criminal matters to attract the wrong sort of attention, and apparently her scumbag ex-husband paid a visit out here yesterday morning."

"What?" Ed's eyes jerked back to Beth. "Her ex was *here,* yesterday? Do you think he did this? Who the hell did this?"

"That's what we're going to find out, Ed. You can't stay, and Kate would like the company while she waits for word on the dogs," Beth said, placing a hand gently on Ed's shoulder.

He was glad Kate had someone like Beth to call, and at the same time, irritated that she hadn't called him.

Beth's phone rang. When she answered it she said, "Yes, actually, he's here already. I'll tell him. Any word from the vet? Hang tough. See you soon."

"That was Kate. She wanted to tell me that you were coming out to run with her today. She's been trying to call you for the last 15 minutes to give you an update, but she's been unable to reach you. I guess you'll have a message from her on your cell phone. I think she'd *really* appreciate your company at the vet's," Beth repeated, knowing she had to get Ed out of her crime scene. "Would you like me to show you the way? I'm going to pick up the evidence the girls 'collected' and get it to the lab this morning."

Beth said good-bye to Chief Jordan and her team and headed out the door with Ed close on her heels.

Kate sat alone in the vet's waiting room, still in her pajamas. She had a blanket wrapped around her—there was blood on it and on her night clothes and hair. She looked like she hadn't slept in a week. When she looked up and saw Beth and Ed she smiled weakly.

"Sorry about the run, Ed. I didn't think you'd be leaving Miami until around 7:00 and I didn't want to wake you just to tell you to run without me in town today."

Kate pulled the blanket tighter around her shoulders.

"I'm just sorry you didn't call me last night. I could have been here with you. You didn't need to do this alone."

Ed tried not to let his disappointment show, but when Kate looked at him, she realized he was upset.

"How are the crime techs doing, Beth? Have they found anything helpful?" she asked.

"Kate, we won't know anything until we've processed everything in the lab. We are finding some good evidence, though. Your girls punctured your intruder's skin pretty good. There are lots of blood droplets. With what we're finding at the house, and the samples of clothing, tissue, and blood on the girls, we'll be able to tell you who your assailant was *if* his DNA is in the system. I'm guessing it will be. I'm going to want that blanket you're using; maybe I can trade it for my FBI jacket?" Beth said, removing her jacket and holding it out for Kate. "What's the doc say about the girls?"

"Sadie is out of danger, but they're still working on Phoebe. She took a shot to the chest when she jumped up and tried to bite the intruder's throat. They had to open her up to get the bullet and repair several internal bleeders. They'll know more in another half hour or so."

Ed sat down next to Kate, helped her put on Beth's jacket, and put his arm around her and pulled her close. She resisted, but Ed persisted and whispered, "Come on, Kate, let me help you through this."

Kate broke down.

Beth, folding the bloody blanket, said, "You're in good hands now, kiddo. I'll be right back." She disappeared through the doors to the operating area.

Ed rocked Kate slowly as he rubbed her back and kissed the top of her head. Her sobbing slowed and finally stopped, but she didn't pull away from Ed. He felt her begin to relax and thought she might have fallen asleep. She was obviously exhausted.

When Beth returned 45 minutes later, she was leading Sadie who slowly limped along on a freshly splinted right front leg. The moment Sadie saw Kate, she hobbled over to place her head in Kate's lap, her tail wagging so hard it nearly knocked her off her splint.

Kate woke and threw her arms around her dog and wept again.

"She'll be right as rain in another month or so, according to Doc Delaney. She was lucky; the bullet was through and through. It clipped her thighbone, or whatever that's called up here on a dog's front leg. She's just starting to come out of the anesthetic. Doc says she'll be really thirsty for the next 24 hours, and that means she'll need to pee a lot. That won't be easy because her balance will be off. Doc also says if she starts to chew and fuss at her stitches and splint, you'll need to put the 'cone of shame' collar on her," Beth reported, handing Kate the conical-shaped collar.

"And Phoebe?" Kate asked without being able to look up at Beth.

"Doc's just finished up. The next 24 hours will be critical. She has her heavily sedated so she'll sleep. If her vital signs stabilize, Doc says you might be able to take her home tomorrow. Kate, she's not out of the woods, but she's strong, and she's got a good chance of a full recovery. The bullet nicked a number of internal organs, but right now, they're all patched up and working. Doc Delaney will be out momentarily. I'm going to head back to the city with these." Beth held up a small cooler containing her canine- gathered evidence and the bloody blanket.

"I'll call you as soon as I have something. You're not staying by yourself tonight wherever you end up—that's not a suggestion; it's an order."

"I have it covered, Beth," Ed said as he stood up.

"I figured you might," Beth beamed at him.

"Let me know where you land tonight, Kate. I'm asking the local cops to post security around your house out here, and Chief Jordan and I will handle security at your house in the city. Gotta run, kids. Take good care of her, Ed, and, Kate, you let him do that. OK?"

Kate nodded.

"Beth, thanks for everything—keep me in the loop."

"Will do. By the way, I called Terry to let him know. And I got two for the price of one. It took them a while to answer the phone, and Terry sounded out of breath when he finally answered. When I heard Suzy questioning him in the background, I understood why," Beth laughed, and even Kate cracked a small, wry grin.

Beth patted Ed on the back and said, "OK, she's all yours. Try to keep her from tracking down the bad guys on her own tonight. Ciao."

Ed sat down next to Sadie and looked at her leg as he rubbed her ears. When he looked up at Kate she was staring at him. He moved back to the chair next to her.

She leaned in and whispered, "I'm sorry I didn't call you last night. I didn't want to be a nuisance, but I see now I should have. Forgive me. I should have called. Thank you for being here."

They sat in silence for another 15 minutes petting Sadie and rubbing her ears until Carrie Delaney came out from the back. Her eyes looked tired, but she was smiling.

"That's one tough doggie you've got there. Really, they're both so strong. I'm cautiously optimistic about Phoebe, but we have to keep her calm. It's best for her to have a couple of days where she's mostly knocked out. We've got her hooked up to IVs and she's resting comfortably. Would you like to see her before you go home and get some rest?"

Carrie eyed Ed as she was talking with Kate.

"Hi, I'm Ed Evert, I work with Kate. We were supposed to go for a run this morning. I just found out about Kate's harrowing night. Thanks for all you've done."

"Well, I thought if Kate could figure out how to get her dogs brought in by the EMS team I'd better damn well be here to greet them. Seriously, Kate, getting Phoebe in here last night saved her life."

"Carrie, she and Sadie saved mine, so I owed them at least that much. I *would* like to see Phoebe, and then I'll let Ed take us home. Ed, do you mind hanging on to Sadie while I run back to see her sister?"

"Nope. We'll just hang out here and keep each other company."

Kate disappeared with Carrie, and Ed knelt and looked Sadie in the eyes. "Thank you, girl. There's a big steak in your future. You saved her life. I should have been there to protect her . . ." Ed shook his head, and Sadie whimpered sympathetically.

As they drove back to her house, Kate made plans for their next 24 hours, again in her element, taking charge. She began by telling Ed they needed to get Sadie into the house, and away from the mob of people who were likely still milling about as they wrapped up the crime scene investigation. Kate listed things she would need in her bedroom to set up an invalid room for Sadie, as well as what she had in the fridge for lunch and dinner. Finally, she told Ed to stop for coffee at the Village Café. While Kate waited in the car with Sadie, Ed ran in and bought three-dozen bagels and a box of coffee and another of orange juice. He knew the cops and agents would appreciate the food.

When they arrived back at Kate's house the scene was still being processed. Cheers went up when Ed set up coffee, juice, and bagels on the lawn furniture in the front yard. Kate led Sadie slowly into her room and lay out a doggie bed, a bowl of water, and another of kibbles on a towel. Kate fed Sadie the tranquilizer, antibiotics, and painkillers Carrie had given her and stayed with her until she settled down on her good side and fell asleep, and then she allowed herself time for a shower to wash away the blood and have another good cry.

When she emerged from her room, Ed handed Kate a large mug of black coffee and half a cinnamon raisin bagel toasted with cream cheese—just the way she like it. She smiled gratefully as she took a long drink of the coffee, then turned to appraise the stained carpet next to the newly installed sliding glass door.

Ed followed her gaze to the spot with the bloodstains. He put his arm around her.

"The FBI team lead said you can have a commercial disaster clean-up crew take a look at the scene tomorrow, but until then, he requests you not touch anything in the living room in case they need to come back."

Kate nodded and looked away from the mess. "Sadie is resting. I gave her the meds Carrie gave me. I think she'll sleep for several hours. Want to take our coffees out on the beach for a short walk? You know, you should probably just go ahead and get your run in; I'm not really up to it."

"Let's walk. I'm not really up for a run yet either. Besides, it's still early. Let's stretch our legs, and then I think you should catch a nap. You only got about 45 minutes at the vet's. You need a good nap today to keep your strength up, Kate."

Kate stared at him for a moment. She looked like she was going to argue, but then said, "You're right." She headed out the front door because the back deck was full of crime scene techs.

They walked along the beach without speaking for several minutes. Finally, Kate broke the silence. "It was pretty terrifying, Ed. The guy never stopped shooting, even when the girls attacked him . . . It wasn't until I drew down on him that he stopped and fled . . . I'm sleeping with my gun from now on. I had to run across the living room to get it out of the safe in the den . . . He just kept shooting at the glass door. He must have fired an entire clip, maybe two . . . He was in the house when I raced back from the den . . . I couldn't get a clean shot away because the dogs were on him . . . It was so dark. I never saw his face. He had on a hoodie and it shaded his face."

Kate stopped talking and they walked a little longer in silence. Ed could tell she was processing. He'd seen the phenomenon before. He decided to just let her talk about her night until she had it out of her system.

"At first, I thought it might be Adam," she said finally.

"Adam? Why would you think that?"

Kate related the story of Adam's appearance on Saturday, and how the dogs had reacted.

"The guy was about the same height and build as Adam. But, he didn't move like Adam—you know how you can identify someone you've known for a long time by the way they walk and move? I'm pretty sure it wasn't Adam. Besides what would he have to gain from killing me—other than vengeance, I guess? And, he would have known the dogs would never let him in. This guy seemed surprised when they started barking."

Kate was silent again. They'd finished their bagels and coffee and had turned around to head back to the house. Ed put his arm around her.

Kate looked up the beach and saw a young couple hurrying toward them. It was Aniston Davis and her friend Jake Fredrickson. Kate made no effort to remove Ed's arm from around her. She stopped and waited for the young couple to reach them when they called out her name.

"Ms. Muldoon, sorry to interrupt, but we saw all the commotion at your house this morning and wondered what in the world happened. Are you all right? We heard the ambulance and police cars last night." Aniston's tone was one of real concern.

"I'm fine; thanks. A man tried to break in last night. Actually, he did break in. He shot out one of my sliding glass doors and came through the hole. I'm not sure what he wanted, or who it was. My dogs stopped him. They were hit by several of the bullets, but I think they'll be OK. Sadie has a broken leg, but she's home. Phoebe is still with Doctor Delaney. Hopefully, we'll get her home tomorrow."

"My God. I am so sorry. Is there anything we can to do help?"

"That's sweet of you, but the cops and FBI are there now and all I really need is a good nap." Kate noticed Aniston eyeing Ed, and she realized her sleep-deprived brain had forgotten to introduce him.

"Aniston Davis and Jake Fredrickson, this is Ed Evert. We work together. Ed and I had planned on taking a run on the beach this morning, but when he showed up, he got more than he'd bargained for." Kate smiled up at Ed as he stretched out his hand to shake theirs.

"Aniston is one of Bill Davis' twin daughters, and Jake is her friend from UF—where he's a senior in prelaw and already admitted to UF Law School next fall," Kate said completing, the introductions.

Ed slipped his arm around Kate again after shaking their hands.

"She's had quite a morning. I'm going to hang around this evening and make sure there're no more issues," Ed said protectively.

Kate watched him carefully and was surprised she had no negative reaction to any of this.

Maybe I'm in shock. I think a nap would be a good idea, she decided.

"He's right about that; I *am* exhausted, and I need to get back to the house. I don't think you have anything to worry about. The local cops are going to set up a security surveillance schedule for our neighborhood, so don't be surprised if you see more patrol cars than normal. Enjoy the rest of your weekend."

Kate and Ed headed toward the house. Ed still had his arm firmly around Kate when they walked in the front door. He guided her into the bedroom, tucked her in, and promised to wake her in several hours.

Sadie was whimpering. Kate opened her eyes with a start and immediately looked at the clock. It was 4:45. She'd been asleep for hours. Ed was rubbing her back gently.

"She sounds like she needs to go out. I'm not surprised with all the water she's had," Ed said. "I'm going to help her up. She hasn't quite figured out the logistics of changing position with only three legs that bend."

Ed knelt down and gently lifted Sadie to standing.

"Come on, girl, let's see about a short walk around the front yard."

Sadie willingly let Ed lead her out the door. Kate slipped on some shoes and followed them.

The cops and FBI were just finishing up their crime scene investigation and were beginning to clear out of Kate's house. The new sliding glass doors were installed, and most of the shards of glass were cleaned up. Kate knew she wouldn't be able to walk barefoot in her living room until the disaster recovery crew finished their work. The bloodstains were dark red now. Kate had already decided she'd get new carpeting in the living room, maybe even do a decorative tile with some beautiful area rugs—she could never leave that carpet there even if it was as clean as new. Several of the smaller items on tables and bookshelves were broken, and she would either toss or replace them. Most didn't look salvageable. And there were holes in a couple of her walls and her sofa. The room was a mess, and she felt violated and depressed.

But these are just things, she told herself. *What really matters is getting my girls well again.*

While they were walking Sadie, Kate made calls to Sophia and Polly to tell them she would likely not be in the office on Monday and why. Then she texted Marcy to let her know she should call her before she left St. Pete. As they were headed back inside, Kate's cell phone rang and Beth's name popped up on the caller ID screen.

"How are the pups?"

"Sadie is sore, but sort of mobile. I haven't heard from Carrie about Phoebe, but she wants to keep her sedated and under observation until tomorrow, at least." Kate scratched Sadie's ears when they perked up at the sound of her sister's name. "How are you? You must be exhausted," Kate asked.

"I am, but planning on calling it an early night in a few hours. Ed still with you?"

"Like a shadow," Kate responded and smiled at him as he steadied Sadie's front haunches while she tried to do her business.

"Shadows can be a good thing, Kate. Let him help."

"I am. Beth, I can't thank you enough . . ."

"Just doing my job. I'll let Terry and Suzy know the status, and I'll call you tomorrow."

Kate and Ed sat on the back deck watching the sky grow pink from the backlight of the sunset. Ed had brought in pizza and beer for dinner, and Sadie was asleep on her mat again.

"Not exactly what you had in mind for tonight is it, Mr. Evert?"

"Nope," Ed laughed. "But I'm really glad I was here to help as much as I could. You're still exhausted and need to get some sleep tonight."

"You headed home after dinner?" Kate asked.

"Nope. I promised Beth I'd watch over you tonight, and I don't want to run afoul of the FBI. I thought I'd stay here and take the night shift with Sadie. She's going to need more meds and another walk around 2:00 a.m., and you need to sleep."

Ed smiled gently at Kate. Kate stared at him.

Who is this guy? And why am I letting him help me? I must be really wiped out. Kate couldn't stop questioning the dynamic that had occurred between them during the day.

"Ed, I really appreciate all your help today. You made a terrible day a lot easier to get through, but . . . well . . . I just don't feel up to . . ."

"Sex?" Ed grinned. "I get that. No big deal. I mean, it's great and all, but you know, we don't have to make a steady diet of it," Ed laughed as he repeated Kate's own words back to her.

She laughed at him and took his hand.

"Thanks for understanding," Kate said as she kissed his hand. "So tomorrow morning we'll collect Phoebe if everything goes well tonight. I'd like to head back to Miami right away if we can. I want to get the girls settled into the house and make sure the dog sitter will be able to handle them both."

Kate was returning to her natural state, organizing everything and everyone.

"The disaster recovery team, my contractor, and insurance agent will all be here in the morning so I can get them organized. I'll leave a key with my contractor. I don't want to be here for the cleanup. Later this week, I can figure out new flooring and whatever else needs to be done. I don't want to come back out here until it's done. Happily, Marcy won't be back until tomorrow, I'll see if she's up to overseeing the contractor's work. Now, if both girls just get better, we won't be much worse for wear when this is over," Kate concluded, laying out her plan for the week.

"Yes, but only if they catch the guy who did this. Then we can rest easy. Until then, I think you should keep your Sig next to you at all times."

"Funny, Beth wants me to store it and never take it out again. I don't think she trusts me," Kate laughed.

"I think we should leave finding and arresting the bad guy to Beth, but you need to be safe."

"Ed, let's clean up the dinner things and take a short walk on the beach, and then I'm ready for a shower and a nice warm bed."

"I'll tuck you in and be there when you wake up." Ed's tone told Kate he was staying because he wanted to help.

And, surprisingly, I'm going to let him, she decided.

Chapter 23

Kate woke to the smell of coffee brewing and toasted bagels. She cautiously opened one eye and looked at the clock on the bedside stand.

Jesus, 8:24! Am I dead? What the hell? The disaster dudes will be here shortly, and I'm still asleep.

Kate quickly looked at Sadie's dog bed and discovered her missing.

"Ed?" Kate called out cautiously as she sat up.

"In the kitchen," he shouted back. "You have just enough time to shower before the repair guys get here. I'll hold them off for you. Then we need to eat and find out if our other girl is coming home today."

Kate reached for her cell phone—it wasn't on her nightstand where she was sure she'd left it.

"I have your cell phone out here," he called out, as if he knew she'd reach for it immediately and panic when she found it missing. "I didn't want it to wake you. Looks like you have two calls from the office, another one from Beth, one from Suzy, and one from Marcy. Haven't heard from Doctor Delaney, yet."

Who is this guy? But, at least I must be feeling more like myself. The fact that he's taking charge is starting to irritate me, she thought.

"How's Sadie?" she asked, swinging her legs off the side of the bed.

"Good. She seems less sore, and she's moving around on her own pretty well."

Kate headed into the shower.

Standing under the hot water as she tried to wake up she thought, *I must have passed out from exhaustion last night. I don't even remember Ed being in bed with me other than rubbing my back for a minute . . .*

Kate was momentarily overwhelmed by a feeling of being out of control and entirely too dependent. She tried to shake it off, knowing she would soon be back in charge.

I must have really needed some downtime . . .

When Kate emerged from the bedroom, there were five men in work clothes talking to Ed. He was pointing out holes in the walls and explaining what had happened two nights before. The scene did not quell Kate's rising anxiety over not being in charge.

"Ah, here she is. Kate Muldoon, this is the crew from Digging Out Disaster Recover. I just gave them a brief overview of the work, but you need to talk to them in-depth about what you want and about coordinating with your contractor."

Ed gave Kate an efficient little smile and winked at her as he walked into the kitchen.

He knows I'm irked because he's taken charge, Kate realized. *I guess that's a good thing.*

Kate turned her attention to the crew chief and began her explanation of what they would be in charge of and what her contractor would handle. As she talked she looked out the sliding glass doors and noticed Sadie limping around on the back deck. She looked reasonably happy, occasionally barking at a nearby squirrel or seagull.

Ed walked back into the living room with a mug of coffee for Kate, and then went out onto the back deck to help Sadie down the stairs to the small backyard, leaving Kate alone to deal with the men.

Smart man, very smart man, she thought, grinning broadly.

Kate finished up with the cleanup crew and barely had time to grab half a bagel before her contractor rang the doorbell. She introduced him to the crew, and then explained what she needed him to handle for her. He gave her a rough guesstimate of costs, the amount of time it would take to put her house to right, and told her he'd have a firm estimate and start date for her later in the day.

The insurance agent rang the bell next. Kate introduced him to the cleanup crew and the contractor, and then left the men to discuss coordinating their work schedules and exchange contact info. Kate walked out into the front yard to make some calls. First to Carrie's office to see whether Phoebe was cleared for pickup. She was overjoyed at the news. Phoebe was ready to go home, but she needed to remain sedated for a few more days. Kate felt a giant weight lift from her chest. Then she called her dog sitter in Miami to explain the situation and arrange for daily care for the week. Kate was not leaving them alone until she was sure they were back to normal.

She wondered again at the miraculous strength and energy working mothers had to summon up when their kids get hurt or sick, yet they know their normal work lives have to continue despite the new problems and added responsibilities.

It will be hard enough leaving the girls with a sitter while I'm at work. I don't know if I'd have the strength to do that if they were human children.

Kate listened to the voice messages from Sophia, Polly, Beth, and Suzy and decided she didn't need to return their calls until she was driving back to Miami after collecting Phoebe.

Then she returned Marcy's call. Marcy was shocked when she learned about Kate's narrow escape and the dogs' injuries.

Kate wondered for the first time if Marcy might have been the target of the attack. She was immediately glad it had been her instead of Marcy who had been home early Sunday morning. Kate made a mental note to share this idea with both Beth and Chief Jordan, but she made a conscious decision not to mention it to Marcy, at least not until she could do it face to face.

Grace Dugan had asked Marcy to stay, and when Marcy learned the beach house would be a work zone and the dogs would be OK staying with Kate in Miami, she decided to return to Miami late Tuesday afternoon. Marcy said she'd stop by Kate's Miami house and pick up the girls and take them back to the beach. Kate was reluctant at first to let the girls go back to the beach without her, but she knew she needed to concentrate on work. Besides, the girls would be close to Carrie Delaney if anything went wrong, so she agreed that would be a good plan.

Kate ran through a checklist of things she needed to do before leaving for the city, including making sure the work crew knew how to lock up and set the alarm system. She also removed her Sig and some ammo from the gun safe and placed it in her purse.

Ed returned up the back stairs to the deck with Sadie—she still hadn't mastered going up the stairs on her own, so he was carrying her. Kate was relieved the dogs wouldn't have to climb stairs at the house in Miami. She didn't think she was strong enough to lift them safely. When he walked inside, Kate brought Ed up to speed on Phoebe while they finished their breakfast of bagels and coffee.

"Where did these bagels come from, Ed?" Kate asked, her brain finally catching up to her surroundings. "These aren't left over from yesterday, are they?"

"Are you kidding? Those cops ate every crumb from that batch. I went out this morning after my run on the beach and grabbed a few fresh ones for us. You were sleeping like the dead. I didn't want to disturb you, and Sadie seemed OK on her own for a half hour. She just curled up next to your bed and went back to sleep. I think she's doing pretty well on that casted leg, don't you?"

"Yes. Carrie said she'd look at her again this Saturday and see how the bone is doing. She's hoping the cast will only have to stay on for three weeks, and then we can use a soft bandage for another three weeks. Carrie will X-ray it next Saturday and give us the word."

Kate unplugged the coffeemaker and headed into her room to pack up a few items. As she was gathering her toiletries she heard her cell phone ringing in the kitchen where she'd left it.

"Ed, I think that's my phone. Can you answer it for me? I'm almost done here," Kate called out from her bathroom.

Kate finished packing her small overnight bag and turned to head out of the bedroom as Ed walked in carrying her cell phone.

"Kate, it's Bill. Apparently, he heard about the break-in."

Kate stopped in the middle of the room, standing completely still, looking at Ed and trying to decide if she wanted to take the call.

"Kate, he sounds really worried."

She continued to contemplate whether to answer the phone. It was an odd feeling. She wanted to talk to Bill and wanted to avoid talking to him.

"I really think you should talk to him, Kate," Ed insisted.

Kate reached out with her free hand and took the phone Ed held out to her.

"Hello? Yes, hi, Bill. Are you enjoying your trip . . . What do you mean . . . It just happened yesterday—early Sunday morning . . . I've been a little busy . . . Yes, I saw Aniston and her friend in town, and then again on the beach . . . Yes, Bill, he is . . . Sadie has a broken leg, and we're going to collect Phoebe now. She had to stay overnight after her surgery . . . We're hoping she'll be OK, but she needs to rest . . . No, he wasn't here. Ed arrived Sunday morning. We were going to take a long training run on the beach . . . You know what, Bill? We were just headed out to pick up Phoebe. I'll be driving back to Miami after that . . . If you want to call again I'll be in the car from about 10:30 until noon. I have a full afternoon today, so that will be my only window to talk . . . Thanks for calling. I'll be fine."

Kate hung up and stuffed the phone into the pocket of her jeans.

"You ready?" she asked Ed who had been watching her intently during the call.

"Yep. I'm coming with you to the vet's you know, right?"

"You don't have to, but I appreciate the help."

"And I'm following you to your house in town and getting the girls settled in. And that's not really negotiable either."

"Ed . . ." Kate was fighting her aversion to being told what to do. "Oh, OK. I'll appreciate the help, but then you need to head into the office."

"Fair enough. And now I promise I won't try to give you any more orders . . . for at least the rest of the day."

Kate laughed. "Deal—you are a very smart man, Mr. Evert."

For once, Ed knew better than to say another word, but his grin said it all.

On the drive into Miami, Kate's cell phone rang at 10:40 and immediately transferred to the car's speakers through the Bluetooth connection. It was Bill.

"Hello, Bill," Kate answered, her voice sounding flat.

"Katie, is this a good time to talk? Are you alone?"

"No, I'm not alone. The girls are in the car with me. But if you mean is Ed here, the answer is no. He's in his own car. Following me back into town. He's going to help me get the girls settled in Miami. I have Anastasia, my dog sitter, coming by this afternoon, and then, hopefully, after that, I'll finally make it into the office for a little while."

Kate knew her tone sounded defensive and brusque, but she didn't care.

"Sounds like you have it under control—as usual."

Bill sounded hurt, but Kate decided she wasn't going to let him get to her.

He chose to ignore me for three months after I turned down his marriage proposal. Then, right after we'd reconnected, he decided to take a Caribbean cruise. He chose not to be here, and I can't help the fact that my life didn't stop simply because he left.

"So, are you having a good time? Where are you? Aniston said you were in Jamaica. She looks great, by the way, and her friend, Jake Fredrickson, seems very nice."

Kate had decided to try to achieve a friendly tone. She realized she was genuinely interested in how Bill was doing.

"Yes, I'm in Jamaica. I want to hear about your break-in, Kate. Do they know who it was? Have they caught him?"

"No, we don't know who it was yet. The house was crawling with cops and FBI agents yesterday. They have DNA and other evidence. So, if the guy's in the system, they'll know who they're looking for soon, even if they might not know where he is. I've left all that to Beth and Chief Jordan. I have my hands full with the dogs and work."

"Kate, I don't think you should be alone. What if he tries again?"

"Bill, I wasn't alone. I had my girls with me. They were so heroic. They never even hesitated. I feel terrible that they're all banged up now. Phoebe took a bullet through her chest wall. Carrie said it narrowly missed her heart and lungs. She's going to be OK, but her chest is all shaved and bandaged, and she's really sore. How's Howie?"

There was a long pause.

"Kate, Howie passed away on our fifth night out. It was quick and painless. I think it was a stroke . . . I gave him a burial at sea. He always loved being out on the boat so much. It seemed fitting."

"Oh God, Bill. I am so sorry."

"Yeah, but he got to go doing something he loved, so it was OK. I knew it was coming. I think he'd been having small strokes for the last several months. I miss him. The boat is really lonely without him on board."

"I can only imagine."

"Kate, I really don't think you should be alone at night."

"Bill, I have the girls, and I have my Sig." Kate hesitated, and then added, "And sometimes I have company."

"Ed?"

"Yes."

There was a long pause in the conversation.

"Do you love him, Katie?"

"I don't know, Bill. It's all pretty new and very confusing right now. It's different than it was with you. You and I have known each other so long and have so much history."

"Do you miss me?"

"I should ask you that question. I haven't heard from you since you left, so I figured you'd sorted things out and decided that communication wasn't . . . necessary."

"But I do miss you, Kate."

"That wasn't exactly clear from the evidence, my friend." Kate paused trying to determine why Bill's comment irritated her so.

Finally, she said, "You know, you really can't have it both ways, Bill." Kate was surprised by her frankness.

"What do you mean?" He sounded stunned.

"You can't say you miss me, and yet not call, or text, or e-mail, or even send a flipping postcard. You can't be off on a grand adventure in the Caribbean and expect everything you left behind to remain unchanged, exactly as you left it, just waiting for your return. You just can't have it both ways, Bill."

Bill was silent for several minutes.

"I guess you're right, Kate. I should have called you every time I thought of you, but then I would have been calling you every moment of every day. Maybe I never should have left."

"Bill, you had places to go, things to do, a life to live. But, you made a choice. You want things to be a certain way. You want certain types of relationships, and I don't fit that mold. You tell me that *I'm* controlling, that *I* have to hold both reigns at all times, and you're right. But, Bill, so do you. You're so used to being the boss giving the orders, the quarterback calling the plays. You're so used to having your orders followed, and never questioned. You don't even know you're doing it. Even when you do it sweetly and gently and maybe with love in your heart—you're still taking the lead, presuming everything is going to be done your way, at your tempo."

Kate realized she had never said these things to Bill. Their brief affair had been over before it really could begin, and then he disappeared out of her life for three months while he tried to sort out why she refused his marriage proposal. If he had contacted her right after she told him she wouldn't marry him, they might have had this conversation then. But he didn't, and the words had remained unsaid. Then after he resurfaced, he quickly left again. Thinking about all this made her incredibly sad, and she sighed heavily.

Bill was silent. Kate hoped he was absorbing what she'd said, but she hated talking about important things on the phone because you can't tell how people are reacting.

He's probably getting mad, she decided.

"OK, Kate. I think I get it. Can we talk about this some more? I've had a lot of time to think things through, and you are on my mind constantly. There are things I want to tell you. And now you have some crazy person after you—trying to kill you. Katie, I just want to be with you and take care of you."

"Bill, I'm a grown woman. I've been taking care of myself for many years, and I like it that way. This thing with the dogs has been very unsettling, and it's the first time I've ever leaned on someone else. I was glad to have Ed's help yesterday. He took care of Sadie through the night, carried her up and down stairs, and got both dogs into the car. But once we're at home in Miami, it will be easier to handle on my own. I don't want to be unfair to Ed, and I don't want to be unfair to you. Bill, I'm rambling. I need to go. I'm fine. They'll catch the guy who broke in, and the dogs will get better. Life will go on. I need to stop talking now."

"OK, Katie. I love you. Do you know that?"

"I don't know any more, Bill, and I don't want to think about it now because there's no answer. I'm exhausted and have to think about other things that need to be handled more immediately. You're there doing your thing, and I'm here doing mine. Listen, Bill, we're almost at the house," Kate lied. She simply did not want to start crying on the phone. She'd had enough drama to last a long while.

"Can I call again?"

"Yes, and I'll try not to have so much drama in my life next time you call, and you can tell me all about your grand adventure. I'm sure it's wonderful."

Kate desperately wanted to hang up, and she wanted just as desperately to tell Bill she needed him and he should come home. But that would not be the right answer, and she knew it.

"OK, Katie. I love you. Please try to know that."

Bill hung up.

Chapter 24

At the office, Kate worked without a break, trying to catch up from being out all morning. She wanted to get out of the office at a reasonable time so she could go home to see her girls. It was already close to 5:30 when her phone rang. Caller ID let her know it was Kevin O'Neil, the CEO of Brighton Industries.

What now? Kate thought, feeling the pressure of her burgeoning caseload and injured dogs at home.

"Hello, Kevin. How are you today?" she said, hiding the irritation of getting a call so close to when she'd hope to leave the office.

"Not very damn good, Kate. We've got a huge problem. I need to talk with you about the damn trial that's coming up."

"All right, do you want to chat now, or shall we set a time for an in-person discussion tomorrow?" Kate asked, hoping he'd say "tomorrow," but knowing he would say "now."

"Now, unfortunately. It's urgent."

"OK. I'm all ears."

Kate IM'd Ed in case he wanted to sit in on the call.

"I just found out Francis DeGracio, one of our quality and safety engineers, has been lying all along about the results of our trials of the auto shut-off function on our series 48 mower. The damn thing failed one out of ten times it was tested on a downhill. Kate, the fucking machine stopped moving, but the motor continued to run. That means that the accident we're about to go to trial on could very possibly have happened exactly as the plaintiff, Jonathan Torres, reported it."

Ed walked into Kate's office and gave her a quizzical look. She motioned toward the side chair, and put Kevin on speaker.

"Kevin, you're on speakerphone now, and my colleague Ed Evert is here in my office. This development means we gave inaccurate information in our discovery responses, and you gave incorrect information at your deposition, Kevin. We have to update those responses immediately, now that we know the truth. More importantly, our chances of winning at trial just dropped to less than 50 percent in my estimation. The jury could kill us monetarily. Plus, you now have a recall to plan and a PR mess on your hands."

"I know. But do we really have to update our discovery responses? Can't we just quietly settle with the Torres family? And then just as quietly recall the damn machines?"

"That depends, Kevin."

"Really? On what?" He sounded hopeful.

"It depends on whether or not you want me to continue to be your attorney. Kevin, you have only one option. You personally signed those interrogatories under oath, and I'm pretty sure you remember swearing to tell the truth at your deposition. Right now, you haven't violated those oaths because you didn't know the truth then. You do now, and you need to amend your answers; it's the same as if you'd lied in the first place."

"But, Kate, that's going to mean terrible press and a huge settlement with Torres."

"Yes, and if you don't do it now and the truth is later discovered, the fact that you committed fraud and perjury will trash the company's reputation, and you could end up in jail. You need to get your PR people working on this. They've got to find a way to spin it so you come across as being betrayed by DeGracio, and you've come forward to do the right thing as soon as you learned of his deception."

"You're right, but damn it, Kate. Assuming I authorize you to revise the discovery, what's next?"

"You get your accounting department to figure out how many of those foot-eating machines were purchased, and whether you can track down the original purchasers. You need to know the size of your exposure. And, your engineers need to figure out if there's a mechanical fix for the problem. Then, you need to begin a recall of every single mower.

"I'll contact Torres's attorney and start settlement negotiation. He's already provided us his expert's valuation of Jonathan's losses, so you'd better be prepared to pay pretty close to that number, minus any mitigation or other economic arguments our expert witness can come up with. Torres's demand was nearly $3.5 million dollars. I'll get in touch with our expert and tell him we need him to go over Torres's valuation with a fine-tooth comb to see if there's any way we can bring down the tab. But, Kevin, this is going to cost you. How much did the company reserve in the event of a plaintiff's verdict at trial?"

"We only reserved a million. To be honest, Kate, I didn't think there was any chance we'd lose, based on our safety testing numbers. Shit, I didn't think one of our own engineers would have the balls to outright lie about them."

"Well, he did and now, if you want to ensure that we don't have a class action staring you in the face, we need to get ahead of the damage, settle with Torres, and buy back or fix every machine that you can track down. And, Kevin, you need to make sure there aren't any other surprises relating to safety testing on other pieces of equipment you've sold in the last 15 years. You're going to have to fire DeGracio, of course, but first, you should find out what he will tell you about other false safety test statistics."

"Jesus, Kate, this is worse than I imagined. I thought we could just quietly settle with Torres . . . I guess I understand, but shit! I'll get my guys here figuring out how many machines we need to recall. Our audit team can start a review of our safety testing, and I'll have the PR folks get to work. Can you talk to our economic damages expert, Dr. Walton, and get him to look at the plaintiff's demand again?"

"Yes, I'm pretty sure that won't take too long. He was ready to testify a month ago. He was prepared to say, assuming the facts as represented by Torres to be true, his damages were more like two and a half million, and that's without any mitigation—which, frankly, at this point, would look like a win. I'll see if I can get Torres's attorney interested in talking about settling in that range. Kevin, we have our work cut out for us. Can you call me tomorrow morning? I want to see if I can reach Dr. Walton tonight and at least leave a voice mail message for

Matt Danson, Torres' attorney."

They said their good-byes, and Kate turned toward Ed.

"A safety engineer at Brighton Industries lied about the damn safety testing records. The mower's motor failed to stop one out of ten times the handle was released on a downhill. The mower stopped moving forward, but the motor kept running and the blade kept turning," Kate told Ed.

"Meaning Torres could have slipped going downhill, let go of the handle, the cutoff switch failed, the motor didn't stop, and his foot could have slipped under the safety guard," Ed concluded.

"Yep, just like he testified."

"Shit!"

" Shit is right."

It was 6:15, she'd done all she could on the Brighton emergency. She was exhausted and needed to head out to relieve her dog sitter soon.

"I think I'll go for a run tonight," Ed said with a sly grin as he appeared in her doorway.

It was obvious to Kate that Ed's running route was to her house and that he wanted to come by the house for sex tonight.

"Hmmm . . ." she said. "Are you sure you have the energy for a run? It's late and we've had a few high-stress days."

Ed just laughed, swung his jacket over his shoulder, bid her good night, and left the office.

On her way home, Kate again considered whether it might be time to end the relationship with Ed. The sex was great . . . phenomenal, actually, she had to admit. And he had shown a side of himself over the last several days that Kate had not seen before—a mature and caring side. But, she still missed the emotional attachment she'd felt with Bill. She wondered if her expectations for a relationship were unrealistic, too demanding, wanting it all. Or maybe she was just not letting herself form the same emotional attachment to Ed. Was she protecting herself from being hurt again? He'd certainly been there for her when she needed him these last two days. He was trying to make it work, that was apparent, and maybe she was only second-guessing herself because of Bill's phone call.

Kate again wondered if she'd made a mistake turning down Bill's marriage proposal. And then she wondered for the one-thousandth time if there was room in the world for a woman who doesn't want to be married.

Kate was glad she only had a short drive home. She was sick of ruminating about the mess. But she knew she needed to deal with it head-on, and soon.

Just as soon as the shit stops raining down on me, Kate decided.

When she pulled into her driveway, it was evident Ed was already there. The dog sitter's car was gone, and Kate could see wet footprints on the pool deck by the faint blue pool light. Her dogs were lying by the hot tub, probably getting their ears rubbed.

Kate waved to Ed and the dogs, then walked into the house as the garage door closed behind her. She turned on the kitchen light, opened the wine cooler, and uncorked a Barolo. Picking up two glasses on her way, she stepped out on the back deck. His running clothes were in a heap on a chaise lounge. She walked over and handed him the wine and glasses and slipped out of her skirt and blouse, tossing them on top of his clothes.

"More," he said.

She smiled and granted his wish, all the while wondering how long she would be able to indulge her sexual urges . . . worrying again she was no different than Adam.

They sipped their wine, rubbed the dogs' ears, and let the hot water dissolve the tensions of the day. Kate let her mind wander over their relationship once again. Ed had moved out of his friends' house and into one of the new condo buildings downtown where he was on a rent-to-own plan that allowed him to create some equity. It also allowed him to develop a social life.

"You know, now that you are living on your own, you need to start dating."

"Are you dissatisfied with the service, madam?" he said in jest, but his eyes registered surprise.

"Ed, what we have is extraordinary, but I feel rather guilty. I'm monopolizing your life. You need to think about your future. You may want a wife and family, and, if so, you probably need to start thinking about that now."

"Seriously, Kate? Are we going to have this discussion again? Now? I'm more than happy with the status quo. Apparently, you're not. Maybe I need to spend *more* time with you. I would enjoy that very much." Ed slid closer to her and began to trace his fingers around her breast, plucking her nipples gently, and then more firmly as she tried to push away. "Let's go inside. I want to make love to you."

"We can go inside, and we will have sex, my young friend, but we will not *make love*," Kate said as she pushed back and stepped gracefully out of the hot tub. Scooping up their clothes and the wine bottle, she called to the dogs and headed into the house. Ed quickly followed, helping the dogs back into the house and onto their dog beds in the kitchen.

As soon as he closed the door behind him, Ed pulled Kate to him, kissing her passionately, and she felt the familiar warmth and desire growing. Ed walked her backward to the stairs, where she surrendered and turned to walk up.

Once in her bedroom, he pulled Kate onto the bed, and rolled her on top of him. He was already hard. She mounted him and began rhythmically riding him, as he held on to her hips. But he wasn't willing to come so soon and flipped her off to the side and pinned her down on the bed while his mouth explored her body. Kate was losing control quickly and begged for him to come inside her. But Ed rolled onto his back, and again pulled her on top, grasping her breasts as she rode his thrusting pelvis. Finally, they exploded and collapsed together.

Ed whispered, "Do you really want to give this up?"

A few minutes passed and finally, Kate said, "No, but we need to. We should at least take a break, and you should consider what you want your future to look like."

Kate rolled to Ed's side.

"I need to tell you some things. You already know my ex-husband, Adam, was an ass and totally self-centered. Not only did he pretty much fuck anything that moved, he also didn't care that many of the women he screwed were looking for something more and believed he was too, because he lied to them. I worry that I'm acting too much like Adam. I don't mean I'm fucking everything that moves. And, I don't think I've been anything but honest with you about this relationship, but I worry that you have more to lose by not pursuing other options than I do. I'm content with this relationship . . ."

"Just content? *Really?*" Ed interrupted. He looked hurt.

"Ed, the sex is wonderful. I'm more than content with that, but our relationship is strictly sexual and intellectual in terms of our work. But, I am truly monopolizing you in both of those areas. You need to pursue other options, or at least think about whether you want other options. You need to see if you'd like to add an emotional aspect to your relationship with a woman. You certainly seem to have that capacity. Your caring over these last couple of days has been wonderful. You need to know if you want to fall in love, get married, have children."

Kate pushed herself up to look at him. Ed's face was blank.

Finally, he said, "What if I love you?"

"Jesus!" Kate fell back on the bed and covered her eyes with her arms.

"Don't tell me how I feel, Kate. I'm pretty sure I've fallen in love with you. I think about you when we're not together. I can't wait to tell you stuff that happens to me when you're not around. I love debating issues with you. I love your brain, the way you think. I love your sense of humor. I care about what happens in your life. I want to defend you from the assholes you have to deal with. I want to protect you, even though you don't want to be protected. And I love making love to you. How is all that not an emotional attachment? I am fulfilled by this relationship."

Ed stopped talking and looked over at Kate.

"Now, you tell me how you feel about me," he whispered.

Kate lay very still. Finally, she quietly said, "Ed, I haven't allowed myself to think about anything but the sex. I don't think anything more than a sexual relationship is even possibile for us. Look, I am older than you. And although the actual number of years between us isn't huge, we're at very different places in our lives. I've had the chance to decide I'm not going to be a mother. I've had the chance to decide that I don't want to be married. I've had the chance to live on my own and know how much, and when, I need to be with someone else. I don't think you've had the chance to make those same decisions, and I don't want to be the reason you don't get to."

They silently lay together on the bed holding hands, staring at the ceiling.

Ed cleared his throat and said, "You're right, but you're not that much older than I am, Kate. And, I've had experiences that you haven't. I know things about myself that you never will. I know I can kill another human being. I know how it feels to be certain you'll die before the morning, and then get that next day by the grace of God. I know what it's like to drive my body to the extremes . . . sure I was going to die, and would have even welcomed death. So, to me, our ages don't really have much to do with anything. I understand what you're saying, Kate, but what if I think about all those things you mentioned and decide I want to be with you, on your terms? What then?"

Kate rolled toward him and put her hand on his chest. "I don't know. I guess we'll figure that out if it happens. But you need to have the chance to decide." They fell asleep in each other's arms; physically, intellectually, and emotionally exhausted.

Chapter 25

Kate and Ed woke early Tuesday morning. Their mood was guarded, each not wanting to bring up their conversation of the night before, and each savoring the intimacy of their night together. After he helped Kate feed, medicate, and assist both dogs outside, Ed decided to run home rather than have Kate drop him off on her way to work.

As she showered, dressed, and waited for the dog sitter, Kate thought about her day ahead, trying to keep her mind off yesterday's conversation with Bill and the night with Ed. She had a number of urgent pending matters that required her full attention. She couldn't afford to be distracted by personal issues, like a confused heart.

Ticking off each pending item in her head, Kate created a mental checklist for her day. Brighton Industries needed her full attention as she tiptoed through the discovery update and settlement negotiation quagmire. The interpleader and declaratory judgment action had been set for hearing on Friday morning, and there were witnesses who needed to be prepared. Marcy deserved a resolution to the question "Was she or wasn't she a newly minted millionaire?" Phillip Bentley was pressing for a final resolution to the worthless claims Bobbi Jo and James had filed against the company. And, she needed to catch up with Beth and learn whether the DNA found after the break-in at her beach house had revealed the identity of the intruder. And if that wasn't enough, there was the construction mess at her beach house and decisions about what materials to use. It was going to be a long day, and she was exhausted just thinking about it.

As she poured herself another cup of coffee, her cell phone rang; it was Beth.

"Kate, I thought you'd want to know right away, but hope I'm not interrupting anything."

"Nope. Just sitting here waiting for the dog sitter and making a list of things I need to get done today. You were on it, so this is great. What's up?"

"We got a hit on the DNA we pulled from the blood droplets and tissue your intruder left behind, thanks to the girls. You'll never guess who paid you a visit Sunday morning."

"Probably not," Kate said. "You could tell me it was Adam, or Zeke Peters, or even Doug the Dick—just about anyone—and I wouldn't be surprised."

"It was our favorite sociopath, Gary Cook. Have you had any direct contact with him other than your brief sighting at the marina?"

"You're kidding! No, not a thing. Shit! That man gets around. But, I have no idea how he would know me or where I live. I can't think why he would have picked me as a target." Kate hesitated momentarily as she took in Beth's news.

"You know, Beth, I wonder if he might have been looking for Marcy Simpson. She's the friend and client who's been staying at my beach house for the last week. I think I mentioned her situation to you. She was named the beneficiary on her ex-husband's $4 million insurance policy. She's Joe Dugan's ex-wife—you may have seen his obit in the *Herald*. He was that well-known cardiologist. Anyway, this is just a wild guess, so it's probably not even close to correct, but I wouldn't feel good not mentioning it in case it turns out I'm right. Marcy and I are about the same build and coloring. Her ex, Dr. Dugan, remarried Senator Ferguson's youngest daughter about 16 years ago. It turns out Dr. Dugan's death is now being investigated as a murder. The whole situation is rife with political intrigue and pressure. Joe Dugan was in the process of divorcing his wife and planning on trying for sole custody of their kids. He was going to make some very damning accusations in the divorce petition.

"Plus, Joe's insurance policies were oddly structured. In addition to the $4 million policy naming his *ex*-wife, he had a policy for his boys, and recently changed the beneficiary on another policy from his wife to the boys. He had no policy naming his wife as beneficiary. That's why his wife and the estate's attorney are making a strong pitch to have the court find the policy naming Marcy was really meant for his wife.

"Chief Jordan arrested Marcy ten days ago because the current Mrs. Dugan and her well-connected daddy pressed for an arrest warrant. The $4 million seemed like a great motive—except Marcy had no idea the policy was current, and she hadn't seen her ex in years. Happily, I was able to get her out of jail, and she's been staying at my beach house ever since. The case is a mess, but it looks like I'm going to be able to show Joe Dugan truly intended Marcy to be the beneficiary, even though she was no longer his wife. I've been trying to convince Chief Jordan to look at Joe's second wife and her lover Zeke Peters as suspects in Joe's death. Given some of the allegations I read in the divorce petition and the underhanded intimidation I've seen from the attorney for Dugan's estate and his father-in-law, I wouldn't put it past them to try to harm Marcy. Beth, I know this sounds farfetched, but do you suppose there's any chance this guy Zeke, the widow, or her daddy put out a hit on Marcy?"

"It does sound farfetched, but, Kate, with $4 million at issue, nothing is out of the question. Any chance your friend got hooked up with some really bad dudes herself and they're looking for payment?"

"No chance whatsoever! But then, you don't know Marcy. She couldn't hurt anyone or even *wish* them ill. Don't waste your time pursuing that angle, Beth," Kate said.

"We need to find this Gary Cook—and fast." Beth said. "At least we know he was in the area on Sunday morning. Hopefully, he's still here. We're going to stake out a couple of places where we know he's been seen. Keep your fingers crossed. I'll keep you informed of our progress. In the meantime, take precautions and stay safe."

Kate was saying good-bye as her dog sitter walked in the back door.

By the time Kate hit the office, she'd decided the only way she would survive this week was to delegate. She called Ed's office.

"Hello, beautiful," he brazenly answered her call.

"Hello, yourself," Kate sighed. *This is why a person should never get involved with someone at the office. I need a sex-free safe zone where I only have to think about work.*

"Ed, I need you to see if you can resolve the Bobbi Jo issue today, or tomorrow, at the latest. Get in touch with the company's health-care carrier and make sure they understand the company disagrees with the denial of benefits for Bobbi Jo's sex change operation. Then put the company's position in a strongly worded letter, and send the letter by e-mail, PDF, and certified mail. And copy Bobbi Jo's attorney, as well as Philip Bentley, Josie Myers, and the state insurance commissioner.

"Then call Bobbi Jo's attorney and tell him she's not getting any money from the company, but also tell him what we've done to back her request for coverage by the insurance company. And tell him the company expects her to be at work Thursday morning and ready to start training for the line foreman job. If she thinks she has a better chance suing the company, she should go for it. If she fails to show up on Thursday, we'll consider her absence job abandonment, and she'll be out of a job. Put all that in an e-mail and a letter after you finished talking to him.

"Next, call James Bell's attorney and tell him the best we'll do for James is put him on another line. Let him know the company expects him to come in and talk to Josie Myer by Friday to make arrangements for a line change. Make sure he understands he's not getting any money from the company, and our offer to transfer him to a different line has a time limit. Also, tell him he'll be expected to sign a settlement agreement stating the line change is in complete settlement of all claims against the company from his date of hire until today."

"Ok, Boss Lady. Roger that. I got it, and I'm on it. I'll report back when I'm done."

"Thanks," Kate said and hung up.

Her next call was to Dr. Jeffery Walton, Brighton Industries economic damages expert. She quickly updated him on the company's urgent need to settle the Torres matter and why she needed him to take one last look at Torres' damages expert's report and wring out everything he possibly could. She was going to have to make an offer to settle, and she wanted to know her best, most defensible position because that would help her decide on her opening offer. She knew she'd have to come up from her baseline, but she hoped to eventually meet the plaintiff somewhere between her baseline number and the plaintiff's expert's full-figured $3,496,452.23.

Dr. Walton promised he'd be back to her by early afternoon.

Matt Danson, Jonathan Torres's attorney, called Kate around 1:30.

"Matt, thanks for calling me back. How've you been?"

"Busy, Kate, very busy. But, I'm not complaining."

"Know what you mean. Hey, what do you think our odds are of actually getting to trial next month? It would be good to put this one to bed."

"Yes, but I wouldn't put it past Judge Kilmer to pass us again. I think he's hoping we'll settle."

"How's Mr. Torres doing? I'm sure he's interested in getting this behind him and moving on with his life. How's his rehab coming along?"

"It's a long slog, and he's an impatient, young kid. His life has changed, and he still can't get his head around that."

"Right. I know it's a long process for him, but I noticed the last medical report seemed to be pretty positive. Have you sent that report to your damages expert? You know you might need to see if a downward revision of your demand is in order."

"I'll send it to him, but, Kate, the kid is young, and that's both a good thing and a bad thing for you. His body will recover faster, and he'll get to maximum medical improvement faster than an older guy, but he's going to live a long time with the disability caused by your company's mower. That means more future damages and more expense for you guys."

"Well, Matt, do you think your client is in the mood to try to resolve this matter short of trial?"

"Probably. He's very impatient."

"Yeah, I get that. Well, we are too. I was just talking with Kevin O'Neil yesterday about the trial. He's starting to talk settlement. Doesn't really want to wait and run the risk of being set over again. I think if you guys came up with something reasonable, we might be able to start negotiations before our final push toward the trial date."

"You've got our damages expert's report. That's our reasonable number. Kate, this injury should never have happened to this kid."

"Probably true. Because Mr. Torres shouldn't have been trying to cut wet grass, in the rain, on a hillside, while wearing flip-flops, no matter whose mower he was using. How about getting me a number that reflects some of his comparative negligence?"

"How about you getting me a number that reflects how much the jury is going to love this kid, and how well he did at his deposition? You know we're still looking for punitive damages."

"And your punitives will be capped at no more than $500,000. Besides, if I'm talking settlement, I'm not going to talk about punitives. Think you can get me a number that factors in his own negligence to get settlement negotiation started?"

"I'll give it my best shot. I'll talk to the kid today and get back to you."

"I'd appreciate that. Any chance you can have it to me by tomorrow morning?"

"Actually, if the kid's home, I can get it for you this afternoon."

"This afternoon would be great. I'd rather explore settlement now, than spend my client's money getting ready for trial, *again*. The sooner we talk, the more generous my client is likely to be, because the more he pays me, the tighter his wallet gets."

"I'll talk to Jonathan and see if I can explain comparative negligence. Let me work on getting you a number."

"By the way, Matt, we've started updating our discovery responses as called for in the pretrial order. We'll be sending you the updates by Thursday at the latest."

"Anything interesting, Kate?"

"We've found some more safety test results that will be included in our update. There were some of situations where the automatic shutoff wasn't as quick as others. We can talk about it when you get the update. Don't forget you still need to update *your* discovery responses too."

After hanging up, Kate felt like she needed a shower to remove the sliminess she felt from her little dance with Matt. While she felt the comparative negligence defense was a strong one, she didn't like the hide-the-ball discovery game her client had played, even if it was unintentional. She needed to present their case as positively and zealously as she could, but within the ethical guidelines. Her client had her dancing too close to that line for her comfort.

Dr. Walton called Kate a little before 3:00 that afternoon.

"Kate, I don't have a huge amount of additional reductions I can get you just based on debunking the plaintiff's expert's numbers. The fact that the kid is only 17 hurts—we're looking at close to 70 years of future damage. Anyway, I've done what I can with that aspect, and I'll e-mail over the updated report. I spent a little time looking through some recent jury verdicts in cases with comparative negligence defenses. Your best bet is going to be trying to get a high percentage of comparative negligence assigned to the kid. I'm sending you some verdicts that should help you. Most of them run in the 25–50 percent comparative negligence range. That's pretty great for our position. I'll get these verdicts over to you right away. Good luck with the settlement negotiations. I understand from Frank that their legal department only reserved a million for this case. I guess that looked reasonable when we all thought the automatic shutoff feature worked flawlessly. Happy hunting, Kate."

"Thanks, Jeffery, I think I'll need it!"

Matt Danson revealed his eagerness to settle when he called Kate back just two hours after their first call.

"Thanks for getting back to me so quickly, Matt. I hope this bodes well for our discussions."

"Hard to say, Kate. My client is motivated, but he has an intense fear of being taken advantage of by a large corporation. I can't really say I blame him. So, we're not coming off our original demand much, but, if we could get this done this week, we'd go for a flat three million."

"Matt, I get that he's worried about being ripped off, so let's do this. Let's assume, just for the sake of these negotiations, that the accident happened *exactly* as your client testified at his deposition. In other words, assume for the sake of this discussion that the shutoff switch failed to turn the motor off immediately when Jonathan let go of the handle. Of course, you know I'm not making that admission, but let's discuss what your damages would look like in that case."

"If that was the case, Kate, I'd start looking for more plaintiffs, and you'd have a class action on your hands."

"Maybe, but you'd have to find those plaintiffs, and we already sent you our claims history in discovery. There just aren't any claims like Jonathan's where the owner hadn't tampered with the mower to override the shutoff function. As you heard, there were quite a few owners who didn't *like* the shutoff feature because it requires two hands on the handle at all times. Some owners thought it was more important to be able to operate their cell phones while cutting the grass than keeping their toes and fingers safe. So, I'm not really worried about a class action. And, if you were honest with your client, you'd have to tell him that, while more plaintiffs in the law suit would increase *your fees*, Matt, adding more plaintiffs would likely *reduce Torres' award*. Your current client receives no substantial benefit if you amend or refile this action as a class. Remember, you're working for Mr. Torres, Matt."

"I'm not coming off the three million number, Kate."

"Well, then, tell me what part of that number reflects your client's own culpability? Matt, he was cutting wet grass, in the rain, on a downhill slope, while *wearing flip-flops*. His own dad testified that he told him not to cut the grass that day because it was dangerous, and his mom testified that she ran out the door after him carrying his work boots when he walked out in flip-flops. Matt, that's some pretty strong testimony supporting comparative negligence. I've got some recent verdicts from Florida, Texas, South Carolina, and Georgia where the juries ascribed between 25 percent and 50 percent of the negligence to the plaintiff in comparable personal injury cases. You know we'll be filing an offer of judgment, and you also know what happens if you don't meet or beat our offer—the judge won't award you your fees and costs. I know you don't want to go *there*. Look, why don't I send you these verdicts. You should discuss them with your client. Meanwhile, I'll take your demand to my client, but I can tell you they'll reject it. They want to know your client has applied a reduction for his own negligence. It's only fair, Matt."

"Kate, we'll take a look at the verdicts, but I don't think Jonathan is going to be persuaded. I've told him you're good in the courtroom and that he could end up getting nothing. But, he seems inclined to roll the dice."

"That's where you come in, Matt. That's where you earn that big fee, your one-third. And while you're at it, talk to him about a structured settlement. A kid as young as he is shouldn't come into money in the seven-figure range, and, frankly, I wasn't all that impressed with his parents' ability to understand the concept of that kind of money either."

"I hear that, Kate," Matt laughed. "I'll see what I can do and let you know tomorrow."

Kate hung up and gathered her things. She was leaving early. She wanted to be there when Marcy stopped by to collect the girls. She was going to insist Marcy take her car out to the beach, it was much more spacious than Marcy's Mini Cooper. She also wanted to call Jamie French, her favorite Garrett Beach cop, and see if he was on duty tonight, and if he'd stop by to check on Marcy and the girls. Kate was worried Cook might make another attempt at completing his mission.

Ed called Kate's cell phone around 6:30.

"*First*," Ed began without even a hello, "Beth left messages for both of us late this afternoon. She's going undercover at The Angler tonight. Gary Cook's car has been spotted in the parking lot again, but they haven't been able to find him. They're concerned he might have left the area. So they've staked out all of the places he's been spotted. They'll be a bunch of teams out. Beth says Suzy's neighborhood is one of the locations they're staking out. You might want to make sure Suzy has company tonight or maybe spends the night somewhere else.

"Also, Terry apparently spotted someone who looks like Cook at the gym where he works out. So, there will be a team working that location as well. I know they're planning on watching your beach house, and Beth said they'd watch your house here in Miami. It's not that far from the marina. Who knows, they might get lucky.

"Oddly, one of the CCT cameras caught an image that looks like Cook being dropped off by an Uber driver at the University of Miami Hospital two nights ago, and even more oddly, he was wearing scrubs. Beth's team canvased the hospital staff and learned a couple of orderlies have seen a guy hanging around the emergency rooms who matched Cook's wanted poster. One of the orderlies even found the guy asleep in an empty exam room one night. He thought he was a doctor catching a few winks between patients. Beth has a team at the hospital as well."

"Sounds like Beth is on her game as usual," Kate remarked. "I sure as hell hope Cook hasn't left the area. With so many leads, it would be a shame if one of them didn't pan out."

"Yeah, well, I asked Beth if I could tag along tonight. I'd like to do something other than sit around *alone*."

The implication of Ed's comment was not subtle. Kate figured he was irritated with her for leaving the office without telling him she was going.

Kate chose to ignore his comment and simply said, "OK."

There was a significant silence.

Finally, Ed continued. "OK." He was clearly disappointed Kate hadn't volunteered to keep him otherwise engaged this evening.

"So did Beth agree to you tagging along with her surveillance team tonight?" Kate asked, trying to bridge the gap between them, and, at the same time, assure herself that she really wasn't a heartless, selfish bitch—it was a hard sell at the moment.

"Kind of. She said she couldn't keep me out of a public bar, and she would tell me when they planned on being there. But, Beth also made me promise I wouldn't do anything foolish, like come armed. Apparently, she felt she needed to tell me that because she wasn't as specific about that instruction when you delivered the ransom money in the Bentley matter. Did you really take your Sig with you, Kate? You never told me that."

"I did, and it really pissed Beth off, but I'd do it again in a heartbeat. I have a concealed carry permit, so it was legal. But, Beth complained I could have shot her or one of her team. I think she was wrong about that, but she's the expert in that area. I just wanted some protection. Don't make the same mistake." Kate laughed at the memory of Beth's ire when she saw Kate's Sig clatter across the floor of the hotel room.

"You want to come along with me tonight, Kate? Beth can't keep you away either, but I'd prefer my date didn't come packing. You might get mad at me—again—and shoot me this time," Ed chuckled.

"I might. I'll see how exhausted I am—it's been a long day."

Kate wasn't sure she wanted to encourage Ed, but she really *did* want to tag along, just in case Cook decided to show up at The Angler. Now that the dogs were with Marcy, her house seemed very empty.

After all, Kate thought, *I've actually seen the guy.*

"Come on, it'll be fun. Cook may or may not show, but in any event, I can fill you in on my discussion with the attorneys for Bobbi Jo and James Bell. It's the best entertainment I can offer—other than aerobic sex at my place."

"What time are you heading out to The Angler?"

"I'll pick you up at 7:30. See you then," Ed said quickly and hung up without waiting for Kate's response.

He's persistent; I'll give him that. Kate smiled, wondering if they'd end up having aerobic sex. Upon reflection, she decided it didn't sound like an entirely bad idea.

Kate and Ed sat in a booth at the back of The Angler eating greasy fish and chips and drinking sparkling water with lime, hoping it would look like a gin and tonic. Beth had agreed if Kate promised to come unarmed, having her at the bar might actually be helpful since she'd seen Gary Cook in person—everyone else would be working from a photograph. Kate had lied and told Beth she'd leave her gun in the car. Instead, it was resting comfortably in the special side pocket of her purse.

Beth's team was sitting in three different groups around the bar and restaurant, appearing to chat casually as they kept a watchful eye on the door. One of Beth's team was stationed in the kitchen monitoring the security cameras with views of the parking lot and each of the doors. The FBI team had invisible ear buds, but Kate and Ed had to rely on their cell phones if they wanted to communicate with Beth.

Kate had to admit this *was* more fun than staying home alone. But, she was again struggling with the guilt she felt when she was with Ed.

God knows, Bill certainly doesn't feel guilty dating other women or leaving me alone for months while he cruises the Caribbean, for heaven's sake. And, when I told him how I feel, and all he said was "I got it." I guess "I got it" too, she thought. *His message was loud and clear. He doesn't think I'm worth the fight.*

She considered ordering a real G&T, but decided that might not be a good idea. Just in case some shit really did go down tonight, she needed her wits about her—especially since she was armed. Instead, she munched her greasy food and watched the door.

"Kate, I'm trying to figure out why you're so reluctant to be with me. You seem to have a great time when you let your guard down," Ed said, reaching over to take her hand.

"Ed, we work together, and I'm your boss. That fact alone is enough to make this relationship awkward and *totally* against my better judgment," Kate replied, fighting the urge to pull her hand away from his. She didn't want to hurt him, but she didn't feel comfortable with his public demonstrations of affection with Beth and her troops present.

Talk about conflicted, she thought.

"Is that it, or is it the whole Bill thing . . .?" Ed asked, letting his question hang in the air.

Kate was silent.

"Do you think Bill is sitting on his yacht in the middle of the Caribbean mooning over you? Seriously, Kate, if he had any feelings for you at all, he'd be here fighting for you. He knows my intentions. He'd have to be stupid not to, and he isn't stupid."

Mooning? Is that what I'm doing? Really? How pathetic is that! Kate thought.

"No, he's not stupid. As a matter of fact, he called back on Monday after his daughter e-mailed him about the break-in. Look, he knows what he wants and what he doesn't want. He wants a wife, and he doesn't want me. You're right, Ed, he's made it clear. Could we not talk about Bill anymore, please? It doesn't feel great wallowing in rejection. I'm trying to move forward. So, please, just leave it at we work together and that is more than enough reason for us to at least be careful."

"Kate, I'm sorry. I didn't mean to make you 'wallow in rejection.' I'm glad to hear you're trying to move forward. I prescribe more rebound sex," Ed grinned.

"Thanks, Dr. More-Sex. I'll take that under advisement." Kate cast him a sideways glance and a small smile.

Seriously, if he didn't work for me what would be the harm? I really do enjoy being with him. Maybe the six years between us isn't really that significant. Kate contemplated her situation as she looked toward the front door.

A man with a beard and baseball cap walked in and walked to the bar with the ease of someone familiar with the place. There was something about his walk that looked familiar, but the beard and cap kept her from making a positive identification. She picked up her phone and pushed in Beth's speed dial number.

"I can't say for sure, Beth, but I think the bearded guy who just walked up to the bar may be Cook. There is something I recognize about him, his build and walk maybe. The beard and cap are new though."

Kate paused to listen to Beth, and then continued, "I think I'll go check it out and see what I think up close." She hung up without waiting for a response.

Ed's head snapped toward Kate, and he held her hand tighter.

"Do you think that's a good idea, Kate?" Ed said as he felt Kate's hand slip out from under his.

"I'll be right back."

And with that, Kate was on her way to the bar. She wiggled in next to the bearded man, bumped his elbow, and when he turned to see who nearly caused him to spill his beer, Kate smiled and looked deeply into his eyes—and saw Gary Cook.

"Hey, I'm sorry. Did I make you spill? I hope not. My bad." Kate was nonchalant, and her voice was friendly.

She turned to the bartender and said, "Could I get two Macallan 15 year, neat. I can't seem to get our waitress's attention. Quite a crowd you've got in here tonight."

While the bartender made her drinks, Kate turned her back to the bar and looked out at the tables. She casually glanced in Beth's direction, took in her grim expression, and nodded and smiled.

"Yep, quite a crowd. I don't think I've ever seen the place this packed."

Kate turned around and smiled again at Gary Cook, taking another deep look into his cold, dark eyes as she picked up her drinks and told the bartender to put them on her tab.

"Bye, and sorry again for bumping you," Kate said as she turned to leave the bar.

Gary Cook said nothing but stared at her as she crossed the room to the booth where Ed was waiting.

"You're crazy, Kate. I know it's crowded in here, but Jesus, there was no guarantee the creep wouldn't try something. And, damn it, he's still staring at you."

Ed took the drink Kate offered, and then slipped his arm around her and kissed her firmly on the lips. "Let's try to get out of here in one piece. I have plans for you tonight."

Kate's phone buzzed. She picked it up as she kissed the tip of Ed's nose.

She glanced at the caller ID. It was Beth.

"Yes, it's him," Kate said as she hit the answer button.

"Damn it, Kate, are you just generally a risk taker? We could have done that," Beth scolded.

Ed could hear the ire in Beth's voice through Kate's phone; he laughed.

"Tell her I'm scolding you too, and that I have my own special punishment in mind for my little risk taker."

"I heard that, Ed. Keep her safe, please. We're going in now, and I want to look up after the arrest and see Kate sitting right there with your arm around her. Got it?" Beth clicked off.

Kate and Ed looked at each other briefly, and then turned toward the bar and watched as two agents walked to the front door and five others converged on the bar area. Beth and another agent walked up behind Gary Cook, their weapons drawn but held discretely at their sides. When Beth was directly behind Cook, she pushed the gun into his ribs and, at the same time, placed her strong hand on his left arm.

"Gary Cook, you're under arrest—" was all Beth managed to get out before she was doused with beer from the stein Cook had been holding in his left hand.

Before he could strike her with the stein, he found himself face-down on the bar with his left arm painfully wrenched behind him, Beth's elbow in the middle of his back, and her partner's Glock screwed into his ear.

"Bad decision, Gary. Now, we can add assaulting a federal agent and resisting arrest to the long list of reasons we're arresting you." Beth snapped handcuffs on Cook as her partner continued to press his weapon into the side of Cook's head.

The crowd in the restaurant finally reacted to the unusual scene at the bar. A couple of women screamed when they saw the guns now held at the ready by every agent in the place. Several bar patrons hit the floor, hiding under their tables from what they thought would be a barrage of bullets.

"Federal agents—FBI," Beth shouted in an authoritative tone, holding her credentials aloft. "Stay where you are. Nobody move while we remove this piece of garbage from the bar, then you can go back to what you were doing before we interrupted you."

Kate watched in awe as Beth nearly picked Cook up by his

handcuffed hands and hustled him out of the bar. The two agents at the door walked outside and held the door for Beth and her unwilling companion.

"Cool," Ed said with pure admiration. "That was just so cool."

"She's a pretty incredible force to be reckoned with," Kate said in agreement.

"Now, where was I? Oh yeah," Ed said and kissed Kate so passionately she felt her resistance melt.

When they came up for air, Ed said, "Drink your scotch. We're heading out. I'm taking you home with me. You haven't seen my new place, and I want more."

Ed signaled the waitress for the tab, and Kate tried to clear her head as she took a long drink of her scotch.

Ed flipped his credit card on the waitress's tray without even looking at the bill. Then he took another drink of his scotch—a taste he was getting used to, thanks to Kate's influence.

The pair sat silently sipping their drinks until the waitress returned. Ed signed the credit card slip, took one last sip of scotch, and grabbed Kate's hand.

"We're leaving now," he said evenly, "because if we don't leave now, I'll embarrass you by having my way with you *right here*."

Ed stood and pulled Kate up next to him.

Why not, Kate thought, already feeling emboldened by the scotch.

Chapter 26

Kate lifted her head from Ed's chest and peered out into the dark loft. In the dim light of the crescent moon and the Miami skyline, she could make out the trail of clothes leading from Ed's front door to his bed. The time on the small alarm clock on the floor next to them said 4:38.

The condo was spartanly furnished, about what Kate would have expected for a bachelor with no money. Just the essentials, with the exception of the large canvas that hung on one of the two walls that wasn't covered by large windows. Even in the dim light she could tell the painting was an abstract, the colors and stokes bold and evocative, and anything but soothing.

Ed snored softly under her as she sat up slowly trying not to wake him. Kate quietly padded to the canvas and stared at it in the shadowy light. It was signed, but Kate couldn't make out the name.

Ed stirred and rolled toward where she stood. "Like it?" he asked.

"Actually, I love it, but it has so much emotion. It must be hard to look at every day."

Kate stood naked, continuing to take in the painting.

"Who's the artist, Ed? I see that it's signed, but I can't make out the name."

"A buddy of mine, a Marine," Ed said simply as he lifted himself up on one elbow to look at Kate.

"Does he live in the Miami area? If he has other works, I think I could get one of the galleries in my neighborhood to show him. The work is very good, and the gallery owners are always looking for new local talent—especially works that aren't pelicans, egrets, seashells, and sunsets."

Kate was still staring at the painting.

Ed swung his legs over the side of the bed, which was really just a box spring and mattress on four wooden blocks. He walked up behind Kate and encircled her with his arms.

"He used to live in Florida, Kate. But he's dead now. And, yes, he has more works. I bought them all from his estate. His wife needed the money, and all she saw when she looked at them was the pain he suffered," Ed spoke softly as he held her.

She turned around in Ed's arms and caressed his face. "I am so sorry. Did he die in Afghanistan?"

Ed released her and walked to the kitchen area of the loft and opened the refrigerator. "I need something nonalcoholic to drink. How about you? I've got juice—orange, grapefruit, cranberry, and water, and some Coke, though the Coke's probably flat by now." Ed said as he rummaged through the fridge. He turned back toward Kate holding up a bottle of orange juice.

"Orange juice sounds good," she said, not pushing for an answer to her question.

She walked to Ed and took the glass of juice he'd poured for her. They were both silent as they continued to look at the painting.

After several minutes, Ed said, "His name is Peter Campbell. He was wounded in Afghanistan during a mission we were on together. His truck ran over an IED. It blew his truck completely off the road. I was in the second truck, and we managed to stop, but shrapnel flew everywhere. We all caught a piece or two," Ed said rubbing his thumb over a scar that ran down his left side. "Pete was the only one in his truck that wasn't killed outright."

Ed paused again. It was clear he was replaying the attack in his mind; his face was tense. He was silent for a long time.

"He lost both legs in that attack. It happened about three months before my tour was up. Pete was just two months into his second tour. That day was one of the reasons I didn't re-up. The whole war seemed so pointless," he paused. "Doesn't sound very Marine-like, does it?"

Kate simply reached out to touch his hand.

"Anyway, when I got home six months later, I looked for Pete and found him at Bay Pines in St. Petersburg. He was waiting for his wounds to heal so he could start rehab, and they had him painting as therapy.

"There are 17 canvases in all. Some of them are really hard to look at . . . He was in a lot of pain, physically and mentally. I went to see him as often as I could."

Ed reached out and pulled her in close.

"Ed, I'm sorry. I didn't mean to bring up something so upsetting." Kate held him close, their naked bodies pressed together.

"The reason I have his painting hanging here is so I *will* remember. I never want to forget the pain he was in and what he gave up. He tried to make it, but in the end, he just couldn't accept his life and broken body. He didn't have any kids and wasn't going to ever have any after that. His wife struggled hard to make the marriage work, but in the end, Pete took his own life. It devastated his wife and their parents, but I think I understand. He didn't want to live as half a man—it's hard for someone who's been so active and strong to accept living as less." Ed let go of Kate and walked over to the window, looking out at the city below. "I know *I* couldn't have accepted it."

Kate sat down on the end of the bed and watched him.

"So, now I have an art collection that reminds me of him and all the guys who didn't make it back in one piece . . . or at all. Sometimes I feel like I have to push myself to succeed because I'm doing it for all of them." Ed's voice was soft, low, and barely audible.

"I won't tell you I know how you feel, because I couldn't possibly. But, Ed, thank you for telling me about Peter. Sometime I'd love to see his other pieces," she whispered.

Somewhere in the loft Kate's cell phone rang.

Where in the world did I leave my purse? she thought as she began searching, following the sound of the phone. *And who the hell is calling me at this ungodly hour?*

Kate located her phone on the fourth ring, just before it rolled to voice mail.

"Hey, Beth, what's up? And why are you calling at this crazy hour?"

Kate said, picking up randomly scattered clothes from the floor as she talked. She pushed the speakerphone button.

"We've been interrogating Gary Cook since we brought him in last evening. I've got some news that I thought you would want to hear right away." Beth sounded exhausted.

"I hope it's good news; it's too early for bad news."

Kate sat down on the bed and began sorting her clothes from Ed's.

"It's good, Kate—a little complicated, but good." Beth took a deep breath before she continued. "We convinced Cook that we had him dead bang based on fingerprint and DNA evidence we recovered from your place. We're working on matching them to other evidence collected at the scene of the outstanding warrants, including the murder charge that's pending in New York. He's looking at some significant jail time in maximum, if not the death sentence in Florida. We think he's connected to the murders that occurred last month up in Lakeland, but we haven't gotten that confession yet. In any event, he'll never breathe free air again, no matter how long he lives.

"It took a while to get him to start talking. Then one of my guys found a video on YouTube showing the most recent botched electrocution using 'Old Sparky' up in Stark. Man, that was gruesome. We showed it to Cook, hoping it would be incentive to get more talkative. Well, it worked, but not the way we thought it would. Cook said he'd tell us more if he could watch the video again—damn sociopaths. You forget how abnormal they are because they look like anyone else.

"Anyway, we pushed him really hard and offered him a preferred prison placement in a federal prison for his confession to the outstanding warrants and any other crimes he came forward with—we have him as our primary suspect on a number. My guys are walking him through all of them right now.

"He said he'd start singing if we could promise him Florida would not seek a death sentence, *and* if we gave him a copy of the electrocution video for a day. We got the local prosecutor to agree to his demands about 2:30 this morning, and old Gary has been a fountain of information ever since. About an hour ago, he got to the crimes he committed here in Miami where he's been hanging out for a couple of months, including his breaking and entering and attempted murder at your place," Beth sighed heavily.

"I swear, every time I think of Suzy with this guy I want to throw up. I guess I can kind of understand it. He *is* handsome and, like most sociopaths, he can be very charming when he wants to be. But, shit, Kate—I swear you can see the devil in his eyes. The bastard could have killed both of you without so much as a moment's hesitation."

"I know. It must be especially creepy now that you've spent so much face-to-face time with him."

Kate shuddered at the thought of Cook in Suzy's house and her own.

"So, he's been here in the Miami area, living out of his car and a gym locker—I guess that's where Terry saw him. He's been hooking up with people who need crimes committed and will pay him whatever he demands. He keeps his money and clothes in his locker at the gym and sleeps in cheap hotels, his car, or with unsuspecting women, like Suzy. He said he also sometimes finds an empty bed in one of the hospitals—apparently, if you're wearing scrubs, their security is surprisingly lax, even around the emergency rooms. He bragged if you act like you belong there no one challenges you. That's where this story gets interesting for you . . ."

"Me?" Kate asked in surprise.

"You and your client, Marcy Simpson. He claims to have information about Dr. Dugan's death," Beth explained.

"Really?" Kate was astonished. "What sort of information?"

"Cook was trying to impress me with his ability to sneak into the hospital," Beth explained. "He claims one night he was sleeping in an empty exam room at UM hospital and a doctor came into the room to take a private phone call on his cell. Cook said the room was dark, and the doctor didn't turn on the lights, so he didn't see Cook.

"And Cook didn't actually see the doctor, just a man in scrubs with a stethoscope around his neck. He might have been a nurse, who knows—everyone assumes a man in scrubs is a doctor and a woman in scrubs is a nurse.

"Anyway, Cook says he heard the doctor say something like, 'Joe confronted me about the DNA test. He even took a swing at me. We need to move fast before he files the divorce papers.' That's pretty much all he could remember. He couldn't give us a description because it was dark and he didn't lift his head to get a good view because he didn't want to make any noise. He also claims he wouldn't be able to recognize the guy's voice because he was whispering."

"Well, it's something. Unfortunately, without an eyewitness, it's all supposition and guess work at this point," Kate sighed. "But it's something."

"Kate, I've got more. Last Friday, Cook was working out at Terry's gym. He said he was talking with a couple of the guys he'd done some 'work' for, mostly petty stuff, but one recent home invasion. A man asked him if he'd be interested in something more serious. Cook, of course, said he would be for the right price. The guy offered him $100,000 to kill a woman. Kate, he identified Zeke Peters as the guy hiring him, and Marcy was the target. After he got her cell phone number from Zeke, he hacked it and found her at your beach place. Cook collected half the money up front and was hoping to try again."

"Oh my God! Beth, what if Marcy had been there? She'd be dead now!" Kate clamped her hand over her mouth as she looked into Ed's stunned eyes.

"My first call later this morning, when people are actually awake and in the office, will be to Chief Jordan," Kate told Beth. "Hopefully, this information will be the ironclad evidence he feels he needs to arrest Zeke, and maybe even Joan. Expect a call from the chief later this morning and encourage him to make the arrest, Beth. Tell him you're thinking of doing it yourself, maybe that will motivate him."

Kate thanked Beth, hung up, and looked at Ed. "Get dressed. I need you to take me home so I can get ready for work. It's going to be an interesting day."

"Why don't you tell me about your day while we shower—I know you believe in multitasking," Ed grinned at her.

Kate shrugged.

Why not? she thought again, and they headed to the bathroom.

Chapter 27

Kate ended her call with Chief Jordan and looked up as Ed walked into her office carrying two large takeout cups of coffee. He sat down at the worktable. Kate joined him.

"That went incredibly well," Kate said, referring to her telephone conversation with Chief Jordan. "The chief finally grew a pair. Beth faxed him a copy of the statement Cook provided in exchange for a cell at the super-max security prison in Colorado instead of the needle or a ride on 'Old Sparky.' The part of his statement admitting to taking money from Zeke to kill Marcy and the conversation he overheard in the hospital was apparently all the probable cause the chief needed. They're issuing an arrest warrant for Zeke this morning."

"What about Dugan's wife?"

"Not yet, but he's planning on bringing her in for questioning this afternoon. And get this . . . He's bringing in Zeke's wife too. He's going to make sure they're all in the precinct at the same time, and that their paths cross before they're questioned. He's going to interrogate Mrs. Peters first and make Joan wait. The chief is hoping to get Joan and Zeke bidding against each other. I guess we'll see how deep their love really is. My money's on Joan giving up Zeke before he figures out his goose is cooked," Kate predicted.

"Sounds like the chief is enjoying himself. I'd love to be a fly on the wall in that interrogation room," Ed mused.

"I agree. So far, Cook has confessed to more than 20 murders, spanning just over ten years, from Seattle to New York City, and down to Florida. The dude is a true sociopath." Kate fell silent, considering the depravity of Gary Cook for a moment. "And our friend Suzy

Spellman is one incredibly lucky woman," she sighed.

"She is, but primarily because she has a friend who managed to extract her ass from an enormous life-threatening crack," Ed replied. "You know, that's a side of Suzy I never caught sight of when I worked for her."

Kate laughed out loud.

"What?" he asked and looked quizzically at Kate.

"I'm just remembering Suzy's reaction when I told the girls you and I were an item. She went ballistic. She told me I was out of my mind getting involved with someone I work with. She was pretty heated. But, at the end of her rant, she admitted she was actually jealous," Kate laughed again. "Turns out, she was hoping to reconnect with you once you were working for someone else. How does it feel being a sex object?"

"Not too bad . . . a little embarrassing, I guess. How much did you tell your 'homegirls' about us?" Ed asked, looking a bit sheepish.

"Don't worry, Ed, none of the *important* details—your secrets are safe with me. Besides, if I gave Suzy details, she might get inspired and try for a threesome."

Ed's reaction was classic. He turned bright pink. Kate laughed out loud again. But now, uncomfortable with the topic of their discussion, given it violated her own "not in the office" rule, Kate changed the subject.

"Anyway, the answer to the big question, 'Who killed Dr. Dugan?' is still open. According to Cook, it wasn't him, and I can't see any reason he would lie about that—except, of course, he's a sociopath, and likely to lie about everything. I'm guessing if Chief Jordan shakes the tree hard enough today, we may soon learn the identity of Dugan's killer. I'd be shocked if Zeke didn't have his hand in it somehow.

"In any event, I'm moving forward with Friday's hearing on the declaratory judgment. There are other people with motives far more compelling than Marcy's, and they actually had opportunity and means. Besides, it's now crystal clear Dugan specifically intended for Marcy to remain the beneficiary on the life insurance policy. It's equally clear he did not wish his wife to benefit from his death in any way. The testimony and documentary evidence we've gathered so far should be sufficient to get the court to release the funds. It's worth a shot, anyway.

"Besides, I want to keep the pressure on, so we can see what Gray and old Fergie will come up with next. Disgraced as he is, Senator Ferguson's still politically a very heavy hitter. Unfortunately, Chief Jordan's political self-preservation instincts have him convinced he needs to proceed cautiously and make sure his theory is well supported by unassailable facts before he lets the accusations fly against Joan. But, I think it's only a matter of time, now."

After her phone call with the chief, Kate had determined she needed to leave the next phase of the Dugan investigation to the law enforcement officers—at least for a while.

"I'm going to call Marcy now and see how she and the girls are doing, then I have to see if I can shake a settlement out of Matt Danson. The Brighton case would be truly ugly with the newly discovered safety test results. I hope we can get it settled. I'd hate for your first foray into civil ligation to earn you immediate membership in the Million-Dollar Club."

"Any chance I can convince you to have dinner with me tonight?" Ed suggested.

"Sure, meet me at my place, and we'll go to my favorite restaurant in the neighborhood. It's the one where I usually meet my 'homegirls' as you call them. It's walk-able and pretty nice. See you about 7:00?"

"Sounds great."

Ed walked out of her office with an enormous smile on his face.

She didn't even hesitate, she just said yes.

He smiled all the way back to his office.

Marcy sounded a little shell-shocked at the news that a sociopath had been arrested with information about Joe's murder, and that Zeke and Joan were under suspicion in Joe's death. She was genuinely weary from the rapidly shifting dynamics of her previously calm and predictable life. Kate had decided to wait and tell her the rest of the disturbing news in person.

"Kate, I can't thank you enough for letting me hide away in your beach house while all this turmoil occurs in my life. By the way, the repairs are going well, and the girls seem happy to be here. We don't go to the beach for our walks yet because the girls still struggle with the stairs, and I didn't want to get sand in their wounds, but we head out the front and walk along the road. They're getting stronger every day, but they still tire quickly."

"I'm glad you're there to keep an eye on the workmen, but I'm sorry you have to deal with the confusion and noise. I was hoping you'd have a well-deserved vacation—I know you haven't had one in years," Kate replied, glad Marcy didn't yet know that Gary Cook had been hired to kill *her*.

"You know, I wonder if my life will ever return to normal. For the first time, I actually miss the routine of working all the time. Oh, I meant to tell you, last night the nicest young officer from the beach police stopped by to make sure everything was locked up and I was feeling secure. His name is Jamie French. He said he knows you, and the girls seemed to know him. He stayed and chatted for quite a while. He told me he'd be patrolling your street because of the break-in."

"Glad to hear he came by. Hope he wasn't intruding," Kate responded.

"Oh, he wasn't a bother at all. It was nice to know someone was checking on me, and besides, he's rather cute."

"Yes," Kate replied, "and quite the flirt. Sounds like you caught his eye. Let me know if you need anything and I promise I'll call as soon as I learned anything new."

Kate's next call was to Matt Danson.

"Hey, Matt. I took your $3 million demand to my client. They're not interested at that price, but said if you'd discount that number based on your client's negligence, they'd think about it. Did you have a chance to read those verdicts I sent over? The ones out of South Carolina and Georgia were especially on point. You need to know we'll be looking for a verdict of at least 50 percent comparative negligence."

"Kate, that's outrageous. My client will never walk again without a significant limp. He played football and basketball on his high school teams. He'd planned on joining the Marines or Rangers once he graduated. All that's changed now. He's looking at numerous reconstruction surgeries on that foot and a lifetime of pain. He deserves every bit of the $3 million, and your client deserves to be punished for creating a dangerous piece of equipment."

"Save it for the jury, Matt. We both know all lawnmowers are inherently dangerous and need to be operated with extreme care—*and in accordance with the written safety directions*. That's why the instructions on the mower's motor housing and the booklet that was attached to it when it was sold say not to use it on wet grass, never mow grass in the rain, and, to quote the instructions directly, 'always wear sturdy footwear.' Flip-flops are clearly not sturdy! His own parents admitted they warned him and tried to stop him. So, even if you're able to tweak a jury's sympathy, and they award your client some enormous verdict, the judge will have to reduce it as a matter of law. The alternative is we just keep it tied up in the appellate courts forever. Your client would be better served getting, say $1 million structured settlement now, rather than waiting for years while the appellate courts reduce whatever verdict you've won— *if* you win, that is."

"Kate, I know you're a great lawyer, but I'm not going to recommend my client take $1 million for his injuries."

"Maybe not, but you need to present the offer to him, and you need to remind his parents that they testified about warning him and trying to stop him. They have to understand their testimony is going to weigh heavily . . . in our favor."

"I'll present the offer to them because I have to, but don't be surprised when they reject it. I'm not even sure they'll authorize me to counter to it."

Kate smiled when she hung up. She loved these cat-and-mouse negotiations. She loved trials better, but her client could get tagged with a huge verdict, and, worse yet, they'd have to pay her to fight it. And Kate was certain that a win, even at the appellate level, was a very remote possibility. Besides, Kevin O'Neil had already told her she had authority to settle for anything under the plaintiff's $3 million demand. He had even promised to pay her a bonus of one-third of any savings she was able to work off the plaintiff's original demand.

Every little bit helps! she thought happily.

Around 6:15, Chief Jordan called Kate to give her an update on his interrogation of Zeke Peters, Zeke's wife, and Joan Dugan. It had been quite a day of 'he said/she said' and finger-pointing. Old Senator Ferguson had even made an appearance at police headquarters, and that had been especially colorful.

Zeke's wife, Mindy, was the first to start the barrage of accusations and revelations. Her denunciations were incited by Chief Jordan's suggestion that Zeke fathered Joan Dugan's first child. The chief explained Joe Dugan had DNA testing done revealing as much. It was a bit of a stretch based on the known evidence at this point, but it was likely to be confirmed. The chief was waiting for the analysis on the DNA he'd collected from the glasses of water provided to Joan and Zeke while they waited their turn to be the target in the interrogation room and from the trace bodily fluids collected from the area rug from Joe Dugan's office. During his interrogation of Zeke's wife, the chief also implied he had evidence indicating Zeke, and possibly Joan, may be implicated in Joe Dugan's death.

According to the chief, Mindy Peters went ballistic, demanding to be excused from interrogation immediately so she could contact her divorce attorney. Apparently, Mindy had suspected Zeke fathered Joan Dugan's eldest son when the kid began to bear a striking resemblance to her husband. As Mindy Peters rushed out of the precinct, she paused just long enough to barge into the glass-walled conference room where Joan Dugan was impatiently waiting with her father and two lawyers.

Mindy had screamed, "You fucking slut! I don't give a flying fuck who your daddy is. You're nothing but a self-centered whore. How many lives have you ruined, Joan? I hope you and that worthless husband of mine rot in prison for the rest of your lives."

With this tee up, Chief Jordan allowed Joan and her entourage of attorneys to marinate a bit longer before beginning their interrogations. He first briefly visited Zeke Peters, who was in another glass-walled room and who had witnessed, if not clearly heard, the encounter between his wife and Joan Dugan. Zeke was sweating heavily before the chief even said a word. But, when asked why he thought his wife was so hostile toward Joan, Zeke stuck to pleading ignorance and said, "Who can tell with women." The chief then left Zeke to stew and went to visit Joan.

With her two lawyers and father sitting in the interrogation room with her, Joan tearfully explained how she had fallen in love with Zeke Peters 18 years ago and ended up pregnant by him before learning he was already married with four children. Joan claimed Zeke was in debt up to his eyebrows to his father-in-law for much of his medical school and several legal bills. Mindy's father had forced Zeke to sign a prenuptial agreement requiring him to immediately repay every cent he owed in the event of a divorce and to relinquish any claim to Mindy's inheritance, which was potentially quite large. As a result, Zeke was unable to marry Joan without cataclysmic results to his bottom line.

Joan then sobbed out her version of Zeke's plot to trick Joe Dugan into thinking he'd slept with Joan and miraculously managed to get her pregnant after just one wild night of drunken partying. The drugs he'd slipped into Joe's drinks had rendered him incapable of even knowing whether he'd actually cheated on Marcy. Zeke had driven them to a motel, and only Joan really knew what happened that night. When Joan told Joe she was pregnant, Dugan did what Zeke told him was "the honorable thing," and divorced Marcy and immediately married Joan.

Joan mournfully claimed she had always intended to divorce Joe and marry Zeke as soon as he was free, but Zeke never made much of his life and wasn't ever in a financial position to repay his father-in-law. Not to mention how much Joan loved the luxurious lifestyle Joe's successful career provided.

After coming clean about the paternity of her first child, Joan categorically denied knowing anything about Joe's intention to divorce her or his plans to obtain full custody of the boys. Unfortunately for

Joan, Chief Jordan had followed up with Steve Sloan, Joe's divorce attorney, before starting this particular line of questioning. The chief had learned Joe Dugan moved out of his house four days before his death after advising Joan of his plans to leave her and seek custody of the boys. Joe found out Ron Gray would represent Joan in the divorce because, according to Steve, Joan had flown into a violent rage when Joe told her his plan, threatening to "have Ron Gray cut off your dick in court if you even dare *even think* about filing for divorce."

After that, Steve and Ron Gray had spent several hours discussing their clients' interests. Gray pushed to find a way to proceed with a quiet divorce and keep the salacious accusations contained in Joe's divorce and custody papers out of the public record. Steve had agreed he would delay filing the papers for four days to give them time to come to an amicable arrangement. Joe ended up dead instead.

Ron Gray, one of the two attorneys in the interrogation room with Joan, immediately recused himself as a material witness, and that's when the party really got ugly. Senator Ferguson started yelling at Gray that he'd better keep his mouth shut, and if he said one word, he'd have him disbarred for violating Joan's attorney-client communications privilege. And Joan began wailing, then screaming, and finally made a mad rush at Chief Jordan, wildly swinging her fist attempting to hit him while screaming, "You fucking bastard! You're ruining everything. I know the governor, you fucker. My daddy will have you fired for this. Tell him, Daddy! He can't get away with this. You'll have his job, right, Daddy?"

When the chief and two of his deputies restored order in the interrogation room, Gray and his associate were escorted into an interrogation room of their own. Senator Ferguson was left sitting uncomfortably with Chief Jordan's biggest, meanest-looking deputy standing over him while Joan was handcuffed, arrested on the charge of assaulting an officer of the law, and read her rights.

Joan did *not* exercise her right to remain silent. Instead, she shouted, "Joe was an ungrateful prig. Without our social connections in Miami, he would have been just another dime-a-dozen doctor trying to eke out a living in this miserable town."

Senator Ferguson repeatedly yelled at his daughter to "shut the fuck up for once in your life."

After she fired her attorneys, Joan decided to switch tactics. She began accusing Zeke Peters of threatening to blackmail her. According to Joan, Joe confronted Zeke with the paternity test results showing Zeke was the biological father of their first son and declaring his intention to divorce Joan and seek custody of all three boys. To top it off, Joe informed Zeke he would be separated from their medical practice. Facing divorce and financial ruin once Joe's divorce and custody papers were public knowledge, Zeke became desperate. He knew Joe's divorce would trigger his own, and that would trigger his loan repayment obligation to his father-in-law that he had no way to satisfy.

Joan maintained that Zeke told her he was going to kill Joe, making it look like a heart attack so they "would finally be able to marry." Zeke believed they could live off Joe's estate and the insurance he knew Joe had taken out for his family. Joan, of course, denied ever agreeing to Zeke's plan and claimed she threatened to tell Joe and the police. According to Joan's story, that was when Zeke turned on her, threatening to spill his guts to a reporter friend with the *Miami Herald*. Joan wept loudly as she declared she'd only kept quiet because Zeke threatened her father and their family with social ruin if she went to the police.

"I didn't really think Zeke would go through with his threat," she claimed. "I didn't think he had the balls. Anyway, he was in for a surprise—since we now know there was really no money in Joe's estate. He put it all in a trust for the boys—I can't touch a dime. I get the house, but that's mortgaged to the hilt—I don't even get anything out of the medical practice—those bastards had a policy on Joe's life, but *they* get the proceeds. Looks like everyone is profiting from Joe's death but me."

Chief Jordan chuckled deeply as he recounted the interrogation scene. Kate wished she could have seen it all firsthand, but thoroughly enjoyed the chief's "play-by-play." After she hung up, Kate called Marcy to check up on the girls, give her the update on Zeke and Joan, and tell her to come by the office on late Thursday afternoon to prepare for the interpleader hearing on Friday.

Kate was ready to make Marcy a millionaire.

"Hey, how would you like to stop by a couple of the galleries in the neighborhood after we're done here?" Kate asked Ed over their dinner.

She had just finished relaying Chief Jordan's report from the interrogations of Zeke and Joan. "You could find out whether they'd be interested in evaluating your friend's paintings and perhaps putting a few up for sale. If you're interested in selling some of them, that is. If they like the work, one of the store owners might even organize a one-man posthumous show and create a market for the paintings."

"We can do that, Kate, if you want to. I didn't buy the paintings to make money. I bought them because they remind me of the sacrifices our troops and their families make every single day. I'm not sure I want to sell them yet, but if I do, I'll probably give Annie, Pete's widow, any profits. She might even be ready to see Pete's work again. When I bought them, she couldn't stand to look at them because of the pain he'd painted. I'd like her to attend a showing of Pete's work. I think it would be good therapy for her. I'll ask her about it over the weekend."

"I understand, just let me know what you decide."

"I've already decided what I want to do after dinner," Ed grinned wickedly at Kate. "That is, unless you're getting too much of me. I'd even commit to making that crazy 6:00 a.m. hot yoga class tomorrow, since we'll miss the one on Friday because of the hearing. How about it?"

Kate stared at him with her usual mixture of desire and guilt. *I wonder if the guilt fuels the desire, or the other way around?* she briefly pondered.

She felt the need for some affection tonight. She needed to feel wanted. *Why not?* Kate thought again.

"Sure," she said, noting the surprise in Ed's eyes.

I guess it's good to not be too predictable . . . keep him guessing, she thought with a wicked grin of her own.

"But, you're going to have to work for your reward."

"What do you have in mind?" Ed responded, eager for an adventure.

"Nothing like that, sailor. First, we're going to discuss the interpleader and declaratory judgment hearing, and specifically which witnesses you will be preparing tomorrow and handling on direct exam at the hearing on Friday."

Kate had decided to give Ed a major role at Marcy's hearing since they would likely settle the Brighton matter.

"Great." Ed's eyes gleamed. "I love litigation almost as much as I love . . . making love to you." Ed winked at Kate when she winced.

Chapter 28

The following day, Ed strolled into Kate's office a few minutes before their first witness preparation session.

"Kate, you'll never guess who showed up at work this morning."

"Bobbi Jo?"

"Yep, but that's not all. James showed up too. Looks like they both took the company's 'take it or leave it' offers. Needless to say, Josie is thrilled, but Phillip Bentley just wants to know when things will finally get back to normal on his production lines. Not a very warm and fuzzy guy. But, I think he's pleased too."

"Great job. And, yes, about the best you'll ever get out of Phillip is 'OK, glad that's over, and, by the way, I need you to help me with this new project.'"

"Unless, of course, you save his kid from certain death or prison. You've given me big shoes to fill, Kate."

"Even that type of result yields only just so much gratitude where Phillip is concerned," Kate laughed, remembering Phillip's words to her when the drug charges against Phil Junior were dismissed. "Clients tend to operate on a 'what have you done for me lately' mentality, Ed. Get used to it. Their highest form of praise is sending you more work. And, you must perform beyond their expectations on each and every task. It's a competitive world out there, Ed. Clients want their work to be your first and only priority, and they want it done brilliantly. Many times you'll think they want it done for free too! But, it's a great way to make a living, all things considered."

"I'm not complaining, and, I mean this, Kate, you really are an inspiration. Why do you think all your male partners are so bent out of shape? You show them how to do it, and you make it look easy."

"Now, that's an admission against interests if I've ever heard one. Don't let any of your fellow males hear you utter that sort of statement. They'll drum you out of the gender," Kate laughed.

Kate, Ed, and Polly were heavily into Johnny Sutton's witness prep when Sophia knocked on the conference room door.

"Kate, you have a call from Matt Danson regarding the Brighton matter. He said it wouldn't take long, and he wondered if you could be interrupted."

Kate stepped out of the conference room, leaving the final preparation for Ed to finish up, with Polly's help.

"Hello, Matt. How are our chances of settlement today?" Kate inquired.

"Not good, Kate. My client and his parents nearly fired me. They came close to kicking me out of their house when I told them you thought they should settle for $1 million. It took me over an hour to explain how settlement negotiations work, and then came the lesson on comparative negligence. Listen, Kate, these aren't sophisticated people. They see a life completely changed because of events occurring in one fleeting second. They're still trying to get their heads around what their future looks like now. They're not fans of the new normal, and to them, it's all your client's fault."

"I hear you, Matt, but, really, save the tugs on the heartstrings for the jury. My view, and my client's, is pretty simple. They manufacture an inherently dangerous piece of equipment, intended to be operated by adults, with a high degree of care, and only under specific conditions—which, as I've said, do *not* include cutting grass during a Florida rainstorm, on a wet hillside, while wearing flip-flops. My client endeavored to make the machine as safe as they could. They spent money on R&D for an emergency shut-off switch—which they didn't have to do. *Consumer Reports* lists their mower at the top in safety.

"You know you don't want to try this case, Matt. Your client could lose out entirely if the jury is persuaded the kid acted like the typical headstrong, rash, 17-year-old male who believes he's 'ten feet tall and bullet-proof.' And, you know that's not a hard sell for me to make. My client really wanted to try this case and make an example of the situation. They only recently decided to talk settlement. I'd take advantage of this opportunity if I were you, Matt."

"Kate, they told me I could go to $2.5 million and no lower. But they want it all at once and not in a structured settlement. Like I said, they're not sophisticated people."

"I don't think that's going to fly, Matt. I'll relay the new demand, of course, but don't be surprised if they reject it. You might want to start getting your folks ready for the bad news. I'll try to get back to you today. I'm out of pocket all morning tomorrow at a hearing."

Kate smiled as she hung up. Her instincts told her the case would settle for somewhere around two million, and she would have saved her client a million dollars.

Kate slipped back into the conference room to observe the last of Johnny Sutton's witness prep, and again was impressed by the gentleman's wit, intelligence, and clarity. The old dude came across as so very charming and credible. Kate knew the judge was going to believe him.

The next witness prep session was Michael Dugan. Michael was bringing his mother with him, and Kate hoped Grace Dugan would be able to testify regarding her knowledge of Joe's insurance policy and his desire to support Marcy through medical school. Since the documents supported this testimony, Kate hoped the judge would allow it. Plus, Grace would likely say great things about Marcy and denigrate Joan Dugan if given half a chance. Kate figured a little gratuitous sentiment never hurt.

She wanted Michael to testify about the conversation he'd had with his brother the last time they were together—when Joe told him he'd named Michael his new personal representative and trustee on the boys' trust. She was hoping to also get into evidence the reasons Joe gave him for changing his will and the trust instrument, and Joe's suspicions about Joan and Zeke. The judge might rule against her—but it was worth a try.

Milton Martin, the second insurance agent on Joe's policy, was the next witness in line for his prep session. And he'd been anything but cooperative. Kate had cajoled him into coming into her office by telling him she'd received documents from the insurance company that he would be shown on the witness stand. She suggested that he didn't want to be caught off guard and deserved a chance to look at the documents before being asked questions about them. The documents contradicted Martin's statements to Terry that he never serviced a $4 million policy taken out by Dr. Dugan. Kate also thought if Martin knew Joan and Zeke were currently being questioned in relation to Dr. Dugan's murder, perhaps Martin would be less "forgetful" knowing his lack of memory was aiding the killers of his former customer. But you never know about people.

If Martin continued to be uncooperative Kate had already decided she wouldn't call him to testify. She could get the necessary insurance paperwork into evidence using Mr. Meardon as the corporate representative to authenticate the documents and provide an explanation of their import. So, Martin was superfluous; however, Kate had hoped he would admit Gray, or Joan, or maybe even Senator Ferguson had tried to influence his testimony. That would be icing on the cake.

Before they began the prep session with Martin, Kate huddled with Polly on the status of the Brighton discovery update. She insisted the updated discovery responses had to be served by hand on Matt Danson today. The settlement negotiations with Matt had all been based on the assumption that Jonathan Torres's testimony regarding how the accident occurred was true. That assumption had taken the safety test results out of the equation, so Kate felt she was negotiating with Matt in good faith, even knowing the test results they originally gave Matt were no longer accurate. Nevertheless, Kate wanted to get the updated discovery to Matt by close of business today, before they reached a final settlement number.

She had explained her reasoning and obligations to Kevin O'Neil, and, after a fairly lengthy discussion, Kevin accepted Kate's sequencing for the settlement negotiation and document production. Polly assured Kate she'd be able to finish the update and drop it off at Matt's office around 3:30.

Milton Martin's prep session was painful. He looked through the documents Kate provided, claimed he didn't recall a thing about Dr. Dugan or receiving administrative fees for keeping the account current. He denied ever trying to sell Dr. Dugan another policy, despite the records in the insurance company's files to the contrary. Midway through the hour set aside for Martin's prep, Sophia interrupted Kate again, this time to tell her Chief Jordan was on the line with some important information and needed only ten minutes. Over Milton's complaints, Kate stepped out of the conference room and handed Ed the list of topics she'd prepared for discussion with Milton and asked him to finish up for her.

"Kate, we got DNA results from both Joan and Zeke. Zeke's match the DNA of the third sample Dr. Dugan submitted for paternity testing. Not surprisingly, Joan and Zeke are unquestionably the parents of the second sample Dugan sent in. It's a pretty safe assumption the second sample is from Joe's eldest son," Chief Jordan recounted.

"Great to have that confirmed. How are your suspects?" Kate asked.

"When we told Zeke about Joan's newest version of the 'truth,' he went into a rampage. We already had him handcuffed, but ended up chaining him to the floor of the interrogation room as well. After shouting things about Joan that I won't repeat to a lady, he got down to telling us his version. There were a lot of similarities to Joan's, with one gigantic exception: Zeke says Joan not only knew about his plan, but she had encouraged him, and get this—she even went with him when he stole the digitalis out of the clinic's drug safe. She had taken Dr. Dugan's keys and the ID badge you need to open their drug safe. Zeke said the clinic's electronic tracking system would show Dr. Dugan's card was used at 2:00 a.m. the morning before his death.

"Zeke said he and Joan used to meet at the office at night. According to Zeke, Joan got a kick out of having sex on the rug in Dr. Dugan's office. After spending several hours with the woman, I don't doubt it and that's why we found the trace evidence.

"Zeke's agreed to plead to second-degree murder and testify

against Joan, in exchange for no death sentence. He's admitted to injecting Joe Dugan with digitalis after he and Joan knocked him down during a struggle at the office. He's claiming it was a crime of passion and not really premeditated. That argument seems totally bogus to me, but the state attorney went for the plea as long as he would testify against Joan. Anyway, we've formally charged Joan with conspiracy to commit murder. We'll add to that as our investigation continues. One more thing, the autopsy results are in. Dugan's body shows signs of a struggle and a small needle mark at the base of his skull, right where Zeke says he injected the digitalis. The poor guy was killed by his wife and supposed best friend in his own damn office."

"What a tragic tale, but wonderful news for Marcy." Kate was elated. "You know Joan's supposed to be in court tomorrow for the interpleader hearing. I have her under subpoena."

"Don't worry, Kate. I'll make sure she's there. Tell your client she's about to get revenge for her arrest."

"I can't wait. See you then, and thanks, Chief."

As she hung up, Kate thought, *It'll be interesting bringing Marcy up to speed this afternoon. Her life has been quite a roller coaster—from broke ER nurse, to suspect in a murder, to target in a hit, and finally (hopefully) a millionaire in a matter of just four weeks. It's enough to give her whiplash!*

Over lunch, Ed and Kate prepped Steve Sloan, and then Ralph Meardon for their roles at the hearing the following day. As lawyers, both men knew what to expect, and the prep sessions went smoothly. Kate invited them both to remain after their turn on the witness stand to hear Joan's testimony if they had time. She promised them it would be interesting.

Before Marcy arrived for her session, Matt Danson called to relay his client's new demand. They would go no further than $2.2 million, and they wanted it in one payment. After giving Matt the appropriate amount of grief about his client's own negligence and listening to Matt's standard sympathy argument about a young man's life changed forever, Kate said she'd discuss the amount with her client and call back with their response before close of business.

She immediately called Kevin O'Neil to let him know the Torres matter could be settled for $2.2 million. In true client style, Kevin announced that if it had been "that easy" to get the plaintiff down to $2.2 million, she should go back with a flat $2 million—never mind the fact that he'd earlier told her anything less than $3 million was approved in advance.

Kate agreed to tell Matt their counter was $2 million and not a penny more, but she hoped he didn't raise his demand after he received the updated discovery. She hung up and called Matt.

"Hey, Matt. My client said they'd go to $2 million lump sum and not a penny more. I'll put our offer in an e-mail as soon as we hang up. By the way, the updated discovery is headed your way shortly. Please take a look at it and let me know if we have a deal for $2 million. My client can issue a check within 48 hours of your acceptance."

"You're making my life difficult, Kate! I'll try to sell my client on $2 million, and I'll let you know. Good luck at your hearing tomorrow, and if I don't talk to you before the weekend, have a good one."

Marcy arrived at the office at 3:00 after dropping the girls off at Kate's city house with the dog sitter. Kate hadn't wanted her to travel into the city with the dogs early Friday morning before the hearing, so Marcy was spending the night with Kate. They were going out for dinner after Marcy's prep session. Ed had pouted like a three-year-old when Kate told him he wasn't invited to dinner and wouldn't be spending the night, but she knew he'd get over it.

Before she began her witness prep session with Marcy, Kate decided to bring her up to date on Zeke's confession and Joan's arrest and to tell her the truth about the break-in at her house. Marcy had listened silently as Kate explained the whole sordid saga. When she explained the attacker, Gary Cook, was a sociopath who was the subject of a multiple-state manhunt and was now in FBI custody, Marcy was stunned.

"My God, Kate, why would anyone want to kill you?" Marcy gasped.

"Well, as it turns out, it wasn't me he was looking for."

Kate looked into Marcy's concerned eyes and reconsidered whether she should continue.

"Marcy, this may upset you, and I'm sorry. But you need to know, the killer was looking for *you*."

"What? How can that be? No one even knew I was there, and nobody could hate me that much . . . or maybe they could . . . Oh, shit, Kate. Did I bring all this trouble on you?"

"Marcy, that's not why I'm telling you about Cook. You need to know the lengths someone connected to Joe's death was willing to go in order to keep you from obtaining the proceeds of Joe's insurance policy. Marcy, we've defeated them, and now all that's left is convincing the court that the insurance proceeds were meant for you. Kiddo, you're very nearly a multimillionaire! How does it feel?"

"Numb, Kate, I'm just numb. And frankly, I won't believe it until it happens, and maybe not even then."

Chapter 29

Ed and Kate flanked Marcy at the counsel table as they waited for Judge Bryson to take the bench. Marcy trembled slightly as she sat silently staring at the witness stand.

No doubt dreading having to sit up there, Kate decided as she gently patted her friend's hand.

"You're going to be great. Take a deep breath and try to relax," Kate whispered.

"It's not easy. The only other times I've been in a courtroom were when Joe divorced me and when I was a murder suspect. Not exactly the best experiences of my life," Marcy whispered back.

"This one may significantly change your feelings about courtrooms, Marcy," Kate said, squeezing her friend's hand.

She then turned to scan the gallery; it was not overly crowded. Kate recognized Dr. Jenkins, Marcy's supervisor at Jackson Memorial. He hadn't said a word to either Marcy or Kate when he arrived this time, and he seemed to find something interesting on the floor to stare at when Kate momentarily caught his eye.

Your guilty conscience is showing, Dr. Jenkins, she thought.

Larry Lewis was also in the gallery—he winked at Kate when her gaze passed over him. She smiled in return. Shirley Warner and Dr. Perez sat next to Larry talking quietly to each other.

As Kate's eyes moved through the rest of the courtroom, she noticed several print media reporters on the front row and several photojournalists lining the back wall. The press was much quieter than she was used to. Kate decided they were probably confused about the nature of the proceeding. She didn't imagine any of them had ever attended a declaratory judgment hearing or even had a clue what a declaratory judgment was. These proceedings usually weren't very exciting or news worthy.

Just wait, ladies and gentlemen, Kate thought. *This hearing may give you material for both a sensational bombshell, and a 'feel good story' all at the same time.*

"All rise," came the call from the bailiff.

Kate turned toward the front of the courtroom as she, Marcy, and Ed rose for Judge Bryson's unceremonious entrance. As the bailiff told them to take their seats, the judge settled in quickly at the bench and looked out at his courtroom that seemed more crowded than usual to him. He looked curiously at the media people in the back and those in the front, taking particular note of the female sketch artist sitting on the front row.

"If you wouldn't mind, ma'am, please draw me 20 pounds lighter than I am."

There was a light twitter of laughter in the courtroom. The young woman's head jerked up from her sketchpad looking worried at first, but when she realized Judge Bryson was joking, she smiled at him and nodded.

"Let's begin. I note there are some folks in the gallery today who may not get to this courtroom very often. Rest assured, I expect the same decorum as my fellow jurists on the criminal side of the courthouse."

The judge then looked at both counsel tables and simply said, "Counsel?"

Both sets of attorneys rose.

"Kate Muldoon and Ed Evert for Marcy Ann Simpson, the named beneficiary of the insurance policy at issue, Your Honor."

"Ron Gray, representing the estate of the deceased, appearing in opposition to releasing the funds to Ms. Simpson."

"I requested an agent for the insurance company be here this morning. Is anyone here for Upton Insurance Company?" Judge Bryson asked as he looked out over the gallery.

A gentleman Kate did not recognize sitting three rows behind her stood up and identified himself as Mr. Hampton Argyle, one of the attorneys at Upton.

"Thank you, Mr. Argyle, you may be seated. I do want to let you know your interpleader of $4 million into our court registry caused quite a stir. I believe it's the highest amount we've ever had deposited. It made everyone feel quite special, if only for a moment." The judge smiled benignly at Mr. Argyle, and there was a second ripple of soft twittering in the gallery.

Judge Bryson was living up to what everyone had told Kate about him. He was serious, personable, and reasonably modest about his role as circuit judge. Kate liked him instantly.

"I believe it makes sense for Ms. Muldoon to present the named beneficiary's position first. Ms. Muldoon, would you start us off?"

"Thank you, Your Honor. Our job today is twofold. First, we will prove Marcy Ann Simpson is the intended beneficiary of Dr. Joseph Dugan's $4 million life insurance policy—despite the fact that they had been divorced for 16 years. Under normal circumstances, that proof alone should be enough for the court to order the release of the funds to Ms. Simpson. But, our proof must include a second point because events over the last several weeks have revealed that Dr. Dugan's death was not, as originally believed, from natural causes. It is now known that he was murdered. For that reason, we believe we must also prove there is no legal impediment to Marcy Simpson receiving the insurance proceeds. To be blunt, Your Honor, we will prove when the funds are released to Ms. Simpson she will not be profiting from a criminal act she committed."

"Thank you, Ms. Muldoon. I appreciate your position. It *is* a bit unusual for evidence relating to a criminal matter to find its way into my courtroom. And, it is rarer that you would have to prove your client's *innocence*. However, I understand your reasoning. I believe your suggestion will eliminate the need for any further hearings on this matter. It seems an efficient way to proceed. Please begin."

Judge Bryson nodded toward Kate, and then added, "I assume, Mr. Gray, you have no objection to Ms. Muldoon's proposal?"

Gray responded simply, "None, Your Honor," knowing it would do him no good to object.

Kate noted that Gray almost looked defeated when he took his seat. *If he wasn't such a jerk, I'd feel sorry for him,* she thought.

"Thank you, Your Honor. Our first witness will be Johnny Sutton." Kate turned and nodded to Ed as she sat down next to Marcy.

Ed picked up Johnny's witness file and the documents he would be placing into evidence through Johnny's testimony, and walked confidently to the podium.

What followed was a charming replay of Johnny's deposition testimony, with the exception of Ron Gray's contribution, which was much lower key—so low key, in fact, as to be nearly nonexistent. Once again, Johnny provided a succinct but delightfully colorful narrative of his encounters with Dr. Dugan over the years. And, once again, he provided his own brand of gratuitous observations and comments, taking special note to again compliment Marcy on remaining "as pretty as the photo Joe showed him all those years ago." The old dude came across as sharp, witty, and oh, so very credible. He often spoke directly to the judge when answering Ed's questions—the judge seemed to love him. At three points during Johnny's testimony, the judge asked follow-up questions, allowing Johnny to meander just a little more and provide more color and detail to his story. With each detail, Johnny became even more credible.

When Ed finished with Johnny, the judge turned him over to Ron Gray for cross.

"I have only a few questions, Your Honor. I don't want to tire out Mr. Sutton."

"Like I told you at my deposition, sonny, I could do this all day. There may be snow on the roof, but there's plenty of fire in the belly."

The courtroom twittered quietly again. Johnny smiled graciously.

"Thank you, Mr. Sutton. After you retired ten years ago, did you ever see Dr. Dugan again?"

"No, sir, I did not, and more's the pity. He was a lovely man."

"Sir, you never saw the original policy after you gave it to Dr. Dugan, did you?"

"That's correct. There was no reason to."

"And, Mr. Sutton, you have no idea whether Joe Dugan ever made any changes to that policy, do you?"

"No, sir, I do not. Like I told that young fella, Mr. Evert, when I was answering his questions just a moment ago, Dr. Dugan asked if Marcy would continue to be eligible as the beneficiary if they were divorced. And I explained she could and that he could easily mark up the original policy or let the company know if he wanted to change the beneficiary line. You know, he was the owner of the policy, so, he could do whatever he liked with it." Johnny smiled at Ron, who looked like a man standing at the end of the plank.

"No further questions," Gray said as he sat down heavily.

"Any redirect, Mr. Evert?"

"No, Your Honor. We release this witness."

"I have a question, Judge Bryson," Johnny said, looking up at the judge as he was just about to leave the witness stand. "I understand why I couldn't be in the courtroom before I gave my testimony, but now that I'm done, may I stay and listen to the rest of the hearing?"

"Certainly, sir. This courtroom is open to the public, and there is no reason to exclude you now that you've testified and have been released from your subpoena."

Johnny grinned ear to ear and happily took a seat two rows behind Kate.

According to their trial strategy, Ed called Ralph Meardon to the stand next.

Kate had decided they would not use Milton Martin because they couldn't rely on his testimony, and, at the end of the day, they didn't need him. Ed would be able to get all the necessary insurance documents and policy history into evidence using Meardon. Nevertheless, Kate had not released Milton from his trial subpoena, and he was currently impatiently cooling his heels in the witness room, still expecting to be called to testify. Kate did not feel the least bit guilty about tying up his morning.

Ed's direct examination of Meardon went smoothly. He managed to get all the insurance documents into evidence quickly and efficiently, providing copies to the judge as Meardon explained the importance of each. Judge Bryson took a special interest in the premium payment history, both before and after Johnny Sutton was the agent on the account. Again, the judge asked several of his own questions, focusing on the fact that Dr. Dugan could have let the policy lapse, reduced the amount, or even change the beneficiary at any time.

On cross-examination, Gray asked whether Meardon had ever met Dr. Dugan—he had not. Then he asked if Meardon had ever seen the original policy that was given to Dr. Dugan—again, he said he had not. Finally, Gray asked when Meardon first met Ms. Simpson.

Meardon didn't need more invitation than that to launch into a recounting of the first meeting with Marcy in Gray's office. As Meardon was about to detail the conduct of Zeke Peters, Gray objected.

"Thank you, Mr. Meardon, that's enough. You've answered my question. These other details are unnecessary and not germane to the issue before the court," Gray said, as he held up a hand to signal Meardon should stop.

"Oh, come now, Mr. Gray," Judge Bryson smiled winningly. "You don't really think that's going to work, do you? Sir, you opened this line of questioning. You know on redirect Mr. Evert will simply ask Mr. Meardon what else he wanted to add about his first meeting with Ms. Simpson. So, let's just cut to the chase here and let him finish his story."

Gray stammered, but Meardon had all the encouragement he needed, and he immediately finished his story, including details of Zeke's rant against Marcy and rushing toward her, tipping over furniture on the way. He added that both he and Argyle had leapt up to prevent what looked like an imminent battery to accompany the already completed assault.

Lawyers can make excellent witnesses when they know what you want the judge to hear, Kate thought as she looked down at the table to hide her smile.

"My," Judge Bryson exclaimed. "I can see why you didn't want *that* testimony to come in, Mr. Gray. But, it may be relevant, so I'll include it in the evidence I consider."

At that, Gray apparently decided he'd done enough damage. Saying he had no further questions, he again sat down heavily.

As Ed rose for redirect, Kate discretely handed him the waiver document Gray had prepared for that first meeting. When Ed leaned down to take the document, Kate whispered in his ear.

"Might as well see if you can get this into evidence too—it might deliver the final nail in Gray's coffin."

Ed thoughtfully reviewed the document Kate had handed him.

Dropping a copy of the waiver on Gray's table, Ed asked to approach the bench with a copy of a document he wanted Mr. Meardon to identify.

Gray exploded out of his chair.

"This document has nothing whatsoever to do with this matter," Gray was almost shouting.

The tension in Gray's voice brought a smile to Judge Bryson's lips. "Well, I guess I'll be the *judge* of that, now, won't *I?*" he said, laughing at his own joke. "Hand me the document, Mr. Evert."

When Ed handed the judge the document he also delivered a copy to Meardon on the witness stand, and then returned to the podium.

Judge Bryson silently read the waiver. Three separate times during his reading, the judge looked out at Gray over the top of his glasses.

"Did you prepare this document, Mr. Gray?"

"I did, Your Honor. But it was never signed, so, it is not relevant here. It's similar to settlement discussions and not permissible as evidence."

"But you prepared it and presented it to Ms. Simpson. Is that where Mr. Evert is headed?"

"Yes, Your Honor, I did, but—"

"I'll allow it. Please proceed with your questions, Mr. Evert."

Knowing he'd already scored the points he needed, Ed quickly completed his questions about the one-sided waiver now in evidence. He then asked one last question.

"Mr. Meardon, was Ms. Simpson represented by counsel at that first meeting?"

"No, sir, she was not. She was on her own, and frankly, she looked quite intimidated—reasonably so, I might add. She was alone in a room full of lawyers and a man who wouldn't stop shouting at her."

Gray was halfway out of his chair with an objection on his lips, but he seemed to think better of it when Judge Bryson shot him a sideways glance. He sank back down into his chair.

"No other questions," Ed said quickly.

"Mr. Gray?" Judge Bryson said, nodding toward Gray, looking at him over the top of his glasses.

"No questions," Gray said, rising barely an inch out of his chair.

Meardon left the witness stand, walked into the gallery, and took a seat next to Mr. Argyle.

Kate called Michael Dugan to the witness stand next. After her brief introductory questions, she directed Michael to the last time he met with his brother.

"Dr. Dugan, what financial arrangements did your brother have in place for his sons in the event of his death?"

"He left two separate insurance policies, each for $1.5 million dollars. The money goes into a trust for the three boys, and I'm the trustee."

"When did you first learn you were the trustee?"

"Well, I wasn't the trustee until about three months before Joe's death. The trust was set up when their first son, Murphy, was born, a little over 16 years ago now. Prior to that, the trustee was Zeke Peters, a coworker of Joe's who'd been a friend since high school. I last saw Joe when he came to St. Petersburg shortly before his death to visit a number of private schools in the area. That's when he told me he'd changed the trust instrument, and that I was the new trustee. He also told me he changed his will to make me the personal representative of his estate. He gave me copies of both his new will and the new trust instruments."

"Dr. Dugan, what was your understanding of why your brother was looking for schools in the St. Petersburg area?" Kate asked.

"Joe was divorcing his wife and seeking full custody of the boys," Michael Dugan responded quickly as he saw Gray leaping to his feet.

"Objection! Not relevant to this hearing and not supported by any evidence before the court," Gray shouted.

"Dr. Dugan, what evidence do you have that your brother was divorcing his wife and seeking custody of his boys?" Judge Bryson asked without acknowledging Gray's objection.

"Well, he told me he was, and he told me why. Joan, his wife was . . . a handful. She had . . . some problems with drugs and alcohol, and she'd been arrested several of times. Their oldest son seemed to be following that same road, and Joe was worried . . . and, frankly, he was tired of Joan's antics."

"Thank you, Dr. Dugan. Ms. Muldoon, is there any corroborating evidence of the impending divorce and custody issue that you intend to present?"

"Yes, Your Honor, it will come in with another witness, Mr. Steve Sloan."

"Mr. Gray, your objection is overruled. Please continue, Ms. Muldoon."

"In that last conversation with your brother, what was your understanding of why you were being named trustee and personal representative after all these years?"

Kate was not surprised when Gray again objected.

"Mr. Gray, everything Dr. Joe Dugan said and did prior to his death is not off-limits here," the judge explained. "Besides, Ms. Muldoon has properly asked what Dr. Michael Dugan understood to be the reason. Let's hear what he has to say, shall we?"

"Do you remember my question, Michael? If not, I'll repeat it."

"I remember the question. I understood Joe no longer wanted Zeke Peters to serve as trustee or personal representative because he had lied to Joe about a very significant fact."

"What was that fact, Dr. Dugan, if you know?"

"Zeke Peters was my brother's oldest boy's biological father."

"Objection! How could Dr. Dugan possibly know that?" Gray interrupted.

"Let's find out. Overruled." Judge Bryson appeared to be having a good deal of fun. "Dr. Dugan, how did your brother know this?"

"Joe told me he had a DNA paternity test run on DNA samples from himself, Zeke, and his eldest son. The results were conclusive."

"Ms. Muldoon, in your presentation of evidence, will there be any corroborating evidence of Dr. Dugan's testimony?"

"Yes, Your Honor, there will be, including testimony from a woman who will testify Dr. Joe Dugan had just learned Zeke had similarly tricked him when they were in high school."

"I thought there would be. Thank you. You may continue."

"Thank you, Your Honor. I am nearly done with Dr. Dugan. Michael, what was your impression of Joe's feelings about Marcy Simpson?" Kate asked, glaring across the aisle at Gray, daring him to object—he didn't.

"Joe loved Marcy. Frankly, so did our whole family."

"Dr. Dugan, do you feel the same way about your brother's second wife?"

Again, Kate glared at Gray as she watched him struggle not to object.

"No, ma'am. In fact, my parents left Miami, where they'd lived their entire lives, and moved to St. Petersburg, because of Joan's behavior. They just couldn't stand it. When my dad died last week, my mom specifically told Joan she wasn't welcome at the funeral services."

"Thank you, Dr. Dugan, and may I add my condolences on the loss of your father. Your Honor, we have no more questions for Dr. Dugan."

"Mr. Gray, I saw you thinking about objecting to some of Ms. Muldoon's questions. Perhaps you have some questions on cross?" Judge Bryson asked pleasantly.

Gray stood and picked up the legal pad he'd been taking notes on. After several moments, he tossed the legal pad back on the table and said, "No, Your Honor."

"Is this witness excused, Ms. Muldoon?"

"Yes, Your Honor."

"Dr. Dugan, you are excused, and you may either stay in the courtroom or leave, whichever you prefer."

Judge Bryson did not seem surprised when Michael joined the ever-increasing gallery.

"Our next witness is Mrs. Grace Dugan," Kate announced.

As they waited for Mrs. Dugan to enter the courtroom, Kate

returned the witness file she'd use with Michael to the file box behind her chair and retrieved the one for Mrs. Dugan.

Grace Dugan looked a bit unsure as the bailiff escorted her into the courtroom. She smiled when she saw her son and touched him lightly on the shoulder as she passed by his seat on the aisle. When Grace saw Marcy sitting at the counsel table she smiled and gave a little wave. After being sworn in, Grace smiled bravely at Kate.

"Thank you again for being here today, Mrs. Dugan. We know you have recently lost your husband, and we are so sorry for your loss."

Grace nodded, and then said, "I'm honored to be here if my testimony assists in setting the record straight. Marcy is a dear, dear woman. She doesn't deserve the shabby treatment she's been subjected to by the Miami prosecutor and police. They should be ashamed of themselves."

Kate glared at Gray as she heard him rustling as if to stand to object, but he remained seated and quiet.

Kate walked Grace through her introductory questions, and then asked, "Mrs. Dugan, did you know that Marcy planned to attend medical school when your son, Joe, finished his schooling and began practicing medicine?"

"Oh yes. They talked about their 'master plan' many times. Marcy had dropped out of med school after only two years so she could get her nursing accreditation and start supporting Joe. It was supposed to be Marcy's turn when Joe finished. I remember teasing them about where having my grandchildren figured into their master plan. You know, that's what grandmothers do."

Grace turned to the judge and said with a smile, "The only thing in life that's not overrated is being a grandparent."

"I wholeheartedly agree, Mrs. Dugan. I have a few of my own," Judge Bryson said with a kindly smile.

"Well, Marcy told me they planned to start their family while she was in medical school. Marcy thought she could handle being pregnant while she was in school. She was always up to any challenge. Joe wanted to make sure she'd get the chance to become a doctor after she'd supported them while he was in school. That's why he took out that big insurance policy naming her as the beneficiary."

Kate breathed a silent sigh of relief that the testimony had gone in to evidence so smoothly.

"Mrs. Dugan, did Joe ever write to you once you moved to St. Petersburg?"

"Oh yes, I got several letters from him every month. They weren't long letters, but he kept me up to date on his sons. I knew he was busy, and I was happy to get the letters, and I felt especially pleased that they were handwritten. There's something much more personal in a handwritten letter. Joe did the same thing when he was in medical school. He was such a great son. I was blessed with *two* wonderful boys."

Grace bowed her head slightly and stifled a small sob.

"Do you need a moment, Mrs. Dugan?" Judge Bryson asked as he handed her the box of tissues from his bench.

"No, I'll be OK. I promised myself I wouldn't cry," Grace said as she pulled two tissues from the box, set it to the side, and gently dabbed her eyes.

"Mrs. Dugan, we're almost done here. I only have a little more," Kate assured her. "Do you think you could identify Joe's handwriting if I showed you a document?"

"Absolutely. Joe did not have a doctor's typically terrible handwriting. He wrote in a lovely script."

"Your Honor, I have a document I would like to mark for identification, but I will place it into evidence with my next witness. Mr. Gray, it is our evidence number 27. Here is another copy," Kate said as she dropped a copy of the original insurance policy on Gray's table and walked to the bench with the original and gave Mrs. Dugan a copy.

"Your Honor, I have given you the *original* of the document. Everyone else has a copy."

"Ah, so this is the original insurance policy Mr. Gray has been asking the witnesses about," the judge interjected.

"Yes, Your Honor, it was found during discovery—"

Kate got no further. Gray bolted to his feet.

"I have *never* seen this particular document before. Up to this point, we have only seen *copies* of the insurance policy. This document has handwriting on the first page and again on page 20 and initials in the corners and elsewhere and a notary stamp. Ms. Muldoon cannot use this document! It was never provided to us." Gray seemed quite self-satisfied, feeling confident his objection would be sustained this time.

"Ms. Muldoon, is that correct?"

"No, Your Honor. In fact, it couldn't be further from the truth. Mr. Gray *was* provided a copy of this document within hours of its discovery. My next witness is chief of police, Steve Jordan. He will explain the circumstances of the document's discovery. We can call him now, and then recall Mrs. Dugan, if necessary, but we shouldn't have to. The police took this document into evidence in their investigation of Joe Dugan's murder, and they have maintained the original from that time forward. Chief Jordon allowed us to have a copy of the original because it was responsive to my discovery subpoena. You'll note, the document you are holding, Your Honor, has the criminal investigation identification number on it, as do *all* the copies of the *original* policy.

"Moreover, when I obtained copies of the documents that Chief Jordan took into evidence, I immediately had copies made and hand delivered to Mr. Gray's office, along with an inventory of those documents. Item number 27 on that inventory stated, 'Copy of **Original** Insurance Policy number 1097-442-56.' The word 'original' is both underscored and in bold type. I can provide the court a copy of the inventory that Mr. Gray signed on receipt of the documents, if you would like, and I can call my paralegal to the stand first to identify the document and inventory and testify about delivering it to Mr. Gray's office, if you would prefer."

"Let's see the signed inventory of documents, Ms. Muldoon," Judge Bryson replied.

Kate retrieved two copies of the inventory and dropped one in front of Gray and handed the other to the judge.

"Mr. Gray, is this your signature on the inventory Ms. Muldoon just provided us?" Judge Bryson asked.

"Yes, but this document must have been doctored, because we never received the original policy."

Now I understand why he's been asking the witnesses about the original policy. He never realized he had it. He probably left the menial task of document review to one of his associates or a paralegal, Kate thought. *I wouldn't want to be at Gray and Ferguson this afternoon.*

"If I didn't know better, Your Honor, I'd think Mr. Gray is calling me a liar *and* accusing me of tampering with evidence. But, I'm sure that couldn't possibly be the case. Perhaps he's just . . . confused. If the court will bear with me one more moment, perhaps I can clear up Mr. Gray's confusion. Ron, do you have your copy of our exhibit list and the attached exhibits?"

"Am I on the witness stand now?" Gray asked indignantly.

"Perhaps, if you'd prefer that," the judge said, "but maybe you could ask your paralegal who is sitting with you at counsel table to find your copy of the exhibit list and exhibits that you received from Ms. Muldoon prior to this hearing." Judge Bryson had quickly figured out where Kate was going. "Miss, I'm sorry I don't know your name," the judge addressed the young woman at the counsel table with Gray.

"Sarah Buford, Your Honor."

"Ms. Buford, are you Mr. Gray's paralegal?"

"Yes."

"Did you help Mr. Gray prepare for this hearing?"

"Yes."

"Did you receive Ms. Simpson's exhibit list and exhibits prior to this hearing?"

"Yes."

"Did you bring a copy of those items to court with you today?"

"Yes."

Sarah Buford's face had turned scarlet by now.

"Would you find those items for me and bring them to me, please?"

Sarah slowly stood up and rummaged in a box behind her chair and came up with a file.

"I want to see that file!" Gray demanded.

"Well, Mr. Gray, hopefully you have *already* seen it, and you can see it again, *just as soon as I am done with it*," Judge Bryson said temperately but firmly. "Unless, of course, you think *I* might somehow tamper with the evidence too. Would you like to come up to the bench and watch what I am doing?"

Gray's face became the color of Sarah's.

"No, Your Honor, of course not. That won't be necessary."

"Good. Now, Ms. Buford, if you would be so kind as to bring the file to me."

Sarah walked the file to the bench and placed it into Judge Bryson's outstretched hand. The judge looked up at Kate and said, "Did you say the document is Exhibit # 27?"

"Yes, Your Honor."

"Ah yes, here it is on the list in *your* file, Mr. Gray," the judge said holding up Kate's Exhibit List aloft. "And it does indeed say, 'Copy of **Original** Insurance Policy number 1097-442-56,' and the word 'original' is both underscored and in bold type."

Judge Bryson then rifled through the exhibits in Gray's file in search of number 27. When he found it, he lifted it up and showed the courtroom, and in particular, Ron Gray, that pages numbered 1 and 20 of the exhibit had handwriting on them. He compared the exhibit from Gray's file to the same pages of the original policy sitting on his desk.

"Yes, Exhibit # 27 in your file, Mr. Gray, looks identical to the original that has been in police custody. It seems you had it in your files after all. Thank you, Ms. Buford. You may have your file back. Ms. Muldoon, you may continue your examination of Mrs. Dugan," the judge nodded at Kate.

"Thank you. Mrs. Dugan, you have in front of you the document we just spend so much time discussing, Simpson Exhibit #27 for identification. Would you please look at pages 1 and 20 of that exhibit?" Kate waited as Grace turned the pages.

"Do you see the handwriting on those pages of Exhibit #27, Mrs. Dugan?"

"Yes, I see where Joe wrote a number of things."

"Let me clarify, are you saying you recognize the handwriting on those pages to be your son's, Joe Dugan's, handwriting?" Kate asked.

"Without a doubt. It's his handwriting, and I can tell you it also says what he felt about Marcy. She was his 'one true love.'"

Mrs. Dugan again tried to stifle a sob and pulled another tissue from the box.

Marcy bowed her head and quietly cried into the tissue she was clutching.

Gray stood to object, but the judge cut him off. "It's OK, Mr. Gray. I'll consider the comment for what it is."

"Mrs. Dugan, how do *you* feel about Marcy Simpson?" Kate asked.

"I love her like a daughter. I've missed her since their divorce. I wanted to continue to communicate with Marcy, but she said she didn't want to intrude. She said since she was no longer family, she felt she should step aside. When Joe Senior died last week, I asked Marcy to come to St. Pete to help me out. She was reluctant to, but once I told her that I'd informed Joan she was not welcome to attend his funeral, Marcy agreed to come up and help me. She was wonderful support . . . just like a daughter."

"Thank you, Mrs. Dugan. I have no other questions," Kate said, relinquishing the podium to Gray.

Gray had apparently decided his case was so weak that he needed to try something risky, and he came out gunning for Mrs. Dugan. In doing so, he demonstrated why widows and children should be handled with great care on the witness stand.

"That was quite some testimony, Mrs. Dugan. Let me ask you, how much of Ms. Simpson's $4 million is she planning on giving you for your assistance here today?"

Kate was instantly on her feet, "Objection, Your Honor! There is no evidence of Ms. Simpson trying to bribe a witness."

Before Judge Bryson could rule on Kate's objection, Grace Dugan jumped in.

"How dare you imply such a thing! That is the most impertinent thing anyone has ever said to me. Marcy would never do such a terrible thing, and I wouldn't take anything from her in any event. If Marcy is awarded the $4 million dollars, she deserves every cent because of what was done to her."

"Mr. Gray, do you have any evidence of an arrangement between Mrs. Dugan and Ms. Simpson regarding the testimony Mrs. Dugan has given, or are you using this hearing as a fishing expedition?"

"It's a fair question, Judge."

"Do you care to rephrase your question?"

"Sure. Mrs. Dugan, isn't it true Ms. Simpson promised to give you some part of the insurance proceeds?"

"It is absolutely *not* true!"

"Well then, isn't it true she promised to give some of the insurance proceeds to someone in your family, your grandsons perhaps?"

"She has done no such thing, and we wouldn't take it from her if she did."

"Mrs. Dugan, $4 million is a lot of money. Other than being married to your son for six years, what in the world did she do that would ever result in her *deserving* $4 million?"

"I'll tell you what that sweet girl did to deserve that money—she loved my son absolutely. She stood by him when they didn't have any money, and she worked to give him a fine education. She put up with the heartbreak of their divorce and with having her dreams for her own future destroyed by that treacherous woman Joe married. Joe's evil and conniving second wife, Joan Ferguson, tricked Joe into getting that divorce. I won't even call that woman a Dugan. She always thought she could get anything and everything she wanted by bullying people and throwing around the fact that her father is a former senator. Besides, it was Joe's wish that Marcy receive that money, and she should have it." As Grace spoke, she shook her finger at Gray like an angry mother scolding a three-year-old.

Gray looked like he stepped on a landmine, and, in a way, he had.

"Anything else you want to try, Mr. Gray?" the judge asked, smiling.

"No more questions for this witness," Gray sighed, slumping down into his chair.

The judge looked at Kate.

She said, "No more questions, and we release Mrs. Dugan."

"Mrs. Dugan, you are excused and you may either leave or perhaps you'd like to join your son, Michael, in the gallery."

"I'd like to do that, Judge. Thank you."

Grace Dugan's eyes never left Gray as she stepped down from the witness stand and slowly walked past him. Her laser-sharp glare nearly cut him in two.

Ed was handling the next two witnesses, so Kate yielded the podium as he announced, "Our next witness is Chief of Police Steven Jordan."

Skillfully, Ed elicited testimony from the chief regarding how and when the documents were discovered in Dr. Dugan's office desk drawer. Ed then walked the chief through each document and as he identified the document Ed moved it into evidence. When he got to the original insurance policy, Ed asked the chief to read into the record the words Joe Dugan had written.

"Marcy Anne Simpson ('Dugan' has been crossed out), my ('first' has been added) wife appears on the beneficiary line on page 1. These changes had been initialed. On page 20, just above Dr. Dugan's signature, there is additional handwriting that says, 'It is my specific intention that this policy remain in place even now that Marcy and I are divorced. Marcy is not aware I have kept this policy current. I hope she will use the proceeds however she wants, but I pray she'll have the opportunity to go to medical school someday. I love you, Marcy. You are my one true love, Joe.' That addition has also been initialed. Both pages have been notarized."

Following this testimony, Ed asked the chief about Marcy's arrest.

"Have you ever arrested Ms. Simpson?"

"Yes, the state prosecutor, Mike Taylor, got a warrant issued for Ms. Simpson's arrest during the first week of our investigation into Dr. Dugan's death. I arrested her, even though I believed Mike was acting prematurely. We had no evidence showing Ms. Simpson was involved in his death. Mike convinced Judge Crawley, because Ms. Simpson stood to gain $4 million and she works in a hospital ER where digitalis is available. That was all he needed for the warrant."

Chief Jordan looked up at the judge and added, "Digitalis was found in Dr. Dugan's blood when he was brought to the ER. The recently completed autopsy done on Dr. Dugan's exhumed body show signs of defensive wounds and a struggle before he died, and a small puncture wound at the back of his neck, likely caused by a hypodermic needle. We actually have charged Zeke Peters with Dr. Dugan's murder, and we have a signed confession from him. He has also implicated Joan Dugan in the attack on Dr. Dugan."

"Thank you, Chief. Did Mr. Peters implicate Ms. Simpson?"

"No. As a matter of fact, we now also know Mr. Peters, and possibly one other person, actually hired a man to kill Ms. Simpson. His name is Gary Cook, and he's now in FBI custody."

"Thank you, Chief."

Ed looked toward Kate, and she nodded.

"Your Honor, we have no further questions for the chief," Ed concluded.

"No questions," Gray said barely raising his head as he spoke.

"Chief, you are excused. You can join the gallery if you would like, or get on with your busy day."

"Thanks, Judge, but I have a prisoner in one of your witness rooms who one of your bailiffs has been kind enough to guard while I provided my testimony. I'll go relieve him."

"Sounds interesting. In that case, I'll see you later."

The judge shot Kate and Ed a curious look.

"Our next witness is Steve Sloan," Ed informed the judge.

Ed quickly took Steve through the introductory questions, and then asked, "Mr. Sloan, did you ever meet Dr. Joe Dugan?"

"Yes, Dr. Dugan was my client. I was representing him in a dissolution of marriage and child custody matter."

Ed next announced he would be asking Mr. Sloan about three documents that had been numbered Simpson Exhibits 20, 21, and 22.

Gray stood immediately, this time holding the documents in question from his own set of exhibits. "Judge, there is no reason these exhibits should be placed into evidence in this case. First of all, they contain attorney-client privileged communications; these documents were never filed. Second, there are sensitive matters alleged in these documents that may damage parties not related to this matter."

"Mr. Evert, why are these documents relevant?" Judge Bryson asked, as he looked over the exhibits he'd retrieved from his bench copy of the parties' exhibit files.

"These documents contain information Dr. Dugan provided to Mr. Sloan for inclusion in the petition for dissolution of marriage which was to be filed in the public record. Contrary to Mr. Gray's statement, the information contained in the documents was *not* intended to remain private communications. Moreover, Dr. Dugan signed them. You will see his attestation at the end of the petition, and Mr. Sloan and his paralegal witnessed his signature, making the petition a sworn statement of the deceased. These documents and the testimony we will elicit from Mr. Sloan will corroborate the testimony of Michael Dugan regarding the reasons his brother was seeking a divorce and custody of his boys. The documents also help to explain why Dr. Dugan left no insurance policy for the benefit of his wife, but left a $4 million policy in place for his ex-wife."

Judge Bryson continued to read through the documents, occasionally looking over his glasses at Steve and Ron Gray.

"While, I understand your objection and reasons for wishing to keep this information out of evidence, Mr. Gray, I can't help you with that. Mr. Sloan can testify about the matters in these documents. He is not precluded from doing so. The information Dr. Dugan gave Mr. Sloan was intended to be included in pleadings filed in the public records. That information was never privileged attorney-client communication. Moreover, these documents will assist the court in understanding Dr. Dugan's rather unusual insurance structure, and that *is* exceedingly relevant. Overruled, Mr. Gray."

Next, Ed asked Steve Sloan to identify the documents, and one at a time, he moved them into evidence. Then, Ed had Steve read aloud specific paragraphs of the documents. After each such paragraph, he asked Steve if the written statements agreed with what Dr. Dugan had told him regarding his desire to divorce Joan and seek custody of his boys. When Steve identified the DNA test results, he explained sample A was Dr. Dugan's, sample B was Dr. Dugan's eldest son, and sample C belonged to Zeke Peters.

When Ed was finished with Steve, he turned him over to Ron Gray. Ron sat several moments looking at the top of his table. He saw no possible advantage in cross-examining Steve Sloan. Indeed, if he did so, Steve would almost certainly mention Ron's own involvement in the divorce and custody dispute.

"No questions," Ron reluctantly said without even standing.

"I'm sorry, Mr. Gray, did you say something?"

Gray realized his error and immediately stood and repeated, "Sorry, Judge, no questions."

"Mr. Sloan, you may be excused. You can leave or join the crowd in the gallery. Ms. Muldoon, how many more witnesses do you have?"

"Two or three and we would like to briefly discuss one of them in chambers."

"Let's do this. Let's take a 15-minute break and we'll meet in my chambers after the break. Court is recessed until 11:30." Judge Bryson banged his gavel and headed off the bench.

Chapter 30

Kate, Ed, and Ron Gray waited in silence outside the judge's chambers until Judge Bryson open the door and invited them in.

"I must say, Counsel, I have never had a civil hearing this interesting in my entire 23 years on the bench. What did you want to talk to me about, Ms. Muldoon?"

"Your Honor, our next witness is Miranda West. She is the woman Zeke Peters got pregnant when they were in high school. She had an abortion at that time, paid for by Joe Dugan after Zeke and Miranda convinced him that he, not Zeke, was the father. About four months ago, Ms. West met with Dr. Joe Dugan to confess her part in the charade so many years ago. That revelation was apparently the impetus for Joe Dugan to send DNA samples of his first son and Zeke Peters to the lab for paternity testing and ultimately changing his personal representative and the trustee of his boys' trust from Zeke Peters to his brother. While her testimony does not bear directly on Marcy Simpson's innocence, it does supply background on Dr. Dugan's unusual insurance and testamentary decisions, as well as the motivations of other actors in this almost Shakespearian story.

"Ms. West will testify in open court if she has to, but she would prefer not to. Because she is not a party and has nothing to gain, and a great deal of privacy to lose, I ask that she be allowed to provide her testimony in chambers. I also ask that this portion of the transcript be sealed. We've been careful not to identify Ms. West in open court in the hopes you will grant this request."

"Mr. Gray, any objections?" the judge asked.

Gray contemplated the request and wondered if he could make

any hay out of embarrassing Ms. West on the stand. He decided he couldn't. "I don't have any objection at this time. I do, however, want to cross-examine her, and depending on that examination, I may request some or all of the testimony be read into the record in open court."

"That seems fair. Ms. Muldoon, is Ms. West available now?"

"Yes, I let her know during the break that we would likely be ready for her next."

"OK, please let the court reporter and bailiff know where we are and that we are ready to proceed with the next witness in here."

Kate excused herself and went to deliver the messages to the court reporter and bailiff, and to tell Marcy where they were and what they were doing. Marcy declined to join them. She said she just wasn't up to sitting in on the testimony of Joe's "first." She looked exhausted.

Miranda's testimony had been quick, and Gray had decided he really didn't have any questions. She cried enormous tears as she told the judge about the ruse she and Zeke had played on Joe Dugan. She said she only came forward after so many years because it was something that had sat heavily on her conscience, and her therapist had suggested revealing the secret might help.

Upon returning to the courtroom, Kate immediately called Joan Dugan to the stand. Ron Gray seemed surprised by this and started rummaging through his paperwork.

No doubt looking to see if I listed Joan on my witness list. Really, Ron, you need to pay attention to these details, Kate thought.

When Kate heard the clang and rattle of leg irons and handcuffs, she turned and saw Joan Dugan walking into the courtroom in an awful orange prison jumpsuit. Chief Jordan had promised Marcy would have revenge for her arrest. It couldn't be better than this scene. Joan looked like a scrawny, scraggily, feral animal as Chief Jordan half-dragged her up to the witness stand. The chief and one of the bailiffs stood next to Joan as she was sworn in.

Kate shot Marcy a sidewise glance; she was staring in open-mouthed awe at the spectacle. When she looked toward Ron Gray, Kate realized he too was staring in astonishment at the scene unfolding in front of him.

"Please state your name for the record," Kate said calmly.

"Everyone knows who I am. And you're all going to be really sorry as soon as my daddy talks to the governor about this travesty. You, and the chief there, are going to be first on my hit list," Joan Dugan responded.

"Your Honor, we request leave to treat Ms. Joan Dugan as a hostile witness," Kate addressed the judge.

"Granted."

"If you think I'm hostile now, bitch, just you wait until I sue you for everything you have."

"Ms. Dugan, you will control yourself and answer Ms. Muldoon's questions. This is a court of law, and you will comport yourself accordingly," Judge Bryson said sternly.

"This is a damn kangaroo court, and everyone is going to hear about it from me," Joan continued undeterred.

Judge Bryson banged his gavel with great force.

"Ms. Dugan, I'm warning you for the last time, one more outburst like that and you will be held in direct contempt of court." Judge Bryson pounded his gavel a couple more times for good measure. "Try again, Ms. Muldoon."

"Your name is Joan Ferguson Dugan, correct?"

"Yeah," Joan snarled.

"You were married to Dr. Joseph Dugan until his death, weren't you?"

"You know I was."

"Isn't it true your husband was going to divorce you and seek full custody of your three children?"

"Yeah, I'd have loved to see him raise those three on his own."

"Ms. Dugan," Kate said as she picked up the petition for dissolution of marriage and petition for custody of the children and read from one of the paragraphs, "isn't it true you have been arrested and charged a total of six times with driving under the influence of alcohol?"

"So what? Drinking is legal, and if you had to put up with my three kids and that sanctimonious husband of mine, you'd drink too."

"And you also have been arrested and charged with illegal drug use and possession at least four times, haven't you?"

"Yes, I've had very good legal counsel and stayed out of jail, isn't that right, Ron?" Joan said as she stared at Ron Gray.

"And you've been arrested and charged with disturbing the peace three times, correct?"

"So? I have cranky neighbors who can't stand to hear me having a good time."

"And, Ms. Dugan, isn't it true you are currently under arrest and incarcerated for striking an officer of the law and for conspiracy to murder your husband, Dr. Joseph Dugan?"

"Look, I'll admit I got angry and hit Chief Jordan, but all he's got is the statement of that lying scumbag murderer, Zeke Peters. I don't know anything about my husband's tragic murder."

"Ms. Dugan, under your husband's will, you receive only the marital home, isn't that correct?"

"That's what you think. I'm getting at least a third of Joe's estate. My daddy told me I get that much," Joan answered referring to the widow's right to claim a third of the marital estate under Florida law. Life insurance, however, passes outside of the estate and is not subject to such as claim.

"And, Ms. Dugan, your husband did not leave any life insurance policies naming you as the beneficiary, did he?"

"No, but everybody thinks he left Miss Goody Two-Shoes over here $4 million," Joan said, as she waved at Marcy. "Some fine husband! And you wonder why I drink and do drugs. My life with his holiness, Dr. Joe Dugan, was no cakewalk. I should have just aborted the kid and stayed single."

"Your witness, Mr. Gray," Kate said, and sat down hoping to watch Ron Gray walk into a buzz saw.

"I have no questions for this witness," Ron quickly answered.

"Chief, you may return Ms. Dugan to the jail. Thank you for your time," Judge Bryson said, looking like he couldn't see the back of Joan

Dugan soon enough.

As she left the courtroom, Joan shouted to Grace and Michael Dugan, "What are you two looking at? Do you see what living with your son and brother has done to me? He wasn't the saint you thought he was. This is all his fault."

"Your Honor, we call Marcy Simpson to the stand."

After being sworn in, Marcy tentatively looked at Kate, then out at the gallery, then to the judge, and finally back to Kate. The echo of Joan's shouts seemed to continue to ring in the courtroom, and Marcy looked completely unnerved. Kate smiled encouragingly; Marcy responded with a wan smile of her own.

Kate quickly took Marcy through the preliminary introductory questions about her education and professional history, and then she asked about her marriage to Joe. Marcy's testimony was succinct, but timid. Kate then asked about the insurance policy, and Marcy recounted her story of the night Joe told her about the policy, and their 'master plan.' Finally, Kate got to the testimony that only Marcy could provide.

"Marcy, did you have anything to do with Joe Dugan's death?"

"Absolutely not. I hadn't even seen or talked to Joe since right after our divorce. I was shocked when Zeke Peters called to tell me Joe was dead. I was even more shocked when Mr. Gray told me about the policy. To be honest, I couldn't imagine why Joe would have kept that policy current all these years. It wasn't until the letters in his desk drawer were found that I could believe he actually *meant* for me to be the beneficiary."

Kate took the packet of letters from the exhibit file and asked to approach the witness.

"Ms. Simpson, I am handing you what has been marked Simpson Composite Exhibit 12. Please take a look at this exhibit and tell me if you can identify these documents."

Marcy rifled through the letters, occasionally pausing and running her fingers across the writing.

"Yes, I know what these are." Her voice caught, and she reached for a tissue from the box on the witness stand. "These are the letters

Joe wrote to me after our divorce. I returned them unread. That's my handwriting where it says, 'return to sender.' I saw no reason to even open them—it wasn't going to change the fact that we were divorced. Apparently, Joe kept them in his desk drawer at his office; at least that's where they were found." Marcy contemplated the letters for a moment longer before handing them back to Kate.

"We move the entire composite exhibit into evidence," Kate said.

Judge Bryson looked at Ron Gray expecting an argument and was relieved that even Ron seemed to know attempting to keep out these poignant and revealing letters was futile.

"The documents will be received, and I would like a few minutes to review them."

Six minutes passed as the judge quickly read through the letters, intermittently glancing at Marcy who sat silently wiping away tears. When he finished he looked at Kate.

"Thank you, Ms. Muldoon. You may continue your questioning."

"Where were you the night of Joe's murder, Marcy?"

"I was at work at the ER at Jackson Memorial. It was the usual crazy busy night. I was substituting for one of my coworkers so she could spend some time with her family."

"How long was your shift that evening?"

"I worked the four p.m. to midnight shift."

"Can you identify this document?" Kate asked, handing Marcy her time records for the week Joe Dugan was murdered.

"Yes, these are my time records for that week. I found out about Joe's death on Thursday of that week. His death had occurred the night before, this Wednesday, the ninth," Marcy said, pointing to the appropriate line item.

"Did you leave the hospital that evening during your shift?"

"No. It's always chaos in the ER on that shift. We don't take meal breaks, and to be frank, it's difficult to find time to go to the bathroom—we're always running from one crisis to the next."

Kate moved the time records into evidence.

"Marcy, did you hire someone to kill Dr. Dugan?"

"Of course not. Joe told me years ago he no longer loved me, but

I never really stopped loving him. Joe was a very good man. I could never harm anyone, let alone someone I loved that much."

"Did you conspire with Zeke Peters to kill Joe?"

"Absolutely not. Zeke Peters is a terrible man. I understand he has confessed to killing Joe. It's hard to believe, after everything Joe did for him."

"Marcy, $4 million is a lot of money. It could provide strong motive to kill someone, maybe even someone you love."

"Maybe some people would see it that way, but I didn't even know about the policy. I really never thought about it after the night Joe told me he had bought it. Like I said, when Mr. Gray told me about the policy, even *I* questioned why Joe would have kept it valid all those years . . . but he did," Marcy said with an incredulous note in her voice. "I know he meant well, but you know, so far, that policy has only caused me trouble."

"Like what, Marcy?"

"Well, getting arrested for Joe's murder, and losing my job at Jackson Memorial because of the accusations against me. I've been sort of hiding out since then because I'm a real *persona non grata*—ever since that article in the *Herald* appeared with my photograph under the headline, '*Killer Nurse?*' Nobody even wants to speak with me. And, to make it more of a nightmare, I just found out yesterday that Zeke hired an evil man to try to *kill* me. My life was very boring until that insurance policy entered it, but it has been nothing but agony ever since."

"Marcy, did you take digitalis out of the drug safe at Jackson Memorial so it could be used to kill Joe Dugan?"

"No. I haven't taken any digitalis out of that safe for any reason for over six months."

Kate showed Marcy the drug safe logs for the last year. After Marcy identified the document, Kate moved it into evidence.

"Can you find your name anywhere on this record showing that you removed digitalis from that safe?"

As she looked through the records, Marcy explained the drug safe and the electronic and paper records that are maintained to keep track of anyone accessing the drugs.

"Here it is, on page 6, this record shows the last time I pulled digitalis, was . . . 1, 2, 3, 4, 5, 6 . . . almost 7 months ago. Usually, if digitalis would help a patient, the EMS team will have already administered it on the way to the hospital. There are lots of safer ways to combat a heart attack."

"Thanks, Marcy. I have no further questions."

Kate glared at Ron Gray as he rose slowly and walked to the podium.

"Miss Simpson, do expect this court to believe that your ex-husband, who divorced you over 16 years ago so he could marry someone else, actually meant to keep the policy current so you would be paid $4 million in the event of his death?"

"I know what you mean, Mr. Gray. It's pretty hard to believe. Like I said, even *I* didn't believe it until I saw the letters and policy and the other things Joe left in his office drawer. But Joe's intention seems pretty clear now. I guess if you're looking for an example of the dead speaking from the grave, this is it."

Marcy looked down at her hands while Ron Gray cast about for a new line of questioning.

"You know what, Mr. Gray? I would exchange that $4 million right now if it would bring Joe back from the dead—even if he would still be married to someone else—I'd do it in a heartbeat. Joe was a great man. He helped a lot of people. He didn't deserve to be murdered by a man he thought was his best friend . . . and possibly his wife, for heaven's sake."

"Miss Simpson, there is no question on the table. Please cease from making gratuitous, self-serving comments," Gray hurriedly tried to close Marcy down.

"Sure, Mr. Gray, but you know, he trusted you too, and you have done nothing but let him down ever since you represented him in our divorce. But, that's something you'll have to take up with your own conscience."

"Move to strike, Your Honor. Miss Simpson, please cease making comments when there isn't a question before you," Gray shouted at

Marcy.

"No problem, I'm done now."

Marcy looked toward Kate who was trying to hide her smile.

"Me too, Miss Simpson, me too. No further questions," Ron Gray said, sitting down with a thud and throwing his witness file at his paralegal.

"Ms. Simpson, you may step down. Anything further, Ms. Muldoon?" Judge Bryson asked.

"Nothing further, Your Honor."

"Mr. Gray, do you have any witnesses to call?"

"No. Ms. Muldoon has done a thorough job of calling every witness who might even possibly have some remote connection to this matter. We have nothing further."

"Yes, Ms. Muldoon *has* done an excellent job of providing the court clear and convincing evidence that Ms. Simpson was the intended beneficiary of the insurance policy," Judge Bryson said. "She has also provided sufficient evidence to convince the court that Ms. Simpson had nothing whatsoever to do with Dr. Dugan's death. She has cleared her client's good name here in open court. I certainly hope that one of you journalists in the courtroom today is from the *Herald* and will provide her with an apology and written retraction of any accusation of wrongdoing.

"I am sympathetic to your desire to bring all this evidence to the court under the circumstances, Ms. Muldoon, even though it lengthened our hearing substantially.

"But now, I have to ask the only question I have left. Mr. Gray, with the overwhelming wealth of evidence, both documentary and testimony, supporting Dr. Dugan's intention to keep Ms. Simpson the beneficiary on the policy even after their divorce, why in the world was the payout of this policy challenged in the first place? And now, with the recent confession of at least one of Dr. Dugan's murderers, why would you put yourself, Ms. Simpson, and this court through the necessity of a hearing? Sometimes, sir, it is better to acknowledge the truth and withdraw from the battlefield."

It was clear the judge's question was rhetorical and he did not wait for a response.

"And now, I am ready to rule. I find that Ms. Marcy Simpson is the rightful beneficiary of the insurance policy in question. I further find there is no legal impediment to Ms. Simpson receiving same as there is no evidence of her involvement in Dr. Dugan's death. Therefore, the funds being held in the court registry related to Dr. Dugan's life insurance policy number 1097-442-56, all $4 million, should be paid over immediately to Ms. Simpson. You may go to the clerk of court's office and arrange to have the funds sent by wire transfer to the account of your choice, Ms. Simpson. And, I personally wish you the best of luck. Please let me know if you use some of the money to get that medical degree—although, to be honest, I'm not sure I'd undertake such an arduous endeavor if $4 million suddenly fell into *my* lap.

"There being no further business before this court, we will stand adjourned until 1:30, Madam Clerk. Court is dismissed."

Judge Bryson banged his gavel, the bailiff called, "All rise," and the judge quickly left the courtroom.

There was a momentary silence so deep you could hear yourself breathe. The media quickly recovered and remembered they were on deadline. There was an astonishing commotion as they began rushing from the courtroom, calling their editors, each hoping to make the end of the noon news cycle.

Marcy stood like a statue, staring blankly at the door where the judge had disappeared. As Kate turned to her, Marcy said, "He really was mine, Kate, and now the money is too. Oh my God, Kate! All that money is mine," and she collapsed sobbing into Kate's arms.

Grace and Michael Dugan pressed forward to congratulate Kate and Ed and embraced Marcy warmly.

Ralph Meardon came forward to shake Kate's and Ed's hands, saying, "I knew that it would be a fight, but I never thought it would be this bad. You handled this matter expertly—but we all knew you would."

Johnny Sutton walked surprisingly spryly to the front of the courtroom, hugged Marcy, and told her she deserved the money. He then shook Kate's and Ed's hands and whispered to Ed, "She's the hottest attorney I've ever met. I hope you appreciate her, kid. I just wish I was in your shoes!"

Ed laughed and turned red.

Steve Sloan hugged Kate and slapped Ed on the back.

Finally, Ed looked at Kate, and they simultaneously threw their arms around each other.

"God, Kate, that was awesome. Thank you for letting me handle so much of the hearing. I love this work!" he whispered in her ear as he held her tightly in his arms.

Kate drew back just enough to look him in the eye. It was clear he'd caught the litigation bug. "You did great, kid," she said with pride. "It's a lot of fun—when you win."

Over Ed's shoulder, Kate saw Dr. Jenkins slinking out of the courtroom.

And then she saw Bill! He was standing along the back wall watching her.

Ed pulled her in tight again and whispered, "I want to celebrate tonight, Kate."

Kate pulled away again and looked at the spot where she was sure she'd seen Bill. But he wasn't there. No one was left in the back of the courtroom. She quickly looked around searching for the tall man she had thought was Bill. But he'd vanished.

Is my mind playing tricks on me, or was he really here? Kate wondered.

Chapter 31

Following their victory lunch, Kate headed back to the office and Marcy headed to her condo for the first time in weeks. She needed some time to process, but she and Kate agreed to meet for dinner on Sunday at The Pelican. Kate thought it was the perfect place to initiate Marcy's new life as a millionaire. Kate was now sitting in her office sorting through the files from the Simpson hearing, arranging them to be stored.

She was haunted by what she had thought was a glimpse of Bill in the courtroom.

Was he really there, or did I imagine it? And if I imagined it, what would cause me to do such a thing? I know I'm tired—exhausted, really, and stressed. Perhaps that's all it was, exhaustion . . . and maybe a little wishful thinking, Kate told herself. *He could call me if he's back, even if only to tell me congratulations, or just a text, anything at all to let me know he's still alive, and thinks of me every once in a while.*

Kate's direct line rang; her heart leaped, but a look at the caller ID display told her it wasn't Bill. It was Matt Danson.

"Hello, Matt. I'm kind of surprised you're calling today. I expected your call on Monday."

She hoped this didn't mean Matt had reviewed the new safety testing reports she'd sent him the day before and no longer wanted to settle the matter.

"Hey, Kate. I reviewed that package of discovery updates you sent over yesterday. The safety testing results were pretty interesting! Looks like that safety shutoff switch on your client's mower isn't exactly bulletproof reliable after all. The switch failed to work sometimes when the machine was on a downhill. That means Jonathan's foot could have easily slipped under the guard and into blades spinning like a buzz saw, just like he said!"

"Of course, your young client was still cutting the wet grass, during a Florida rainstorm, while wearing flip-flops, which is what made his foot slip in the first place," Kate responded, hoping she could keep the settlement discussions on track. "Those safety testing reports change none of that. Remember what I said when we first started our negotiations. I said, 'Let's assume for the sake of our negotiations that everything your client said in his deposition is true.' So, our settlement discussions have been in total good faith."

"OK, Kate, but I want to find out where those tests results were when you first responded to my discovery requests. I'd hate to think you were playing hide-the-ball with me. You've always been a straight shooter in the past."

"That hasn't changed, Matt. If I'd been playing hide-the-ball, the ball would have stayed hidden. I would have beaten your pants off at the trial and your young man would have gone home empty-handed. As it is now, he has the opportunity to get a $2 million payday. So what's he say to $2 million?"

"He says he feels like he's getting screwed by a big corporation. He barely trusts me, and he thinks you're Satan's mouthpiece."

Kate laughed. "Seriously, Matt? Is that him talking or you? Listen, I got those documents to you as soon as I found out about them. These test results only recently came to light. One of Brighton's safety engineers had been sitting on them. I've read my client the riot act about discovery obligations. And, like I said, it doesn't matter if the test results show the shutoff switch works only 50 percent of the time, or—as the test results show—90 percent of the time. Your boy's recovery is still going to be reduced by his own negligence, and I'll appeal any other outcome."

"I hear you, Kate, and, believe it or not, Jonathan has given me the authority to settle at $2 million, if your client really can produce a check for that amount in 48 hours. The kid wants it over, and he wants big bucks in his pocket to replace his lost sense of invincibility. Call your client; tell them we have a deal, Kate. And, by the way, don't be surprised if you find me back with a dozen new plaintiffs. I believe I may have discovered a new cottage industry for myself. I'm going on a campaign to find people injured by your client's mower. If I find them, you'll have the pleasure of talking to me on a regular basis."

"I'll relay the message to my client—both parts of it. I'll get back to you on the timing of the check. How about we make it Monday at noon rather than a strict 48 hours, since we're talking about the weekend."

"Sounds reasonable. I'll tell my client this is his last 'poor' weekend. Next weekend he'll be a millionaire."

"I know, and it worries me—try to counsel him a little about what he should do with that money."

"I will, but I know it will fall on deaf ears. He's already picked out a bright red Camaro and a powerboat to match. His folks have picked out a powder-blue Cadillac. You can't protect them from themselves, you know."

"So true, Matt. Have a great weekend. I'll talk to you on Monday."

Moments later, Ed walked in. "So, do we get to celebrate or not?" he demanded, looking as if he expected to be disappointed by her response and ready for a fight.

"Yes, we can do that. But, I need to get home and see how the girls are doing. If they're doing well enough to be on their own tonight, I'll let the dog sitter go home for the weekend and I'll make reservations for a really great dinner somewhere in my neighborhood so we can walk there and back—that way, we can drink with impunity," Kate winked at Ed again. "I don't know about you, but I intend to have a martini, and then get lost in a lovely bottle of wine."

"Should I bring a toothbrush?" Ed asked, breaking their rule, but pretty sure Kate was breaking it too.

"Yes, and running shoes. I'm going to need a long, slow run in the morning to sweat out all the toxins I'm planning on consuming tonight."

Ed, feeling emboldened by their talk, walked over to Kate's desk, leaned down, and lightly kissed her cheek as he whispered, "And a little aerobic sex will help with that too."

Kate didn't pull away, and instead, she reached out and touched Ed's knee . . . and slowly ran her hand up his inner thigh.

"Whoa. Look who's breaking all the rules *today*," Ed said as he turned bright pink.

"Be prepared to be surprised, Mr. Evert. Very, very surprised." Kate winked again.

She was feeling unsure and covering it up with bravado. She wanted to celebrate Marcy's win. She wanted a great meal, and an excellent bottle of wine, and she wanted to celebrate by making love with someone who wanted her.

Kate removed her hand from Ed's thigh.

"I'm going to be heading out of the office pretty soon. I'm feeling like a neglectful mother. Dinner reservation for 7:30, OK with you?"

"Yes, more than OK. I've got a couple of things I need to finish up before I head out. I'll be at your house as soon as I can. I miss the girls too."

Ed turned to leave but stopped and turned to face Kate.

"You know, this is the third time you've agreed to spending time with me without an argument. Aren't you weary of such a steady diet of me?" he teased.

"Oh, I'm enjoying the diet, but you're *not* good for me. You're like chocolate, Ed."

Chapter 32

Saturday morning dawned bright and sunny but not too hot or humid as they started their long, slow run down to the marina. The vision of Bill in the courtroom still haunted Kate, and she secretly wanted to see if the *Leona* was in her usual slip. She wasn't.

As they ran, Kate again considered the state of her love life. Her night with Ed had been most enjoyable, but she'd decided being with Ed really was like a steady diet of chocolate. You think you want it, but it's just not good for you, and eventually, you have to stop eating it.

She'd been quiet during their run, and when they returned to her house, they took their water bottles into the backyard for some stretching.

"What's on your mind, Kate?" Ed asked as they finished, "You've been super quiet this morning."

"Just thinking about my unhealthy steady diet of chocolate. You've become an addiction, I think!" she winked. "Race you to the shower," she shouted over her shoulder as she sprinted in the house and up the stairs.

As Ed washed her back, he began kissing her neck and murmured, "Care for some more chocolate, Kate?"

When she turned around to face him, she couldn't help but notice he was already getting hard.

"Did you start without me, Mr. Evert? That's very unfair," she giggled.

"I can catch you up really quickly. I know just where you like to be washed," Ed said as he began caressing her breast with his sudsy hand and pressed her back into the shower wall.

"Here, and here," he whispered, gently washing her breasts, and then slipping his hand down her stomach, finally reaching his goal. As he slipped inside her, he rocked her up until she was standing on her toes. His strong hands held her bottom, as again and again, he pressed into her until neither could wait any longer.

"See, chocolate can be very tasty after a nice long run," Ed whispered into Kate's ear, his hands exploring her again.

"Yes, and extremely addictive, I'm afraid," she responded, enjoying the sensation of his warm, soapy hands on her body. "But, I need to get my day started. Carrie Delaney promised she'd give the girls a quick checkup if I can get them to Garrett Beach this morning. Then, I'm going to the house and check on the renovations and make some choices my contractor asked about. And then, I going to enjoy a much-needed dose of alone time . . . *without* chocolate."

"Oh, come on, Kate. We haven't been together *that* much," Ed pouted.

"Enough. Let's not overdo it."

"Whatever!" he continued to pout as she reached out and turned off the water.

"Why don't you see what your buddy Ben is up to this weekend? I don't think you've seen him in months," Kate suggested.

"Are you kidding? Ben can't get away from the wife and kids and apparently babysitters are even harder to find in Miami than a pond without an alligator! But, since you're ditching me, I think what I will do is call Annie Campbell, Pete's widow. I've been meaning to see how she's doing. I could talk to her about putting some of Pete's work on exhibit."

"That's a wonderful idea," Kate agreed.

Ed needs to get more involved with other people in Miami, people his own age and at his stage in life, Kate thought, again feeling guilty about monopolizing his time, not that he complained about it.

Carrie had pronounced the girls' progress "very good, and on their way to a full recovery," and a much-relieved Kate spent Saturday and

Sunday morning at the beach, puttering in her small yard and walking her girls on the beach. On Sunday, before she headed back to Miami, she gave them a nice warm shower and gently massaged their tender muscles. The three of them had a wonderful, quiet time together, and Kate was grateful for the solitude and time to think about her "chocolate addiction."

Over the last few days, whenever Ed wanted to have sex, her internal response had been "why not?" But, she was beginning to think she knew the answer to that simple question. She just wasn't good at casual sex. She never had been. It wasn't so much that she wanted "a commitment," but she did want substance, something more than just sex, something more than just "chocolate." She felt a great affection for Ed, maybe even a type of love. It was puzzling. But, she had finally decided that maybe the answer to "why not?" was because she wasn't *in love* with him.

The issue was still on Kate's mind Sunday evening as she dressed for her dinner with Marcy back in Miami. She'd decided she was going to tell Ed she needed a break, and he needed to respect her decision and not pressure her because she was afraid she'd give in. She needed to see what it felt like to be on her own again, with no man in her life. And, Ed needed to see what it was like without her in his. She knew he'd try to talk her out of her decision, but she vowed to remain firm, no matter how great her "chocolate" craving.

She was looking forward to her dinner with Marcy. At one point they'd been like sisters, and she hoped they could be again. Kate wanted to bounce her "man dilemma" off Marcy and get some advice. It wasn't like her to be unsure about a situation or to waffle between positions—but that's where she was.

Returning to The Pelican had been an excellent idea. The maître d' even seemed to remember her, and he casually chatted with her as he walked them to the table she'd requested—the one in the bay window, the one where she and Bill had dined not that long ago. Kate and Marcy looked smashing and were the objects of numerous lecherous stares from the male patrons, which they totally appreciated. Marcy had spent part of the day on Saturday at the spa, and part of the day Sunday shopping. She certainly looked every bit the newly minted millionaire she was.

They chatted like old friends over cocktails and dinner, catching each other up on the parts of their lives that didn't involve murder and litigation. Marcy's condo wasn't really damaged, except for needing a new front door, and her superintendent had already taken care of that. It also didn't appear that Gary Cook had taken anything from her place, but he'd made a terrible mess of it. Cleaning it up had been quite a task, but she'd taken the opportunity to do some "purging," getting ready for her new life. After the article appeared in the *Herald* on Saturday, setting the record straight, Marcy had received numerous calls from the very same friends and neighbors who'd been reluctant to talk with her when the whole world believed she was a murderer. Now, they were more than happy to visit with their millionaire friend.

Kate shared her thoughts about ending her fling with Ed. Marcy confessed she hadn't guessed that Kate and Ed were an item, which made Kate feel better. She'd been feeling like they were wearing bright red signs that flashed "these two are having sex." And, Marcy understood Kate's desire for a relationship offering more than sex. She confided that the same feeling had been what kept her from getting serious about the men she'd dated after her divorce. She had wanted the same substance in those relationships that she'd had with Joe, and she simply never found it. As they were finishing their dinners, Kate asked Marcy if she had decided what she was going to do now that the insurance issue was settled.

"Is medical school in your future, Marcy?"

Marcy smiled shyly. "Yes, as a matter of fact, it is. One of the things I did while I was biding my time at your beach house was look into where I might actually be admitted. I have two years of UF medical school from my first time around, and I'd hoped to be able to transfer at least some of that credit. Unfortunately, I'm much older than the usual med school applicant, and medical schools are all so competitive, they have their pick of candidates. I'm decidely outside their target market. But, Kate, if you look outside the U.S., you can find good schools that take 'nontraditional students,' like me. Granada has an excellent one. While I was at your beach place, I submitted my application for next term. Guess what was waiting for me when I picked up my mail from the condo mailbox on Friday?" Marcy said as she pulled a letter from her purse and handed it to Kate. "I've been accepted! Can you believe it? I'm really going to get to go back to medical school after all these years. Thank you, Joe Dugan." Marcy saluted the air with her wineglass.

"How absolutely fabulous, Marcy! When are you headed down there?"

"In just three days actually! I also applied for my passport while I was at your place and paid for expedited service. It was in the mail I picked up on Friday as well. I've decided to list the condo for rent while I'm gone. The condo association has a relationship with one of the local realtors of vacation properties. I want to maintain a home base here. But, I don't want anything more elaborate than what I have because I've already decided what I'm going to do with my medical degree."

"Of course you have. I would expect nothing less," Kate laughed at the wonderful, but drastically different direction Marcy's life was rapidly taking. "Do tell, what are you going to do?"

"I want to do a rotation in trauma care, and then join Doctors Without Borders. I've already contacted them about my interest, and they said I'm just what they're looking for. I'm so psyched, Kate! It feels like a dream come true."

"You *should* be excited, and you deserve this opportunity. But don't forget, you have several tough years ahead of you."

"I know, but it will be something I *want* to do, not something I *have* to do, and I already know I love practicing medicine and that I will be good at it. The time will fly by. But, Kate, I want to ask you something. I've never been outside the country, and I wondered if you'd consider coming down to Granada with me for a couple of weeks—totally my treat! I owe you so much, and I could really use the help finding an apartment and getting to know the area before classes begin in a month. Any chance you'd be able to get away?"

"I'd love nothing more!"

Kate immediately pulled out her phone and checked her calendar, making sure there wasn't anything she couldn't delegate to Ed. "Looks good, Marcy. I actually think I can make this work. I just need to talk to Ed about covering for me on a couple of hearings and seeing if he'll keep the girls for me while I'm gone."

Kate wanted to toast Marcy's exciting new future with a glass of champagne, and as she looked to find the waiter, her eyes caught a fleeting glimpse of a very tall, well-tanned man chatting with the maître d'. Kate's stomach dropped as she stared. This was no mirage—definitely *not* a hallucination. It was Bill in the flesh. And, standing next to him, was an exotically beautiful woman with long, black hair.

"My God," Kate gasped. "Marcy, don't look now, but Bill Davis has just arrived with an absolutely stunning woman on his arm. I feel like I've been punched in the gut. Well, I guess that settles the Bill matter. He *is* back, and he hasn't bothered to even let me know. And now I see why. Good God, I have been so foolish . . . carrying a torch for someone who has already moved on so completely and who has so little regard for my feelings. At least now I'm finally convinced I can move on as well."

The waiter appeared at her table, and Kate ordered a bottle of their best champagne rather than a couple of glasses. She was happy they'd taken a car service to the restaurant because right now, she felt she needed to climb inside a bottle.

"I think we'll drink our dessert. This one is my treat, Marcy. You'll have plenty of time to take me to dinner, so stop worrying about it," Kate added when Marcy began to protest.

"Are you sure you want to stay, Kate? I can see Bill and his friend now. She *is* glamorous . . . looks European to me. Oh dear, I think he's walking this way. Are you going to be OK?"

"Hello, Katie. I see you've stolen my favorite table," Bill said, standing at their table grinning down at her, looking gorgeous, and making her heart ache and her stomach churn.

"Hello, stranger. I see *you're* back in the country. How long have you been home?"

"Just a couple of days. I saw you in court last Friday. That was quite a win."

"Bill, I'd like you to meet Marcy Simpson, my very great friend and recent client. It's her win really."

Bill extended his hand to Marcy, and said, "She's quite the lawyer, isn't she?" He grinned at Kate in the same sexy way he always had.

Kate didn't understand. Was he trying to make her feel awful . . . Did he not know how devastating it was that he hadn't called her or tried to reach out to her at all? And now he was dining with this totally dazzling woman. Kate wondered how much pain a heart could feel before it went completely numb.

"Yes, she is a wonderful lawyer *and* a great friend. We're celebrating *our* win," Marcy replied as she looked at Kate and marveled at her strength—she didn't look the least bit ruffled.

"Well, congratulations," Bill added and turned to Kate. "I expected to see Captain Protective with you, Kate. I saw him at the hearing. You're training him quite well."

"Ed is out with friends. I'll give him your regards when I see him again," Kate replied.

The sommelier arrived with the champagne and stood off to the side.

"I wonder if we might have our champagne on your lovely patio. My friend and I would like some air, and we wouldn't want to monopolize Mr. Davis's favorite table. I'm sure his lovely date would prefer this view," Kate smiled sweetly at the sommelier as she stood.

"Of course, Ms. Muldoon. Please follow me," he said as he led the way.

"Kate, can we talk?" Bill gently caught Kate's arm as she started to leave. "I have some news."

"Yes, it certainly looks that way." Kate's eyes turned toward Bill's date, and she smiled. "I'm busy right now and really don't think this is a good time. You know how to reach me. *Good-bye*, Bill." Kate pulled her arm away and followed the sommelier out of the dining room.

Epilogue

Two Months Later

The caterers were nearly done setting up the beach area where the ceremony would take place. Thousands of small white lights filled the back deck and yard. It looked magical—the perfect venue for a wedding.

Her recently completed, "forced remodeling" project had miraculously come together a week before the big day, and Kate loved the results. As she looked around, she decided you'd never know the house had been the site of a shooting spree by a sociopath in search of her friend Marcy. Kate smiled as she thought of Marcy now up to her eyeballs in medical school and loving every minute of it.

Best of all, Phoebe and Sadie were both fully recovered, and running in and out of the house, and up and down the back stairs each time someone took food into her small backyard.

Happily, the weather was cooperating. A cool breeze had picked up, and the sky had only enough clouds to reflect the colors of the setting sun. It promised to be a spectacular outdoor wedding.

The guests had all arrived. The plan was for everyone to gather up at the house for cocktails and hors d'oeuvres, and at precisely 7:00, Kate was to escort them to the chairs set up on the beach facing the bower, with the ocean as a backdrop.

Kate had already caught sight of the brides—they looked splendid and flushed with excitement . . . just the way brides are supposed to look. Beth's brother, Frank, and Melissa's mother and sisters, represented their families. Beth's parents had declined to attend, but Beth was neither upset nor surprised. Her folks had never been able to embrace their daughter's sexuality. Kate thought how sad it was that they would not be here to witness this beautiful celebration. Suzy and Kate were the designated bridesmaids, and Terry and Frank were the groomsmen. Phoebe and Sadie were standing in as flower girls, and they were already decked out in their flower-laden collars. Beth and Melissa would be walking each other down the aisle between the white folding chairs on the beach. Chief Jordan, an ordained elder in his church and a Florida notary, had agreed to perform the service. Everything was set.

Kate watched as the guests milled about chatting. She noticed Ed talking with the FBI agents. She decided he was probably picking their brains on whether—and when—he should submit his application. She'd hate to lose his help, but maybe not seeing him every day would be the answer to how they moved forward. Ed had been reluctantly giving her space to figure out what she needed, and he swore he'd been exploring what he wanted too. As she watched him, she realized she could fall into bed with him on a moment's notice. It had been a struggle reigning in her "inner slut"—celibacy was difficult.

After a few more minutes, Kate linked her arm in Chief Jordan's and asked, "Are you ready to get this party started, Chief?"

"I am, if you are."

Together, they walked out onto the deck, and Kate announced it was time to move down to the beach for the ceremony. Gradually, the crowd walked down the path and found their seats.

Kate and Suzy stood at the front of the crowd on one side of the bower with the girls lying at their feet. Terry and Frank stood on the other side. When Chief Jordan took his place under the bower, the flute and guitar music began. Kate could see Beth and Melissa heading down the path to the beach arm-in-arm.

The tightening in her throat and the tear that suddenly sprang to her eye surprised her.

A light supper was being served, and people had plates of food balanced on their knees or on the small tables set up in the yard and on the deck. The wedding service had been beautiful and brief, and as hardened as Kate thought she was to the institution of marriage, even *she* was touched by how right it had seemed for these two women. Silently, Kate said a prayer they'd always be just this happy, but she knew they'd have many challenges ahead of them—far more than most newly married couples—but, they seemed up to the task.

Suzy and Terry were playing grab-ass while they stood at one of the high-top tables—thinking nobody could see them fondling each other's rear ends. Kate just laughed to herself. Terry was rapidly approaching the all-time "Suzy Spellman Relationship Duration Record," and Suzy showed no signs of growing tired of him.

Maybe this relationship will actually last, Kate thought, and she realized she sincerely hoped it would.

Chief Jordan left his wife chatting with Melissa's mother and escaped to talk to Kate.

"Kate, I've been wanting to tell you, I submitted grievances to the Miami Bar Ethics Committee regarding Mike Taylor, Senator Ferguson, and Ron Gray."

"You're kidding!" Kate was genuinely shocked.

"No, Kate, I'm not. It's about time Mike and old Fergie got their hands slapped, and maybe Gray will think twice next time he decides to use his law license to take advantage of a layman. I just heard back from the committee yesterday. Ferguson has voluntarily surrendered his license. He wasn't practicing anyway, but the committee is going to force Gray and Ferguson to delete his name from their letterhead. I heard he's thinking about moving out of the area. It seems, since his daughter's incarceration, he's finding it difficult to live in Miami in his newly disgraced status. The committee wants to suspend Taylor's license for a year. My grievance wasn't the only one filed against him over the last three months. And they're going to recommend a public reprimand for Gray. I don't know if either of those recommendations will stick, but at least the committee is attempting to take some action against them."

"That was quite a risk, Chief. All three of those men are heavily connected. You put your career on the line when you filed those grievances."

"Well, you won't be calling me 'Chief' much longer."

"What?!? They've gotten you fired? That's absurd—it's not right! Chief, I'll represent you—*for free*—if you want to sue to keep your job."

"Thanks, Kate. That means a lot. But, I already have a new job all lined up, and it pays better."

"Seriously? What is it?"

"Police Commissioner!" Jordan chuckled.

Kate threw her arms around him, and then toasted him with the champagne glass she was holding.

"Well done, Chief. When does the promotion happen?"

"It will be announced in two weeks. My wife's proud, but she's already complaining that she sees me too little. By the way, Beth told me Gary Cook was sentenced to multiple life sentences, and he's in the super-max facility in Colorado. I guess it's justice, but it seems far too little for the pain and suffering he created."

"At least he won't be able to continue to harm people, Chief. That's something. What's the latest on Joan Dugan and Zeke Peters? I haven't heard from the prosecutor's office—not surprising, I guess."

"Peters has already inked his deal. He claimed it was a 'heat of passion' murder. He pled to second-degree murder and assault with a deadly weapon, which really sucks because Dr. Dugan's murder was most certainly premeditated. He also pled to the conspiracy to commit murder charge for hiring Cook to kill Marcy. He got a total of 25 years, but he'll likely be out in 18. Plus, his attorney got him a pretty cushy jail assignment in Tarpon Springs. I hear he's working in the infirmary there. I wonder how many of his fellow inmates are going to show up at the infirmary for a flu shot and end up having a heart attack instead," the chief laughed heartily at his own joke.

"What about Joan?" Kate asked. "That woman is just nuts."

"Well, that's exactly what her defense counsel says too, and, apparently, they've got a shrink that says the same thing. They're working out a deal for a plea to attempted murder. The last I heard, the prosecutor's office was thinking about going for it. She'd only serve 10 to 15 years, and likely it would be in the minimum-security facility in

Lakeland, the one with a psych ward. We'll see how *that* works out."

The chief's wife walked up and slipped her arm in his.

"Enough shoptalk now, you two. Ms. Muldoon has hostess duties to perform, and we're going to go do some networking—you need to do more of that now, Steve," she said proudly.

"Congratulations again, Chief. You deserve it!" Kate said as she scanned the lawn looking for Suzy and Terry—they were nowhere to be seen.

It was 10:45. The caterers finally finished cleaning up the last of the food and serving pieces and removing the bower and chairs from the beach. Her house and yard were back to normal, and there was nothing left for Kate to do.

Feeling wound up from the party and not ready for bed, she decided to take the girls for a walk on the beach. Phoebe and Sadie turned south once they reached the sand, heading off in the direction of Bill's house. Kate had been avoiding walking or running that way since she'd come back from Granada. But, she decided at this hour the chance of running into Bill was nearly zero.

He's been home for over two months, and he still hasn't called me, she thought sadly.

When she reached Bill's section of the beach she looked toward his house. There were lights on. She considered stopping by, just to say hello and tell him she hoped they could be friends again. But it was really too late.

Too late in so many ways, she thought as she walked along, enjoying the cool breeze and moonlight.

THE END

Preview from Book Three
Prologue

Devena Elan

The small group spilled out of the Ritz Residences condominiums onto what appeared to be an empty sidewalk. At the center of the group was a tall, slender woman wearing a broad-brimmed hat, large sunglasses, a loose-fitting tank top, and a long flowing skirt. She was surrounded by a gaggle of children of various sizes and colors. If they were to hold still long enough for you to count them, you would learn there were seven of them, ranging from 3 to 13 years old. But they didn't hold still. Some ran ahead, and then raced back to the woman, some circled her, a couple of them rushed over to pet a passing puppy. The smallest of them, a little girl, lagged behind the swarming group but still remained within their ever-contracting and expanding circle.

The sidewalk was suddenly no longer empty. Men and women with cameras and microphones seemed to appear out of thin air, leaping out of parked cars and streaming out of shop doors as even more journalists rapidly joined the throng.

The news was spreading like wildfire on Twitter and Snapchat: Devena Elan was taking her children for their daily walk.

Devena and her children seemed to barely notice the hoard of circling photographers snapping photos and shouting questions at them. Although she occasionally smiled her Madonna-like smile, she did not stop or respond to their questions. Instead, she and her pack continued to meander forward.

She was regal in her posture, her movements slow and graceful—a sharp contrast to the rapid, random movement of the children, and the bustle and shoving of the paparazzi.

At the first intersection, Devena paused long enough for all of the children to catch up so they could cross the street together. She was the calm in the eye of a hurricane standing on the street corner, taking inventory of her charges, literally counting noses. She came up one short, and her eyes darted back in the direction they'd come.

She spotted her youngest, now a quarter of a block behind her and no longer walking. Instead, the little girl was standing as if paralyzed in the middle of a small circle of paparazzi blocking her path to her mother, their cameras greedily lapping up the delightfulness of this little girl's sunny golden curls and large green eyes.

Devena said something to the six children now ready to cross the street before starting back in the direction of her littlest daughter. She was no longer smiling attractively, and her movements now emitted neither grace nor fluidity. Her gate was urgent and fierce.

One of the male photographers reached out with one hand and touched the hem of the little girl's dress, pulling it up to her shoulders revealing her ruffled bloomers. The cameras lapped away. The photographer then reached out and started to untie the shoulder strap of the little girl's sundress. The cameras kept lapping.

Devena ran toward the group of photographers encircling her daughter, pushing several aside as she bore down on the man undressing her 3-year-old.

The crunching sound of Devena's fist breaking the man's jaw could be heard up and down the sidewalk. It was followed by the cracking sounds of her violent rib-breaking kick administered after she swooped down to gather her daughter in her arms.

Devena stood in the middle of the paparazzi glaring at each of them, memorizing their faces and the organizations they represented. The vultures immediately retreated, abandoning their fallen comrade to deal with his pain and broken bones on his own.

Then Devena strode victoriously to the group of children waiting for her at the corner, cradling her 3-year-old protectively.

Just another walk in the park with Mom, her 13-year-old daughter thought as she rolled her eyes, and they all trouped across the street and off to the restaurant where Dad was waiting for them.

"We had a *deal*," Devena said through angry tears. "We told them we wouldn't hide from them, we'd let them take photographs of all of us as long as they didn't try to touch us or interfere in any way with the kids. We had a *deal,* and he *broke* it."

"I know, sweetie," Spike said, patting her arm. "But, you know you can't count on those vultures to keep their word."

Spike had seen the "Momma Bear" transformation himself the few times he'd tried to discipline one of their unruly mob in a manner Devena did not approve. Once, she'd even managed to blacken one of his eyes and fracture a rib.

And she supposedly loves me, Spike shuddered as he recalled the event and thought of the damage Devena could unleash on a member of the paparazzi if she truly thought one of her precious kids was being harmed.

Why we needed seven kids in the first place is way beyond me. Spike again mulled over the question he'd never been able to answer.

Two, or three max would have been just fine if she had to keep up with the rest of the starlets who'd, for no apparent reason, decided the "baby bump" was the new sex goddess look. Spike found the whole thing mystifying. *And why did we have to travel the world to find more than our own naturally occurring kids? If you want to adopt, then adopt, but for crying out loud, there are plenty of kids right here in the good ol' US of A that need adopting. No reason to travel to third world countries just to find a baby.*

Though bewildered by the whole phenomenon, Spike had kept his mouth closed. There was just no reasoning with Devena on the subject of their kids. He'd lost every fight he'd ever had with her on the subject. She was that way with all of her projects.

So, now they had a motley crew of seven "unique and genuine individuals," as Devena called them. Between the seven kids and her damn causes throughout the world, Spike barely even saw Devena these days. Their once-idyllic, sexy life, jetting from one hot spot to another, was now just a fading memory.

It's no wonder I spend so much time away on the set of any movie project that will have me. That's what happens when you have seven wild children and a crazy woman at home making your house an insane asylum. No wonder we can't hang on to a nanny.

As Spike gloomily pondered the sorry state of his life, he looked over at the kids' table where pandemonium had broken out—again.

Thank God we're in a private dining room with soundproof walls; otherwise, even this restaurant would have kicked us out. We're running out of options and may need to leave Miami just to find a restaurant that will feed us. Spike was lost in his gloomy self-pity.

The knock at the door was barely audible over the noise from his progeny. Spike got up to investigate, certain it was the manager coming to tell them to keep down the noise or they'd have to leave.

"Sir, I am sorry to interrupt," the young maître d' began as he winced at the crash emanating from the wild tribe inside the room. "There's a policeman here who says he needs to speak with your wife."

Spike looked past the maître d' and saw a large man in full police uniform standing down the hall 10 feet away.

"OK, just a minute. I'll get her." Spike ducked back into the private room.

Now what? he wondered, crossing the room to where his wife sat in serene mediation amidst the din.

"Devena, there's a cop out in the hall who wants to talk to you. Do you know anything about why he might be here?" he inquired.

"Not sure, but it could have something to do with the possible theft I reported this morning—my pearl and emerald brooch, the one you gave me in Thailand, has gone missing. I'll go talk to him." Devena rose and floated to the door.

Not without me, he thought. *You're not leaving me here alone with this mob.* He hurried after his wife.

In the hall, Devena flashed her attractive, full-lipped smile in the policeman's direction. "How may I help you, Officer?"

The policeman paused long enough to swallow a few times and absorb the full effect Devena has on a man when she focuses her unfiltered sexual energy on him. Spike thought he saw a flash of awe and terror envelop the cop's face before he recovered his composure.

"Ms. Elan?" the cop managed.

"Yes, of course. What can I do for you?" she replied.

The cop handed Devena a document. She unfolded it. Spike looked over her shoulder and read the heading on the paper: "*Arrest Warrant*."

"Ms. Elan, I'm placing you under arrest for assault and battery on one Myron J. Pierce at 12:35 this afternoon. You will need to accompany me to headquarters for booking."

"Whatever are you talking about? Is this about that horrid photographer who was undressing my baby in public so he and the rest of those wretched paparazzi could photograph her? I wanted to file a charge against *him* for child abuse, but my PR person said it would be ill-advised."

"Well, ma'am, you can always do that down at headquarters. But you will need to accompany me, and, ma'am, if you come along willingly, I won't have to put handcuffs on you." The cop was struggling to maintain his composure.

"*Excuse* me? Are you saying that I am going to be treated like a common criminal, Officer . . ." Devena looked at the man's name badge pinned to his chest, "Reynolds?"

Devena's eyes had a frightening cast to them now.

"No, ma'am. I certainly would rather you just came along with me to headquarters so we can get this worked out." The cop had caught the dangerous gleam in Devena's eyes, and he was beginning to backpedal.

A pregnant pause followed as Devena considered the publicity angle of appearing in a photo in handcuffs. She decided the potential downside outweighed the upside.

"Well, Officer, since I know you're just doing your job, I will come with you. But, really, this is all just a huge waste of time."

Devena turned to Spike. "Darling, would you please take the kids to the surf shop. I promised them they could each pick out a few things before we returned to the hotel."

She then turned back to the cop. "All right, Officer Reynolds, let's get going. I have a massage appointment at 4:30 at the Ritz, so we need to get this done quickly."

"What? Wait, Devena, you can't leave me here alone with this mob. They'll eat me alive. Can't I come with you?" Spike felt fear rising in his throat just thinking of facing their pack of free-range kids without backup.

"We can't leave the little darlings here by themselves, Spike. Don't worry. I'll take care of this and meet you all for dinner after my massage. Ciao, honey." Devena turned to leave, but then as an afterthought, turned back to Spike. "Oh, and what was the name of that female attorney here in Miami that Frank Hanson told us about at his cast party several months ago? You know, it's the same one July Moon was raving about a few weeks ago. Kate something Irish. What was it?"

"Kate Muldoon. The media calls her the 'Defense Counsel to the Stars,'" Spike supplied.

"Yes, that's right. Please call her and tell her to meet me at police headquarters immediately. I want to file a complaint against the monster that was molesting our little Jenner. Thanks, sweetie, see you later."

Devena floated away next to the policeman. Spike turned to the maître d'. "I need the lunch bill and a van to meet me in front of the restaurant in 10 minutes," he said breathlessly. "We aren't going far, just back to the Ritz. It's only a couple of blocks, but I'll pay him $500. I'm not even going to *try* to herd this gang back there on foot by myself."

Next, Spike called all three of the nannies they had on standby and told them to meet him at the front door of the Ritz in 15 minutes. He needed reinforcements. Panic was setting in.

Spike dug into his jeans pocket, pulled out a Xanax, and popped it into his mouth. Swallowing hard, he pulled out his phone and began a Web search for Kate Muldoon's phone number. Once he found the number, he pressed the call button and waited for the Xanax to kick in.

Note from the Author

Read about my other novels as well as some of my short stories online at lizmathewsauthor.com. You can also follow me on Facebook and Twitter.